TWELVE

BY TRISTAN K. HODGES

TWELVE by Tristan K. Hodges

This is a work of fiction. Although based on historical stories found in the Bible, the events and characters described here are products of the author's imagination.

Paperback ISBN: 978-1-63337-808-7
eBook ISBN: 978-1-63337-809-4

Storehouse Media Group
7643 Gate Parkway Suite 104-676
Jacksonville, FL 32256
www.storehousemediagroup.com

Cover image via iStock / credit: Lalocracio

Dedicated to Yasha, Yeshua, Jesus ...
the same yesterday, today, and forever.

Love is patient and kind,
love does not envy or boast,
it is not arrogant or rude,
it does not insist on its own way,
it is not irritable or resentful,
it does not rejoice at wrongdoing
but rejoices with the truth.
Love bears all things,
believes all things,
hopes all things,
endures all things.
Love never fails.

1 Corinthians 13:4–7

LIST OF CHARACTERS

Yasha ha Natzeret .... *Jesus of Nazareth*, leader of the Twelve

Kefa .... *Peter*
Arye .... *Andrew*
Yaakov.................................. *James*
Yochanan............................. *John*
Faivel.................................... *Philip*
Natan .... *Nathaniel*
Mattiyahu .... *Matthew*
Toma.................................... *Thomas*
Yaakov ben-Chalfai................ *James Alphaeus*
Taddai .... *Thaddeus*
Shimon .... *Simon the zealot*
Yehudas................................ *Judas*

Yochanan the Immerser......... *John the Baptist*
Magda................................... *Mary Magdalene*
El'azar .... *Lazarus*
Miryam................................. *Mary*
Marta .... *Martha*

Uri Ohred .... prime minister of Israel
Nakdimon............................. deputy prime minister
Saidoreh .... prime minister's wife
Salome .... daughter of Saidoreh
Peres Peliat .... president of Israel
Moshe Reuven....................... head of Shin Bet
Zvi Goren .... director of Mossad

Mohammed Mustafa............ president of Palestinian Authority
Isan bar-Abbas...................... Palestinian terrorist

TWELVE

PROLOGUE

PRESENT DAY JERUSALEM

One by one, eleven men slink into the empty safe house as dusk approaches. An unexpected late-April spring rain takes them by surprise. Most have hardly slept in the past three days. Eyes are bloodshot, clothes unwashed. Inside, tangible fear ricochets around the tight rooms. Few words are spoken; no one is sure if hostile ears might be listening. Tension is high, nerves afire.

Kefa instructs Taddai to make sure all the doors and windows are secured and shaded—they don't need any more surprises. Once every entrance is double-checked, the men congregate in the largest room next to the kitchen. Dishes lay askew in the sink, remains of Turkish coffee litter the counter. A pronounced mustiness hangs in the air.

Yaakov quiets the group and begins to go over the recent events. Their leader is dead. They are on the run. Government agencies feel victorious in decapitating the cell, forcing them underground. Different political groups are trying to take credit, the opposition flying back and forth. Governmental factions had united for a short time, trying to squash the Israeli cell known as the Twelve, but twenty-four hours after the execution, they're absorbed in conflict, each claiming to have saved Israel from a coup d'état. Even the major earthquakes from this morning and three days prior—something Jerusalem hasn't seen in years—can't shake people out of their stubbornness and prejudices. Pockets of rubble line the streets, especially closest to the Temple Mount. Everything feels like it's about to crumble.

TWELVE

Emotions for the eleven are raw. The man who has led them in the fight for justice and peace in a nation of volatility lies dead. He was a hero, a face for so many downtrodden and misunderstood. He stood out wherever he traveled; such was his demeanor, his message. And his closest followers are left confused and mourning.

Yasha ha Natzeret. Their beloved leader.

Only he could have taken twelve diametrically opposed Israelis and brought them together under his shrewd leadership. Only he could have stepped into the great divide between their beliefs, their politics, their pasts and bridged the seemingly impossible gap. Everything became secondary as they'd been gathered together in a collective mission, an upside-down objective. Even still, one of the Twelve defected and double-crossed the group. Nobody saw that coming. Immediately after, events spiraled at a dizzying rate, culminating in Yasha's death. Now, they're reunited after hiding for the past few days—Faivel had contacted everyone via back channels, as they'd all been scattered throughout Jerusalem. The cell has managed to stay intact, however imperfectly.

Natan jumps in, voicing concern for their safety. "Should we disperse or stay together in Jerusalem? It might be too dangerous to continue the work," he confesses fearfully. The Twelve know all too well the risks involved.

Will government agents hunt them down? Or did the blood of their leader satisfy them? No one knows. The answers, it seems, are hiding as well.

While Yaakov paints a doleful portrait of circumstances, Yochanan, his level-headed brother, delivers opposite news. Essentially, he detonates a bomb.

"Someone has seen Yasha alive," Yochanan reports. "This morning."

Yaakov gives him a cynical look. *Don't be ridiculous*, he thinks.

"Impossible!" declares Shimon.

Yochanan replies, "And two others said they saw him outside the city."

"*What?*" shouts Mattiyahu, sharply. "It's a trap."

Toma vocalizes his utter disbelief, rattling off the details of Yasha's demise. Everything they saw. Everything they read. The beatings, the blood, the execution. "Unless I see…," he says, shaking his head, "I won't believe it." His blunt vow disdains those who would believe otherwise.

Ben-Chalfai also grapples with the announcement. His scientific mind tells him, once again, that being raised from the dead is impossible. Despite the evidence, despite previous episodes.

Something's afoot. Shouts of disbelief and voices tainted with confusion volley between the men. The group has evolved into a tightly knit unit over the course of the last year. None of them would've imagined this to be the case, as all twelve men joined the cell with differing worldviews and strong biases. Their idiosyncrasies, attitudes, and even demeanors didn't mesh well in the beginning. But Yasha had given them an opportunity, given them a purpose to lay everything aside and focus on a greater good. As a result, they've chosen to risk potential hazards, keeping the purpose alive. All because of Yasha.

"Who saw him?" Mattiyahu asks. He looks at Kefa pointedly. "Have *you* seen him?" He wants proof, wants a legitimate explanation for this conundrum.

Yochanan looks at Kefa, who stands up to address the group. Kefa pauses, aware of the disunity between his heart and mind. He wonders about the report. "No," he replies, "but the casket's empty." That much he can verify.

He explains that it was Miryam, Marta, and El'azar, people they know and trust. At sunrise, they had set out to locate where Yasha was being held when they bumped into Magda, the Israeli Defense Force (IDF) soldier who gave Yasha the crimson guitar after the terrorist attack. She confided to the three siblings—against government protocol—that the coffin of their leader was empty. No explanations or elaborations. Just facts. Magda, baffled yet hopeful for a miracle, was headed

to report the phenomenon to her superiors, who naturally were going to be furious.

Once Magda left, the siblings decided to search for more answers. Maybe Yasha had been intentionally placed in someone else's coffin. Maybe he had been moved to a new location. They were deep in conversation when they rounded a corner and literally bumped into Yasha. At first, they didn't recognize him, but when he greeted them by name, the siblings gasped in shock. They started to express their colossal excitement, yet Yasha told them not to draw attention. He wanted to surprise others around Jerusalem too. The three siblings promised to stay with Yasha wherever he went, but he instructed them to find Kefa immediately. To let him know that death did not win.

After listening to Kefa, the other ten men argue in circles, the majority processing out of heightened emotion. Yochanan tosses in tokens here and there. Natan voices rage that Yasha's life was exchanged for the Palestinian terrorist, that the murderer walked free while the do-gooder was summarily killed.

"Isan bar-Abbas never got his comeuppance," he says, gritting his teeth.

"Infernal *terrorist!*" Shimon spits.

"Wait!" Faivel interjects, holding up his hands. "Maybe it's true." All eyes turn to him. Faivel feels like he's about to hit the jackpot. That he's finally about to solve Yasha's riddle. "Didn't he say, *'Tear down this Temple, and in three days, I'll put it back together'*?" The others look at him in silence. Faivel continues, "Crazy as it sounds, maybe he was referring to himself. Maybe he brought himself back like he did for El'azar!"

Everyone stares at Faivel. Five seconds elapse while they all consider this theory. Was Yasha being metaphorical? Was he giving them a clue? Has it been exactly three days?

"You're reaching," says Shimon, shaking his head and breaking the tension.

"By a camel-ridden mile," Taddai adds.

"Wouldn't he have come to us by now?" Ben-Chalfai says.

The group erupts again into deliberations. The idea of this impossibility challenges all remaining members of the Twelve. Over the past year, they had witnessed hundreds of miracles, even experienced some themselves, but *this*? Coming back from the dead by his own doing? Can they believe it? Some of the eleven men think it's a ruse to lure them out of hiding in pursuit of their trusted leader. Others believe conspiracies abound. No one is to be trusted, least of all anyone in government. Too much has happened since Yasha called them to follow him. None of them can prove anything. Until they encounter Yasha themselves, that is.

As the noise in the room grows to a sustained volume, the men suddenly hear a door shut in the front of the house. Voices stop mid-sentence. Bodies freeze in fear. Kefa glares at Taddai. He silently mouths, *"Didn't you bolt the doors?!"*

●●●

OFFICE OF THE PRIME MINISTER

Two IDF officers arrive from the outskirts of Jerusalem. They've recently come from the holding place where the corpse of the Twelve's leader resides. Except now it doesn't. The prime minister of Israel, Uri Ohred, has gathered his top intelligence officials together: Moshe Reuven, the head of Shin Bet, Israel's security agency, and Zvi Goren, the director of Mossad, Israel's national intelligence agency. Unsettling news has made its way to the top.

The male IDF officer hands a cell phone displaying photos of the empty metal coffin to the prime minister. Ohred cannot believe the images. The security measures taken to guard the body were extreme. The only person who had the vault codes was the prime minister himself.

TWELVE

He struggles over the possible explanation. Either Yasha's body was relocated by others, or he relocated himself. Ohred groans and presses his fingers against his eyes. Both options are ridiculous. Yasha cannot simply disappear.

Officer number two, a female, explains what they discovered: no sign of forced entry or vandalism, no witnesses, and no explanations other than that of the guards assigned to watch around the clock.

"Bring them in," Ohred barks.

The guards enter with downcast eyes. They cannot meet the piercing glare of the prime minister. Their own lives are in jeopardy as they failed to safeguard the corpse of the Jewish revolutionary. Ohred upbraids the guards for allowing the body to disappear. When asked, they offer no explanation, save a weak one—they had fallen asleep. One guard suggests foul play. This infuriates the prime minister. Negligence is inexcusable. For some minutes, he rants with extreme profanity, letting deep tensions surface. Ultimately, his name is on the line.

"Out! Both of you!" he yells. "You're done here!"

Silence fills the office once they depart. The female officer begins to offer a suggestion, but Ohred holds up his hand, demanding quiet. Scenarios of chaos explode in his head, and he tries to focus. He clenches and unclenches his fists repeatedly. People will go crazy with anger, with fear…potential riots, potential civil unrest. The country's been focused on rebuilding after the two recent earthquakes—one this morning and the other three days ago—while simultaneously jockeying for credit of the death of Israel's most notorious alleged traitor. The scenario before them, however, would resurrect focus on Yasha and the Twelve. Stories and accusations would travel as fast as social media messages. Allegations of subterfuge would surely be on every tongue. The government's spin against the Twelve had worked. Lies and propaganda served a plate of manipulation that was naively devoured by the public. People were even relieved that Yasha, a touted threat, had been dealt with.

All that ground cannot be lost, Ohred thinks, fuming. *Yasha's a thorn in Israel's side. A thorn in* my *side, specifically.* He must remain in control of his country. This small group led by one man will not be his undoing. *Somehow, they must've breached the system; any preternatural option is simply implausible. Where are they hiding their leader? What are they planning?* He believes the future of Israel lies at stake.

"Sir, if I may?" Moshe Reuven says.

The prime minister looks out the window but nods his head in approval.

"What if the Palestinians are involved? We'll be worse off than before, the final deceit surpassing the first," Reuven suggests. The thought had occurred to them all.

The prime minister takes a swig of bourbon that sits on a credenza near the window. Rain slides down the panes. The liquor's burn is painful, but like lightning, a solution comes to him. This may or may not be the work of the Palestinians, he considers, but pointed accusations would certainly ignite more unrest. He must pin it on another faction, he decides. Ohred spins around and points at Moshe Reuven, the head of Shin Bet.

"Say this: his friends—the cell—came by night and stole him away. Spin the story," he demands. "The guards were drugged, the camera tapes looped, the body confiscated in order to blackmail the government. Create false evidence."

Looks are exchanged around the room. Eyebrows raise and lips press together. The elite IDF officers have high-level clearance, yet the Shin Bet director feels uncomfortable that they're still present. Everyone must strictly adhere to the spin that the situation is the fault of the Twelve, not of the Israeli government. The female soldier grows angry at the decision. She cannot prove what happened to the body, but she knows intuitively that members of the Twelve are not responsible. Unbeknownst to the prime minister, she's met them.

TWELVE

"With all due respect, sir," the female soldier says, "that would imply a manipulation of Israel's sophisticated security agencies by untrained, inexperienced men." A heist by amateurs.

Prime Minister Ohred glares at her momentarily. She's young and beautiful but clearly more intelligent than he gave her credit for. Over the years, her acute analytical nature and remarkable intelligence had led to a rapid promotion. A quick glance at her badge indicates her name and region. Magda, a Galilean. But her black skin and slight accent indicate that her roots began elsewhere. Africa definitely, Ethiopia presumably. The prime minister revels in the fact that Jews from across the globe make their way to *Eretz Yisrael*, some wanting to defend the land and people. Even though she wasn't born on Israeli soil, she's earned great respect for protecting and defending the small country. Ohred glowers at her for a moment, knowing that she's right but not wanting to acquiesce. His pride won't allow it.

For a year now, Magda's been following the activities and progression of the movement led by Yasha. She even donates anonymously and covertly to support his campaign of peace and love. He forever changed her life. Twice. Her instincts confirm that members of the Twelve didn't kidnap the body. Something miraculous has happened, she's sure of it, though she has no proof.

Early this morning, before sunrise, she'd set out for the place where his body was being kept in order to pay her respects. Only a high-ranking officer could access the location without permission. The prime minister had ensured complete security and isolation. To her surprise, she'd found the guards asleep, the metal coffin empty. Alarmed and confused, Magda felt like something unexplainable had happened. She left quickly to look for him and to inform her supervisor. En route, she'd run into El'azar and his sisters, Marta and Miryam, unofficial members of the Twelve, desperate to find where their leader had been hidden. Magda informed them— breaching the rules of conduct—that the coffin was empty. All four had

been shocked at the discovery. All four had felt a supernatural presence in the atmosphere as they conversed.

Like the prime minister, Magda tries to piece together the events, the facts. Everyone grasps at straws, herself included. She may not understand how and why, but she trusts her gut that tells her more is at play than meets the eye. She feels giddy at the prospect of another unexpected miracle—perhaps the greatest one yet. Could Yasha have done the impossible for himself just as he'd done for El'azar four months ago? She knows that everyone in the room remembers the El'azar incident when Yasha pulled his friend back from the grave. Imagine the ramifications if Yasha pulled off his *own* resurrection!

More than ever, she is drawn to Yasha, wanting to be a part of whatever's happening that defies reason and nature. If her instincts are right, this unexplainable phenomenon is huge. Not just on a political level but on a human and spiritual one. The reality will be explosive and utterly world changing. Now, though, her IDF position may be on the line for defending the Twelve. Yet she takes the risk.

"I cannot prove it yet," she tells the prime minister, "but the Twelve are not responsible. I assure you."

Ohred acknowledges her position but denies its truth. No explanation is off the table. The heads of intelligence again discuss half a dozen options from every angle possible. The Palestinians? The Twelve? Outside groups or governments? There are many options, he agrees, but there's only one right one. He trusts his gut. Even though the members of the Twelve had scattered in recent days, he believes they are the force behind their missing leader, no matter how clumsy and inadequate they might seem. Two of them have been convicted of crimes and previously incarcerated, after all.

Silently, Ohred wrestles with this unimaginable dilemma, shaking his head. His plan will work, he'll make sure of it. He is a master manipulator. The thought of failing the administration and the citizens of Israel causes

his stomach to clench. But another terrifying thought flashes through the prime minister's mind. If the president of Israel, the State's highest figurehead, finds out, the repercussions will be severe—forced resignation and public humiliation. The political embarrassment will outscore all the investigations into his administration's previous corruption, something Ohred denies vehemently.

The prime minister circles back to his personal theory, the one he will enforce. "Members of the Twelve were angry and distraught at the death of their leader, mere hours before Passover began, no less. So, they've retaliated by stealing Yasha's body. The Twelve are responsible, and we have proof—*that* is the narrative!" He knows that Shin Bet and the Mossad will comply without coercion. He worries that the two IDF soldiers, on the other hand, may not. "And when this news gets to the president's ears," he continues, facing the soldiers, "we will make sure you don't get blamed." The guards who fell asleep were directly under the soldiers' command.

He scribbles something on a piece of paper. It's an amount of money the soldiers have never seen in their bank accounts. They are being bribed at the highest level to remain silent and adhere to the narrative. He makes sure the soldiers accept the money without question or opposition; the choice is not theirs. One will save the money, the other will donate back to Yasha's cause. With a wave of his hand, Ohred dismisses them.

Quickly, he and the intelligence heads, Moshe Reuven and Zvi Goren, lay out the details for a press release. More spin, more lies, more manipulation. He will not suffer another insurrection in this country. Not during *his* administration. Though it has the potential to be a public relations nightmare, he determines to control the situation, swearing to hunt down each member of the Twelve and their missing leader. This blight on Israel's annals must be erased.

• • •

THE SAFE HOUSE

Every one of the eleven men holds his breath. Hearts pound, eyes dart. Shimon reaches for a handgun hidden in his waistband. The shadow of a man appears first. Natan feels his knees buckle and stumbles backwards a few steps. Faivel grabs him to keep him upright.

"Who got through?" Yochanan whispers. Shin Bet? IDF? Mossad?

"Maybe it's Toma's evil twin," Yaakov mutters. He glances at Toma, who's as pale as death.

Suddenly, a man appears in the doorway near the kitchen. He does not speak but gazes at the eleven.

"A ghost!" cries Mattiyahu, his eyes huge.

"Peace to you," the man declares.

The backlight on the man casts an eerie glow on him, as if he were transparent. The eleven Israelis think it's the spirit of their deceased leader. Waves of terror ripple through the room, forcing some to eye the back door in hopes of escape.

"Commander?" Faivel mumbles.

Kefa gasps, voice raspy, "Yasha?"

Oddly coincidental, thinks Yaakov. They were just talking about Yasha, and he appears out of nowhere? As if he'd been listening to their conversation?

This isn't happening, Toma thinks. *Stuff like this just doesn't happen.*

The others remain immobile, trying to process the aberration.

Their leader steps forward. He offers a broad smile. "Don't be upset. Don't let all these doubting questions take over."

Toma moves and positions himself behind Taddai, who is frozen in place. Shimon's hand becomes sweaty as he intensely grips his gun. *Is this a joke?* he wonders. *How could Yasha possibly be alive?* They all saw him arrested and tried for treason. His death was broadcast in the papers and on every media outlet. It cannot be real.

"Look at my hands, look at my feet—it's really me!" he says, walking closer. Instinctively, the men move back, dubious of the sudden apparition.

"Touch me. Look me over from head to toe. A ghost doesn't have muscle and bone like this," he chuckles. Yasha holds up his hands in the manner of surrender and smiles at Shimon. The evocative gaze penetrates his heart. Shimon loosens his grip on the gun, feeling guarded albeit somewhat foolish.

Toma is visibly shaking. He stares at Yasha, silently absorbing his changed countenance. It's as if nothing had happened. As if the physical thrashing wasn't just a few days ago. Their leader looks not merely alive but better somehow. Toma has harbored doubts about him and the group, about their mission even, since he joined. The impossible follows this man relentlessly. Now, Toma's doubt and confusion have reached a new level. If only he would allow his heart to arrest his mind.

Yasha lands his gaze on him. He knows Toma's nature consistently wrestles with skepticism, with apprehension, despite the fact that Toma has witnessed miracle after miracle. Despite his own supernatural incident. Yasha gently instructs him, "Take your hand and stick it in my side." The place where he'd been slashed by a soldier in order to verify his death.

Just moments ago, Toma had declared to the group that he couldn't believe Yasha to be alive. That he would have to physically touch Yasha's wounds to even consider such an unbelievable miracle. Had Yasha overheard? Toma forces himself, completely terrified, to swallow his fear and prove that what they're seeing isn't a ghost.

Gathering courage, he moves forward slowly. Once he touches the leader's torso, he exhales loudly. Both men let out a fractured laugh. A dozen questions fly through Toma's head. *How is he alive? When did this happen? Can this be real?* The impossible nature of the reality before him— alive after being dead for seventy-two hours—staggers Toma. He remembers that instance with El'azar, but this is different. Yasha pulled off his

own resurrection? His mind spins, thoughts moving in tight circles. *Maybe I'm hallucinating*, he thinks.

The leader hears a message internally. A gentle, instructive voice. *LOVE IS PATIENT AND KIND.*

"Don't be unbelieving," Yasha instructs Toma, addressing his propensity to doubt everything. "*Believe!*"

Toma whispers as the truth sinks in, "My God…" *Yasha is alive!*

"Toma," Yasha chides kindly, "So, you believe because you've seen with your own eyes." No faith required, no trust. He puts a gentle hand on his shoulder. "Even better blessings are in store for those who believe without seeing."

Toma doubts he'll ever achieve such levels of faith. *At least Yasha hasn't turned his back on me*, he thinks. No question the others will home in on this flaw—his propensity for doubt. They'll probably give him a nickname, in fact.

Toma looks around the room, embarrassed and self-conscious. Had Yasha somehow heard when he refused to believe until he saw, and perhaps touched, Yasha again? Toma shrugs his shoulders. "I didn't know he was just going to reappear and walk in here," he says, chagrined.

Yaakov mumbles, "What you don't know could fill the Dead Sea."

And with that, the collective tension breaks. Yochanan, then Mattiyahu and Arye move in and grip their leader in a hug. The embrace is deep, backs slapped, faces cupped. The rest welcome him back, one at a time, some laughing with relief, some tearing up. Intimacy and camaraderie of men bound by oaths of allegiance and a committed mission tested by fire.

"I *guessed* it," says Faivel, proudly. He raises his fists in celebration. Faivel, at last, has interpreted Yasha's mysterious message. He feels victorious in this one thing.

Yasha smiles and hugs Faivel. "Well done," he says. "I always believed you could solve it."

TWELVE

Kefa, though, stands fixed, the shame of his recent denial of knowing Yasha rendering him immobile. The others don't know, but Yasha does. He stretches out his arms, waiting.

Kefa takes a step, and Yasha rushes over, embracing him. "I'm sorry," Kefa whispers in his ear, tears filling his eyes. "I'm so sorry. I'll never forgive my…"

"Water under the bridge," Yasha answers. "And you must. I have." Yasha lets go of him, their eyes now connecting. "Don't worry, Kefa, you'll have many opportunities ahead to vouch for me."

A few of the men begin to whisper aloud previously unspoken thoughts. How many people know? Does this mean their revolution is alive again? A level of excitement buzzes in the air. Their leader, though, offers no answers. Instead, he looks past them into the kitchen and takes them by surprise for a second time.

"Do you have any food here?"

Voices halt. Did they hear him correctly? Food? How can he desire food at such a precarious time? Arye, oozing with nervous excitement, grabs a dirty plate to wash, which slips and falls loudly into the sink. A few of the others jump.

"Sorry," he offers, sheepishly, "I have butterhands."

Yasha guffaws. Arye's jargon always makes him laugh. "Butter*fingers!*"

Yochanan moves to the refrigerator and rummages through until he finds something edible. Some leftover falafel beef, a small piece of broiled fish in lemon sauce, and stale flatbread. He creates a quickfire dish out of the basics. The men watch their leader eat with ravenous force. It settles any last concerns that he may still be an apparition. He compliments Yochanan on making something delicious out of ordinary ingredients. A true talent. He's been hooked on his food since the first day they met.

Faivel peeks out of the curtain covering the front window. "Were you followed?" he asks, scanning the area. Eyes bloodshot, face haggard. His

gray-streaked afro is misshapen and unkempt. It's been a rough few days. "Shall we stay here?"

The leader nods. With a mouth full, he answers, "Stay here in the city."

Their excitement grows as it seems he is saying that their mission will be resumed. The government will be stunned that he's back. The people will be just as astonished. Maybe the shock will give them time to make inroads in the city—an uprising of supporters could prove to be stronger than any attempt by the administration to control matters. The circumstances have been flipped, and the power now lies with them.

"Do the officials know you're alive?" asks Shimon excitedly. He's eager to put up a fight after being run underground.

The leader smiles, eyes twinkling.

Not all of the Twelve are as animated as Shimon. Natan, Toma, and Ben-Chalfai appear otherwise—fearful, jumpy. They're in uncharted waters and feeling unsteady. Nothing like this has ever happened!

"Don't be intimidated," Yasha says to his men. "Eventually, everything is going to be out in the open, and everyone will know how things really are. So don't hesitate to go public now. Don't be bluffed into silence by the threats of bullies. There's nothing they can do to your soul, your core being. Save your fear for God," he says, "who holds your entire life—body and soul—in His hands."

"What are we going to do?" asks Yaakov.

The leader of the Twelve stands and looks at his men, wiping his mouth. He understands their nature, their strengths and weaknesses. None of them ever knew the entire plan—it was hidden in order to be revealed over time, through demonstration and deed. Even now he wonders if they fully understand what has happened, what is currently unfolding. He knows they sense an opportunity for vengeance—some more than others—and are eager to redeem themselves. If they only knew the impact they would wield and the influence they would carry for future generations, the dark fear hovering in the corners would go unnoticed.

Natan asks, "Are you going to restore Israel now? Is this the time?"

"You don't get to know the time," Yasha answers, "That's not your business."

"What, then, is the plan?" Kefa asks, vocalizing untethered thoughts. He feels the familiar tendency to prove himself, but he shifts that thought to focus on the group. He needs to assert his allegiance. The denial still haunts him.

The leader's voice is strong, direct. He instructs them that they must stay together in Jerusalem until a specific package arrives for them. A package containing great power and impact. The contents will enable them to withstand governments, to cross impassable borders, and to influence entire nations with their agenda. An opportunity of this magnitude has never existed. No government, no people groups will be able to stop the reformation.

Images of weapons and military arsenals race through some of their minds, yet they know their leader is counterculture by rote. Would he step up his approach to spreading his message of political and moral reform? Would he finally lead Israel in the avenues of lasting national and governmental peace? Even though some doubt that he would lead using forceful means, they hope to show strength worthy of notice. A true deliverer, a perfect Messiah.

None of the Twelve, however, understand that the package cannot be seen, cannot be controlled. It's power beyond their imagination. Yasha's last gift to them will be the unmatchable force of heaven in spirit form—the exact power that raised him from the dead. And that exact power will indwell them forever.

Bringing them back to the present, he says, "You're the first to hear and see it. You're the witnesses." He moves his arm over the room, referring to his reappearance, the meal, and the conversation. His return changes everything.

Mattiyahu, the group's sole lawyer, prefers being a legal counsel to that of a witness, to having more control over a situation. He shifts his

overweight body back and forth and fidgets like a distressed witness in a court of law. Old habits die hard. But he knows the control belongs to Yasha, so he reminds himself to trust.

"What comes next is very important," Yasha says. "God authorized and commanded me to commission you: Go out and train everyone you meet, far and near, in this way of life," he adds, "then instruct them in the practice of all I have commanded you." Yasha looks each of his eleven men in the eyes, sensing their fears, their hopefulness. "Even as I was sent," he commands with great intensity, "I now send *YOU!*"

It's a call of great risk. A call of martyrdom. They understand the magnitude of the assignment: to carry on the mission of transforming a nation and, beyond that, an entire world via counterculture methods. To usher in an entirely different kind of domain. It's a radical mission and one of ultimate sacrifice.

Without warning, he vanishes before their eyes.

1

THREE DAYS EARLIER

A mob of angry Middle Eastern men and women fills the square near the Temple Mount. Some are waving signs, others flags, and a few are holding high a photo of their president. There is a swaying of the crowd as the people move forward and back. A barrage of men in military uniform hovers on the edges, their fingers tense on the trigger. Voices rise into the atmosphere, the cacophony bouncing off the buildings. The shouting seems haphazard for a while, but it settles into a monotonous chant.

"Death! Death! Death to him!"

A blank jumbotron screen looms high over the crowd, displaying only the time. 3:33p.m. Suddenly, it jumps to life with an image of the Israeli prime minister, Uri Ohred. The crowd yells louder, fury and revenge filling the air. He begins speaking to the residents of his country. If subtitles were absent, none of the demonstrators would know the content of the press conference, such is the noise. Vague remarks appear on the screen, written in Hebrew and Arabic.

Then, breaking news as two pictures, side by side, fill the screen. On the left, Palestinian Isan bar-Abbas; on the right, Israeli Yasha ha Natzeret.

Both men look roughed up from their time in custody. Yasha, though, has clearly been beaten worse. Members of the Twelve stand dispersed around the square, mostly incognito, as they've been hiding since Yasha's arrest five days ago in the Bethlehem café. Arye gasps at the sight of Yasha. Ben-Chalfai feels tears pricking his eyes. Yaakov clenches his jaw, anger filling his heart. *They completely pummeled him*, he thinks. *He's hardly*

recognizable. Toma, Taddai, and Yochanan struggle with the injustice of Yasha's punishment—how could such a peaceful man inspire such hatred in others?

On the screen, the two faces of the prisoners generate shouts from the crowd. Convicted of terrorism that killed innocent civilians in Jerusalem last year, bar-Abbas has been held at the highest security Israeli prison. Yasha, a revolutionary leader in opposition to the Israeli government, has been detained for treason at a Palestinian jail after being recently captured.

A deal has been made. In order to avoid a civil war, the Israeli and Palestinian governments have come to an agreement. But the crowd doesn't know this. The event has already taken place in the middle of the night, but they are led to believe their opinion matters.

The face of the prime minister again fills the screen. Now is the time to apportion their destinies. Both men will pay a price for their choices, according to Ohred, yet in truth, only one will be sentenced to judgment. The other will eventually go free to enjoy a second chance—a nod to the first century *Pesach*, or Passover, practice of releasing one prisoner. Israeli ordinances decree ultimate payment for the highest offenses. But he taunts the crowd, seeking approval.

"A prisoner exchange," Ohred announces. "And accountability to follow for the man attempting to start a civil war in this land."

The crowd's roar rings through the air, growing louder, shouting approval. The facts remain regarding these two offenders, the prime minister explains, though no one cares to listen. Justice must be served. In the minds of Israelis and Palestinians alike, terrorism and treason are taken seriously, yet only one will ultimately pay the price. The Israeli people, both enemies and former supporters of Yasha, won't tolerate a traitor in their midst. Treason stands an unpardonable sin.

Propaganda against Yasha and the Twelve rose to new heights within the last week. A smear campaign stamped with high-level espionage changed the political landscape in Israel. They were branded by the

government and the media as a guerrilla organization. Not even the prime minister's various scandals come close to the seriousness of treason, especially for a country surrounded by active enemies.

Media-run stories first claimed that Yasha's cell had been funneling large sums of money to the Palestinians earmarked for massive terrorism with plans to sell out and destroy the State of Israel. Even an insider to the group was named as a source. Accounts had been rigged, money laundered. After that, allegations of plans to take down the Dome of the Rock and start a war with Islamic states throughout the Middle East circulated wildly. Israeli intelligence had falsified the claims, shoveling a scripted narrative down the throats of every man, woman, and child. Yasha and the Twelve had planned to start Armageddon.

Proof, of course, resides squarely inside the tightly controlled Intel Community. One man, according to authorities, has put an entire nation at risk of destruction—he betrayed his own country, betrayed his closest followers and supporters. Israel must make an example of Yasha. To show strength. To warn others.

A mob had set all of Jerusalem in an uproar. The people had loved Yasha until they hated him—flipped on a dime by cancel culture. They attacked every safe house looking for the Twelve, wanting to drag them out and make a public spectacle of them. But the houses were empty, the men scattered. A frenzy fueled by a deceptive government has made for civil unrest in the name of pursuing recompence.

Corporal punishment remains the only option. Israel must protect itself against foreign invaders and internal enemies alike. Prime Minister Ohred has made good on his promise to sway the people against Yasha, even his previous devotees. Yasha's inner circle of men hides, afraid their fate will be the same as his. Endless media coverage inflating the falsely accused leader has bombarded the airwaves, calling for justice to be served. And so, they chant.

"Death! Death to him!"

TWELVE

• • •

Inside closed walls, away from the crowd, Yasha stands before a large group of officials. A hooded prisoner, he wobbles back and forth, barely keeping himself upright. The guard holding him up yanks the hood off, and there's a collective reaction. Yasha ha Natzeret looks like he just had a session with the warden of Evin Prison, Iran's notoriously torturous penitentiary. Blood drips from every area of his head, stripes of red stream down his back. Just as he begins to fall over dead, the lead guard grabs him and growls, "Not time yet."

The man in authority nods his head. Two more guards then grab the prisoner and drag him through a corridor into a dark cell reeking of sulfur and urine. They throw him to the ground on the dank, stone floor. He barely makes a sound. About a dozen people watch: among them soldiers, secret service, government officials, a rabbi. The man has made a lot of enemies.

Orders have been given at the highest level. Treason is punishable by execution, especially when the offender refuses to cooperate. Any attempt at conspiring to subvert the government is met with the ultimate punishment. In the eyes of the Israeli government, Yasha and the Twelve succeeded in their sabotage attempts. Swift punishment is mandatory.

The guards pick up the thick ropes and tie one to each wrist with such force that immediately the skin is cut to the bone. His feet are tied together in the same fashion. His head hangs limp, but he's still alive. One breath, then two. The ropes on his hands are threaded through iron rings on opposite walls, where two guards yank at the same time. Yasha flies up with a jolt—his blood sprinkling the area from the sheer force—and releases an agonizing wail. If it wasn't for the wood-paneled walls installed to dampen all sound, his screams would have thundered down the halls. A third guard pulls the rope attached to Yasha's feet, and his knees, which were barely touching the floor, swing back. He's now suspended in the air, stretched three ways.

The lead guard walks up close enough to Yasha's face to hear the shaking breath fall from his mouth. The guard taunts him, calling him obscene names in a few different languages. He asks questions that go unanswered.

"Do you hear that?" Trickles of noise, of cheering, float in the air. "They chant for your death," he snarls.

Silence.

"People hate traitors. You think you've won them over because of some silly good deeds? They *despise* you."

Silence still.

Patience is growing short. The guard grabs Yasha's hair and yanks his head up. He wouldn't be recognizable to most, maybe not even his mother.

"Bravo, ruler of Jews," he sneers. For months, Yasha talked about ruling and prevailing from a higher place. A heavenly place, with love, peace, and joy. But such ambitions get battered by rulers of the world. Their governments, their kingdoms must be protected at all costs. The guard spits on him and punches him once more. Yasha's head falls back down as he slips in and out of consciousness.

The director of Mossad, Zvi Goren, mocks him. "He saved others—but he can't save himself. King of Israel, is he? Then let him get himself out of this situation; we'll *all* become believers then!" His disdain for Yasha and his references of a greater kingdom has steadily grown over the past twelve months. The mass influx of visitors into Israel seeking a miracle has encouraged nefarious characters to infiltrate his country, to threaten the tight security that he's established as director of Israel's national intelligence agency.

Silence fills the cell. Thick air grows thicker. Everyone is content to stare for long minutes, waiting for the end.

Yasha sucks in a long, labored breath, breaking the silence. Then a faint whisper. *"Eli...my God...why have...You...abandoned me?"*

Everyone has turned on him. All of the Twelve, government leaders, ordinary Israelis and Palestinians. Bearing the weight of the world, he is the scapegoat. A sacrificial lamb, as it were. What remains misunderstood, though, is the fact that Yasha fulfills the role willingly. A sacrifice not forced but offered. One day people will understand. One day members of the Twelve will take up his mantle, will continue his mission, and will reach the world with his divine love. They, too, will operate in supernatural, miraculous power. While it seems now that this is the end of Yasha and his purpose, in fact it's the beginning of a worldwide metamorphosis.

Moshe Reuven, the head of Shin Bet, Israel's security agency, stands in the corner. He and his organization track what happens inside every square inch of Israel's borders. Yasha and his followers crossed established boundaries set by the Israeli government, which is why he'd been forcefully arrested, interrogated, and convicted. With thick condescension, Reuven says, "He calls for Elijah." Clearly, the prisoner is delusional and experiencing hallucinations.

A third guard picks up a small metal cup holding caustic, murky liquid and begins walking toward the man. His interactions with Yasha in the past few weeks have left him with a bag of mixed emotions. He feels caught, having sympathies in both camps. Yasha is a rabble-rouser and enemy of the state, to be sure, yet he is captivating and benevolent to so many. Above all, he loves the unlovable, just as Yasha's cousin, Yochanan the Immerser, had said months ago in a different prison.

"Don't be in such a hurry," Reuven says, with fierce derision to the guard. "Let's see if Elijah comes and saves him." He mocks everything.

Ohred looks at his watch. He hadn't planned on executing Yasha today, just hours before Passover. But the mounting political tension, pressure, and urgency had come to an apex. He feels stretched taut, ready to snap. Ohred—and all of Israel—needed to be rid of Yasha once and for all.

Suffocating from suspension, Yasha tries to gather his breath. He sputters some sounds while the room waits to hear any final words. Bloody drool slips from his mouth, splattering the floor. After a few attempts, he utters a final, guttural cry—its shrill force causes everyone to wince. He then whispers three words that perhaps only a father could detect.

"It is finished."

He finished the work he was sent to do: accomplished victory over earthly parameters, invaded the natural with the supernatural, and bridged the gap no other person could. Instantly, his body goes limp.

Now, the only noise in the cell is a faint ticking coming from the antique watch on the wrist of Zvi Goren. Even death cannot stop time. After a minute, Goren nods to a guard to verify Yasha's death.

"See to it."

The second guard pulls out a switchblade and takes aim. A slice the width of a hand opens in Yasha's side, but he doesn't move. Water and blood pour out, and as soon as it hits the floor, the ground begins to shake. A low rumble at first, then a noticeable quaking. No one can remember the last time Jerusalem had an earthquake. People look around as the stone floor cracks open and the roof begins to crumble down. The bare light bulb blacks out and explodes. The shaking grows incrementally stronger, and Reuven, Goren, and others all run from the holding cell, leaving the third guard—the conflicted one—alone with the dead man. With a violent crack, the walls split from the top down, instead of from the foundation up. Again, the impossible has happened.

That's when he knows the truth.

Holding onto the doorway, eyes huge with fear, he sees clearly for the first time. Though no one is there, he gasps, "This man was *innocent!*"

Quickly he ducks out, leaving the suspended body hanging amidst the rubble.

2

TWO HOURS EARLIER

A group of Palestinian teens laugh and cajole in a house tucked in East Jerusalem. One of their siblings, a young boy named Yishmael, has brought them something unexpected. Something meaningful and valuable to the Jews, their enemies. Eyes widen and hands reach for the lacquered guitar that belonged to the leader of the Twelve. The boy discovered it in a corner of his father's café in Bethlehem the night Yasha was arrested by the Palestinian Authority. Yishmael was thrilled with the treasure that lay in his hands. He would most certainly be hailed as a hero for stealing the instrument, especially considering the arrest and allegations brought against Yasha. And so, he is. Praises for the boy's bravery fill the room. Allah is proud.

The older boys take turns stroking the guitar. None of them know how to play, but two have heard it strummed before—the day the Jewish leader pranced around with it by the Jaffa Gate in the Old City's walls. Within minutes, the bargaining begins. Who does it belong to now? Wouldn't the thief's family have rightful ownership? Not everyone agrees. Rank and ties among the Palestinian groups surely takes precedent. Voices grow louder and more spirited. At last, the boy who found the guitar offers a solution. They will roll dice for it.

Shouts of cheering and competitive banter echo around the room. Two sixes determine the winner. They sit in a circle on the floor, the space in the middle their gambling arena. Round and round they play, the tension and anticipation building. After a handful of minutes, the victorious

8

combination is thrown. Half the boys celebrate with the winner, the other half groan and fall into silence. Perhaps it's luck. Perhaps it's fate.

Both emotions pulse through Yishmael as he surveys the others. Slowly, reverently, he picks up the prized guitar. He gazes into the dark red, glossy lacquer, and an image catches his eye. He expects to see his own reflection, but the face of the rightful owner stares back. The same face that has performed miracles throughout Israel and the West Back since last April.

That night, Yishmael suffers a disquieting dream. In it, he holds the treasured guitar, plucking the nylon strings. Suddenly, the leader of the Twelve appears and holds out his hand toward the boy. He's been caught. Afraid of retribution, Yishmael shrinks back, heart pounding. But the man merely smiles, quelling the fear. His hand reaches toward the boy, who looks at the instrument and begins to hand it over. The man slowly shakes his head, eyes offering forgiveness, offering love. Unspoken words find Yishmael's heart: *Keep it.* The proffered hand extends closer, waiting, and the boy understands at last. He cautiously grabs hold of the hand and rises. Heat and peace flood his being with such intensity that it wakes him instantly.

3

ONE DAY EARLIER

Deep inside the ancient walls of Jerusalem, Yasha sits in a bare interrogation room. Moshe Reuven and Zvi Goren, representing Israel's highest offices of security and intelligence, glare at him intensely. An IDF soldier guards the room.

Moshe Reuven, the longtime head of Shin Bet, begins to forcefully prod Yasha about the Twelve. Of his doctrine, of their plans. A small contingent takes part in questioning this man who has led the strongest revolutionary movement in their nation. He has unofficially enlisted thousands, if not more, into his ideology, posing the greatest threat to the established government. It's an underground movement set out to defy and replace, undermining law and order. Though Yasha is entitled to explain and justify himself, Reuven's mind has essentially been made up.

The Shin Bet—responsible for safeguarding state security, exposing terrorist rings, and interrogating terror suspects—keeps a tight rein on the activities within Israel's borders. It provides intelligence as well as protection. The agency answers directly to the prime minister. Reuven looks at his watch—10:00 a.m. Time is of the essence.

Yasha, black and blue from a previous interrogation, sits motionless as questions bombard him in rapid-fire approach. How did he acquire his inner circle of twelve men? Were they recruits or volunteers? Was there money involved? Why those men in particular? Yasha says nothing. He will not give them the satisfaction of an answer. If they're in the intelligence community, why bother asking? Shouldn't they already know?

His silence infuriates Reuven. Doesn't Yasha understand that the Israeli government and intelligence agencies retain full control? That his fate rests squarely in their hands, or so they claim?

After long minutes, the detainee finally gives a calm answer. "I've spoken openly in public. I've taught regularly in meeting places and the Temple Mount, where the Jews all come together. Everything has been out in the open. I've said nothing in secret."

Reuven and the IDF soldiers grow more annoyed with this answer. They know. They've been watching and following this renegade for many months. And they hate playing games.

Sensing this, Yasha continues to push back. "Why are you treating me like a conspirator? Question those who have been listening to me." He looks at each man as though holding a highly confidential secret behind his eyes. "They know well what I've said."

Out of nowhere, a fist strikes Yasha on his cheekbone. He rights his head again and feels for the blood that has erupted from his skin. The IDF soldier snarls, "How dare you speak like that!"

Yasha touches his cheek again and examines the dollop of blood on his finger. "If I've said something wrong, prove it. But if I've spoken the plain truth," Yasha says in a low voice, "why this slapping around?"

Another crack against the left side of his head. The military baton draws blood from a few areas. His arms move up in self-protection, but the club finds uncovered spots, inflicting concentrated pain. Globs of spit are hurled at his face and neck. They slide down his skin, mixing with the blood. He hears an unspoken message reverberate in his heart. The familiar, peaceful voice.

LOVE ENDURES ALL THINGS.

Yasha wipes his face, smearing blood on the back of his hand. Even his enemies are the object of a greater love; his assignment does not exclude them. "I arrive on the scene, tell you the plain truth, and you refuse to have a thing to do with me. Can any of you convict me of a single

misleading word, a single sinful act? But if I'm telling the truth, why don't you believe me? Anyone on God's side listens to God's words." He pauses a beat, eyes boring into theirs. "*That* is why you're not listening." They're on the wrong side of this conversation. On the wrong side of history.

Eyeing Yasha with suspicion, Reuven says, "Where did you come from?"

Yasha withholds an answer.

"You won't explain? Don't you know that I have the authority to pardon you, and the authority to…*kill* you?"

Yasha looks him full in the face. "You haven't a shred of authority over me except what has been given you from heaven. That's why the one who betrayed me to you has committed a far greater fault."

Reuven starts to deny this but stops himself. How much does Yasha know of the clandestine meeting with one from his inner circle? Betrayal and duplicity are part of the job. The ends always justify the means. The administration officials are the ones in control, not Yasha. They will change the truth, bury it even, to direct the narrative. Sophisticated plans will shift allegations and blame. Treachery, conspiracy, and deceit are all being deployed. The organization goes to great lengths to cover its tracks.

On cue, Zvi Goren steps in. His agency, the Mossad, is responsible for counterterrorism and covert operations. Unlike the government and military, the Mossad's powers are exempt from the constitutional laws of the State of Israel. And such power can be wielded however deemed necessary, independent of legality.

"Any individual that expresses views which the Israeli government considers an incitement to violence may face criminal penalties," Zvi Goren says. "I'm referring to your threat on the Temple Mount."

Silence. Yasha knows they don't have all the information, that his words are different from their words. When he spoke a few weeks ago of tearing down the place of worship and rebuilding it within three days, he was referring to himself, not the Dome of the Rock. But, of course, they

can't understand that. Not yet. A few days from now they will experience the shock of their lives.

"There's also sufficient evidence that you are a spy for the Palestinian Authority."

Again, Yasha stays silent. He knows that this is all part of the plan. The level of spin against the leader of the Twelve multiplies by the day. No need for facts or confirmation to verify the ruse. The war of words rages on. The people in the region are turning. Truth is elusive. Falsified evidence is produced to dupe the public, even members of the Twelve. Everything is a setup to eliminate Yasha so that the Twelve will fall apart. So that their movement will die, forever to be forgotten in Israeli history.

"Documents, protected accounts, surveillance tapes..." Goren says. "And then, of course, there's the incident at the refugee camp in the West Bank back in February."

Yasha gives no reaction, save a slight smile. He remembers those faces, that hunger... for food, for hope.

"Strange that you would be trying to provoke another intifada by destroying the Dome of the Rock and yet also be working with the Palestinian Authority to unleash terrorism amongst the Israelis," Goren accuses. "Playing both sides, perhaps?"

Yasha holds his tongue. He doesn't need to give them the satisfaction of an answer. They have already decided his fate, he knows. Regardless of protocol, regardless of truth. Whether they claim he's working for or against the Palestinians, the truth, like him, will be buried.

"It would be *irresponsible* of us to allow you to destroy the State of Israel with the help of the Palestinians," Goren says slowly, emphasizing certain words, "and then to turn on them and destroy the Dome of the Rock. All in the name of setting up your own government...your own *kingdom*."

Yasha whispers, eyes closing, "Your kingdom come, Your will be done..."

Goren scowls at him. "Needless to say, espionage against the State of Israel is taken quite seriously. There are, basically, no opportunities for bargaining. In fact, you have very few options at all. Either you cooperate and provide detailed information about the Palestinian Authority's plans or face the alternative." No need to detail the alternative. Everyone knows what happens to people who oppose Mossad.

Yasha sighs deeply, eyes still closed. His twelve cell members flash though his mind, each one chosen for a purpose. He loves them like brothers. The rescue mission is almost complete: to pull them from a life dictated by the world. To enable them to see things from a higher perspective. To love, even one's enemies—the one who betrayed him, included.

There is no need to defend himself. Yasha knows what few people do. Justice will be miscarried. The innocent will be reckoned guilty. As quiet as a lamb being sheared, he sits composed, allowing the administration to cut off truth.

"We take silence to mean an admission of guilt."

After long minutes of waiting, Moshe Reuven speaks. "The State of Israel finds you guilty of treason. The plot to take down the current administration via espionage with the Palestinian Authority is your crime." A crime for which there is no pardon.

Yasha tilts his head back, neck muscles taut, blood and mucus still clinging to his skin. One of his cell members betrays him, he betrays the government, or so the story goes. Like the goat upon whom all sin was transposed in ancient times, he bears the hands of the iniquitous upon him. The scapegoat. Eyes now open toward heaven, as if he can see through the ceiling. Unnatural peace blankets his demeanor. He's willing to die—for the Twelve, for the rest.

The Shin Bet director whispers to his equal. "Are we in agreement?"

"No choice. He is guilty," he answers. He beckons the guard over and speaks into his ear. The decision has been made.

The IDF soldier steps in front of the notorious leader of the Twelve. Shackles are placed upon him again.

"We have a law," Reuven says to Yasha, "and by that law, you must die." He then turns back to the soldier and coldly gives instructions. "Beat him…within an inch of his life."

4

THE NIGHT BEFORE

The *Adhan* wakes Saidoreh with a start. She's thankful, this one time, for that piercing Arabic sound in the pitch dark—the early morning Muslim call to prayer. Otherwise, she would still be asleep, still suffering the worst nightmare yet. No other noise can be heard in the home she shares with her husband, the prime minister—only the Adhan reverberating throughout the Jerusalem sky, seeping into her bedroom.

Normally, Saidoreh dreams of the wild religious man known as the Immerser. The one with long dreadlocks and piercing blue eyes. The one who had publicly called out her legal and moral infractions a year ago, humiliating her worldwide. Saidoreh had to retaliate, to take control of matters. She had had no choice. Since then, the nightmares have tormented her. No matter how hard she tries, she cannot shake them or the sensations they leave. *How long will the dreams continue?* she wonders. How long can she live feeling drained, scared, and completely unnerved? Her guilt and the graphic night terrors pull her further and further into darkness. Even the anti-anxiety meds and sleep aids cannot combat the unseen forces.

Tonight, however, the nightmare was about a different man—the one named Yasha, who's been traversing the country with a gaggle of followers, preaching religious ideologies and performing impossible feats. Like a diviner, she has seen his gruesome death even though he's still alive, albeit in a covert detention center. Saidoreh rubs her face and exhales a shaky breath. She then rolls over and grabs her phone. 5:04 a.m. Her husband,

Uri Ohred, is not there. In fact, his side of the bed remains untouched. She pulls the covers over her head, trying to push out the horrific images she's just seen. After ten minutes, she realizes that sleep is futile and that she must talk to Uri. Otherwise, her conscience might erupt.

Normally, she is the picture of control. Her iron will matches that of her husband—a steely determination forged by years in a hostile environment. But following her recent decisions, a shift has occurred, and she cannot manipulate her predicament. Thus far, she has told no one, not even Uri. Nothing has ever rattled Saidoreh's confidence to the core. Not when her first husband served in war, not when scandals broke out within her second husband's administration, not even when she heard rumors of planned assassination attempts against Uri. But the night terrors that occur every time she closes her eyes will not relent. She's never experienced anything like it, and she remains powerless. The only thing she can do is confess.

Saidoreh sits up, pops a pill for her nerves, and dials her husband.

• • •

The offices are dark save for one room. The Israeli prime minister has been awake all night, sleep as far away as peace in his country. He sits in a leather chair across from the president of Israel, Peres Peliat—a large, imposing figure. The two are friends as well as administrative allies. Ohred knows he does not have to include the president in the final plans, but extra support never hurts. That, and it makes him feel superior in an underhanded way.

"Now," the prime minister asks the aging head of state, "what shall we do?"

Ohred's rage against everyone—Yasha, Nakdimon, Yehudas, the Palestinian Authority—sends his blood pressure soaring. He believes the latest events were set up as retaliation against him. He was clearly double-crossed by his deputy, Nakdimon, a man he once trusted implicitly.

Cameras don't lie. Everyone is subverting his government, and everyone must pay. First and foremost, the leader of the Twelve.

Now that Yasha is back in Israeli custody, a decision must be made. He'd been seized by the Palestinian Authority three days ago—a surprise to the Israeli government—at the behest of the former deputy prime minister. Just yesterday, Ohred and Mustafa, the Palestinian president, had agreed to a prisoner exchange. Yasha now waits in a Jerusalem prison. Ohred believes that Yasha has been trying to ignite a civil war between the Israelis and Palestinians. His words and actions declare as much, despite what some might claim. Ohred is determined to silence Yasha and the aspirations of the Twelve. Then and only then will the prime minister peacefully enjoy Passover.

"There must be punishment," says Peliat.

They cannot simply execute Yasha without just cause and proof. Even with proper justification, the State of Israel has protocols for killing one of its citizens. Legal channels demand attention. There must be a foolproof course of action. Ohred is tired of Yasha and the Twelve. Charges brought against him must leave no room for doubt. True or not, the accusations will prevail, and Yasha will cease to be a problem.

Like a flash of light, the answer arrives. Ohred poses it to President Peliat, weighing the merits, waiting an approval.

Before the president responds, a blaring ring tone fills the office. Saidoreh's number looms on Uri's screen. His wife never calls unless it's incredibly urgent. He holds up an apologetic hand. Before he can greet Saidoreh, her words stumble out, flustered and scared.

"Saidoreh, calm down," Ohred says, seeking clarification.

In between shaking breaths, she tells him what's been happening. The nightmares, the eerie presence that haunts her, the visions of the future. The wild religious man from the past, the leader of the Twelve at present. At the end, she makes an impassioned plea. "Uri, please," she begs, "don't get mixed up with judging this man."

A tense pause fills the air. The timing of her statement alarms him. He looks at his watch. The exact moment they were to decide the fate of Yasha which would ensure a favorable outcome for his administration in this matter? Impossible. How could she have known? What has happened?

"What are you saying?"

"I've just been through a long and tortured night because of dreams about him," Saidoreh explains. "Yasha and the Immerser were together, laughing and talking about their family, about the future. The scene changed suddenly, and both men were covered in blood. They reached out for me, calling my name over and over!"

Though the relationship between Yasha and the Immerser wasn't known when she had the Immerser jailed then subsequently murdered months ago, it cannot be ignored any longer. Her nightmare confirmed that the Immerser's blood is already on her hands, but maybe she can save Yasha, his cousin.

"Please," she begs, "let him go." Maybe then the demons will let her go.

Ohred can hear tears in his wife's voice. Saidoreh never cries. Despite the constant nightmares and sleepless nights since the Immerser's death, her resolve has never cracked. Until now.

The prime minister feels unnerved and for some minutes begins to second-guess himself. A sharp chill rushes through him. He re-focuses on his wife, soothing her worries, making vague promises. When he hangs up, President Peliat eyes him suspiciously. Ohred shakes his head, dismissing any questions before they are posed. He silences the voices in his head that challenge his judgment. He must stay focused, despite any unexpected last-minute appeals. Despite any uncertainties. Too many things haven't gone to plan; there have been too many last-minute surprises. Ohred can't take the pressure, the persistent aggravation. By tomorrow night, before the start of Passover, Yasha will have been brutally interrogated and summarily executed.

TWELVE

The prime minister and the president pick up where they left off.

"Your decision?" Ohred asks, eyebrows raised.

President Peliat nods, giving his approval. "Do what you must."

This decision, however, could easily backfire on Ohred—something he cannot afford. Again, he plays through the calculations, understanding the inherent risks. Treason, in his opinion, is an immediate risk to Israel's security that must be quickly eliminated. In the end, he ignores Saidoreh and banks on his own instincts. He is rarely wrong.

5

FOUR MINUTES EARLIER

Kefa, the first member of the Twelve, stands beside a large metal trash-can, warming his hands over the fire. Servants and officers of the Israeli Defense Forces hang about there as well. Night duty. The temperature seems to be getting colder. Dawn draws closer yet seems further and further away. The large courtyard nestled in the Old City of Jerusalem creates a tunnel for the wind to whip through on this breezy April night. For a while, voices are low and hushed; small clouds of breath make a rhythmic appearance. Kefa rubs his hands together, thinking of the past few days. He hasn't slept all night. Hasn't spoken to anyone, not even his brother, Arye, another member of the Twelve.

No one has seen Yasha since his arrest in Bethlehem three days ago. All members of the Twelve had scattered like frightened rats, himself included. He was the first to be chosen and the first to run. Shame burns in his chest. Hours after fleeing, he had berated himself for being a coward, for running away. He then forced himself to return to the city, despite his instincts to protect himself.

Kefa cannot believe that one of the Twelve became a turncoat, that their leader was handed over to the authorities seeking to shut down the cell. Anger swells up in him. Betrayal is unforgiveable. Yet Yasha had predicted this, hadn't he? Why is he surprised? Yasha often announced events before they would happen. But news of the turncoat's unexpected death shocks him even more. He wrestles with mixed feelings of sadness and satisfaction. Kefa tries to pinpoint when Yehudas had turned on

Yasha and the tight-knit group. Did he make a deal with the Israeli government? Did they blackmail him? Why was the Palestinian Authority involved?

Kefa's thoughts spin out of control. Events around him spin out of control. Where are the others? Hiding, no doubt. This, too, makes Kefa incensed, yet he feels their fear. Will the government come for the rest of them? What are they going to do to Yasha? Kefa is insistent on staying in relative proximity to their leader, in Jerusalem proper. He will not abandon Yasha now, not after all that has happened. Didn't he make that promise? Under his breath, Kefa vows to stay strong, to stay close, fueled by his disdain for the choices the other cell members have made. His pride proves relentless.

Emotions surge through his heart as he gazes at the fire. Twisting, turning, whipping him in different directions. Kefa is lost in thought as the recent days flash through his head. He doesn't realize the people in the courtyard are talking about the Twelve. A young soldier squints at him across the fire, pointing a finger in his direction.

"You," she says, her tone full of accusation, "I recognize you..."

Kefa snaps to attention. All eyes are on him.

"You were with Yasha ha Natzeret," the female soldier says, emphatically.

Everyone knows the name Yasha, leader of the Twelve, the most controversial figure of late to traverse the land of Israel. Rumors of plots to take down the government and start a civil war have spread for weeks. Allegations of sponsoring Islamic terrorism via backchannels raged throughout all communities. News reports and social media blasted the group again and again. Lies, deception, and accusations grew as did the number of citizens who had once supported him. People's loyalty seemed to have shifted in the wake of 'Indisputable' evidence. Once he was viewed as a dynamic humanitarian, now a traitor to their country. Truth, as Kefa knew, could be manufactured.

Fear flashes in Kefa's eyes, and he panics. He pulls his hat down lower over his bald head in an attempt to hide his face. "I don't know what you're talking about."

Immediately, he feels a stab in his gut. The pain is sharp, and Kefa sucks in a breath. Moments pass, and the pain now crawls up his belly like a vine. The sensation of being squeezed overcomes him. He shuts his eyes tight, willing the conversation to end, willing the internal discomfort to end.

But the soldier ignores him and says to her companions, "Yes, yes! He's one of them!"

They begin to talk about recent events, about government control. They've seen videos circulating in the media proving the subterfuge of the Twelve. Kefa knows the videos are manufactured using advanced artificial intelligence (AI) technology. Faivel, the fifth member of the Twelve, even demonstrated how they create them through computer images and voice copy capability. But Kefa also knows explaining this to the soldier won't make a difference. The voices around him reflect a collective sense of anger and frustration moving throughout the holy land. They take turns glaring at Kefa.

Kefa shakes his head emphatically. "I swear, I never laid eyes on the man."

Stubbornness and arrogance have always been his Achilles' heel. For years, an overly self-confident attitude and behavior had dictated the course of his life. Until he met Yasha, that is. Yasha had not only confronted Kefa with this weakness but had shown him how to overcome it. To focus his energy on the collective mission instead of on himself. To submit to Yasha's authority. He had been doing so well, in his opinion, until Yasha was arrested and taken away.

Now, the vine of shame grows higher, grips tighter. His breathing becomes more difficult. He pulls the upturned collar of his coat together and shoves his hands deep into the pockets. Somehow, he's sweating despite the cool temperature. He hunches his shoulders and keeps his gaze low, pulling his hat lower. How much do they know? Have they been sent to trap him? He nervously wonders if they will apprehend him like they did Yasha. He determines not to let that happen. His mind spins, his eyes dart around looking for an easy exit.

"You've *got* to be one of them. You've got it written all over you."

But Kefa curses and swears, his voice loud and defensive. "I don't know the man!"

Without warning, a wailing cry blares before dawn. Kefa looks up toward the dark sky. The 5:00 a.m. muezzins ring out from loudspeakers at the top of countless minarets across Jerusalem. The Adhan is inescapable. Kefa remembers the haunting words that Yasha had spoken to him just a few days ago. *Before the sound crows out, you'll deny me three times.* He feels the vine wrapping tighter, now around his heart, constricting blood flow.

Lightheaded, he stumbles backward, losing his balance. He can't breathe. He wants to run, but his feet seem stuck in the cobblestones.

Again, the muezzins call out, sending violent chills across Kefa's flesh. Tears form in his eyes, panic rises in his throat. How did Yasha know? How did this perplexing man know Kefa better than he knew himself? The weight of it all—the last twelve months, the unexpected turn of events, the prophecy, the denial—is too much. Anger, confusion, shame. The sting of it all hurts badly. Kefa doubts himself and everything he thought he understood. How could he let Yasha down like this? How could he not keep a simple promise? He denied knowing the one person that he swore he never would deny. When confronted, he crumbled. Not once, or even twice. Three times in a matter of minutes! The thought causes his stomach to lurch. Kefa turns, stumbles down an alley, falls against the stone wall, and retches violently.

After he's spent, Kefa weeps.

6

ONE DAY EARLIER

Mohammad Mustafa, the president of the Palestinian Authority, sits quietly with Prime Minister Ohred behind closed doors. An emergency 7:00 p.m. meeting was arranged in light of the situation at hand. Both governments have been played. Both heads of state are furious. Obligatory pleasantries foregone, they each reach for their preferred vice: the president, his cigarettes and the prime minister, his bourbon.

Unbeknownst to both leaders, the former deputy prime minister of Israel, a man named Nakdimon, had taken government matters into his own hands less than forty-eight hours ago. Without approval and without sanctions, he singlehandedly altered Israel's plan to arrest Yasha, leader of the Twelve, after Passover. Pitting Israel against her Palestinian neighbor, he dropped alarming top-secret intelligence in the hands of the Palestinian Authority, forcing them to apprehend Yasha before the high holy day. Nakdimon had gambled with Yasha's future as well as the future of Israel and Palestine. A civil war could erupt at the drop of a hat. Precious real estate is at stake. Neither country seeks an escalation in conflict, but both will defend this parcel of land to the death.

Given the urgency and surprise of recent events, Ohred and Mustafa share their frustrations and ire over Nakdimon's decisions. Ohred assures Mustafa that Nakdimon, currently missing in action, will most certainly be found and punished accordingly. Even though he was always a loyal citizen and dedicated official of the State of Israel, Nakdimon will pay. His rash decision will cost him his life. Traitors are not tolerated.

25

Little time has been allotted for each government leader to formulate a plan. Events are moving fast. Time is of the essence. Mustafa will hold Yasha as collateral, of course. Rebuffed, he will seek ways to come out ahead in this situation. Both men calculate their next moves critically. Ohred looks intently at Mustafa, weighing the potential outcomes of his undisclosed proposal. He's hoping it will diffuse any plans of retaliation for Nakdimon's sabotage. Though uncertain, it's worth taking the risk.

"I'm thinking of releasing bar-Abbas," Ohred says. In this case, he is willing to release his highest profile prisoner for what he wants. Just one man.

Mustafa's eyes flash with surprise. A year ago, the Israeli government apprehended and convicted a young Palestinian terrorist by the name of Isan bar-Abbas. He'd used explosives to kill fourteen people and wound a dozen more. The Muslim government wishes he had blown himself up as well, thereby achieving martyrdom. Now, however, he sits in an Israeli cell, no doubt being tortured. The fate of bar-Abbas hangs between these two officials.

Mustafa cannot believe that the Israeli government is considering letting bar-Abbas go back into Palestinian territory. His people will go wild. Even he understands that releasing a convicted terrorist with blood on his hands might insight more terrorism against Israeli citizens. Why would the prime minister release bar-Abbas when Israel holds many other less violent Palestinian citizens?

There's a catch, he recognizes. There's always a catch.

Mustafa smokes his cigarette for a long minute, fumes filling the room alongside his thoughts. He feigns ignorance, recalling the meeting with his top official yesterday after Yasha had suffered through an intensive beating at the hands of his security forces. Mocked, battered, spit upon. Yasha endured it all as Mustafa had watched from a video monitor in a protected room. The information that he was hoping for never manifested. In an instant, Mustafa's anger toward Yasha had shifted to the Israeli government. Now, Mustafa sits a few feet away from the prime minister playing the part.

He offers the release of two Israeli soldiers captured at the Lebanon border for bar-Abbas. Ohred purses his lips, shakes his head. Mustafa offers to renegotiate on the controversial land settlements that seem to be a persistent thorn between the two nations. Ohred declines. Clearly, he wants one thing and one thing only—Yasha, leader of the Twelve. The same man who currently sits beaten and pulverized in a dingy West Bank cell. Not a soldier or a criminal, Mustafa thinks, just an ordinary man who wages a different kind of campaign in Israel. A man considered too dynamic to be safe, even though neither he nor his followers use weapons of any kind. Yet words can be more effective than firearms.

"What shall I do then with Yasha, the Jew?" Mustafa asks. Ohred's statement of potentially releasing bar-Abbas requires a response—a quid pro quo approach to keeping the peace between two hostile nations that comprise an incredibly small area in the greater Middle East.

For months now, the prime minister has been waging a slanderous campaign against Yasha and the Twelve, scattering seeds of doubt, distrust, and disinformation all over Israel. Pockets of accusers seep into popular gathering places, stirring up people into believing that Yasha is destroying their country. Using small mobs and endless negative media, the prime minister adds layer upon layer to his groundwork of lies. The tide has now turned against them. Yasha must be held accountable to the government and the people of Israel. Justice must be carried out.

A smile crosses Ohred's face. Everything is progressing. In the end, each man will get what he wants.

Bar-Abbas for Yasha.

The two heads of government determine suitable terms of condition. The prisoner exchange will take place under the cover of night to avoid any more unrest. News will eventually be leaked to the press and show up in the headlines. After that, each side will steer the propaganda.

Both prisoners have vocalized discontent with the status quo in Israel and Palestine. Both have raged against the corruption of the government. And both have taken matters into their own hands: one as an aggressive peace-monger, the other as a violent warmonger.

Bar-Abbas will enjoy a homecoming celebration and be elevated in status by his fellow Palestinians. He will be visited by President Mustafa and praised for his bravery, resilience, and activism for his people. Substantial monetary compensation will be deposited in his account. Mustafa assumes the Israeli people will welcome Yasha's return, as he has made a positive impact on hundreds if not thousands of lives. Only the prime minister knows the truth. The last part of his plan has yet to be fulfilled. An intensified, unwarranted response by both Mossad and Shin Bet has complete sanction. Secrets in these organizations run deep. Corruption runs at all levels. The spin against Yasha and the Twelve will be so intense that even some of his cell members will turn against him.

"We have a deal, then?" Ohred asks, hand outstretched.

Mustafa nods. Hands clasp.

Yasha's final hours are set.

7

THREE HOURS EARLIER

News of Yasha's interrogation reaches Yehudas, the eleventh member of the Twelve, and he loses all resolve. Everyone knows how the Palestinian Authority interrogates suspects in custody. Yehudas assumes correctly that Yasha will be severely beaten—a given under the circumstances of imprisonment by the enemy. A cold fear ripples through him.

Almost the last to join, he was the sole member of the Twelve to outright question some of Yasha's actions and intentions. Fear, indignation, duplicitousness have all led him to this situation. Over the past ten months, Yehudas's persistent state of offense had been the unavoidable bait, his inescapable downfall. Hadn't Yasha called him out just two nights ago when they were eating Passover dinner in Bethlehem, claiming that Yehudas would betray him? After Yasha's declaration, embarrassment and resentment had sent Yehudas running from the second-floor room. One decision led to another, and Yasha's prediction had come to pass. Now, he wrestles with regret and seeks to atone for his transgressions.

Yehudas feels betrayed, ironically, as foreign interrogation wasn't part of his agreement with the Shin Bet, Israel's internal security service. Arrest and detainment, certainly, but not any involvement with the Palestinians. That betrayal stings more. Why would Shin Bet do a bait-and-switch? What is Yehudas missing? The hatred he holds for the system turns inward.

He manages a 4:00 p.m. appointment with the head of Shin Bet, Moshe Reuven, the man he has connived with all along. Yehudas enters the large office with bloodshot eyes, smelling of stale alcohol. He throws darts of accusations in fierce succession.

"This wasn't the plan!" Yehudas yells. "Lies and breach of confidence! A betrayal of our agreement," he fumes, shaking with indignation. "What," he demands, "is going to happen to Yasha?"

After a lengthy pause, the director explains in a cold voice that the leader of the Twelve, the man in question, has sabotaged multiple governments. His declarations and demonstrations on the Temple Mount brought the Israelis and Palestinians to the brink of war. Action was required.

"But why did *they* arrest him?" Yehudas shrieks. "*Your* men were supposed to meet me."

The director squints, measuring his words. He cannot reveal to Yehudas that Nakdimon, the deputy prime minister, double-crossed the government. That the ambush surprised everyone, including the prime minister and heads of the intelligence community. Contingency plans have already been set into motion. A challenge for the Israeli government to regain control, but not impossible.

Ignoring the question, Reuven says, "I don't owe you any explanations."

"You never answered me," Yehudas states. "What will happen to Yasha?"

"Justice as the State of Israel sees fit."

"I handed him over assuming he would be detained, not wrongfully battered by some bureaucratic thugs or the Palestinian Authority."

"Your mistake," Reuven retorts.

"But Yasha hasn't done anything wrong, anything illegal," replies Yehudas.

"That's a matter of interpretation."

"What is the crime?!" Yehudas demands. "You owe me that, at least." He knows that the bargain they struck heavily favored the government.

Despite the millions of *shekels* he received now resting in an offshore account.

Moshe Reuven glares at him. "Sedition."

Yehudas goes white. Yasha will be tortured by the Palestinians *and* the Israelis. All because of him. His body trembles. His world spins. The irony stabs him in the gut. He begins to crumble inside, all former resolve disintegrating. He knows how the Israeli government handles sedition. The decision has been made, apparently, without proper channels. Without a trial. There will be no second chances for the leader of the Twelve. Events are spiraling wildly.

"Suffice it to say, he will be punished accordingly," Reuven says, confirming Yehudas's thoughts.

"I handed him over to you so that the Twelve would dissolve. That the *momentum* would die. Not *Yasha!*"

"Yehudas, you've been compromised from the beginning. You were waiting for your chance to play the high stakes. An opportunity ripe for picking. Don't make this about something else."

Yehudas shakes his head, angry tears forming. An enormous sadness descends. He throws on the man's desk a small notepad with the offshore account numbers and amounts of deposits made. Blood money. His lust for wealth and control has created more problems and solved nothing. The security he's craved vanishes.

"I've sinned. I've betrayed an innocent man to death." A man who gave only love and acceptance to Yehudas. He shakes with fear, voice cracking from sudden tears. His greed and arrogance have caught up with him. This money and all the money he slowly pilfered from the coffers of the Twelve has become meaningless.

"What do I care? That's *your* problem," Reuven answers sharply. He nods at the notebook. "You got what you wanted."

The director's assistant buzzes the phone. She announces that the prime minister is on the line. No doubt the call concerns Yasha. He picks up the receiver and waves Yehudas out of the office. Snubbed and rejected, he walks out, slamming the door. In disgust, the director throws at the door the notepad full of numbers.

Yehudas fumes with anger and shame. Both sides have repudiated him. He has nowhere to turn, no one to trust. He can feel the walls of guilt closing in on him. Forever he will be branded a traitor and thief. With ultimate clarity, he knows that the Israeli government is going to kill Yasha. Nakdimon had said as much. He had tried to warn the Twelve and had spoken directly to the leader himself in the dark of night. Yehudas didn't want to believe the truth. Nobody did. But deadly plans crafted at the highest level are almost always seen through. Who's to say they won't kill him as well? If Yasha is expendable, certainly Yehudas is. Panic surges through his body.

The distraught cell member winds his way through the back streets of Jerusalem, mumbling to himself. His hair disheveled, his clothes dirty, Yehudas looks and sounds like a madman. His strictly Orthodox family wouldn't recognize him. Without realizing it, he ends up at the end of a darkened, polluted alley with no way out. This solidifies his frustration. He lets out a guttural cry, pulling at his hair, pulling off his *kippah*, a traditional Jewish head covering. He circles the dead end like a caged animal, throwing his fists against the stone wall, kicking trash. Tears pour down his face; agony pours from his heart. Despair conquers him.

He has failed his family, failed the Twelve. Failed himself. He wonders if the other cell members would even care if he died. Some of them—Kefa and Shimon and Yaakov—probably want to kill him themselves after the betrayal. Yehudas falls to the ground, face pressing into the gravel and well-worn stones. For untold minutes, he lays there immobile. Anyone looking down the alley would assume the worst. He appears dead. Feels dead inside.

Natan was right, he thinks, remembering the conversation from Passover dinner. *This albatross will kill me.*

Twenty minutes later, Yehudas slowly emerges by the main thorough-fare. The streets are loud and congested. People move along, engrossed in their activities. Yehudas, focused and determined, walks straight toward the curb, causing people to bump into him. Some yell, others curse him. He doesn't hear anyone. Cars weave down the street, horns sounding here and there. Yehudas seems to be caught in a fog. His eyes are glazed, his forehead damp with sweat. His kippah dangles from his hand. From the left he notices an Egged bus barreling down the road. Route No. 476. Yehudas glances up at the sky, unable to offer a confession. No plea for forgiveness. He can never forgive himself. Why should God? Closing his eyes tightly, he steps into the street.

The bus rams full speed into Yehudas; his head smacks against the windshield, splattering blood in all directions. No. 476 screeches to a halt, and Yehudas's body drops to the street with an ugly thud. Clothed in traditional Orthodox black and white, he lies unmoving. A woman, hold-ing the hand of her young daughter, screams shrilly. She picks her up, tramples the kippah, and runs in the opposite direction. Chaos breaks out on the thoroughfare. Seconds later, police and ambulance sirens wail as loudly as missiles.

Yehudas, the betrayer of the Twelve, has betrayed even himself.

8

THE DAY BEFORE

Smuggled into a West Bank detainment center during the night, the leader of the Twelve now sits in an undisclosed facility run by Palestinian Security Forces. It's 6:00 a.m. and mostly quiet. His orange jumpsuit bears the foul odors of the previous owner. The hard metal chair rocks on uneven legs. Men speaking in Arabic file in and out of the room. Minutes later, the door shuts, and two pairs of feet can be heard moving into position—one near the door, the other right in front of him. Yasha braces himself as he cannot see anything. The black hood feels suffocating.

A fist suddenly knocks the side of his head, nearly sending him off the chair. He groans and seems to mutter something. A second blow arrives.

"Prophesy," one guard mocks. "Who hit you?" The other guards laugh.

No answer. The guard hits him a third time. His head slumps forward.

Back and forth, the Palestinian men hurl nasty accusations and insults at him, language used by the foulest of mouths. They shout in his ear; they spit on him; they kick the chair legs until it tips over, bringing the man tied to it down as well. A swift boot to his side causes a gasp and sharp coughs.

Without warning, the man and chair fly upright, the hood yanked off. Bright lights assault him, forcing him to squint. Patches of blood freckle his face. They give Yasha mere seconds before launching questions.

"What is it these men testify against you?"

Yasha keeps silent, answering nothing.

"Going to play stupid?" the guard yells.

Another interrogator approaches. His nose is a mere inch from the prisoner's. Garlic, coriander, and cigarette odors funnel into the impossibly small space between them. "Are you the one provoking Israel and Palestine?"

Silence.

"Stirring up the people?"

Silence.

"Tell us!"

Yasha says calmly, "If I said yes, you wouldn't believe me."

The men eye each other curiously.

"And if I asked what you're really saying," Yasha continues, "you wouldn't answer me."

"You undermine government, you defy laws of the land, you endanger people…"

After a beat, Yasha replies, "Are you saying this, or did others tell you this about me?"

"Do I look like a Jew?" snarls the first interrogator. "Your own nation delivered you to us."

Both Israel and Palestine have reason to suspect and punish the revolutionary tactics of the Twelve. Information has been shared. Intelligence has crossed boundary lines.

The second interrogator punches Yasha hard on the left cheek. The smack of flesh echoes in the small room. Behind his back, Yasha's hands are bound, blood drools from the cut. He grabs a fistful of Yasha's beard and yanks. Screams and blood erupt simultaneously.

"What did you do?" the interrogator asks, holding a thatch of hair.

Closing his eyes, Yasha inhales deeply with unseen determination. Long breaths in, slow ones out. "My territory doesn't consist of what you see around you. If it did, my followers would fight so that I wouldn't be handed over to the Jews. But I'm not that kind of leader; not the world's kind of leader."

The first interrogator asks, "So, are you an insurgent or not?"

Yasha answers, "I was born and entered the world so that I could witness to the truth. Everyone who cares for truth, who has any feeling for the truth, recognizes my voice."

The guards look at one another. The first bends down again, leveling his eyes with those of the prisoner. His voice is low, firm, and demanding. "What is truth?"

Moments pass with only breathing to be heard. It's clear to the guards that their guest has finished talking. They again begin using torture methods to interrogate Yasha, but he says nothing. The camera attached to the ceiling above the door captures everything.

Palestinian Security Forces watch the live video streaming from the interrogation room. They compare what has just transpired with witnesses who testified about the alleged plot to start a civil war with the Palestinians. Israeli intelligence divulged documentation of Yasha's clandestine plot with one claim. *I will destroy this temple made with hands, and within three days I will build another made without hands.* Destroy the Dome of the Rock and remake a government of his own.

The guards ask Yasha about this claim. To verbally assault Allah and their holy site would be tantamount to terrorism. It would warrant death.

"What do you have to say to the accusation?"

Silence.

Suddenly, a mass of saliva and phlegm smacks Yasha in the face. He closes his eyes as part of it slides down his cheek. A deep breath escapes, and he looks them in the eye.

"Any country in civil war for very long is wasted. A constantly squabbling family falls to pieces."

Astounded, the guards look at one another. What exactly does Yasha mean? His answers chaff them. One way or another, they will get him to confess. They are in control, not Yasha. Both guards strike him again, one right after the other.

Yasha lets his head hang. Pain sears from all angles. His breathing shallows, his cuts seep fresh blood. He hears the gentle voice.

LOVE BEARS ALL THINGS.

"One last chance," a guard snarls. His breath assaults Yasha's face. A fusillade of accusations batters him. Curses of blasphemy and indignation fill the air.

The other guard adds, "Aren't you going to answer anything?"

After long moments, he speaks. "Here's what I have to say: from here on, I will take my place at God's right hand," Yasha says. "The place of power."

The guards don't like this answer. Power over this region? Over the people, over the governments? "So, you admit it?"

"You're the ones who keep saying it," Yasha answers.

They exchange glances, silently agreeing. "Why do we need any more evidence? We've all heard him as good as say it himself."

Indignation flies throughout the Palestinian Authority leadership, and they threaten to retaliate by killing Yasha. Undoubtedly, this would make both sides happy. The Israeli government hates him; the Palestinian government suspects him. Both feel threatened by the forces that drive him. Both want him silenced.

Believing that Nakdimon had been operating on official state business, Mohammed Mustafa, the Palestinian president, had immediately moved on arresting and interrogating Yasha. No Jew was going to tear down the Dome of the Rock and rebuild a new structure. Not in his lifetime. Nakdimon had given Mustafa a time and location to intercept Yasha last night. True enough, he and his twelve companions were in a café in East Jerusalem. Now, Yasha sits in this West Bank detainment center, beaten to a pulp, presumably guilty.

But many hours later, after careful investigation, the Palestinian Security Forces come up lacking. None of the testimonies substantiate.

Inconsistencies run rampant; stories do not corroborate. Some offer a false witness, others a more credible bit. Most feel that Yasha is a decent man, citing the aid he proffered to hundreds of people in the West Bank refugee camp. The Palestinian Security Forces, to their chagrin, deduce that Yasha was planning no such assault on the Dome of the Rock. The intelligence that they received from Nakdimon, Israeli's former deputy prime minister, has fallen flat. They've been tricked.

Mustafa seethes internally, hiding true emotions behind endless cigarettes.

A high-level official steps into the room where Mustafa stands with his men. They have been watching from the small video monitors down the hall, reviewing the interrogation as well as the false information gathered. This can only mean the Israeli government has misled them. Betrayed by Nakdimon. Lies woven are now exposed. Were they concocting an entire plot out of sheer contempt for Yasha, too afraid to eliminate one of their own? Or perhaps it was for international political gain? Either way, no matter the deputy's motives, they've been double-crossed. Israel will pay.

Yet unbeknownst to Mustafa, Nakdimon was terminated less than two weeks ago by his boss, Prime Minister Ohred. He no longer holds the rights and privileges as an employee of the Israeli government. He has operated purely on his own, without any authority—a fact neither government is privy to. The hasty plan to have the Palestinian Authority arrest Yasha is unequivocally unsanctioned. For the moment, only Nakdimon knows this.

Mustafa and his men confer on a plan of action. His top official interjects with an idea to appease the situation, reminding everyone that Israel holds Isan bar-Abbas. The man convicted of terrorism in the streets of Jerusalem.

"What is more important?" he asks. "To retaliate against the Jews or to save a Muslim brother?"

In the end, they can always renege. Make a deal to get what they want and then retaliate anyway. Mustafa considers, his pride smoldering. Righteous indignation needs an outlet.

"Yes," he instructs. "Two can play at that game."

Truth is not necessary. Agenda is.

9

THE NIGHT BEFORE

Eleven cell members and Yasha sit scattered throughout a corner café directly north of Herod's Gate in East Jerusalem. The April rainstorm has passed through, leaving the paved streets empty and slick. Tables and chairs sit vacant outside the café; umbrellas drop their last bits of water. Doors on both sides of the café sit open, the warm glow of lights reflecting off wet streets. All seems to be peaceful, yet peace is elusive.

It's late, close to midnight, and the restaurant is ready to shut down for the night. The Palestinian owner and his young son, Yishmael, make the nightly preparations. They watch Yasha and his men, wary as their fame runs the gamut. Rumors of miracles pitted against rumors of government subversion. The owner doesn't like the fact that they chose his café in all of Jerusalem. His intuition flares a warning.

Suddenly, the owner's mobile phone rings. It's his uncle in Bethlehem. The one he hasn't talked to in fifteen years. A family fallout had severed their relationship, the offense too great to forgive. On both sides. In shock, the café owner listens, unable to hang up for reasons he can't name. His uncle apologizes, seeks to reconcile. He wants to make things right again between them. The owner cannot believe his ears.

"Why?" he asks. "Why now?"

After a moment, his uncle speaks with a softened voice, tears forming. He thinks about the unexpected conversation in the upper room of his house just hours earlier.

"Because of Yasha," he says. "The Jew."

The café owner's head snaps up, searching his establishment. Yasha sits only a few meters away. Unbelievable coincidence. Goose bumps cover his body.

Yasha gives him a knowing look. And a slight smile.

Like the owner, the cell members are on edge, sensing something in the air. No one gets up to leave. Low conversations amongst two here and three there pepper the room. Empty cups of coffee sit waiting to be bused. Just then, Yasha abruptly stands, the metal chair screeching, and tells eight of the guys to stay put while motioning Kefa, Yochanan, and Yaakov to follow. He approaches the owner and places a hand on his arm. A strange heat envelopes him. Yasha tells him to wait a bit longer before closing. He nods, speechless, phone still against his ear. The four men head to the back of the café past a door that leads to a small back room.

"Wait here," Yasha says to Yochanan, Kefa, and Yaakov. "And watch."

He disappears through another, smaller door, shutting himself away. The three men look at each other, knowing there is no answer. So, they sit and wait. Yaakov checks his watch; the minutes tick by. Kefa checks the door every so often, unsure of what he's been instructed to watch for. Yochanan sits with his back against a wall, humming softly to himself. Soon, though, the tiny dark room grows warm, and their eyelids grow heavy.

Behind the door, Yasha speaks to his unseen Commissioner. Kneeling, he shakes with the reality that lies before him. "It's time. Display the bright splendor of Your servant, so the servant may in turn show Your bright splendor. You put him in charge of everything human, so he might give real and eternal life to all in his charge. And this is real and eternal life. That they know You, the one and only true God. And me, whom You sent. I glorified You on earth by completing down to the last detail what You assigned me to do."

Yasha hears soft yet strange noises coming through the door. But he turns back to prayer, his devotees filling his thoughts. "I spelled out Your character in detail to the men and women You gave me. They were Yours in the first place; then You gave them to me, and they have now done what You said."

He pauses, listening, but all is quiet. "The world has never known You, but I have known You, and the devotees know that You sent me on this mission." He continues to pray, to search his soul—for the present, for the future.

The adjacent room is too quiet. Yasha has a hunch his men have nodded off. Slowly, he opens the door.

"Kefa!" Yasha says sternly. The three men bolt awake, shame settling on their faces. "You went to sleep on me? Can't you stick it out with me a *single hour?*" Kefa averts his gaze, as do Yaakov and Yochanan. "Stay alert, be in prayer, so you don't enter the danger zone without even knowing it. Don't be naïve. Part of you is eager, ready for anything; but another part is as lazy as an old dog sleeping by the fire."

Yasha slips through the small door again.

Yaakov gently kicks Kefa's boot. "Old dog," he mocks with a grin.

Despite some bruised pride, Kefa offers a half smile, shakes his head, and rubs his face. Trying to stave off sleep. Trying to heed Yasha's instructions. He told all three to keep watch, yet Yasha called Kefa out, solely. *Obviously, Yasha's favorite,* he thinks. More is expected of him because he's more important. He was the first to be called into the Twelve, after all. The only one, in fact, to have been given a new name by Yasha—"the rock." Soon enough, though, Kefa will feel the effects of his unwavering hubris. Pride always comes before a downfall.

Behind the closed door, Yasha prays in such earnest that beads of blood-tinted sweat slide down his face. With every thought, he plummets deeper into a black hole of distress. Groans escape his parched lips. "I feel bad enough right now to die. This sorrow is crushing my life out. God, if there is *any way,* get me out of this!" He sits in silence for an answer that doesn't arrive. Minutes tick by. The silence reverberates in his ears, the message loud and clear. He collapses at this understanding.

Yasha agonizes, knowing what is coming. Squeezing his eyes tightly, he pushes out self-preservation and obeys. "If there's no other way than this, drinking this cup to the dregs, I'm ready. Do it Your way." He steels himself against the coming evil, focusing on the imminent treasure. *I can do all things with Your help*, he thinks, rising from his knees.

Emerging, Yasha again finds Kefa, Yochanan, and Yaakov sound asleep, a light snoring floating through the stuffy air. "Are you going to sleep on and make a night of it?" Yasha asks with disbelief. He kicks their legs with the side of his foot. "No—you've slept long enough. Time's up!"

In the belly of the café, the other cell members linger, waiting for their leader to re-emerge. Some of them feel rebuffed that they weren't invited into the back room, some relieved. The past few hours of preparing for and eating the Passover dinner in Bethlehem were adventurous enough. Add to that the unexpected confrontation between Yasha and Yehudas, which caught everyone by surprise.

Taddai plucks softly on Yasha's red guitar. Yishmael, the café owner's son, stares at the instrument, longing to hold it. He doesn't know how to play, just wants to pretend. It's obviously worth a good deal of money. The striking crimson color mesmerizes him. Taddai smiles at him, but he shies away.

Faivel and Natan sit nearby, bantering about the merits of current literature. Natan tries to convince his best friend that the old masters remain superior to current authors; Faivel believes otherwise. Arye, ben-Chalfai, and Toma play hearts with a deck of cards that Arye always carries in his back pocket. Toma consistently loses to his utter amazement. Mattiyahu stands by the side door, watching the sky change as the clouds break and shift; he wonders about Yehudas—where he went, what he's doing. Shimon keeps checking the time. He, like most of the others, feels eager to move on for the night. Feels too vulnerable here.

Moments later, strange noises approach from outside, and the café's occupants snap into sharp awareness. Out of nowhere, Yehudas bounds into the café from the front entrance, out of breath and sweaty. Another man, Nakdimon, stands just outside in the shadows, communicating on his mobile. He'd traced a signal from one of the Twelve, pinpointing the specific location. Yehudas had literally bumped into Nakdimon hours earlier after leaving dinner with Yasha and the others. Both men were surprised, their conversation brief. He had warned Yehudas that the government was mobilizing, but Yehudas oddly didn't react. Nakdimon wondered if somehow Yehudas already knew.

An hour later, Yehudas found a note that Nakdimon had dropped into his jacket pocket, with instructions to call him immediately at a certain number. Yehudas knew it was related to the plan. The one he had set up with Shin Bet. Everything was still a *Go*. Tonight was the night. Although Yehudas thought it odd that Nakdimon had confirmed the order instead of Shin Bet, he was too jittery and distracted to question the inconsistencies. He just needed to hand Yasha over and then escape the madness.

"Yehudas!" Mattiyahu says, surprise and concern in his voice. He knows something isn't right. Yehudas's eyes are bloodshot, his mannerisms haphazard. *He looks more disheveled than Faivel*, Mattiyahu thinks. *Maybe he ran out of pain medication. Maybe he's having a nervous breakdown.* His traditional uniform of white shirt and black pants look as though he's been in a fight. Mattiyahu and Yehudas had known each other for years before joining the Twelve. They'd worked together as business partners, of sorts. They'd even become close friends. But over the past few months their relationship has frayed. The normal chip that Yehudas wears on his shoulder seems to have doubled in size. He bristles at just about everything. Mattiyahu doesn't know what has come over Yehudas, but he doesn't like it.

"Where is he?" Yehudas demands, scanning the café. No one answers. "*Where?!*"

In the back room through the door, Kefa, Yochanan, and Yaakov hear voices. Yasha says to them, "Get up. Let's get going. My betrayer has arrived."

Yaakov's head pops up. Betrayer? Did they hear him right? They look toward the front of the café, trying to determine who is causing the commotion. Something isn't right. A look of alarm crosses Kefa's face. *Does he mean Yehudas? He just disappeared a few hours ago in Bethlehem, how could find us here?*

Yochanan places a hand upon Yasha's arm, trying to hold him back. Yasha, though, shakes his head, and Yochanan's hand slips away.

Once the four men step through the threshold back into the café, an irreversible charge is set into motion. Yehudas turns to face Yasha and smiles tightly. At that moment, a group of Palestinian forces—intelligence officers, soldiers, undercover agents—moves into the café from the side entrance. All are armed with weapons. A few who were smoking stamp out their cigarettes. Yehudas spins around, and shock registers on his face. These are not Israeli forces, but members of the Palestinian Authority! *What is happening? Where is Nakdimon?* Yehudas has been betrayed at the highest level. Nakdimon has set him up. He fumes, cursing himself, cursing the government.

What Nakdimon had neglected to explain to Yehudas was that the plan had been altered without the prime minister's authority. When Nakdimon couldn't convince Yasha to flee a few hours ago, he took matters into his own hands. Nakdimon deemed Yasha to be safer in the custody of the Palestinians, who will soon discover his innocence, rather than the Israelis, who are out for blood. Safer, at least, for the short term. He will then use connections to have Yasha extradited out of the West Bank, far away from the epicenter. His message of love and compassion and the fight for international justice can go on. It must.

Confusion overcomes Yehudas. Now he's caught in the middle—the exact thing he fears. He begins to panic and fights the urge to run. A shadow moving outside catches his eye. Only the promise of money keeps him rooted to the spot. The sooner he turns Yasha over, the sooner he will get the second half of his payment. Then he plans to escape on a plane to South America, disappearing from all the chaos and deception.

"Yasha!" Yehudas shouts nervously.

"What's going on?" Kefa demands of Yehudas as he charges toward him. His imposing size and strength are intimidating. He doesn't intend on letting Yehudas get the upper hand.

Ignoring Kefa, Yehudas looks at Yasha and speaks with forced pleasantry. "Commander! Commander!"

Yasha frowns at Yehudas. "Friend, why this charade?"

For a split second, Yehudas freezes, his hesitation causing more fear to shoot through him. Can he really hand over Yasha? Can he kiss the money goodbye? It's too late, he decides. Everything is in motion. Yehudas approaches him and quickly kisses both of his cheeks. A greeting or a farewell? Just as fast, he looks away.

"Yehudas, you would betray me with a kiss?"

Without warning, the soldiers descend upon Yasha and seize him. They yank his wrists together in front of him, securing them with plastic ties.

"Yehudas is getting on my top nerve," Arye murmurs to Yochanan. His outburst against Miryam, the Passover dinner, and now this.

Yochanan nods, acknowledging the confession. *Agreed*, he thinks.

Yasha addresses his arrestors. "What is this—coming out after me with guns and knives as if I were a dangerous criminal? Day after day I've been teaching, and you never so much as lifted a hand against me."

Ben-Chalfai glowers at Yehudas, his blood pressure rising. Did he just hand Yasha over to the Palestinians? Was this always his plan? Is he really going to do this? Things are moving way too fast. His scientific mind tries to make rational arguments for the unfolding events. But even he knows something more is at play here. Something orchestrated and unstoppable.

Kefa mouths a question inaudibly to Yaakov: *Attack?* Yaakov nods. They will not go down without a fight. Kefa relies on the fact that Yaakov is thick-skinned, unafraid, determined. Kefa, on the other hand, feels the need to constantly prove himself. While Yasha has been teaching him to become more disciplined, he often still loses the battle against impulsiveness. Arye and Yochanan notice the looks between Kefa and Yaakov. Both feel that their loyalty is being put on the line. Both hope the café doesn't turn into a small massacre.

Yasha turns and faces them. Nothing escapes him. "Let it be. Even in this." He makes eye contact with each of his cell members. "It's a dark night. A dark hour."

The Palestinian intelligence officer nods to a soldier, who pulls out a black hood to throw over Yasha's head. But Kefa jumps forward, surprising everyone. He deftly unsheathes a hidden knife and lunges at the soldier. An awkward maneuver by the soldier saves his life but sacrifices his ear. Instantly, the ear smacks the ground. The man grabs the right side of his head and falls to his knees, screaming in pain. Blood shoots from the hole as he rocks back and forth, crying out to Allah to avenge him.

Guns appear around the room, moving and pointing at Kefa, Yasha, and the others. Threats in Arabic and Hebrew ricochet around the cafe. The Arabs yell at the cell members who are forced to raise their hands and voices in defense. Natan and Toma dive under tables, bracing for bullets. Neither wants to be caught in a crossfire. The café owner pushes Yishmael down behind the bar. He prays in earnest that Allah keeps them alive.

But Yasha, completely unalarmed, kneels down next to the wounded man, picks up the ear, and holds it to the man's head. The screaming suddenly stops. The man on the ground touches his head and ear, eyes wide with fear and awe. He gasps. The blood has stopped, the searing pain vanished. His ear feels completely normal—as if it had never been severed. He falls backward as if to escape. *Who has the power to do that?* he wonders.

Everyone is stunned at the miracle. It happened so fast that some of the Palestinians believe the whole incident was an apparition. Yet the blood pooled on the ground proves otherwise. Members of the Twelve understand, as they've seen Yasha perform miracles for the past year, yet they too are surprised that he would heal an enemy sent to arrest him. The café has gone eerily quiet.

Yasha looks up at the faces around the room. "Put your weapons back where they belong. All who use weapons are destroyed by weapons."

Toma whispers to Natan as they cower together, "I *hate* weapons."

"Such milquetoast," he answers, the irony not lost on him.

Most guns are slowly lowered, and a few knives sheathed. Yasha stands and helps the previously injured Arab soldier to his feet. Officers quickly surround Yasha, forming a human shield between him and his followers, who shift and agitate, unsure of what to do.

"Who are you after?" Yasha asks.

"Yasha ha Natzeret."

A deep sigh that carries the weight of eternity surfaces. "That's me."

Some of the cell members look to Yasha for direction. They stand ready to fight, ready to defend his honor, their honor. He knows their thoughts, their hearts. "Don't you realize that I am able right now to call and twelve companies—more, if I want them—of fighters would be here, battle-ready?" he says, looking at his devotees. "But if I did that, how would prophecy come true that says this is the way it has to be?"

While Yasha aims to soothe their fears, the adrenaline and commotion bouncing around the café leaves them unsure of what is happening and who is in control. Soldiers have moved into place to arrest every member of the cell—aside from Yehudas, slinking toward the exit—once the signal has been given. Yasha knows their intentions. He says, "I'm the one you're after, so let these others go."

Though he's done no wrong, committed no crime, Yasha is willing to submit to the authorities on the condition that his companions go free. He chooses to offer up his life, his future, so that his friends will not have to. Everyone in the café assumes the authorities hold ultimate power over Yasha, yet he demonstrates to his friends and enemies alike the opposite.

He has volunteered to go. It is the ultimate sacrifice, and one sacrifice is enough.

The Twelve realize the momentous impact of Yasha's command. Even Yehudas. Only later will they truly understand the eternal significance of his choice. It will embolden them to fulfill his last command to them— the one he will give after returning from the dead. But now, in the café, fear and guilt fill them as they wait for the decision. It could easily go against them.

The intelligence officer thinks for a moment, weighing his options. Eyes dart around the café; half the men hold their breath in anticipation. The Palestinian officer jerks his head toward the exit.

"Only the one. *Go*."

In a split second, the black hood comes down on Yasha's head, taking him into custody. Each of the Twelve feels a sense of relief, yet it comes at a cost. There are no guarantees of the future. None would have guessed the events of the past year, much less today. In a moment, their leader was arrested and taken as the sacrifice for the group. The intensity inside the café feels stretched in all directions. Enmity, apprehension, confusion, and betrayal all vie for position.

Once the soldiers and officials vacate the café, the panicked cell members run like rats. None follow their leader. Just as Yasha had prophesied hours earlier.

In a corner, the crimson guitar leans against the wall, a treasured token left behind.

10

THREE HOURS EARLIER

At ten minutes past nine, Yasha moves from the Bethlehem house back towards Jerusalem. He and the eleven others pass near the Bethlehem Inn Hotel on Manger Street and the Walled Off Hotel, opposite in décor and theme. Adjacent looms a concrete wall, twenty-five feet high, snaking between Israel and the West Bank. Graffitied messages and images of ire and hope, political and personal, layer atop one another. Paintings of a military helicopter juxtapose social notifications which abut a mountain scape with white block letters spelling BETHLEHEMLAND, Hollywood-style. A hodge podge of voices, ideas, and narratives.

Out of the dark shadows a man appears, running toward Yasha with unclear intent. Some of the Twelve brace together, some stop cold, but Kefa moves in front of Yasha, his hand on the knife in his belt. Five seconds later, they see the face of Nakdimon. They all know him as the prime minister's right-hand man. But they do not know the latest developments.

"Run for your life!" he whispers fiercely. "He's on the hunt. He's out to kill you!" Even though his name isn't mentioned, they all know this decision has come from Ohred, the prime minister of Israel.

"How did you know we were here?" Shimon asks Nakdimon. Even the Twelve didn't know they'd be in the West Bank a few hours ago.

"Probably a happy accident," Yaakov retorts cynically.

Nakdimon ignores the obvious question, as Israeli intelligence has eyes everywhere. Maybe Faivel's ability to block tracing isn't as good as he claims. The cell members exchange nervous looks. Faivel silently vows to re-scramble the lines of communication. He has grown close to the others and doesn't want to bear the blame for letting them down. *It's just another puzzle to solve*, he thinks.

Yasha notices Nakdimon shaking—alarm flashing in his eyes, urgency pulsing through his veins. He smells of fear. Yasha could tear away and run for the hills. Catch a plane, never return. But that would be foregoing his duties. He must finish the mission he was sent for.

"Tell that fox that I've no time for him right now," Yasha replies.

Nakdimon looks at him sternly. Didn't Yasha hear him? His life is at stake, immediately! "The prime minister's assassins are watching, ready to strike. He is perfectly capable of killing anyone he views as a threat. Ohred will protect his ability to remain in power at all costs. I'm risking *my own* life just by warning you! Yasha, you must go, now!"

"How do we know he's telling the truth?" Toma asks. He doubts the honesty of government officials. Are all their lives in danger? Yasha isn't visibly rattled. Maybe this is a ruse.

"They met earlier," Nakdimon answers pointedly, "to discuss the fate of 'the one stirring up Jerusalem and all of Israel,' according to Ohred. Every top official was there, and everyone agreed to neutralize what they view as a threat."

Yasha places a hand on Nakdimon and purses his lips. His fate, unbeknownst to everyone, was set before the foundation of the world, not by any man. "Today and tomorrow I'm busy clearing out the demons and healing the sick; the third day I'm wrapping things up."

No one understands what he means. Will his resistance movement be complete within three days, they wonder? Things are gaining momentum; now is not the time to quit.

"Besides," Yasha says with a sly grin, "it's not proper for a prophet to come to a bad end *outside* Jerusalem." Bethlehem sits a little more than eight kilometers to the south of Jerusalem. The place of his birth, not of his death.

"How can you be so apathetic? Don't you understand? They're waiting for you when you cross the checkpoint," the deputy declares. Only a government insider would know those details. "You must go! You *must!*"

Yasha sighs heavily, knowing what the informant says will surely come to pass. The hourglass has been turned over.

Yochanan glares at Nakdimon with his arms crossed tightly, hands near his armpits. His signature stance. "You're the deputy prime minister, blowing the whistle on your own administration. Something isn't right." The others nod, agreeing. Nakdimon shouldn't be trusted.

"That's right," Arye chimes in, "you're cut from the same piece of cheese."

Nakdimon gives him a funny look.

"Cloth," Kefa sighs, shaking his head. "Cut from the same piece of *cloth.*"

Arye shrugs. "Same thing."

It's hopeless, Kefa decides. His brother will always be a half-inch shy of vernacular perfection. Yasha, meanwhile, suppresses a grin. He loves Arye's idiosyncrasies.

"I know what I'm talking about," Nakdimon says again.

Though he sought out Yasha on two previous occasions, Nakdimon hasn't been consistent in his behavior. The previous time, he and undercover agents tried to detain Yasha at a peace rally, and the time before that he showed up unannounced and alone at their safe house, genuinely seeking answers. No one knows his true motives. He acts conflicted, caught between two worlds. But what Nakdimon doesn't tell them is that Prime Minister Ohred terminated him ten days ago. If he can get Yasha to escape, it will rob Ohred of the satisfaction of killing him. Nakdimon is no longer torn between entities—he is committed to seeing Yasha succeed and his previous boss fail.

"Do you have evidence?" ben-Chalfai asks. "Did you hear it firsthand?"

Nakdimon pauses then shakes his head.

"Of course, no evidence," Yaakov says sarcastically. "Who needs evidence?"

"You just have to trust me," Nakdimon answers.

"Sure," Yaakov retorts, glaring at him, "as much as a prison guard giving a probing entrance exam." Ben-Chalfai's eyebrows shoot up. Faivel winces at the thought. His brother, Yochanan, coughs, covering his snort at the memory. Both brothers once had to endure that required humiliation, though Yaakov certainly had it worse.

Nakdimon begins to plead again, but Yasha stops him.

"I appreciate your concern. You took a risk by coming here and warning me. But I cannot leave. My mission has not yet been fulfilled."

The informant shakes his head in frustration, in disbelief. How can he carry on a mission if he's killed?

"Why don't you believe it's true?" Nakdimon demands. "Why are you unafraid? The cell will disintegrate, and everything you've worked for, everything you've done will fall apart. Why would you be willing to let it all crumble into nothing? You're making a mistake of epic proportions! This is no game. The government *will* find you, and they *will* kill you. The decision has been made at the highest level."

"Don't listen to them," Yasha says. "Just trust me."

"*Please!*" Nakdimon begs.

Yasha places a hand on his shoulder. With clarity he says, "The time has come for the Son of Man to be glorified."

"Martyrdom?" he blurts out. "Is that what you're thinking? That's foolish! You can't establish any new supporters or followers if you're dead. People need you!"

Nakdimon finds Arye's eyes in the dark. Silently, he pleads with him to make Yasha understand. Maybe he will listen to Arye, the resolute, trustful, reliable one. Make him listen to reason, Nakdimon hopes. What else will convince him?

"Yasha, please!" he pleads one final time. "Leave Jerusalem… or better yet, leave Israel altogether!"

Kindly, with eyes of compassion and resolve, Yasha shakes his head. Nakdimon feels defeat. He's done all he can—for now. He'll have to come up with another plan. He will not accept Yasha's decision. He will get Yasha out of the country before it's too late. Slowly, Nakdimon disappears back into the shadows.

Yasha looks around at his companions, his devotees. Their personalities are as varied as precious metals and gemstones. Each of the Twelve was chosen for a reason. Each has captured his heart in a particular way. They're a microcosm of humanity, an irreplaceable treasure, the most important thing in the world. And Yasha must capture it. The price—what he will have to pay—will cost him everything.

Unlike Yasha, the Twelve are concerned that they're also going to be hunted down and taken out. While their leader seems unphased by Nakdimon's alarming information, they begin to fear the worst. Especially now that Yehudas has left.

"When I sent you out and told you to travel light, to take only the bare necessities," he asks, "did you get along all right?"

Confused, they nod, wondering what Yasha means.

"Certainly," says Faivel.

"We got along just fine," adds Taddai.

Toma asks, "Why?"

"Because this is different," says Yasha. "Get ready for trouble. Look to what you'll need; there are difficult times ahead. Pawn your coat and get a weapon." He resumes his path toward Jerusalem, the epicenter of the world.

Kefa touches the knife in his belt again. Shimon and Taddai nod assent. The Zavdai brothers, Yaakov and Yochanan, understand full well what happens when caught with weapons. Mattiyahu runs through legal scenarios in his head trying to determine a positive outcome. But others in the group are less confident. Why do Toma and Natan feel like criminals when all they've done is spread peace and compassion? Arye and ben-Chalfai, too, shake their heads in confusion. Faivel wonders if they're being watched and recorded. Sensing their thoughts, Yasha understands.

"What was predicted long ago, that 'He was lumped in with the criminals' gets its final meaning in me. Everything written about me is now coming to an end."

Yaakov fears it might be the end for them all. He won't do more time in jail, however; those days are over. He will disappear if necessary. Of course, he will convince Yochanan to do the same, knowing his brother holds the same distaste for Israeli prisons. They can hide and make food from practically nothing, which is the only positive thing to have come out of their incarceration.

"What do we do?" asks Faivel. Various calculations run the gamut in his head.

"Watch for the circling of the vultures," Yasha replies with a reference that he's used before. "They'll spot the corpse first. The action will begin around my dead body."

Frantic looks bounce between members of the Twelve. Is Nakdimon right? Will the government take Yasha out to silence him? What about the rest of the group? Nothing illegal has been done, yet they all know that the Israeli government does what it sees fit under the guise of national interest.

Toma doubts that all this will end well. Even though Yasha has eluded government forces until now, he simply cannot imagine a good outcome. And didn't Yasha just confirm that? Action around his dead body? Toma realizes he's more afraid now than when he was fighting an incurable disease a year ago. Once again, he feels that his whole world is in limbo. Once again, he understands that change is required of him—to leave the old behind and to embrace the new, however uncertain. Doubts fill his head, yet he doesn't want to leave the group. Whatever is coming is surely better than what was in store before Yasha rescued him.

TWELVE

"Maybe we shouldn't cross back," suggests Arye.

"Waiting in the West Bank won't be much better," offers Faivel. "The Palestinians don't exactly want us here."

"But the Israelis potentially want to kill us," Toma says, nervously.

"A grim quagmire," Natan grunts. To be honest, both options terrify him.

All eyes turn to Yasha. He's listening while deep in thought. His gaze lies fixed in one direction. They've come to understand his mannerisms. They've learned to follow his cue. Yet standing at the crossroads between Palestinian territory and Israeli territory, between life and death potentially, they feel unsteady.

"Yasha…" Kefa begins.

"We go," he says.

Once they pass through the Bethlehem checkpoint back into Israel, Yasha—resolved and prepared—moves toward Jerusalem. His operation continues. The Twelve assume he's heading for the Jewish quarter in the Old City, but instead he makes his way toward the Armenian quadrant.

The Old City lies divided into four sections, the Muslim and Jewish quarters flanking the Temple Mount, and the Armenian and Christian quarters sitting further west. Eight gates rim the periphery of the Old City, only one of which stands barricaded. They enter through the Zion Gate at the south end. Shimon, the Zionist and sole zealot in the group, decides this is symbolic and that something profound is about to happen. *It must be*, he thinks. By now the Twelve know that Yasha follows directions from an unseen source. Better to follow than to ask questions that will, most likely, remain unanswered.

Walking down the narrow streets towards East Jerusalem, Yasha runs his hands along the ancient walls, feeling centuries of stories. Voices cry out to him from the stones. Years of injustice and violence mixed with seasons of triumph and celebration. His eyes start to mist and stare seemingly unfocused, his voice catches in his throat.

"Jerusalem, Jerusalem, if you had only recognized this day and everything that was good for you! But now it's too late. In the days ahead, your enemies are going to bring up their heavy artillery and surround you, pressing in from every side. They'll smash you and your babies on the pavement," Yasha proclaims. "All this because you didn't recognize and welcome God's personal visit."

The eleven cell members reveal their alarm, eyeing each other nervously. What is he talking about?

"Jerusalem, Jerusalem," he whispers hoarsely, "killer of prophets, killer of the messengers of God…"

Three or four members of the Twelve lean in to hear what their leader is saying. They glance at one another, trying to read his mood. Full stomachs from the Passover meal a few hours ago seem to be making their minds sluggish.

"How often I've longed to gather your children…gather your children like a hen, her brood safe under her wings—"

"Yasha?" Mattiyahu voices, trying to get his attention.

Yasha shouts into the night, "But you refused and turned away! And now it's too late."

Kefa replies, "When did we refuse you? We will *not* turn away from you…"

The leader groans. Sadness and compassion show on his face. If only they knew, if only they understood. He swiftly turns to them, eyes blazing with knowing.

"Before the night's over, you're going to fall to pieces because of what happens to me. You're all going to feel that your world is falling apart and that it's my fault. As was proclaimed, 'I will strike the shepherd; the sheep will go helter-skelter.'" The men look at one another, some shaking their heads, some muttering under their breath. All are confused. But Yasha continues, "You don't believe me? In fact, you're about to make a run for it—saving your own skins and abandoning me."

Kefa responds, proudly. "Even if everyone else is ashamed of you when things fall to pieces, I won't be."

Stopping, Yasha looks directly at Kefa with forceful compassion. "Shimon, Shimon," he says, using Kefa's given name, "stay on your toes. Satan has tried his best to separate all of you from me, like chaff from wheat. But I've prayed for you in particular that you not give in or give out. When you have come through the time of testing, turn to your companions and give them a fresh start."

"Yasha," Kefa says, "I'm ready for anything with you. I'd go to jail for you." While his declarations are sincere, his tone smacks of superiority—more passionate, more outspoken, more committed.

"You might want to consult Yaakov on that," Taddai says under his breath.

Yochanan and Yaakov exchange glances. Clearly, Kefa has never spent time inside Israel's judiciary system.

Yasha responds to Kefa, "Don't be so sure." His intensity grabs everyone's attention. "I'm sorry to have to tell you this, Kefa, but before the Adhan penetrates the dawn, you will have three times denied that you know me." The sound of his repudiation will echo against the Muslim call to prayer.

Shaken, Kefa replies to Yasha with vehemence. "Even if I have to *die* with you, I will never deny you!" People at the end of the alley look their way.

Arye grabs his arm, attempting to quiet his brother. *Why does Kefa always feel the need to prove himself?* he thinks.

Thunder booms overhead. Wind rushes in and gusts against faces illuminated by lightning. The inky sky an ominous sign.

Yasha places a hand upon Kefa's shoulder. He opens his mouth to respond but thinks twice. Silence is more powerful.

Mattiyahu suggests that the cell keeps moving to not get trapped in the alley. Natan, as always, keeps an eye out for Yehudas. No one knows where he went. Just hours ago, right in the middle of the Passover meal, Yehudas disappeared, looking spooked yet resolved. Natan supposes that any of the Twelve would react the same after the dire prediction that Yasha had dropped. He tries to assemble the pieces together but can't. Natan feels nervous, his sense of foreboding strong. The day has evolved far differently than any of them imagined. Except, perhaps, for Yasha.

One drop, then two. In mere seconds, the heavens open their storehouses again. The second rainstorm today. Yasha and his eleven men quickly duck into a café to wait out the storm.

11

NINE HOURS EARLIER

The beaches of Caesarea are empty. The heavens have dumped their torrents of water, the sand now pockmarked and cold. Spring rains have restored the dry land. A line of dark clouds hovers over the place where land meets the Mediterranean. Half a mile or so offshore, scattered clouds bathe in midday sun. Beams of light stretch down like heavenly fingers.

Yasha walks alone on the wet sand, coat drawn tight, hood covering his dark hair. He needed solitude, needed quiet. The constant demand for attention, the growing pressure of notoriety, the hand of government closing in. Time alone is rare. He walks head down, thinking of his mission, his purpose. He thinks of the Twelve, of his family in Galilee, of those who support him and those who oppose him. He tries to regain focus. Thoughts of what's happened and what's about to happen whirl together in his mind. He feels a tightness in his chest—compassion for those who embrace him as well as for those who don't.

Minutes later, he hears the internal voice.

LOOK UP.

Yasha stops, taking in his surroundings. A brisk wind ripples his jacket. A pair of seagulls banter in the background. Suddenly, the sky catches his attention. The demarcation in the clouds is impossible to miss. He stands under the swath of dense, dark sky. Just beyond is the light. He knows with clarity its message: even though the evil and confusion and deception hover and the pain must come, a promise of glory and of light awaits. Yasha takes a deep breath, nodding slightly to the unseen voice.

From behind him, his companions emerge from afar. They've been searching for days, ever since Yasha literally disappeared from the Temple Mount. Like a bizarre supernatural stunt, which has now been performed more than once. Yasha's a wanted man, by friends and enemies alike. Four of the Twelve approach him. The rest stand on the far side of the beach, watching. When Kefa and Arye, Natan, and Yehudas arrive at Yasha's side, they exchange looks. Who will break his reverie? Yasha stares straight ahead out over the Mediterranean into the distant light.

"Yasha?" Natan whispers. He turns and faces the four cell members. "Everybody's looking for you."

Yasha smiles tightly. His popularity has grown; he's become the talk of the nation. His speech, his teachings so forthright, authoritative, and confident. Only Yasha knows how quickly that adoration will flip to contempt.

Looking at Arye and Kefa, Yasha tells them, "Go—secure the next place so we can have dinner together." Passover is quickly approaching, mere days away. They will not forego this celebration, this appointment.

"Where?" Arye replies. "Where do you want us to do this?"

"Bethlehem," he informs them.

"Why there?" Yehudas asks suspiciously. "That's in the West Bank. Passover should be celebrated on Israeli soil." His voice has an edge to it. He notices that his pulse begins to escalate. What is Yasha planning? He has an uneasy feeling about this. Yehudas needs Yasha to be closer to Jerusalem should the need to signal Shin Bet arise. Nobody knows that Yehudas has agreed to cooperate with the authorities.

Yasha studies Yehudas thoughtfully. "I prefer a flexible heart to an inflexible ritual."

Arye assumes correctly that Yasha has chosen Bethlehem for a reason, that he has a well-thought-out plan. Arye trusts Yasha wholeheartedly. Unlike some of the others, he feels an excitement for this festival meal together. He loves not only Passover but loves the fact that Yasha is keeping them on their toes by directing them to a town in the West Bank.

Bethlehem, *Beit Lechem*, means "The House of Bread." It carries significance for Yasha, as he was born there in a Jewish enclave surrounded by Palestinians. Born behind enemy lines. Bethlehem: the city that ignited a rescue operation encompassing nations and peoples who oppose one another. Yasha holds a certain affection for the place.

"Keep your eyes open as you near the city," says Yasha. "A man carrying a water jug will meet you. Follow him home."

Kefa and Arye make eye contact, unsure of how this will play out. One brother feels hesitant, the other intrigued.

"Say to the owner of whichever house he enters, 'The Commander wants to know if the rooms are ready.'"

"Do you know this man?" Yehudas asks. He tries to keep his voice steady, light. He cannot seem too eager or too concerned. But what is Yasha devising?

Yasha ignores the question. "He will show you a spacious room on the second floor. Go, make sure it's prepared." He turns back to the Mediterranean and closes his eyes, ending the brief discussion. Yehudas opens his mouth to ask more questions, but Natan grabs his arm and shakes his head. Clearly, Yasha has given them all they need to know. The answers will become obvious soon enough.

The four walk back to the others and relay the instructions. Most of the others are curious, yet Yehudas seems thoroughly edgy—a fact that isn't lost on Natan. The men wonder if it's a goose chase of sorts. Another riddle for Faivel to solve. Is this something that Yasha has been planning since they saw him last a few days ago? A mysterious place to have the Passover meal? And in Bethlehem? To be sure, his signature methods are unorthodox. Yet even when the Twelve doubt, they are inevitably surprised by the outcome.

• • •

Late-afternoon, Arye and Kefa arrive in the West Bank and move in the direction of Bethlehem University. They wonder aloud how they're going to find the man Yasha described. As they approach the old city, something odd catches Kefa's eye. Hunched over a wheelbarrow, a middle-aged man pushes a load of old plastic jugs down the road. The brothers look at each other, eyebrows raised. Arye shrugs and jogs across the street to investigate. Kefa follows a few steps behind, assuming it's a waste of time. When Arye prods him to hurry, Kefa knows, incredibly, that they've found their man.

Every jug in the wheelbarrow holds potable water. Arye inquires of a place to meet, and the man informs them that his elderly father has a house nearby. They are welcome to follow him home. The next safe house. Kefa wonders how Yasha knew. *Can he see into the future? Does he know everything that's going to happen before it occurs?* These thoughts unnerve Kefa, challenging his confidence and self-assuredness. Maybe that is why Yasha sent him on this mission? Arye nudges his brother onward, a huge smile draped across his face, for as every bit as Kefa struggles, Arye believes.

The room where Yasha and the Twelve convene later that evening sits above the elderly man's house. Fifteen steps built into the side of the stone-clad structure lead to a narrow wooden door. No railing, no adornments—only one small window looking out into the alley. Before holding men, it held storage. The host and his son are surprised by all thirteen men showing up at their door, but they hesitate only for a moment as Yasha nods and diffuses any uncertainty with a loving smile. The government would pounce upon the house if they knew the Twelve were inside. Bad blood runs back and forth across Israel and Palestine like well-worn missile paths. But this doesn't bother the host as he's heard stories from the refugee camp. *The messages that Yasha proclaims are far better than the political nonsense that spews from the officials,* he thinks.

Yasha takes the Palestinian man aside and speaks in hushed tones. He tells him that God sees him, that God knows his heart. That the plans for his life are full of hope and future success. Yasha looks into his eyes, senses deep pain that's decades old. He tells the man to call his estranged nephew, the one in East Jerusalem who owns the café. It's time to reconcile, Yasha admonishes. He places a hand on his shoulder. Heat and peace saturate him. The man tears up, wondering how Yasha knows. The leader of the Twelve explains that pain and wounds can be mended. They are real but don't have to remain. Forgive yourself, forgive him. The man sighs heavily, his pride warring against his conscience. He closes his eyes, nods ever so slightly. He knows that he needs to, but can he?

Within no time, the host's son brings food to the Twelve and their Commander. An array of lamb dishes, cous-cous, flat breads, and eggplant fares fill the room with highly seasoned aromas. Not the traditional Passover menu, but Yasha thanks the host for sacrificially providing, especially given the group's size. Doesn't matter if it's kosher, doesn't matter if it's different. Soon the Twelve begin dolloping portions onto plates. Some sit in groups talking about recent news, while others pack their stomachs with the delicious Middle Eastern fare.

Arye mentions that a few European countries are trying out a new strategy for football league players. "Helmets to prevent concussions," he says with a mouth full of food.

"Ha!" Shimon laughs. "You're lying."

"God as my witness," he replies. "They look ridiculous, but at least they'll save their skulls."

"Amazing that hasn't caught on," Yaakov retorts. The others chuckle.

"What?" he asks innocently. "Why is that a stretch to believe?"

"Arye," says Mattiyahu, "you'd trust a stranger with your bank codes."

He shrugs. "I like to assume the best in people."

Natan singsongs an old Yiddish quote. "You are smart, smart, smart—"

And Yochanan, Yaakov, Taddai, and Shimon join in simultaneously, "—but you are not-so-smart!"

Everyone laughs. The room swells with an air of camaraderie. Over the past year, they've bonded significantly. Months of varied experiences—some supernatural, some tense, all unexpected—have united them. Their initial distrust, their former disdain for one another has turned into something strong. Something collective. A coalition of brothers that will have impact for centuries to come.

"It's true," Kefa grins at his brother, slapping him on the back, then pulling him close. Arye blushes but revels in the attention.

Yasha smiles, absorbing the moment, the innocuous banter. He loves these twelve men. Twelve different personalities, twelve outlooks on the world. Though they come from various factions of Israel and walks of life, they all offer significance. They are being knit together into a beautiful, strong tapestry. Even so, Yasha knows, tapestries can tear.

Eventually, the leader of the Twelve moves the conversation into Passover mode. The real reason they are here together, sharing a meal. Candles are lit, rituals are performed, history is recited. Passover connects the past with the present and the present with the future. A collective understanding and calling—of their Jewish heritage, of their story as a unique people. What the Twelve do not yet realize is that their leader will be their future atonement. He will sacrifice himself for the rest. He will be the embodiment of Passover.

Yasha looks over his men, discerning their strengths as well as their weaknesses. Each of the Twelve has chosen to follow him, for one reason or another. Suddenly, Yasha grows intensely pensive, as if something has shifted in the atmosphere. The noise in the room wanes, and Yehudas takes notice that Yasha broods.

"Yasha," Yehudas asks, "what's bothering you?" He senses volatility in the atmosphere. He knows some of the others have become leery of him, especially Toma and Natan. His fight or flight instincts light up.

Yasha gives him a furtive glance. Flashes of the future appear before his eyes like a succession of gunshots. *Bam, bam, bam.* Long interrogations, severe beatings, brutal death. The reality is that the authorities are closing in, that their evil will succeed in part against him and the broken, hurting people he's met. That his chosen twelve are still woefully naïve despite his attempts at transparency.

"There's great irony here," Yasha says, thinking of the past few months and of the future. "Proclaiming so much love yet experiencing so much hate!"

Grabbing a piece of flatbread, Yasha breaks it in half and gives thanks to God. He knows that in a short time his body will also be broken for many. Bread is the staff of life, he explains, half a piece in each hand. It sustains man, is his most basic necessity. The bread of life is available to everyone—for tonight and every night.

Baruch atah Adonai, Eloheinu Melech ha'olam, hamotzi lechem min ha'aretz. Blessed are you, Lord our God, King of the Universe, who brings forth bread from the earth.

"Remember me," Yasha says, tearing off another bite. "Every time you break bread."

That's odd, thinks ben-Chalfai. *Remember him? Is he leaving? Where would he be going?* His linear thinking is deeply ingrained. He looks at Faivel, who shrugs slightly.

Yasha picks up a cup of red wine, offering a symbol linked to his own blood. Again, he recites a Jewish blessing, for the fruit of the vine.

Baruch atah Adonai, Eloheinu Melech ha'olam, borei pri hagafen. Blessed are you, Lord our God, King of the Universe, who creates fruit of the vine.

"Take this and pass it among you. As for me, I'll not drink wine again until the kingdom of God arrives."

Taddai whispers wryly to Shimon, "Could take a millennium or two..."

Faivel assumes this is another puzzle. Their leader consistently speaks in strange phrases. He tries to interpret the meaning, to stay ahead of the rest. He struggles over and over. If only Faivel allowed his heart to lead the way, his mind would follow.

"What does he mean?" Faivel mutters to himself.

"Just go with it," Yaakov suggests. "Might save you some time." He knows that Faivel—pensive, expressionless, systematic—will stay up all night over this one.

"You must never let familiarity breed contempt," Yasha continues. "Whenever you eat this bread and drink this cup, you are retelling the story—"

"The story?" asks Faivel.

Yasha smiles at him. "All that has happened. All that is about to happen."

Faivel processes the leader's words, twisting and turning them like a Rubik's cube. *What is about to happen?* he wonders. *Another miracle? Or maybe something sinister?* Eventually all the sides will fall into place; he just craves more details.

"I've told you everything...so that trusting me, you will be unshakable and assured, deeply at peace. In this godless world, you will continue to experience difficulties. But take heart," Yasha says with mysteriously wide eyes, "I've conquered the world."

Yehudas's head snaps up, his eyes locking with Yasha. That must be the plan, Yehudas fears. Conquering not just Israel but the whole world. This information makes Yehudas shudder inside—with distrust, with disbelief, with dread. Would he really attempt such a thing? Other cell members—namely Kefa, Shimon, Yochanan, and Yaakov—see it differently, perhaps as a scenario full of promise and glory. But for Yehudas, this state-ment cements his decision to turn Yasha over to the authorities. Even after meeting with the director of Shin Bet last week and receiving half of the money, Yehudas has vacillated over his decision. He cannot deny the good Yasha has done—the widespread benevolence, the supernatural acts. But he also cannot ignore his intuition telling him that the Twelve will be silenced sooner or later. Now, Yehudas reaffirms that he must stop this grassroots reformation. The other eleven will be furious over the betrayal. But Yehudas feels he has no choice.

Suddenly, a sadness clouds over Yasha.

"I have something hard but important to say to you," he con-fesses. The room falls quiet. Every ear is curious, every mind trying to guess what's coming. "One of you is going to hand me over to the conspirators."

Eeriness fills the space. They're stunned into silence. Yehudas freezes in fear. *Did Yasha just read my thoughts?* He barely allows himself to breathe, hoping Yasha will not call him out. That Yasha won't reveal his plans, his motives, or his deception at stealing money from the group. Yehudas wills himself to play dumb, to react as the others do. *Nobody has to know*, he thinks. *Maybe Yasha won't disclose anything after all.*

The rest of the cell reels at the shocking news. One of them is going to betray Yasha? Impossible! Each man looks strangely at one another. Aren't they all companions in this mission? Don't they all fight for the same goals and purposes? Yasha senses what they are thinking and explains that the Passover table is inherently a great equalizer. Every man comes with his own history, for better or worse, no matter their socio-logical, economic, or religious background. Yochanan and Yaakov know incarceration; Taddai knows military humiliation; Toma knows incurable disease. Grace is available for all at this meal. Though their pasts cannot change, their futures are not set. They all have a choice. They are all sus-ceptible to betrayal.

One voice breaks the silence. Then two. Half of the twelve nervously ask the million-dollar question.

"Is it me?" ben-Chalfai inquires.

"It's not me, is it?" asks Mattiyahu.

Yasha pauses, letting the atmosphere grow heavy with dreaded anticipation. *Who will it be?* they wonder.

"It is one of you," he answers, "who I eat with daily, one who passes me food at the table." But they've all done this. Any of the Twelve could be the impending traitor. Hearts around the room pound anxiously. Hardly a breath is heard.

"I'm entering into a way of treachery well-marked by the Scriptures," Yasha says, "but the man who turns traitor on me—better never to have been born than do this!"

Kefa silently prays it's not him. He would rather die than betray his leader. Is his destiny already determined? He decides not and makes a vow to *never* deny his connection to Yasha. But have their roles been preordained? Do they still have a choice in events yet to come? They walk a line of unseen realities. They follow a leader notorious for demanding trust. Didn't Yasha just demonstrate that he can see into the future when he spoke about the man with the water, the one who owns the house they're now sitting in?

Yehudas swallows hard. *How much does Yasha know? Is he aware of the meeting with Moshe Reuven last week? Does he know about the promised money? Will the plan with Shin Bet be exposed?* With every passing moment, he grows more anxious. His eyes dart around the room, his cheeks flush. *So much for keeping a neutral appearance*, he berates himself. He sweats profusely. But he must play along, ask like the others. Fear grips him. His throat dries up. All instincts tell him to stay mute. But he cannot. He must force himself to speak.

"Yasha," he says quietly, "it isn't me, is it?"

No one in the room seems to breathe. Food has become meaningless. The answer, everyone knows, will be explosive to the group.

Yasha looks at Yehudas and sighs acutely—a sound full of resignation, sadness, and pain. "Please, no more pretending. Don't play games with me, Yehudas."

Yaakov smirks and shakes his head. *Imagine that*, he thinks. He's disappointed but not surprised.

"That's one heck of an albatross," Natan says quietly.

Mattiyahu groans and looks at Yehudas with a pained expression; maybe he can stop Yehudas before it's too late. The others feel relieved. The ball on the roulette wheel hasn't landed on their number.

Then Yasha dips a piece of flatbread in lamb stew and hands it to Yehudas. "Go, do what you must. Do it and get it over with."

Yehudas takes the bread and chokes it down. No question that Yasha knows what he's about to do. Something shifts inside Yehudas, and a cloud comes over his eyes. He glares wildly at his fellow companions as if they seek to hurt him. Again, he is called out in front of the others; again, his embarrassment turns to shame and then indignation. He backs up, stumbling over his chair. Immediately, Yehudas bolts from the room and out into night's early hours.

The remaining eleven sit in a stupor. Where is Yehudas going? What is he planning to do? Are their lives at risk? Probably no more so than they have been for the past year. Close on the heels of relief comes anger for some of the inner circle. How could Yehudas willingly betray the one they've followed and emulated so closely? And how could Yasha just let him go?

Looking around the table, Yasha asks, "Do you also want to leave?"

A heartbeat of silence. Eyes shift, wide and questioning. Arye shakes his head.

"Commander," says Kefa, "to whom would we go? You have the words of real life. Eternal life. We've already committed ourselves, confident that you are of God."

Heads nod in agreement. Voices affirm the general consensus.

Yasha smiles, swells with affection for his men. "Haven't I hand-picked you, the Twelve? Still," he proclaims, looking at the door, "one of you is a devil!"

The eleven men try to process it all. Yasha's words, Yehudas's actions, the opposing forces of supporters and naysayers, the government faction—how does it all fit together? Is it part of some grand plan?

Yasha sighs, "Now is the Son of Man glorified, and God is glorified in him." All ears and eyes remain fixed on their leader. The tension in the room holds steady. They have no idea what's going to happen next, what Yasha will say next. But instead of escalating their fears and doubts, he turns the tables once again. He gives them instructions.

"Let me give you a new commandment: *Love* one another. As I have shown you love, show others. This is the very best way to love." He drinks red wine from the small glass and smiles with deep tenderness. "This is how everyone will recognize that you're my devotees—when they see the love you have for each other."

Even for Yehudas? The one Yasha just declared a traitor to the Twelve? How can they love outsiders when they can't love one from within?

Natan waits a few moments then asks about Yehudas. "What's he going to do? What will happen to him?"

Yasha nods, understanding his concern. "Everyone's going through a refining fire sooner or later…" His eyes glaze over as thoughts of the future pound him. That fire won't be for Yehudas alone.

"Terrific—can't wait," says Yaakov with a straight face. If it's anything like prison, he might reconsider.

"What about the rest of us?" asks Mattiyahu.

"Is there a plan?" says Yochanan.

"What's going to take place now?" Toma worries.

The atmosphere has morphed. An hour ago, they were laughing and celebrating Passover and the history of the Jewish people, their ancestors. Now they sit in bewilderment as Yasha has just announced a gigantic rift in the Twelve. Taddai bounces his knee nervously, military tags clinking together. Ben-Chalfai takes deep breaths to calm his speeding heart. Yaakov cracks his knuckles and makes fists. Something big is about to happen. Something life changing. They can all feel it.

"This is what the Son of Man has done: He came to serve, not to be served—and then to give away his life in exchange for many who are held hostage."

Hostage? The eleven men grapple with their leader's words. Strong images and predictions unnerve Yasha's followers. Events seem to be speeding up. Emotions feel chaotic. Walls seem to be closing in. The eleven become leery of the future; former assumptions become unreliable.

Should they go out and get ahead of what's coming? Should they fight back against those who seek to dismantle and demolish them? Preserve what they've built and believe in? They ask question after question, desperate for guidance.

"Be preservatives yourself. Preserve the peace," Yasha instructs. "Count on it that God will notice."

He stands, looks at his watch, and moves toward the door as if keeping an appointment. The cell members stare, unsure of what to do.

Kefa jumps forward and asks, "Yasha, where are you going?"

He stops and turns to face his beloved followers. "You can't follow me where I'm going," answers Yasha. "You will follow me later."

"But why?" Kefa replies. "Why can't I follow now? I'll lay down my life for you!" His heart has spoken faster than his brain. Such impulses seem to dominate Kefa. His brother, Arye, looks at him with huge eyes. He understands Kefa's strong connection with Yasha, but he's alarmed at the confession. Willing to die for him? Leaving the family business to follow Yasha and change Israel is one thing, giving your life for that mission is quite another.

With raised eyebrows Yasha says, "Really? You'll lay down your life for me?"

He considers this manifesto. A deep sigh emerges. He shakes his head slightly as if to say *Think again*. Then Yasha flicks his hand and bids him to follow. The rest of the men scramble so as not to be left behind.

12

FIVE DAYS EARLIER

Yehudas wakes in a cold sweat. The dream rattles him to his core. Men clad in black, faces covered, had captured him and every member of the Twelve. They'd been blindfolded and taken to a remote place in the desert. The twelve Israeli men kneeled in a line, shoulders almost touching. Systematically, each member of the cell was beheaded. Strangely, though, Yasha was absent. Yehudas could hear each time the sword struck the head of a fellow member. He didn't turn to look, though the blindfold and his thick tears would've made it impossible to see. Screams and moans erupted from the others, but Yehudas remained silent at the end of the line, shaking with unmistakable fear. One by one, the men entered eternity.

At last, Yehudas's time had come. He felt the presence of his executioner close behind him. As he squeezed his eyes tight, he repeated *O God, O God!* As soon as he felt the cold steel touch the back of his neck, Yehudas launched up in his bed.

It was only a dream. A nightmare. His apartment, sterile and cold, retains an eerie feeling. He trembles all over and tries to capture his breath. His heart borders on combustion. The images from his subconscious, gruesome and shocking, penetrate his psyche. It was too real.

Yehudas believes it's prophetic. If the Twelve keep making converts, their enemies will surely kill them. The whole business has gone too far. It's one thing to be a peace activist, but it's another to enrage people along the way. Yasha clearly threatens the authorities. His presence as well as his proclamations seem to antagonize those running the country. *If they feel that Yasha is a threat, then why haven't they done something? Arrest him or deport him maybe?* Yehudas racks his brain for a sound reason, yet the dream's tentacles still shroud his thoughts. He bounces back and forth between the images from his nightmare and what the authorities are possibly planning. He doesn't want to get caught in the middle.

Again, he feels his loyalty deviating. While he never sided with any government or political faction, he was never wholeheartedly with Yasha and the Twelve. He had joined to appease Mattiyahu, his unofficial business partner, and to rebel against his *Haredi*, or strictly Orthodox, upbringing. Yehudas once thought that Yasha was everything missing in Haredi Judaism: intimate, non-judgmental, kind, powerful. A true representation of what religion should look like. Yet it terrified him. Still does.

He wrestles to make sense of it all—his unfortunate past, his current place in the Twelve. Why did Yasha invite him into the cell in the first place? True, he had felt compelled to join, but his misgivings have never abated. Now he feels trapped between two worlds—he can't go back to being strictly Orthodox yet can't forge ahead into the unknown with Yasha. In truth, he fears for his life. To him that's more important than any message, than any movement.

And then it hits him. Yehudas realizes that the authorities need someone on the inside. Without help from a member of the Twelve, they can go only so far. Yasha has eluded them and continues to spread his mantra of peace and acceptance all over Israel and Palestine. He's stirring the pot too much. Let enemies be enemies, as they've been for centuries. Why try to establish friendship between sworn adversaries? Lines that were drawn many generations ago have been blurred. Hundreds of people believe in the message of Yasha, yet others are deeply offended by what he approves of and allows. Yehudas is one of them.

The fact that Yasha let Miryam, one of Yasha's most devoted supporters, fawn over him a month ago with priceless gifts had crossed a well-defined boundary. And kissing his feet? It had turned Yehudas's stomach. What he deemed inappropriate behavior had appalled him. And worse, Yasha had reprimanded Yehudas in front of everyone for blasting the woman and questioning the entire display. How could Yehudas not have been embarrassed and offended?

He now understands the threat that Yasha poses. The counterculture revolution will either succeed wildly, or it will be decapitated like the men in his dream. In a flash, Yehudas decides that he must help facilitate its end. To save his own life. To save others.

• • •

Three hours later, in the back seat of a black town car, the head of Shin Bet sits opposite from Yehudas. All the windows are dark, as is the cloud-filled night. The digital clock reads 3:14 a.m. Moshe Reuven smokes a cigarette and offers one to the eleventh member of the Twelve, but he refuses. His nerves can't be quenched.

Yehudas, quivering and tense, flips the business card—the one bearing the name and number of Israel's security agency—over and over, turning cartwheels under his fingers. A member of Shin Bet had casually bumped into him four days ago, soliciting his help as an insider, giving him a card bearing the director's name. How long had they been following him? Did they provide all the cell members with a card or just him? He suspects they saw a weakness in him and are trying to exploit it. Yehudas distrusts everyone earning a government paycheck. The director is no exception. Pleased at Yehudas's unexpected offer to help, Reuven had immediately informed the prime minister.

After long minutes, Yehudas begins talking about the leader of the Twelve—*his* leader for the past ten months. The only thing Yehudas wants to do is offer information and receive security. He can hardly believe that he even got mixed up with the Israeli cell, but that's water under the bridge. He answers questions the director throws at him like baseball pitches, quick and curved. Reuven needs inside info on Yasha's plans, his objectives, his security measures, and his devotees known as the Twelve. Of course, the Israeli government has been tracking him; of course, they know of the safe houses and history of all the members.

In fact, intelligence agencies are aware that Yehudas has been pilfering some of the Twelve's monetary supply for himself, unbeknownst to the group. Offshore accounts have been traced and verified. Shin Bet had been on the verge of exposing Yehudas—presenting the option to save himself by handing over Yasha or to go down with the group—when he suddenly came forward. But that information remains in the director's corner. Moshe Reuven feels confident that Yehudas would rather save his own skin by turning Yasha over. No need, now, to force a choice.

What they need is confirmation of Yasha's intent. His concrete plans. While he doesn't use violence with weapons, he promotes something just as powerful—indoctrination and insurrection.

"You fear the people," Yehudas says. The director remains silent, but his eyes confirm that truth. "What will you give me," he continues, "if I deliver him to you?"

"Protection, immunity," says Reuven. "The usual things."

But Yehudas shakes his head. He needs more.

"Are you asking for money? A *bribe*?"

Yehudas thinks a moment, then nods. "Protection and immunity aren't enough by themselves. Monetary compensation will complete the deal." Remuneration is essential. While he has successfully filched a considerable amount from the Twelve's reserves during the past few months, it's small potatoes in comparison to government funds.

Greed, uncertainty, and fear maneuver Yehudas. The love of money lays at the root of highest evil—to betray Yasha. Money doesn't equal security and protection, yet Yehudas believes otherwise. Always has. His blind faith in money led him to pilfer and skim from the abundance of others, year after year. Manipulation is second nature to him. What he practiced before joining the Twelve, he perfected thereafter. Some of the other cell members have questioned his activities, but Yehudas hides the nefarious activity well. Yasha has known all along, of course, yet has never said a word. Why Yasha hasn't called him out is a mystery. Another one to add to the cache of what makes Yasha so enigmatic. Now, the same evil that Yehudas seeks to escape—the evil that is coming for the Twelve—ensnares him coldly.

The director writes a figure in a small notebook. "Ten," he offers. The number on the page reads ten million shekels, Israel's monetary currency.

Yehudas looks out the window and considers the offer. He turns back and looks Reuven in the eyes. "Thirty." Roughly eight to nine million dollars.

The director guffaws but sees that Yehudas isn't joking. He knows Yehudas holds the key to this predicament. He inhales his cigarette and exhales a veil of smoke. "Agreed."

Yehudas doesn't know if he's relieved or terrified to continue. Negotiation had taken mere seconds. *Something is wrong*, he thinks. *That was too easy.* Everything feels out of control. Suddenly, images of exotic destinations that thirty million shekels can provide flash through his head. His only escape from this madness. He'll go hide, make a new life for himself far from the epicenter of the world. He hears the hamlets of New Zealand are nice. Maybe they have a small synagogue there. Or maybe he'll leave Judaism behind forever.

Reuven hands Yehudas the notebook with an offshore account number. "The first half will be transferred within an hour and the second half upon fulfillment of our verbal contract. Apprehension of the target must be secured for the deal to be final."

"As you wish," Yehudas says, understanding the parameters. "I'll contact you when it's time."

"No one must see it," Reuven states. "No one must know."

Yehudas nods, praising himself for years' worth of successfully kept secrets. Nobody will be the wiser. He thinks of a handful of places Yasha retreats to when needing solace from the crowds. It shouldn't be too difficult to arrange a place of arrest. He will have to take Yasha by surprise though. The other eleven, no doubt, will be livid.

A thick stream of smoke is blown into the air. Before dismissing Yehudas, the director asks, "Why are you giving him over to us?"

Yehudas sighs deeply, unsure of how much to divulge. His doubts about what the cell is doing motivate him, but it's more than that. The dream flashes again through his mind. A new wave of fear rips though him.

"I...I..." he stammers, unable to finish.

"It doesn't matter," Reuven replies. He leans over and unlatches Yehudas's door. Clearly, the meeting is over.

Yehudas stands rigid in the blackness of the mid-April night. As the town car screeches away, the pit in his stomach enlarges, and he feels increasingly nauseous. For a split second, regret shoots through him. But he knows events are set in motion. There's no turning back now.

13

FOUR DAYS EARLIER

"They're *cousins*?!" barks Prime Minister Ohred, slamming the Sunday morning newspaper down on his desk. The office walls reverberate with his fury.

Pictures of Yasha and Yochanan the Immerser—the Twelve leader and the untamed religious influencer—headline an article detailing their family connection and spiritual unity. Their unconventional approach to reformation, both morally and practically, flies in the face of political correctness and the Israeli government.

"How did this *detail* go unnoticed?" he yells.

His deputy, Nakdimon, stands in the corner, face pale and clammy. The press secretary, the head of Shin Bet, and the director of Mossad sit in uncomfortable silence.

"Sir, if I may?" the press secretary begins.

He looks at her impatiently. His nod is subtle.

"That paper is notorious for printing stories under heavy bias," she says with caution. "Perhaps they are—"

"We assumed incorrectly that Yochanan was a lone wolf," Moshe Reuven interrupts. "His parents are dead, and he has no siblings."

"And you stopped there?" Ohred asks incredulously.

"He lived in a kibbutz in the Eilat wilderness for the past twenty years. Ate from local sources and spewed premeditated ideologies on life and death, according to his fellow residents. Wasn't a threat to anyone—wasn't even on the radar until he began speaking out against this administration."

"But then he suddenly came out of the wilderness and into Jerusalem," Ohred laments, face red with rage. This wild man from the desert keeps haunting him. He assumed that all references to the Immerser had been buried months ago. Saidoreh, Ohred's wife, had seen to it that the Immerser was silenced for publicly humiliating them. What Ohred doesn't yet know is that Saidoreh, too, is haunted by the Immerser through relentless, vivid nightmares. A secret that will eventually break her.

"Yes," says Reuven, "he had gathered a small but vocal crowd together and moved north, picking up additional followers here and there. He'd called out for people to adjust their way of thinking and living, to 'immerse' them into God's way and God's government, whatever that is. Most had written him off as being mentally unstable. He spoke of no family whatsoever. Never connected with anyone."

"But according to the story," Ohred says, picking up the paper, "they were close years ago, Yasha and the Immerser. They grew up together in Galilee. Shared similar sympathies, lofty goals of making a lasting impact here in Israel. But then years passed without any contact between them." He throws it down again in frustration.

"We do know that Yochanan met Yasha at a peace demonstration months ago," adds Reuven. "And we assume it was an unexpected reunion of sorts. Their interaction was brief, according to witnesses."

"That was also right around the time of the bar-Abbas incident," Zvi Goren offers. Mossad, his agency, had eventually tracked down the Palestinian terrorist responsible for killing multiple Israelis and Palestinians in one attack. Now, bar-Abbas occupies a solitary cell in an undisclosed prison.

"Was the Immerser involved in any way?" asks Ohred.

"No," replies Goren.

The prime minister tries to assemble the pieces. Eyes shift around the room. No one wants to take the fall for this.

"Someone explain to me why this *journalist* has uncovered a vital bit of information that my intelligence community has not," he demands.

Goren begins, "Sir, we—"

"Stop!" Ohred barks, holding up his palm. "Save the excuses. Are there other family members that cause concern?"

"No," Reuven says. "Like I mentioned, the Immerser's parents are dead, and he was an only child. Yasha's father is dead as well; his mother and brothers live mostly in northern Galilee. For some reason, they are not included in the inner circle. They don't make much contact."

Odd, for sure. Unless there is something deeper. The prime minister shelves that thought for later.

"I predict there's going to be some retaliation in regard to the Immerser," Director Goren says flatly.

"That would be foolish," Ohred replies. He will not get caught and be exposed for manipulating circumstances involving the Immerser. The story of the Immerser's self-inflicted death will remain official. Prisoners can be known to induce a hunger strike in hopes of getting attention. In the Immerser's case, he took it too far. Or so the public believes.

"Still," Goren continues, "many saw him as a man of justice, in spite of his comments and accusations of this administration."

The prime minister narrows his eyes, remembering the political embarrassment. His face flushes again with resentment. "If there is a rebellion against the Israeli government, it will cost many lives," Ohred assures. He wishes only for peace in his country, but he will use the IDF by whatever means necessary to obtain it.

"Perhaps the disruption at the Temple Mount/al-Aqsa Mosque is setting the stage," Reuven offers.

Four days ago, a small riot had broken out at the holy sites. The prime minister knows someone must take responsibility for this latest unrest. The Temple Mount security forces fall under his jurisdiction. Everyone present knows this too. Naturally, Ohred deflects hoping to shift the focus.

"Increase the special police unit solely for the Temple Mount compound," Ohred instructs Nakdimon, his deputy. "What do the security cameras show? Do we know who ignited it?"

"Different rumors have emerged as to who instigated the situation, but one name keeps popping up."

They all know.

Yasha. Leader of the Twelve.

Prime Minister Ohred wonders why turmoil seems to follow Yasha regardless of his claims for peace and justice. Clearly, he is toying with the current administration, setting traps and destabilizing their control. This thought infuriates Ohred, as his time in office is no game. Moshe Reuven had volunteered months ago to concoct a plan to stop Yasha in his tracks. Timing, though, remains crucial. Any move by the government must be above reproach; their jobs are on the line. But so far, Yasha and the Twelve have remained inviolable. Ohred, Reuven, and Goren are beginning to run out of patience.

"The leader of the Twelve was seen ascending the Temple Mount, but soon after the crowds erupted, he disappeared from the cameras. Vanished, actually." Reuven endures the looks of contempt. He has no explanation, just recorded proof.

Ohred asks, "And the others?"

"The cell members scattered in different directions," Reuven answers.

"Were all twelve of them there?"

"From the tapes, it doesn't look like it."

"Who was missing?" Ohred probes.

"Yehudas and Mattiyahu, but that doesn't mean they weren't involved."

"Explain."

"They could easily have been orchestrating opposition from the Arab quarter, spreading provocations about the Temple Mount," offers Reuven. Distrust of strictly Orthodox Jews in Israel runs high, as they often war against and undermine the established norms. They assume, incorrectly, that Yehudas still operates under the beliefs of his acutely religious family, even though he left the sect not long ago. Some habits die hard, the officials believe.

"But where's the evidence?" Ohred demands.

A distinct silence fills the room. Between the recent rocket attacks in Ashkelon by Hamas, and the Temple Mount skirmish, and the news that Yasha is related to the Immerser, Ohred's nerves stretch taut. His hemorrhoids flare. More and more, the prime minister is convinced that Yasha's involved in espionage. Especially after his outright display in the West Bank refugee camp. No one believes he was only serving the poor. If Yasha is trying to specifically pit the Palestinian Authority against him, he will pay a high price. Whatever the State of Israel decides to do with the cell known as the Twelve, the Palestinians will not interfere in its affairs.

"Or maybe Mattiyahu and Yehudas are weak links in the group," Ohred says, redirecting the conversation. "They're an unusual pair. We should approach them…"

The Shin Bet director nods. "Actually," he interjects, "we have tracked down some hidden accounts. Yehudas seems to be quite adroit at hiding money." His agents will make contact, feeling out where true loyalty lies. They can easily scare them with threats of arrest or worse. Doubtful that Yehudas or Mattiyahu will talk, as the group seems tightly knit. But there are always means of persuasion. And there is always luck.

"What about El'azar? Is he involved in this?" Ohred asks, referring to Yasha's close friend.

"No," Reuven replies. "Aside from setting up safe houses around Israel, El'azar seems to refrain from the Twelve's activities. He stays close to his younger sisters, Marta and Miryam. Especially since his unfortunate encounter with Hamas's rockets in Ashkelon and his subsequent experience with death mere months ago." *Life is unpredictable—even more so with Yasha involved*, he thinks.

Shin Bet had dutifully tracked down the safe houses that El'azar, with the help of Faivel, had set up for the group. "One location, though," he admits, "had slipped through the cracks but was recently discovered."

The prime minister glares with intense disdain. *Unacceptable*, he muses. The most sophisticated intelligence agency in the world was out-maneuvered by some amateur renegades. He reaches for his bourbon.

Ohred paces, thinking about the situation from sharp angles. The momentum behind this cell is growing, despite his efforts to the contrary. The Israeli people seem impervious to the smear campaign and media tactics that have always worked in his favor. He's even started planting opponents around the city to heckle and taunt them. The Twelve stir up the country, flipping normalcy on its ear. Jealousy drives him to madness.

"I will not tolerate a group of twelve men and a handful of naïve followers to unravel what has taken me *decades* to build. These people," he seethes, "these traitors and turncoats to Israel are out to destroy the world."

There must be a way to bring them down without igniting the public into a rage. This one man and his twelve accomplices are causing huge cracks to appear up and down the country. People either love him or reject him. Most fall into the first category, which makes the prime minister highly anxious. There is power in numbers, and Yasha's followers seem to multiply by the day. Time is running short. Action is required. Eventually, Ohred believes, Yasha will make a mistake. Nobody's perfect.

Suddenly, Moshe Reuven's phone buzzes with incoming messages. One after another, he scans them quickly, then reads them a second time.

"There's new information," he says.

"What now?" Ohred demands.

"Witnesses say Yasha was trying to cleanse the sacred area, inviting all to genuflect, physically and spiritually."

Worshipping, whether kneeling or standing, on the Temple Mount/ Haram al Sharif has boundaries. Yasha claims to stand for justice and promotes anti-violence, yet his outbursts are deemed aggressive and volatile.

"He apparently quoted phrases from the *Tanakh*," he continues, referring to the Jewish Holy Scriptures.

"That certainly wouldn't agitate the Muslims," the press secretary says sardonically.

"Anything specific?" Ohred asks.

The director scrolls through the messages. He reads only one aloud. The one with the proof. "Yasha was heard saying: 'I am going to tear down this Temple, built by hard labor, and in three days build another without lifting a hand.'"

Ohred slams his hand on the desk. He turns abruptly to Reuven and points. "How much money has been hidden by Yehudas?"

"Enough to fund a mission as foolish as destroying the Dome."

Yasha's proclamation backed by enough finances to make it happen? Sheer coincidence? Not a chance, Ohred thinks. *It's double proof.* Yasha's trying to insight a civil war. It's the moment, the event, they've been waiting for. Now an arrest can take place on grounds of plotting a crime—proving that crime will have to come later. If the Palestinians spread the word that the Dome of the Rock is in jeopardy of destruction, waves of suicide bombers will be unleashed in Israel. Hamas, Hezbollah, and outside Muslim countries will rush to defend their sacred territory. The prime minister envisions apocalyptic scenarios never before witnessed in the holy land, not even with the Six-day War or the Yom Kippur War. His heart pounds, his acid reflux burns. The sooner they control this situation, the better.

"Did you hear that? After that, do we need more witnesses?" Ohred looks around the room at his intelligence team. "Are you going to stand for it?" he demands. Because he will not.

Nakdimon stands up and faces his boss. It's now or never. He feels Yasha is innocent, and so he plays devil's advocate. "Yasha often talks in codes or offers odd-sounding allusions," he says.

"Sounds more like a strategic blueprint to me," Ohred spits. He will not be persuaded by his deputy, who has seemed to recently fall under the spell of Yasha and the Twelve.

"They are a devout group," Nakdimon continues, "committed to spreading right living to vast numbers of people, regardless of race or religion. Yasha promotes peace as a matter of principle, as a matter of global restoration."

"Or they're an apocalyptic group as their statements and actions suggest!" The prime minister grows angrier by the second. At his deputy, at the Twelve. His fuse runs short. He decides within seconds to terminate Nakdimon. For questioning his judgment, for failing to detain Yasha months ago.

After a brief discussion, the intelligence group agrees to surround the last known safe house and conduct arrests. Troops in the Old City as well as surrounding neighborhoods will be reinforced.

"Find him," Ohred growls, "and bring him to me. I want him dead."

"Dead?!" exclaims Nakdimon. "Why dead? What's he done?"

Nakdimon's face blanches, his breathing halts. Ohred and Reuven cannot be serious. *Why are they so blind to Yasha's heart? To his ministry?* he wonders. *Why are they willing to acknowledge only the negative ramifications that Yasha and the Twelve have on the State of Israel? Those things pale in comparison to the good he's doing and to the lives he's changing.*

Moshe Reuven and Zvi Goren give each other a look. During their last meeting with the prime minister two months ago, Nakdimon had left the room to take a phone call. In his absence, the decision of Yasha's fate had been proposed. Plans would be executed at the opportune time. Both the Shin Bet and Mossad understand the art of war. It's how the State of Israel has survived for decades. Surrounded by enemies, the tiny country has a long history of taking out individuals before they show aggression against the homeland. To rise and kill first, according to the *Talmud*, the primary source of Jewish religious law.

Nakdimon reads the silence, knowing he doesn't have all the information. He presses his boss further. He needs to stop whatever has been set in motion. Yes, Yasha has flipped Israel on its ear, causing a myriad of issues. But does he deserve to die? Definitely not. Nakdimon needs to buy some time.

"Sir, Passover is two weeks away. We don't want a riot on our hands."

He's right, of course. With all the stress and chaos of late, the feast had slipped Ohred's mind. The holy days demand pause. Arresting Yasha now could potentially set crowds of people up in arms. A few weeks would give him time to craft the details of a feasible plan, one that would be highly effective but also easy to disguise. He'd have to cover his tracks flawlessly.

"Unfortunate timing," Ohred muses. He breathes deeply. "Two weeks, then, and he's mine. From this moment, he's as good as dead." He dismisses the group.

Nakdimon gathers his coat, asking himself if he should warn Yasha. As if Ohred could read thoughts, he meets his deputy at the door. Nakdimon takes deep breaths, finding some resolve to tell his boss that there might be another way. As he begins to speak, Ohred holds up his hand. He simply shakes his head, guessing Nakdimon's intentions. No more playing games. His muddy brown eyes, cold and determined, are locked onto his deputy's.

"Your sympathies seem to lie outside of this administration."

"With all due respect, sir," Nakdimon says, "I am a loyal citizen of Eretz Yisrael. I have given my life to protecting and defending this nation that I love. But I don't believe Yasha's trying to sew discord. He is—"

"I know what he is," Ohred answers. "And I will *not* tolerate it. Nor will I tolerate betrayal."

"But—"

"You are officially relieved of your duties."

Stunned, Nakdimon opens his mouth, but no words form. After years of allegiance and devotion, he's terminated without warning. Or reason. But the deputy prime minister knows that he'll have no recourse against his boss. The only way to fight back is to warn Yasha. Nakdimon removes his badge, hands over his keys. He feels betrayed himself and confused, though not necessarily surprised. The Israeli government doesn't allow even a hint of insubordination. He wants to express his frustrations and sentiments to Ohred, as they've spent years together. Instead, Nakdimon nods and bids him farewell.

Once the prime minister is alone, he pours himself another bourbon. He shuts off his office lights and moves toward the window. He closes his eyes, takes a deep breath. He wonders how there is yet another enemy on the horizon, one from within. *Will Israel always be a land of volatility? Will peoples and cultures always fight to control this small stretch of earth?* He reflects for a moment on the history and future of Israel. He's come too far and believes too much in the destiny of this land. He will not abandon his calling or his duty to protect this nation. No matter the supposed humanitarian agenda of Yasha and the Twelve, it doesn't align with his agenda. It must be stopped.

The tentacles of a plan take shape quickly—to frame the leader of the Twelve and to abate all aggression from the Palestinians against Israel. It will require the participation of insiders and outsiders, of Jews and Muslims. He will ultimately use Yasha's words and deeds against him. With some creativity and bending of laws, the prime minister believes he will emerge victorious. Now that Nakdimon is out of the way, he won't have anyone looking over his shoulder. He won't be monitored, won't be second-guessed. He looks at his watch and calculates the number of days until the plan is set in motion. The timing must be perfect. Passover or not, Yasha will pay the price.

14

ONE HOUR EARLIER

Uri Ohred sips strong Turkish coffee, picks up this morning's edition of *Haaretz* after skimming *The Jerusalem Post*. He thinks, *Please let today be a nothing news day.* Just one day of banal, insignificant pieces would be nice. He flips through rather quickly, scanning headlines. Page seven stops him in his tracks. Side by side are pictures of Yasha and the Immerser.

SUNDAY OP-ED
"FRIEND OR FOE?" by Yitzak Yonat

To many, Yasha ha Natzeret looks like the face of peace and altruism. He has been seen caring for the poor and helping people in crisis. Some witnesses claim he can even perform the miraculous: healing the sick, multiplying provisions, reversing mental illness. But others claim him to be a charlatan, aiming to trick people into believing they are getting something for nothing. There's no such thing as a free lunch, as the saying goes.

Yasha is often accompanied by a handful of Israeli men, a group that includes blue collar workers, law and finance professionals, former IDF soldiers, and a questionable Haredi Jew. They are known as the Twelve—a tight knit cell with Yasha as its nucleus. Naturally, Shin Bet is tracking them closely, developing files on each member. While no miracles have been performed at their command yet, their humanitarian efforts are well documented. They seem to be following the lead of Yasha, waiting for him to plow the collective path.

While all of this may seem harmless or possibly phony, there are two pertinent questions that need to be answered. First, where does the Twelve get funding? With no employer, no crowdfunding, no trust fund, Yasha's monetary backing is as mysterious as his supernatural signs. True, his cell members do hold jobs—at least when they're not seen traipsing around with him from city to city—though it's highly unlikely they provide any substantial financing given their professions. None of these men has ties to political connections, either.

According to an inside source close to the group, Yasha has been taking charitable donations for the group, hiding them in unmarked accounts, and using a small portion to fund his campaign. The rest of the money is then funneled, unbelievably, over the border and into the hands of the Palestinian Authority, a practice that began after some "miraculous" incidents at a West Bank refugee camp two months ago. No surprise, all monetary tracks have been efficiently covered. Despite the absence of documented proof, these global unmarked accounts linked to the cell are considered highly suspect in this regard. The money, of course, is then earmarked by the Palestinian Authority for terrorist activity inside Israel. What better satisfaction is there for the Palestinians than wreaking havoc on Israelis using their own financial resources?

Naturally, members of Yasha's inner circle deny these allegations, claiming absurdity and incongruity. They refute this "ridiculous claim," saying it goes against everything that they work to accomplish. Yasha's integrity and honesty would never allow him to participate in such deception, they insist. Perhaps he is being framed.

TWELVE

That brings us to the second question: What is Yasha's motive? Why, in the face of giving hope and healing to the citizens of Israel, would he aid and abet the enemy? Why would he fund terrorism that kills his own countrymen? Why dole out compassion and mercy with one hand and slide dirty money across enemy lines with the other? Is he blackmailing or being blackmailed? Is it political? On face value, it doesn't make sense. Why go through all that trouble, all the smoke and mirrors? The answer, I believe, can be found with one simple connection: Yochanan the Immerser, his *cousin*.

Back in January, Yochanan the Immerser—a well-known, self-appointed prophet of God—died in an Israeli prison following his arrest for defamation threats against Prime Minister Uri Ohred and his wife, Saidoreh. The government claims his death was suicide by starvation, yet those close to him from the kibbutz where he'd lived for twenty years proclaim otherwise.

"He would never choose to end his life," a close resident explains. "Yochanan lived every day with a simple joy, thankful for everything and everyone here. He wanted to make a deep spiritual impact in Israel and felt like that was his calling from God. Obviously, he upset the prime minister and his wife by calling out their immoral and illegal affairs. I don't believe Yochanan would suddenly abort his mission. Seems like a governmental coverup to me."

Another kibbutz resident describes the Immerser as quietly confident, wanting others to live free of worldly demands. He was a self-proclaimed messenger of God, along the lines of the Tanakh prophets, they say. His passion for justice and right living were admirable, yet his strong opinions and public statements against the highest authority landed him in hot water. According to eyewitness accounts, Yochanan was abducted in the night by an IDF raid and thrown into a Jerusalem prison. He remained there for months in solitary confinement, per specific instructions.

Guards revealed that he had attempted contact with his cousin, Yasha ha Natzeret, the man leading the Twelve. Perhaps he was expecting assistance in getting released from prison. Perhaps he was sending coded messages. No one knows for sure what the two cousins had planned. The prime minister, who was responsible for landing him in jail, was sure to be surprised by Yochanan's unexpected death, or was he? Those who knew Yochanan best cried foul play.

Surely, Yasha, like Yochanan's kibbutz friends, was devastated by the news of his cousin's death. Though they grew up in opposite parts of the country, being only six months apart in age, they remained in touch until young adulthood. Yasha's mother, Miryam, and Yochanan's mother, Elisheva, are cousins. They often spent holidays together from the time of pregnancy to the time when their boys became young men. Distance had kept the grown men apart for almost twenty years, but a local peace rally had brought them together again. They became a pair of radicals in the fight against government corruption and abuse of power.

Only time will tell what Yasha plans to do next. Will he continue to crisscross the country in search of those who need help the most? Or will he pretend to care while finding means to punish the Israeli government through sponsored terrorism via backdoor retribution, all in retaliation and honor for his dead cousin? At the end of the day, the real question remains unanswered: Is Yasha a friend or foe?

Ohred fumes for long minutes. Israel is supposed to have the most sophisticated intelligence community in the world, and yet this slips by them? *Unbelievable*, he thinks. Abruptly, he picks up the phone and barks at his aide. He expects Reuven, Goren, Nakdimon, and the press secretary in his office within an hour. No excuses. Prime Minister Ohred swears loudly and walks to his credenza. Teeth clenched, he pours himself a finger of bourbon; the coffee has been abruptly replaced. This bit of unexpected news is forcing him to break his promise to Saidoreh, his wife, about not drinking before noon. He resents his intelligence community for this. He resents Saidoreh.

"I will not lose control of this matter," he vows to himself aloud. *"I will not."*

15

FOUR DAYS EARLIER

Passover looms close. Excitement and anticipation zip through the crisp early April air of Jerusalem like electricity through coated lines. Preparations are being made in countless households, plans for worship set weeks in advance. High holy days bring passion of heart and spirit to thousands of Jews. Yet across town, this same excitement ushers in general uneasiness for those who worship a different god. Those who control the holy sites, the al-Aqsa Mosque and Temple Mount, suffer their neighbors the season of celebration.

Mid-week the thread of peace frays. A handful of Jewish men finish praying at the Wailing Wall and ascend the wooden ramp to the Temple Mount's Mughrabi Gate. They cannot pray there—as dictated by the Palestinian Authority and enforced by the Israeli government—but seek only to breathe deeply of the air atop their holy site. Despite the restrictions by their enemies, they claim to still feel the presence of their god, Yahweh. They walk across, slowly and solemnly, toward the Gate of Mercy on the eastern side of the complex. But instead of freedom to soak in the atmosphere, they are greeted by a group of masked Arab youth. Some are shirtless, others wear simple white tanks, but all don a *keffiyeh*, the cotton headdress commonly worn in Palestinian communities. Only their eyes remain unhidden.

The harassment begins. The Jewish men are too close to the Dome of the Rock, though they have no intention or ability of entrance. Even though any form of worship or religious display by a non-Muslim is prohibited and enforced by the local authorities, people cannot trust. Age-old controversy stirs up passionate defenses. The veiled youth hurl insults and threats toward the Jewish men. Claims of provocation fly up and out like combustible sparks. The Jews turn to walk the other direction, trying to focus on connecting with Yahweh rather than fighting their enemy. But the verbal assault continues to rain down, bombarding everyone in hearing distance. Pushed too far, the Jews turn and fight back. Words as weapons of warfare.

Approaching the Temple Mount area from the Mount of Olives come Yasha and the Twelve. The group passes by the Golden Gate, sealed centuries ago by Muslims, and stops by the Lion's Gate just meters ahead. Near the Lion's Gate entrance, metal detectors stand guard, granting permission for the weaponless. But weapons come in many forms. Yasha enters the Old City into the Arab quarter from the east, as fearless as a lion, yet he will depart the city days from now as a sacrificial lamb. A mysterious paradox. None of the Twelve know this, however.

A desire to worship at the holy site pulls Yasha closer. The Wailing Wall awaits them as it has awaited generations of devoted people for hundreds of years. They have no intention of creating strife or provoking conflict—a core of their peaceful methodology. Most things aren't worth fighting over.

Yet some are.

The Twelve pass by a cluster of Palestinians huddled around a makeshift shrine. On the ground lay large posters, the face of Isan bar-Abbas with a thick, raised scar running below his right eye, at the center of each. Candles and trinkets line the edges. Some kneel, others stand, offering homage to a captured militant.

Isan bar-Abbas, the Palestinian arrested for carrying out an act of terrorism in Jerusalem, sits in jail awaiting trial by the Israeli authorities. His fellow Palestinians hail him a martyr for the cause despite the fact that he's alive and in detainment, not in paradise with seventy virgins. They are drumming up support for him and calling for his release.

As Yasha nears them, a passionate older woman thrusts a flyer in his face. She is short, face lined with years of struggle, hands betraying arthritis. Perhaps she's a relative or neighbor. Yasha pauses, knowing that he cannot respond to the fact that he recognizes bar-Abbas. He stares at the photo, feeling the dark eyes jump off the page. Eyes so dark that you cannot tell where the iris ends and the pupil begins. Eyes dark with hatred and evil. Of all the people nearby, Yasha alone knows what bar-Abbas has done and what will happen to him. How his own life is inextricably tied to bar-Abbas. The man behind the eyes. He is being lauded by the Palestinians, but nobody really knows the demons that torment bar-Abbas and drive him to terrorism.

The men with Yasha catch a glimpse of the face on the flyer. Eyes shift nervously, bouncing from the woman to Yasha to the image of bar-Abbas. Everyone knows the act of terrorism that led to his arrest. In fact, most of the Twelve were in the vicinity the day it occurred—only Shimon, Mattiyahu, Yehudas, and Taddai had yet to join the cell. It wasn't until later that they discovered the name and face of the architect behind the event. The face on the flyer. But the woman does not know this.

She grabs Yasha's shirt, yelling in his face. "Injustice! Control! Oppression!"

Tension climbs higher than the old walls, and Yasha can feel himself stiffen. Her tears and pleas bombard him over and over. She assumes he cannot understand Arabic, but Yasha knows.

Suddenly, shouting from the Temple Mount distracts Yasha and his men. All attention shifts off the shrine for bar-Abbas to the voices of hate. Tension and fear fill the area in a matter of seconds, and more than half of the Twelve brace for a potential situation. *Not a good sign*, Natan thinks. He feels like they are always on the periphery of conflict, though their consistent line of attack is peaceful. Bringing peace into areas of tension carries its own risk. Not everyone wants peace.

TWELVE

Without announcement, Yasha follows the voices up to the Temple Mount. Toma hesitates to trail him, while Kefa quickly catches up, Yochanan and Yaakov in tow. Seven others ascend the ramp, but Yehudas holds back, watching from a safe distance. He senses volatility and the potential for an uprising. Fearful for his safety, Yehudas moves among the old walls to an unseen vantage point where he can observe what's coming. The less he gets embroiled, the better. Certainly, time spent with Yasha and the cell known as the Twelve has labeled Yehudas an activist, yet he feels apprehensive of such branding. His fellow cell members will no doubt realize his absence and form their own judgments. They probably wonder why Yasha invited him into the group. Truthfully, so does Yehudas. There must be a reason. Nothing their leader does is by accident. Yehudas questions what his purpose is in all this. What is his role?

Mattiyahu suddenly notices Yehudas going the opposite direction, so he turns around and tails him. *Where is he going? What's he doing?* wonders Mattiyahu. He feels the need to keep an eye on Yehudas, who has become erratic in the last month.

Across the open Temple Mount area, a long line extends from the stone kiosk sitting between the al-Aqsa Mosque and the Dome of the Rock. Scores of souls wait to pay the entrance fee for holy sites. Red flags go up inside Yasha—money chargers at worship sites. He considers it blasphemy. A low growl emerges from his throat. Fire burns in his eyes. *Give to the government what belongs to the government; give to God what is God's.*

Near the Gate of Mercy, also known as the Golden Gate, a swell of faces ripples in the late afternoon light. Jewish prophecies from centuries ago declare that the Messiah would enter through this gate, a sea of deceased people resurrected in his wake. From the east comes salvation, they say. Perhaps that is why the Gate of Mercy was sealed up long ago. But perhaps salvation and resurrection begin in the hearts of men. An internal work. Yasha silently revels at the thought of his presence there.

His assignment, of course, is to awaken hearts to life. The juxtaposition between indignation against unrighteousness and compassion for lost souls wars in his chest.

Voices have grown louder, more impassioned. The atmosphere pulses with volatility. Yasha sees the Arab vigilantes hassling the Jewish men, who have begun to retaliate, and his heart tightens. No matter the race or belief, he does not tolerate verbal or physical harassment. It is degrading and demoralizing and simply profane. The yelling, the fighting grows heated, and a crowd surges around them. The leader of the Twelve is greatly disturbed. The metal detectors, the entrance fees, the subversive and greedy attempt to control property as well as souls outrage him. All protesters and troublemakers atop the holy site steal the freedom to worship. It all defiles the base level of human rights. Suddenly, with a loud voice that overshadows the others, Yasha breaks into the conflict.

"This place was designated as a house of prayer for all nations!"

Heads turn, the yelling lessens, people stop to listen. He has their attention and intends on keeping it. Yasha points to the Temple Mount surface, a frequent flashpoint of violence. It is a duty and a right to allow freedom of worship at this holy place.

"This place was designated as a house of prayer for all nations!" he shouts again. "For *ALL* nations," he shouts indignantly. Turning his finger toward both the Arabs and Jews, Yasha glares at his fellow countrymen. "But you've turned it into a religious bazaar—a hangout for *thieves!*" He shakes with indignation.

Such language quiets the crowd momentarily, as if they weigh the verity of his words. But generations of mindsets are not easily changed.

"That's where he cuts the line," Arye comments sotto voce.

"Draws," ben-Chalfai replies.

"What?" Arye asks.

"Draws the line."

Right. Exactly right, Arye thinks, as his eyes remain fixed on Yasha.

Murmurs quickly turn into heated accusations, and both sides feel incited to riot. Toma, who had reluctantly ascended the Temple Mount, notices the Temple Mount police and the Waqf brigade approaching from opposite directions. He grabs Natan's arm, his face pinched in distress. Should they run? Is this going to end badly? Toma tends to question, internalize, and speculate everything.

Natan understands. "Not good. Might be more than a kerfuffle," he predicts to Toma. "More like a donnybrook." The sixth and eighth cell members swap side glances. Both are highly concerned.

But Yasha, unafraid, launches into an exhortation about race and religion, about respect for one another and honor for one another. Culture cries out for hate and violence and murder. Even the Immerser had been used as a pawn for the greed of an immoral nation. What has happened to basic decency? How wicked it is to bring hatred and intolerance onto holy ground! The sanctity of human life has all but disappeared, he cries.

"Get your things out of here!" he growls at the men. "Zeal for this place devours me!"

Kefa and Yaakov move in closer, with Shimon and Taddai—one a political activist, the other a wounded IDF soldier—right behind, ready to defend their commander. They are passionate about their country and people, fighters at heart. Adrenaline is pumping and zealous hearts yearn to make an impact alongside their leader. Fists are ready, devotion strong.

Angry shouts lob from both Arabs and Jews. "Who are you?! What right do you have to be here?!"

Pushing through the crowd comes a Muslim cleric. His approach is calm yet calculated. "What permit can you present to justify this? Who sanctioned you to be here?" he asks Yasha.

With matched confidence and composure, Yasha replies, "First let me ask *you* a question. You answer my question, and I'll answer yours. About the Immerser and his war against corruption—Who authorized it: heaven or humans?"

Everyone in this volatile region has heard of the Immerser, of his proclamations. The Immerser, an Israeli, had spoken out about the divided country, blaming Israelis and Palestinians alike. His voice, his mantra pointed to a better way of existence, counteracting decades of antagonism. True, he seemed to offer an enlightened message, but was he divinely appointed or merely earthly motivated?

The cleric considers Yasha's question. If he's honest, he could admit that the Immerser was a positive, even spiritual, force. But he would never, as that might cause the Muslims around him to grow more agitated. He deliberates with a few of the Muslim men closest to him. Their hands gesture wildly, their voices rise higher. No conclusion or agreement can be found. In the end, the cleric believes it doesn't matter.

"We don't know," the cleric answers.

"Then neither will I answer your question," Yasha responds.

Protests against Yasha's presence and diatribe grow by the second. Surges of tension ripple throughout the crowd. Some look for a fight, others fear it. To Toma's astonishment and disappointment, Yasha gives no indication of backing down. Neither does the collective anger. Shimon's adrenaline soars—he's finally going to witness Yasha taking control of their beloved nation. The Messiah he's always envisioned.

"What a generation!" yells Yasha. "No sense of God!"

"Give us some evidence that God is in this," the cleric replies. He, too, has heard rumors of Yasha's impossible feats, the stories from the Palestinian refugee camp. He, too, doubts their validity. "How about a miracle?"

"You're looking for proof, but you're looking for the wrong kind. All you want is something to titillate your curiosity, satisfy your lust for miracles. The only proof you're going to get is what looks like the absence of proof."

What kind of proof is that? Shimon doesn't like this answer.

Onlookers demand some evidence. "Validate the rumors!"

"Demonstrate!" they cry.

Yasha studies the faces around him. Calmly, he says, "Tear down this Temple, and in three days, I'll put it back together."

Now that's more like it, Shimon thinks with excitement.

Shouts rain down like bullets. "He's inciting a riot, a civil war!" they declare. An uproar of angry voices fills the air. No one understands that Yasha's reference points to himself. Muslims assume he means the Dome of the Rock, the third holiest site in Islam. Jews assume he aims to build the next Hebrew Temple. From the perspective of everyone surrounding him, these words are an unequivocal threat—gasoline thrown on an existing fire. Generations of lives and stories layer one atop another in Jerusalem, everyone wanting control of the stones in this great city.

Taddai says nervously, "I hope he knows what he's doing..."

Natan stammers, "Look at that stonework! Those buildings!" He understands the beauty and history of the Muslim holy sites. He has studied ancient Middle Eastern culture and architecture for years. He's scholastic, moralistic, and highly conservational.

Yasha turns and answers, "You're impressed by this grandiose architecture? There's not a stone in the whole works that is not going to end up in a heap of rubble."

Surging together, the crowd advances on him. Palestinians and Israelis both fume at his proclamations. They will not tolerate sacrilege and perilous talk. Yasha claims to be a messenger of peace, yet he's escalated tensions here on the Temple Mount. If only they could understand his heart, his motives, his prophetic statements.

"Let's go," Yaakov urges. He speaks into Yasha's ear, "Take it elsewhere." The warning is clear, arrests will soon be made. And Yaakov has no intention of seeing the inside of an Israeli prison again. Yet Yasha stands firm amid the swell. He doesn't see, however, the small cameras placed high around the Temple Mount that have zoomed in on him, his face captured for government eyes.

The masked Arab demonstrators escalate the tension, causing the police and brigade officers to infiltrate with force. Jews and Arabs alike point fingers Yasha's way, as if to pinpoint a verbal arsonist. They begin to move toward him, yet he manages to slip through the crowd and security forces in the blink of an eye, vanishing instantaneously. Miraculously.

But where did he go? It's not possible to disappear in such a dense crowd. Confusion adds to the collective tension.

Faivel wants to find Yasha but assumes the authorities will be in pursuit. Ben-Chalfai grabs his arm, pulling him in the opposite direction. Yaakov and Yochanan make for a different exit, evading the police like seasoned criminals. All the others slip out of the fracas as well, hoping to escape unnoticed. Even Shimon, always wanting to be part of history in the making, knows he cannot stay. Security forces manage to disperse the crowd from the elevated area, yet the clash that began at the holy sites spills out into the streets of Jerusalem's Old City. An uproar among the people continues for hours, the collective anger flammable once again.

Mattiyahu and Yehudas watch the entire escapade from their respective places of hiding, though Yehudas isn't aware that Mattiyahu is keeping tabs on him. Yehudas caught a brief glimpse of Yasha before he disappeared and feels provoked at his enigmatic leader. Before he thinks it through, Yehudas decides that Yasha seeks to undermine the delicate balance between Arab and Jew, between government and residents. Yehudas cannot deny all the miracles he's witnessed, all the positive inroads that Yasha has made for Israel and beyond. But he believes it's all going to end badly for Yasha and the Twelve if things continue to move in a contentious direction. The government will take them all out if need be.

Yehudas knows that he's walking a thin line. He contemplates contacting the appropriate authorities but decides against it for the moment. He doesn't know who to trust, and he doesn't want to end up on the wrong side of a bad situation. Self-preservation and self-doubt comingle in his head. *What am I doing with the Twelve? Why was I chosen? How will I escape if need be?* Yehudas has no answers.

Unlike most of the other eleven, he questions his own commitment to the selective group. Even after roughly a year. He's not sure what he believes about Yasha's mission, the purpose of the Twelve, the end game. Especially after the contentious episode at the Bethany safe house a month ago. He still fumes over Yasha's untenable attitude. Over his proffered grace. And today's altercation at the Temple Mount only sends up more red flags. *This is all wrong*, Yehudas thinks. *Things have gotten worse.* Could he secretly approach the authorities? Could he forsake the group? Forsake Yasha? He wonders how long it'll be before everything implodes, though, scarring them indefinitely.

He doesn't know it yet, but Yehudas will soon be approached by Shin Bet. All he'll have to do is pull the trigger. Everything else will shatter.

16

ONE MONTH EARLIER

Yasha wipes his mouth with a cloth napkin. He sighs, full of contentment. Yaakov and Yochanan cook like chefs at a five-star Michelin restaurant. After dinner on this early March evening, the Bethany safe house shifts into a mode of relaxation. Everyone but Marta, that is, who cleans furiously, doing dishes, clearing tables. Her brother, El'azar—not counted among the Twelve but a close friend to Yasha—begins humming softly, the sound unfamiliar to all the others. Except for Yasha. He knows the melody that comes from a heavenly piece, from the time when El'azar tasted four days of glory. His t-shirt reads L'CHAIM. *To life.*

A few locals wait outside the house to catch a glimpse of the celebrities, Yasha and El'azar. Recent events have stirred up the neighborhood. The miracles continue, surprising even the hardest of heart. A buzz in the air around Jerusalem persists despite the fact that authorities seek to squash the cell known as the Twelve and persuade El'azar to remain quiet about his experience. Cable networks and news programs jockey to be the first to broadcast his story. So far, El'azar has been cautiously vocal.

Yasha locates his beloved crimson guitar and begins to play, the music soft, peaceful, and incredibly beautiful. The entire house becomes still, all ears listening to a heavenly gift. Each of the Twelve watch him, analyzing and assessing their leader. El'azar closes his eyes, letting the notes flow through him.

Miryam, his youngest sister, tears up at the captivating sound. Her heart swells as Yasha plays—for everything he is, everything he's done, especially for her family. A single drop falls down her rosy cheek. With shoulder-length, straight brown hair and large, brilliant blue eyes, she radiates beauty even when heavy-hearted. She is the youngest and most sentimental of the three siblings, all four years apart.

Marta, the middle sibling, works to clean up, ruled by her obsessive-compulsive nature. Spotless housekeeping drives her endlessly. So much of life she cannot control—this one thing she can. Marta's blue eyes match her sister's, as does the color of her hair, though it falls in long, soft waves. The small gold nose ring remains the only sign of a rebellious choice made while at university.

Miryam, Marta, and El'azar are a tight-knit trio, orphaned by default after a terrible accident took their parents' lives a few years ago.

Yasha continues to play, drawing the room into a deeper, nonverbal connection with him. Who can offer such beauty, such peace? Abruptly, Miryam goes to the back room and retrieves something—a treasure that her family has owned for generations. She then edges toward Yasha and waits. When he finishes playing, Miryam quietly slips down by his feet and holds the small box in her hands. Yasha looks at her, the most tender expression on his face. Miryam gets caught up in his gaze, forgetting her tears, ignoring the others.

"I have something for you," she says. Her voice quivers with nervousness, her hands tremble slightly.

She slowly opens the box, lifting her watery eyes to meet his gaze. Her sister, Marta, remains frozen as she watches Miryam present a family heirloom with vast monetary worth. Though it rightfully belongs to Miryam—Marta has her own family heirloom—the thought of giving it away feels to Marta like a gamble for her future. *What is she doing?* thinks Marta, alarm rising within. Before their deaths, the siblings' parents explained that each child had a special gift, a treasure of Israel, that could be sold to the Antiquities Department for a great sum. It was to provide for their future should their financial situation ever become dire.

Only her brother, El'azar, understands. He puts out a hand to stop Marta approaching.

Oddly, it looks as if Miryam's offering her hand in marriage to Yasha. Half the cell members, especially Natan and ben-Chalfai, grow embarrassed at the intimacy. Inside the box sits not a ring but a minted coin from the first century. It bears the image of Herod's Temple. The worth is astounding.

Small gasps escape from members of the Twelve. Only Toma and Taddai resonate with Miryam's sacrifice of thanksgiving. Both men had been locked in places of despair—physically for Toma, mentally for Taddai—but Yasha had stepped in and rescued them. Tore through the shadows of their souls and gave them new life. Taddai has since given thanks for his past experiences, as they were the catalyst to meeting Yasha. He wouldn't wish PTSD on his worst enemy, yet he also wouldn't change his story. Look where it has brought him. No more weariness and confusion. No more searching for peace. Yasha's love and grace is now the air that he breathes. He understands Miryam's heart.

Quietly, almost inaudibly, Miryam pours out her soul to Yasha. Her thankfulness for saving her brother, El'azar, is immeasurable. Once again, she kneels before him, and once again, her tears cascade. Just as they had in the morgue three months ago. They fall onto Yasha's feet as she confesses her regrets about doubting him. He has singlehandedly saved their family from more extended grief and trauma. The death of their parents was enough to endure; losing El'azar permanently would have sent her into a bottomless depression. Miryam feels that everything she has belongs to Yasha. He has given her above and beyond what she could ask or imagine.

Without caring what the others think, Miryam bends forward and gently kisses the tops of his feet, now wet with her tears. Yasha runs a hand over her silky straight hair. She has offered more than a gift worth incredible monetary value. She has offered her heart. And pouring her heart on him has moved his heart.

TWELVE

Across the room, Yehudas bristles at Miryam's actions. Unlike Taddai, he's angered at the offering. The blackness at the periphery of his heart creeps toward the center. He has principles; shouldn't Yasha as well? Clearly, this act is not kosher. That treasure belongs in safety—in the hands of the Israeli Antiquities Department. It rightfully belongs to this country. Yehudas feels it's a betrayal by her family of Jewish history. He murmurs under his breath against Miryam. Others begin to murmur as well. But Yasha ignores them. He's focused on her sensitivity, her humility, her surrender.

"That's criminal! A total waste," Yehudas finally says. "That could've been sold for many, many wages and handed out to the poor." The tinge in his voice is unmistakable. His strictly Orthodox principles, buried deep within his core, declare this presentation offensive. A strict observance of Jewish law has always guided him, no matter the fact that his religious status has changed. The value of the coin could have gone toward the restoration of the Temple, a tenet held by the Haredi community. It could have gone to any number of worthy causes for the State of Israel.

"Leave her alone," Yasha turns and replies sternly. "Why are you giving her a hard time? She's just done something wonderfully significant for me." He pauses, watching the resentment swell in Yehudas's heart.

Embarrassment takes over Yehudas. *Why is Yasha being hostile? Why is he defending Miryam?*

Yasha looks around the room, making eye contact with his devoted followers. "You will have the poor with you every day for the rest of your lives. Whenever you feel like it, you can do something for them..." he explains. "But you won't always have me."

Kefa immediately feels a foreboding in his gut. He knows that despite the good they dispense to the people of Israel and Palestine, certain factions hate them. He tries to make sense of the conflicting facts. Somehow, Yasha always offers love yet causes offense simultaneously. He fears that in the end, the authorities will have them railroaded.

Yehudas senses the same. His instincts for business run deep, and he knows the government will make deals that support its cause, even at the expense of life. He wonders if that's what Yasha means. *Does Yasha know something the Twelve don't? Or does he plan on disappearing to save his own skin?* Yehudas wrestles with questions he cannot ask. He feels indignation rising within him at an alarming rate. And Yasha's calm attitude only fuels his ire. *This indecent display of affection by Miryam is insulting,* he decides. Yehudas slams his palm on the table and jumps up. All eyes move in his direction.

"Ridiculous!" he fumes.

Yasha notices the blackness now covering Yehudas's heart. Though it pains him, he knows this is part of the plan.

"Yehudas," Mattiyahu reaches out.

"No!" Yehudas shouts. "This is all wrong!"

Taddai, Yaakov, Shimon, and Faivel exchange glances, their previous conversation outside looming in their thoughts. Yehudas is becoming a loose cannon. Is he turning against the group? Against Yasha? He wouldn't dare.

"This! This waste of a gift!" Yehudas declares.

"Yehudas," Arye admonishes objectively, "don't rock the rocking chair."

"It's *boat*, Arye," Yehudas growls, "and stay out of it."

"Be careful," Yasha advises Yehudas. "That critical spirit has a way of boomeranging. You may well end up on the wrong side of it one day."

Yehudas shrugs off the comment. His exasperation builds and cannot be diffused. "And what about the Immerser? You've said nothing of your cousin. It's been over a month. How can you be silent? There's no talk of anything. How can you sit here calmly with presents and music?" he says with derision. "We must avenge...*you* must avenge!"

At the mention of the Immerser, Yasha closes his eyes and breathes deeply. The pain is strong. "Stay your anger. Don't insist on getting even;

that's not for you to do," Yasha instructs. "I'll take care of it. Nobody's getting by with anything, believe me."

"What will you do?" Yehudas demands. "It's already March—your cousin was murdered at the end of January!"

Yasha waits a beat. He knows that his followers don't see the whole picture. They can't possibly. There are always layers to what he says and meanings that transcend the natural. Sometimes his men connect with Yasha's intentions, but largely not. They're too busy looking at what's in front of them instead of what's beyond.

"Don't you realize that I have my shelves well stocked, locked behind iron doors? I'm in charge of vengeance and payback. And the day of their doom is just around the corner, sudden and swift and sure."

Shimon swells with the notion of settling the score. He nudges Taddai, the member most recently engaged in military affairs. They will volunteer to help put a plan into action.

"But when? And *how*?" demands Yehudas.

Yasha hears the soft voice.

LOVE IS NOT SELF-SEEKING.

"By turning my cheek," Yasha answers with finality.

"Oh, fantastic!" Yehudas spits, throwing up his hands and turning away.

Did they all hear him correctly? He's going to stand-down? Vengeance and payback by turning his cheek? It makes no sense. Surely, Yasha and the Immerser's families expect more. It will be seen as betrayal, plain and simple. El'azar tries to figure out what's happening, what's going on that the others are missing. He understands that they're playing chess with someone far superior, that they're always a few moves behind. Shimon sighs loudly, disappointed that any action has been delayed, though Taddai is secretly glad. He has seen enough violence in his short life. Weary from war, jaded from civil service, he still bears the perpetual dark circles under his eyes as if they were scars.

"Why can't you trust me?" Yasha asks.

Yehudas stares at him, incredulous. "Actions speak volumes, and you need to act! Eventually, people will make the connection and expect a response. Retaliation is the only way!" he demands.

"Somehow I don't think he's going to listen to you," quips Yaakov.

Yasha nods and says, "There's trouble ahead when you live only for the approval of others, saying what flatters them, doing what indulges them. Popularity contests are not truth contests. Your task is to be true, not popular."

Natan points at Yehudas. "The prime minister and Saidoreh feel satisfied that the Immerser has paid with his life. *You'll* feel satisfied when *they* pay…" he says. "It's a schadenfreude merry-go-round." Nobody wins.

Toma cocks his head, puzzled. Faivel hides a smile by whistling softly, drawing an imaginary circle with his index finger.

Yasha looks at his chosen twelve, then at El'azar and his sisters. "There's no telling who will hate you because of me. Stay with it—that's what is required. Stay with it to the end. You won't be sorry," he says, waiting a beat, "you'll be *saved*."

But Yehudas seethes. There's no reason for passivity, no excuse for cowardliness. Yasha won't defend members of his own family, yet he'll move mountains for strangers? Yehudas can't abide such seeming insanity.

The other eleven cell members absorb the change in Yehudas's behavior. None of them like it, especially Mattiyahu, his business partner of late. *I've got to reason with him*, Mattiyahu thinks. *He cannot accuse Yasha of being a coward and expect the others to agree. Yasha has proven himself again and again to be reliable and powerful. Why can't Yehudas see that?*

Mattiyahu plans on reminding Yehudas that they were invited by Yasha to be part of something bigger, something outside the norm. They may not fully understand Yasha's methods, but they must believe—in him, in what he's doing. But the animus in Yehudas's heart will prove unyielding. With Yasha's last decision, his fuse has officially been lit.

17

THREE WEEKS EARLIER

The prime minister calls an 11:00 a.m. meeting with Nakdimon, Moshe Reuven, and Zvi Goren. Alarming developments have reached him. Decisions must be made. A plan must be executed.

Everyone gathers in the tight office, the warmth providing a reprieve from the February chill on this overcast morning. Once they've gotten situated, Nakdimon, the deputy prime minister, informs the group of news about a man named El'azar. He is not an official cell member of the Twelve, just an active contributor.

"Turns out that El'azar was killed by one of the rockets Hamas launched into Ashkelon back in December. He was in one of the Twelve's safe houses, ironically, when the rocket hit. His sisters arrived hours later to find him unconscious after they couldn't contact him. He was taken to Barzilai University Medical Center where he underwent emergency surgery for sustained injuries. But due to complications, he later died." Nakdimon pauses, unsure of how to proceed.

"Is there more?" asks Reuven.

"Well, sir, El'azar is now alive."

"Pardon me?"

"Alive. And apparently back to normal, as he was before the attack," says Nakdimon, "according to his family, that is."

"How long was he dead?" says Goren.

Nakdimon clears his throat. "The hospital and morgue have it as multiple days. Four days to be exact."

The department heads give the deputy prime minister a strange look. Not possible, even with superior medical attention. Goren hesitates to ask the million-dollar question, though he knows he must. "Do they know how it happened?"

Nakdimon nods. "You're not going to believe this."

"Try me," he replies.

"It was Yasha, leader of the Twelve."

Moments of quiet pass as the news is absorbed. El'azar's resurrection at an Ashkelon morgue probably wouldn't be as important, but the event happened at the command of Yasha. He claims to make peace, yet the things he does bring anything but. Word has spread, and the people are stirred up.

"Why is Yasha always showing up in places of tension?" Ohred growls to himself. He wonders if Yasha is linked somehow to the militants fighting from across the Gaza border. Could he possibly be involved in the conflict between the Israelis and her neighbors? He seems to be everywhere these days. As if there needs to be extra attention on the Hamas situation. Ohred wants the fighting and the news coverage to end. For many minutes, the room is silent as the leader of Israel works through what *has* happened, what *is* happening, and what's *going* to happen.

Over the past few months, reports of unbelievable occurrences have permeated the country: Yasha feeding thousands from nothing at a refugee camp; Yasha eradicating incurable disease; Yasha changing lifelong deformities. Impossible feats. Clearly, he is trying to change normal culture and established society. Nothing rattles him, especially the government. His motives can't be trusted or ignored any longer. He has crossed a line.

Ideas are thrown around the room, some sensible and others untenable. The prime minister shakes his head at them all. Moshe Reuven broods alongside Zvi Goren. Nakdimon watches his superiors carefully.

"This has to be the Immerser come back from the dead," Ohred spits out in horror. "That's why he's able to work miracles!"

"It's nothing but hocus-pocus. He's probably made a pact with the devil," Goren comments.

"There's never been anything like this in Israel," Ohred grumbles. He feels like he's going crazy. "It's the Immerser, sure enough," he guffaws. "I cut off his head, and now he's back alive." Some sort of retaliatory reincarnation. He half believes his own sarcastic comment.

Goren and Reuven exchange glances. Ohred's decision to execute the Immerser three weeks ago is top secret. Only a handful of people know the truth, not what the public was told. Even Nakdimon was probably unaware, until just now.

What is it with Yasha? wonders Ohred. Political factions, non-profits, humanitarian aid—yes, of course. But unexplainable phenomena, again and again? Not in all the decades he's been in power. That's all contained within the *Torah*, the first five books of the Bible. Sure, God did miracles then but not anymore. He's a realist, as all rational thinkers are.

The prime minister puts forward a question to the group. "What do we do now? This man keeps on doing things, creating God-signs." His mocking laugh sends shivers up Nakdimon's spine. "By now it's known all over town that a 'miracle' has occurred and that Yasha is behind it." El'azar is living proof.

Suddenly, Nakdimon's phone rings. He looks at the caller ID and excuses himself from the room. Ohred watches his deputy with a mix of emotions. He hates being interrupted. But he hates the idea of secrecy even more.

Moshe Reuven apprises the others of current information. Dozens of rumors and gossip columns are circulating through the cities. Half the people feel that Yasha's a humanitarian, the other half that he's selling snake oil. But the numbers of people following Yasha have escalated in the wake of El'azar's testimony. It's difficult to refute living evidence. Reality must be faced.

Goren replies, "If we let them go on, pretty soon everyone will be following the Twelve, threatening to remove what power and privilege we have. These men are disturbing the peace. They are dangerous Jewish agitators subverting our law and order."

Raising people from the dead in broad daylight will certainly invoke fear and instability among the various factions of Jerusalem. Those who worship Allah will make false accusations against those who worship Yahweh and vice versa. For being a so-called pacifist group, the Twelve and their leader stir up an atmosphere of strife.

Stoically, Reuven listens to the various arguments made. Ideas circle around and around. Bribery, blackmail, coercion, intimidation…nothing is off the table.

"Perhaps we can silence them with veiled threats," Goren says. "Maybe imprisonment, maybe extradition?"

Viable options, indeed, though complicated. Ohred wants to avoid this cell from popping up again in the future. A roundtable discussion ensues, voices strong and opinionated.

"What leverage do we have?" Ohred asks his team.

"None so far," confirms Goren.

"Any suggestions?" Ohred demands.

The room falls silent. While lines of impropriety aren't an issue, no one wants to take the fall in case things go awry.

"*Something*," Ohred declares, "must be done. We can't have Yasha walking around this land, raising the dead wherever he goes. Just think of the Mount of Olives!" The largest Jewish cemetery in Jerusalem holds more than 150,000 graves. It cannot suddenly spring to life with resurrected bodies. Imagine the confusion and conflict that would ensue! Imagine the chaos!

After some minutes, Moshe Reuven grabs everyone's attention. The oldest man in the room, the head of Shin Bet, essentially ends the conversation. He will be the one to stick out his neck. "Don't you know anything?" All eyes are on him. The men know him well enough to understand he has already arrived at a decision. "Can't you see that it's to our advantage that *one man* dies for the people rather than our whole nation be destroyed?"

Again, the room goes quiet. The proposition holds enormous ramifications. Surely the supporters of Yasha and the Twelve will protest and demonstrate. They may even revolt. It's a risky move.

Reuven looks at the prime minister. He waits for approval. Ohred lets out a deep sigh, taking into consideration the potential complications. He looks to Goren, the head of Mossad, who gradually nods in agreement. Ohred weighs his options and acquiesces. "Find a way."

The timing must be perfect, the execution impeccable. No trace leading back to any government agency. Months from now, this mentality will change, and Ohred will strike while the iron's hot. With fearlessness, with impunity.

Yasha will, in the end, pay with his life.

At that moment, Nakdimon re-enters the room. He can feel an intensity in the atmosphere. *What have they decided? What will happen to Yasha and the Twelve?* Just as he sits, the prime minister abruptly dismisses the meeting. He leaves the aforementioned details to Shin Bet. Frequent updates are expected.

Nakdimon tries to read their faces as they exit. His intuition screams that something is amiss. He knows that circumstances often bend toward violence in the name of national security. He wants to avoid this scenario for Yasha and the Twelve. As deputy prime minister, he walks a fine line between loyalty to Prime Minister Ohred and following his instincts, which increasingly favor the revolutionary cell. His feelings are torn.

"Sir?" Nakdimon says, hoping for clarity.

"Yasha is to be blackmailed," Ohred lies, "and forced to capitulate. There is enough evidence of provocation that necessitates our decision." He conveniently leaves out the conversation that occurred while Nakdimon took a seemingly urgent phone call. *We will both keep secrets then*, he thinks. No need to tell Nakdimon that Yasha's fate has been decided. Ohred doesn't need to manage another wild card.

Nakdimon sits stunned. The decision is completely unwarranted, he believes. He must find a way to dissuade his boss from making this huge mistake. *Perhaps God will show a way*, Nakdimon hopes. After all, Yasha claims he's been sent from God. A fact that Nakdimon wrestles with. Why would God send someone who has turned out to be so controversial? Wouldn't His emissary be adored by all ends of the political and social spectrum?

Nakdimon knows that Yasha is different, not just some spiritual guru. His actions dictate as much. There's a balance between the love that he offers and the truth he proclaims. A beautiful dichotomy. But not everyone is convinced. Not everyone senses a deeper mission at play. While Nakdimon may not believe that Yasha is straight from God, he does believe that Yasha isn't deserving of punishment. Nakdimon must defend his instincts, defend Yasha against the government. What if he truly is from God? What if time proves it? Does Israel really want to have his blood on their hands? This decision could haunt them for generations.

Hastily, Nakdimon gathers his things, his thoughts still spinning. With any luck, he'll make Ohred see the error of his ways and convince him to be on the right side of history. If not, Nakdimon will come up with a plan. He cannot sit by and be silent. He must act.

18

TWELVE DAYS EARLIER

Faivel receives an unexpected message from a blocked number. He tries to decode its origins but fails. The instructions tell him to show it to the leader of the Twelve and none other. Out of respect and a sense of dread, Faivel obeys. He hands his device to Yasha with the encrypted message. A video. It takes Yasha a moment to gather what's happening in the footage.

"Cousin…" he whispers.

The face of the Immerser stares at him from a dark cell. He looks ragged and tired. Another man stands behind him, though only his torso shows in the frame. The person holding the camera shifts to get a better angle. A deep voice asks for any last words. Long moments pass, then the Immerser mouths silently at the camera. At first Yasha doesn't catch it, but on second viewing, he reads his lips: *I forgive you.*

Yasha knows. Words meant for Prime Minister Ohred and his wife, who threw him there following their public confrontation. Yasha assumes they have seen the video but wonders if they caught the parting message.

At the end, a gruesome image freezes in the frame. Yasha closes his eyes, feeling a huge knot form in his gut. He begins to sway, about to fall over. He is grieved and disgusted—but it's more than that. He knows that the act is prophetic for his own life. Speaking the truth often has consequences.

He drops the device to the ground, wordless. The cell members look around; they know that Yasha has just seen something abhorrent. The device is quickly retrieved and passed around. They're equally as horrified as their leader, especially Yehudas. He wonders if this is a bad omen.

"The Immerser is your cousin?" Yehudas asks. His surprise is matched by the other eleven men. *Who else knows? Has the footage gone viral?*

Faivel eventually determines that the video is a week old. He tells Yasha as much, indicating how much power the government wields over its citizens. *Did the prime minister give the order? Does he know that Yasha and the Immerser are related? If so, the dangers for Yasha—and us—have exponentially increased*, he thinks.

The cell members look at each other, unsure of what to do next. Ben-Chalfai paces back and forth, Shimon fishes for a cigarette. Toma and Natan scan the area to see if they're being watched. Even though they're outside Jerusalem, government eyes are everywhere. Toma is having second thoughts about this group. Doubt and fear are certainly making their presence felt, pushing him to escape. Only the reality of what Yasha has done for El'azar, for ben-Chalfai's nephew, and for himself keeps Toma rooted in the Twelve. Miracles of that proportion can't be ignored.

Yasha suddenly retreats, putting space between himself and his devotees.

"Where are you going?" Mattiyahu yells. Already his mind spins with solutions and preparations of a plan. Violence against a relative demands payment, revenge, or both. Again, he offers to bring legal charges against the government. Again, he will be denied that opportunity.

Yasha doesn't answer. He simply heads east, away from Jerusalem toward the Jordan. He aims to walk into the barren land alone, yet his companions, unless instructed otherwise, remain close.

"What does this mean?" Kefa asks as he grabs Yasha's arm.

He stops, a deep sigh emerging. "What it means is that the truth is too close for comfort—and they are uncomfortable." He investigates their faces, seeing deeper into them and into the future. Knowing the end from the beginning carries a certain weight, something Yasha cannot share with his Twelve. With a shake of his head, he continues his undisclosed quest.

"But what about the Immerser?" Kefa inquires.

Yasha stops. He turns and looks at them for a long moment, tears dividing his face. Words stick in his throat, emotions swell higher. "What did you expect when you went out to see him in the wild? A weekend camper? Hardly!"

"Commander?" Faivel asks, looking for clarification.

"What then? A sheik in silk pajamas? Not in the wilderness, not by a long shot!" Yasha says, voice ragged.

The cell members look at one another, certain that their leader has gone mad. With fear? With grief? They cannot decipher what he says.

Yasha continues, his voice raised, *"What then?"*

"A messenger from God?" ventures Arye softly.

"A messenger from God?" Yasha repeats, leaning in, pointing his finger. "That's right, a messenger! Probably the greatest messenger you'll ever hear."

But the Immerser is gone.

Yasha looks at them intensely. "Let me tell you what's going on here: no one in history surpasses the Immerser, but in the system God prepared for *you*, the lowliest person is ahead of him. For a long time until now, this way of life has suffered violence…" He puts his hands together as if in prayer, bringing them close to his face, symbolizing an urgent message. *"Yes, violent ones are trying to snatch it away!"*

A cold, February wind blows through them. They pull their coats tighter against winter's sharpness. The Twelve wonder about the meaning of his words. They debate his intentions even though they have seen nothing but goodwill. And now he speaks of violence? Does he intend to avenge his cousin? That will incite more problems than they care to imagine. Shimon, Yehudas, and Mattiyahu hope it will lead to a more aggressive demonstration. Shimon longs for passionate Zionists to topple Israel's compromised government. And to participate in such a mission would be a dream fulfilled. Yehudas maintains that it's Yasha's duty to retaliate, and Mattiyahu backs him up both morally and legally.

None of the Twelve are following Yasha's thoughts. The shock has seemingly gotten to him. They stare at him, wondering what to do. He speaks in riddles, which Faivel tries to solve faster than the others. It infuriates him that he cannot decipher the meaning.

"Are you listening to me? *Really* listening?" he challenges.

"The people love you," says Arye, "just like they loved the Immerser..."

Yasha answers, "He came fasting, and they called him crazy. I come feasting, and they call me a lush. Opinion polls don't count for much, do they?"

Yasha turns abruptly, resuming his mission to find solitude. He heads for open country. At first, the Twelve stand glued to the spot, unsure if they're invited, yet as their leader retreats further into the distance, they decide to follow. Yasha walks without aim, silent. Only his thoughts and a trailing group of men keep him company.

• • •

Late that afternoon, the leader of the Twelve crosses into the West Bank territory, landing at a refugee camp. His cell members are confused and curious. Has Yasha gone there intentionally or simply wandered in? Cautiously, they follow suit. Yehudas, however, bristles at the thought of crossing into the camp. He senses potential disaster, smells it like lamb on a spit.

What Yasha and his cell members see in the refugee camp overwhelms them. Rubble lines the streets, graffiti tattoos the buildings, garbage piles up in corners. Children, sick and crying, are scattered throughout; the elderly wrapped in wool blankets stare with sunken eyes; mothers move about with dark circles and haggard looks; people wander uselessly while others sit and deteriorate. The smell of dirty animals and human waste makes Yasha's eyes water. He wanders through the camp, looking into the sad, sunken eyes of fathers and mothers, children and grandparents. They stare because he stands out, because he's obviously not Palestinian. But Yasha carries his own sadness—for his beloved cousin, for humanity at large. A great compassion rises violently within him as does a sense of justice for the Immerser.

He hears the voice.

LOVE DOES NOT KEEP A RECORD OF WRONGS.

Not the wrongs done to his cousin at the hands of Israelis. Not the wrongs done to innocent people at the hands of Palestinian terrorist Isan bar-Abbas. And not the wrongs done when nations rise up against nations.

"This crowd is breaking my heart," Yasha says softly.

He begins to touch people. Compassion and purpose drive him. He heals a man with bandaged legs, a child with an eye patch, people with fevers and disease. Word travels fast through the camp and those curious move in closer to him, even though he's an outsider, maybe an enemy. Within minutes, a UNRWA camp worker begins interrogating Yasha like a reporter, assaulting him with questions and accusations. The worker's organization, known as UNRWA, United Nations Relief and Works Agency, supports the relief and human development of Palestinian refugees. But Yasha remains silent and moves throughout the camp offering undercover restoration. The camp worker goes in search of additional forces to impede him.

Some of the young men feel threatened in what they do not understand, but the older men and women hush and restrain them. Soon it is clear to everyone that there is nothing to fear. They go and bring the sick, the dying, the maimed—anyone who needs a physical touch, anyone afflicted by the ravages of poverty and war. Patiently, Yasha addresses each problem and reaches out to all who need him. Some of the refugees offer profuse thanks, yet others remain skeptical and distrustful of a Jew. The camp workers try and wedge between Yasha and the refugees, demanding that he leave the camp, that he's causing chaos in the streets. But the refugees push the workers aside, eager to get something life changing from this strange man, their desperation driving them forward. Ultimately, all the UNRWA workers can do is watch.

Eventually, the people settle down and Yasha begins speaking, yet only the people closest can hear him. After some minutes, a man brings him an old megaphone. He nods and gauges that the entire camp will hear his every word. Silently, he prays for words.

"You're blessed when you're at the end of your rope. With less of you, there is more of God and His rule. You're blessed when you feel you've lost what is most dear to you. Only then can you be embraced by the One most dear to you. You're blessed when you're content with just who you are—no more, no less. That's the moment you find yourselves proud owners of everything that can't be bought. You're blessed when you've worked up a good appetite for God. He's food and drink in the best meal you'll ever eat. You're blessed when you care. At the moment of being 'care-full,' you find yourselves cared for. You're blessed when you get your inside world—your mind and heart—put right. Then you can see God in the outside world. You're blessed when you can show people how to cooperate instead of compete or fight. That's when you discover who you really are and your place in God's family."

Yasha pauses, scanning the crowd. Though he is not one of them, they remain riveted at his feet. They struggle to weigh his words against the words they've been taught—words of a religion that often promotes violence over peace. Along the edges of the crowd, Palestinian security forces stand guard ready for potential unrest. But none comes.

"You're blessed when your commitment to God provokes persecution. The persecution drives you even deeper into God's kingdom."

Murmurs run through the crowd. Persecution comes at them from many directions. Names of politicians and government officials, Israeli and Palestinian alike, bounce from mouth to mouth. The UNRWA workers stiffen as people look their way.

The Twelve chafe at the radical teachings of Yasha. Even in their religion, no one ever talks with such language. They are unsure in this tense location what to do. They stand on edge, ready to defend their leader if need be. Knowing their hearts, Yasha makes eye contact with his close companions; this message is for them too.

"You're familiar with the old written law, 'Love your friend' and its unwritten companion, 'Hate your enemy.' But I'm challenging that. I'm telling you to love your enemies. Let them bring out the best in you, not the worst."

Jews and Muslims have been at enmity for centuries, dating back to Avraham's sons, Yitzchak and Yishmael. Half-brothers from the same father, fighting for respect, attention, and inheritance. Hating the enemy is genetic; it is ingrained. Loving them is not.

"If all you do is love the lovable, do you expect a bonus? Anybody can do that. If you simply say hello to those who greet you, do you expect a medal? If you only give for what you hope to get out of it, do you think that's charity? The stingiest of pawnbrokers does that."

The refugees look at the Twelve as well as the UNRWA workers stationed around the crowd. They murmur under their breath, eyes full of distrust.

Yasha continues, "If someone slaps you in the face, stand there and take it. If someone grabs your shirt, gift wrap your best coat and make a present of it. Don't pick on people, jump on their failures, criticize their faults—unless, of course, you want the same treatment. Don't condemn those who are down; that hardness can boomerang. Be easy on people; you'll find life a lot easier."

The refugees bristle at Yasha's teaching. It blatantly contradicts what they've been taught for generations. Distrust of Jews is a bedrock of Palestinian life. Had Yasha not gone through the crowds earlier healing them and setting them free of mental and physical suffering, they would've run him out of the camp. Instead, they sit riveted, comparing his tenets against the tenets they've always been told. Deep-rooted beliefs die hard. But undeniable actions of miraculous nature trump those beliefs, at least for the time being.

"Can a blind man guide a blind man? Wouldn't they both end up in a ditch? An apprentice doesn't lecture the master. The point is," Yasha warns, "be careful who you follow as your teacher."

People shift, voices give doubt.

The top UNRWA staff member steps up to Yasha's face. "Show us your credentials. Who authorized you to be here, to speak and act like this?"

Yasha answers, "The One who sent me gave me orders. Told me what to say and how to say it. I'm not making any of this up on my own."

"Who is it that sent you?"

"Whoever believes me, believes not just me but also in the One who sent me. Whoever looks at me is looking, in fact, at the One who sent me."

"Again, who sent you? And sent you to do what?" The UNRWA worker is getting perturbed by Yasha's evasion.

Yasha smiles with genuine affection. The man before him has unspoken needs just as the refugees do, though he hides behind his status. People in positions of authority do not cause Yasha discomfort. Ultimate authority resides elsewhere.

"I am light that has come into the world so that all who believe me won't have to stay any longer in the dark."

The staff worker squints his eyes, trying to interpret Yasha's proclamation. He begins to answer, but Yasha places a hand on his shoulder. A sense of peace, of surprise contentment falls on the man. There is no fight here.

Watching, Yaakov and Yochanan begin to wonder how much longer they will be at the refugee camp. Surely word has traveled outside these walls. They feel like sitting ducks in this environment. Neither of them can tolerate the feeling of being trapped in close quarters.

Yochanan grabs Yasha by the elbow and speaks in his ear. "We're out in the middle of nowhere, and it's getting late. Dismiss the people so they can go and get some food." He, too, feels his stomach growling.

Yasha answers, "There's no need to dismiss them. You give them food."

"Sure," Yaakov deadpans, patting his pockets, "here's some gum. That should hold them over."

Again, Yasha says, "You do it. Fix supper for them."

"Are you serious?" Yochanan asks. "You want us to go spend a fortune on food for their supper?" His calm, level-headed nature balks.

Yasha smirks but persists. He looks around, taking an inventory. "What do you have?"

No one seems to know about food for the hungry refugees; everyone looks to someone else. A woman overhears their conversation and motions that she has something to offer. Leaving and returning within moments, she approaches carrying a small pot of hot brown stew and a square of flatbread, enough to feed one family. There are hundreds present.

"But that's a drop in the bucket for a crowd like this," says Toma. Does Yasha really believe this single serving will make a dent?

Yaakov and Yochanan assess the resources as they often created meals from limited supply. But they shake their heads, telling Yasha there just isn't enough. It's not possible.

Arye sighs with disappointment. "Guess we're back to square zero."

Shimon chuckles.

"What?" Arye asks.

"So close, Arye," Kefa says, "so close." The others grin in amusement.

Yasha, of course, has a different agenda. He takes the metal pot and prays a blessing over it. Then he instructs his cell members to begin dishing it out. They look at him incredulously. Yasha turns to the crowd and bids them to come and get a ladle full of stew in a cup or a bowl or whatever they have. About a quarter of the people rush off to grab a container, their stomachs pleading for sustenance. The rest mill about, certain to get nothing.

Ben-Chalfai and Arye step forward and start pouring stew while Natan and Taddai form lines for the refugees. Kefa takes the flatbread, rips it in half, and hands it to Yochanan. They begin tearing off small pieces for each person, quickly realizing that the amount never diminishes. Yochanan looks at Kefa for confirmation that the miracle is happening before their eyes. They confide this to Arye and ben-Chalfai, who watch the pot of stew as each portion is doled out. It, too, never reduces. Astonishment hits their faces, and they look around for Yasha. But he has disappeared into the crowd.

After an hour, the end of the line comes into view. While physically tired, the Twelve are emotionally charged from the unexpected evening. Most are still processing the miracle, vacillating between excitement for having witnessed the event and awe at the person who had performed it. Their collective respect and admiration for Yasha is tightening their bond. They find Yasha, knowing he, too, needs food.

"Commander, eat," Yaakov says, handing him food. "Aren't you going to eat?"

He replies, "I have food to eat you know nothing about."

Puzzled looks cross the faces of his men. What food? Something different than what they've been parceling out? Food is literally multiplying before their eyes, and he speaks of other sustenance?

Toma asks, "Who could have brought him food?"

Ben-Chalfai shrugs.

Overhearing, Yasha says, "The food that keeps me going is that I do the will of God who sent me, finishing the work that He started." Faivel and Natan exchange knowing glances. Mattiyahu elbows Yehudas. Sent from God himself? Who else can explain such miracles and mysteries?

They all marvel at having a front row seat to witness heaven touching earth. What an experience!

Suddenly, it seems clear to Kefa what Yasha is doing. His power goes deeper than what's tangible; it penetrates the soul. He's not just helping the poor and needy. He's not just calling people out of a normal life into a deeper one. He's offering true transformation. He's transforming the world, one person at a time.

Night has now fallen. The refugees find their way to bed, drifting to sleep with full bellies and echoes of Yasha's voice and counterintuitive teachings in their heads. Some whisper thankfulness into the dark night, others confess their doubt and distrust of Jews. Nothing is ever free, they've been taught.

The UNRWA workers who watched the events unfold from the sidelines whisper in the dark. It's clear that the cell of Jewish men needs to be reported to authorities. Even though they offered food and medical attention for free, they aren't to be trusted. Everyone has an agenda. The seniormost UNRWA worker scampers back to his office and makes the phone call. Yehudas watches from a distance; he's the only one who notices. Like the camp workers, his hackles have also been raised, though for different reasons. They're still in the West Bank after all. The sooner they get back on Israeli soil, the better.

19

ONE WEEK EARLIER

The clock reads 1:00 a.m. Saidoreh finishes washing her face, preparing for bed. Wearing a silk bathrobe, she emerges from the bathroom and hears a specific knock on the door. She cinches the robe tighter and cracks open the bedroom door, knowing who waits on the other side. Her security detail apologizes for the late hour but has something she needs to see. Something extremely important. He hands her a small video device and says goodnight.

Once she has shut the door, she perches in the middle of her bed. Saidoreh knows full well what awaits her. She takes a deep breath. She had orchestrated the entire thing, of course. Yet watching the procedure gives her mixed feelings—disgust, anger, nausea.

The Immerser needed to be silenced, that's all there was to it. The opportunity presented itself, and she grabbed it. No one ever denies that she possesses strong convictions and determination. Few people want to challenge her. For good reason. She often makes decisions equal to that of her husband, the prime minister.

Saidoreh hits play a second time. Though the images are dark, she clearly sees the guards as well as her enemy in an orange jumpsuit. The video zooms in on his face. His intense, blue eyes radiate in the darkness, his dreadlocks frame his face. She raises the volume and listens, holding her breath. Voices last only a minute or so. Then the video goes black.

The prime minister's wife walks over to the large window overlooking the city of Jerusalem. Something about the video bothers her, but she cannot pinpoint what. Saidoreh closes her eyes and replays it in her mind. The man who disgraced her publicly appears surprised but somehow at peace. Suddenly, she understands.

Saidoreh grabs the video device off the bed and throws it into the fireplace. The last, low flames of a dying fire lap the metal and plastic. She stares at it as if it were the Immerser himself. His last words—his message of peace—shake her. *How dare he?* she fumes. She doesn't need his forgiveness, doesn't want it. Saidoreh feels the familiar flames of rage but then remembers that he will not be sending any more messages. To her or to the people of Israel. Vindictive laughter rises from her belly.

The Immerser does not have the last word. News of his death will soon be released, and she decides to control even that. Her fingerprints will not be on this. *No one will ever know,* she vows. Grabbing a pen and paper, she scribbles out the markings of a press release for her husband's cabinet.

Yochanan "the Immerser," a self-appointed Israeli political prisoner fighting against the current administration, was found dead in his jail cell in the early morning hours. Authorities ruled it a suicide. An ongoing hunger strike led to unforeseen complications that expedited his death.

Saidoreh, currently unaware that the Immerser and Yasha are cousins, feels victorious in defeating her enemy. Both speak the truth in boldness. Both create a measure of unrest in Israel. They are no friends to corrupt government. But these two rogue Jewish citizens will not upend the delicate balance of authority in the Middle East's only democracy.

She walks back to the large window overlooking the city to draw the curtains. To her amazement, snow has begun falling. An unexpected front has swept in this late January night. Now a thin, soft blanket of white covers everything—a rarity for Jerusalem. From the domes, spires, and minarets that loom over the city to the empty cobblestone streets, lights reflect off the snowflakes. A dreamlike golden glow envelopes everything. It looks like a peaceful town, one that isn't walking a tightrope of turbulence.

She believes that the snow is symbolic. That her decisions to protect her husband's administration, and Israel in general, will usher in serenity and peace. Content, Saidoreh smiles and sighs. *If you look closely enough,* she muses, *there's beauty in the chaos.* Like Jerusalem's streets, however, the truth will end up being quietly and artfully covered.

What Saidoreh doesn't realize at this moment is that she has ignited her own demise, essentially damning herself while trying to save her reputation and that of her husband. Beginning tonight, she will dream of the Immerser, the intensity of which will become unbearable. Night after night she will lose sleep, stop eating, and self-medicate. Saidoreh will try and hide her nightmares until she cracks. Months from now, the final one will bring her to make a decision—an impassioned plea to her husband that will not unite them but divide them. She will try to save the Immerser's cousin from the same fate of death, hoping to save herself in the process. But Yasha's death, ironically, is the only thing that can save her.

20

AN HOUR EARLIER

The dark Israeli prison cell throbs with quiet. The temperature drops as the hours tick by. January has proven to be a colder than average month. Though it's midnight, the Immerser sits with his back against the gray wall, softly whispering violent words. Words of praise and thanks. He knows that his life is set on a prophetic track, established by and through God. From the beginning, he has been the forerunner to his younger cousin, Yasha. His message of pursuing peace, right living, and seeking God has been fundamental. Dozens adhere to his teachings; dozens more follow him like a guru. Baptism through truth, baptism in truth. *Everything has gone according to plan*, he thinks, *until now.*

The Immerser wonders if he's gone too far. He had called out Prime Minister Ohred and his wife on grounds of consummate impropriety— adultery and massive corruption. Neither of the couple had taken the public accusation well, especially Saidoreh. Her outrage, masked by political practice, blared. She isn't a dignitary to mess with. The woman's manipulation knows no bounds. It's because of her that the Immerser now resides in jail. Been there for months.

He debates his actions, wondering how his incarceration will affect the campaign he's waging. What purpose does it serve to be stuck behind bars? Maybe he should have kept silent. The Immerser shakes his head to clear his thoughts and rests it back against the wall. He decides that he made the right decision. Such inappropriate behavior at that supreme governmental level is inexcusable. How can people change for the better if tolerance of everything rules?

A key in the cell lock startles the Immerser. A burly guard glares at him, though he cannot read the man's face. Something is happening. Normally, the guards don't visit this time of night. Normally, his cell remains locked. He hopes it's a good sign.

"Your time has come," the guard says in a low growl.

"Really?" he asks, rising.

He notices a second guard approaching. He's holding something in his hand. The Immerser can't make out what it is in the dark. As the smaller guard enters the cell, a glint of light reflects off the object. He sees it and sucks in his breath.

The larger, stronger man grabs the prisoner's arms and ties his wrists together behind his back. The plastic band tears into his skin. Tears load his eyes, the reality clear. He will not be released but instead killed. He wars within himself, feeling as though his mission isn't complete. Yet the situation deems otherwise. He closes his eyes for a moment and prays silently.

Why, God? Why now? Why this early?

Within seconds, the Immerser feels the answer. He has completed his job.

Peace fills his soul.

The large guard shoves the prisoner down on his knees. The Immerser opens his eyes. Heat overtakes him, the presence of love filling the dark space. *These guards are just pawns in the hands of a corrupt government,* he decides. Kindness settles in his heart. The Immerser begins telling them about God's love for them both. That love trumps all wrongdoing, all malevolence, all offense. That nothing in this life or the next can separate them from God's love, if they chose to accept that. It's not too late, there's still time. The guards, however, reject his passionate pleas, his ideology and theology. They insist that nothing can save them now, not after all they've done and seen. But the Immerser doesn't give up. As a last appeal, he urges his executioners to seek out the most perfect form of love represented in a human. He smiles as he thinks of his cousin.

"Go," he instructs, "find Yasha ha Natzeret."

The guards exchange glances. "The leader of the Twelve?"

The Immerser nods. "Tell him I sent you. There is none greater than Yasha."

"Not for long," the first guard replies. "If he continues to speak out the way you have, his fate will also be sealed."

Both guards and the Immerser know about the revolution that Yasha wages. More than political speech and humanitarian events, he seeks to bring pieces of heaven to earth. Miracles, signs, and wonders. Things regular people cannot explain. It's a threat to some, salvation to others. *Somehow, most fail to understand that he is commissioned by God Himself,* the Immerser thinks. *Much like me.* And nothing can stop what God has ordained.

Closing his eyes again, the Immerser murmurs a prayer for his cousin. The second guard passes the saber to the other man. He now holds a smaller object—one less sharp but nonetheless powerful.

"What are you doing with that?" the large guard asks.

The second guard points a video device at the prisoner. "For Saidoreh."

The first guard looks back at the prisoner. "What is your name?"

The Immerser stares at the camera, eyes red, dirty face lined with tears. He tries to speak, but his voice suddenly fails him. He sees his breath against the cold air, reminding him that earthly life is a mere vapor of breath in time. Here and then gone. Eternity, on the other hand, is a different story.

The guard knocks him hard on the side of the face.

"Yochanan," he says. "The Immerser."

"Do you have any last words?"

His lips move slowly. He's looking directly into the camera. If the prisoner's saying something, it's inaudible to the guards. *Maybe he's praying,* they think. *Perhaps making peace with God.*

"No?" the large guards barks. His voice booms around the tiny cell. He grabs a handful of the Immerser's dark, wild dreadlocks and yanks his head back. The man looks at his fellow guard who nods, indicating that the footage is still recording. "As you wish."

In one swift move, the blade cuts through neck. The guard lets go of the dreadlocks, and with a sick thud, the prisoner's head hits the stone floor. Blood pours out, running free. The guard captures the execution. Then he zooms in on the decapitated flesh and holds there. After five long seconds, the video goes dark.

21

ONE MONTH EARLIER

"Let's go back near Ashkelon," Yasha declares.

Four days ago, a teenager had arrived from Ashkelon, at the request of El'azar's sisters, with a message for Yasha. El'azar had ended up on the wrong end of a rocket launched from Gaza and was subsequently hospitalized in critical condition. Yasha knows that both Marta and Miryam are confused and offended that he didn't rush to the hospital when presented with the facts of their brother's precarious situation. What they don't realize is that Yasha wants to teach them a lesson—a lesson in truth. Facts are logical, analytical, and full of reason. But truth is perspective. And experience.

Yasha begins to pack up what few belongings he retains. The cell members are surprised but not exactly thrilled at this decision. Confused, they feel it's not safe to venture into dangerous territory. That, and they're tired from traveling up and down the country. Not to mention, a certain faction has begun vocalizing opposition against Yasha.

"You're going back?" ben-Chalfai asks incredulously.

"We," Yasha says. "*We* are going back."

"Quick observation:" Taddai offers, "there are rockets raining on Ashkelon, and some people might be out to kill you."

"He's possibly in a state of fugue," Natan offers.

Doesn't he remember that the prime minister locked up his cousin, the Immerser, in an Israeli prison for crossing the wrong people? He's been there for months now, and nobody knows how long he will be confined.

All communication with him has ceased. Taddai and Arye fret that the same could befall Yasha. What, then, would happen to the Twelve?

Yasha replies, "Are there not twelve hours of daylight?"

Ben-Chalfai, Taddai, and the others remain perplexed. They shouldn't be surprised necessarily; Yasha usually makes counterintuitive decisions.

"Anyone who walks in the daylight doesn't stumble," Yasha continues, "because there's plenty of light from the sun. Walking at night, he might very well stumble because he can't see where he's going."

"What is he talking about?" says Toma under his breath.

"I'm going with environmental hazards," Taddai whispers back.

"This is the verdict," Yasha adds. "The light has come into the world, but men loved the darkness rather than the light because their deeds were evil."

Hannukah, a celebration of light, was mere weeks ago—a celebration that points prophetically to him. Will his followers catch this revelation? Will anyone else? He gave Nakdimon the same message four months ago when Nakdimon sought him out at the Bethany safe house. He, too, seemed unable to process Yasha's meaning. Perhaps one day, after Yasha has returned to God's right hand, they will understand.

Yasha looks around the Galilean safe house, making sure he's picked up the odds and ends he needs. Only Yaakov mimics the leader. He has become Yasha's self-appointed bodyguard. His size, tattoos, bald head, and full beard intimidate most people. The others just watch, feeling hesitant to leave the safe house. They try to reason with Yasha about the potential dangers that lay waiting for them all, especially him, in Judea.

"Are you going to see El'azar?" asks ben-Chalfai, who assumes he's still in critical condition. Maybe he can use his connections in the medical world to gain access to the hospital. Depending on his wounds, it might take a miracle for El'azar to live.

Yasha nods and sighs deeply. "Our friend El'azar has fallen asleep. I'm going to wake him up."

TWELVE

The doctors were projecting that the severity of his wounds would most likely kill him. Only a matter of time, they said. Which is why Marta and Miryam sent the messenger four days ago to plead with Yasha to come at once. But Yasha thinks he's only sleeping? How does he know this?

"If he's gone to sleep, he'll get good rest and wake up improved," ben-Chalfai says cautiously. He is hopeful that El'azar will pull through and defy the odds. *Sick people sleep in abundance, aiding the healing process. That's proven scientifically. What's the reason to wake him?* he wonders. *Can't the hospital staff take care of things?*

Faivel's wheels turn, trying to decode Yasha's statement. He understands that Yasha doesn't waste words, nor does he mince them. Yasha has been dropping veritable riddles in his lap from day one. And he's determined to solve one sooner or later. Preferably before any of the others.

Yasha groans, seeing that his companions do not understand what he's saying. "El'azar is dead."

Natan gasps. Yehudas turns away. Toma begins to tear up. Faivel hits his thigh with a fist and makes a defeated face for the loss of a friend and for missing Yasha's coded statement. He wonders how this information has reached Yasha since none has ventured far from the safe house in the past few days. Communication, both in and out, has been extremely limited. But Faivel also realizes that Yasha hears and knows things that the Twelve do not.

What they do understand, however, is how much El'azar loved Yasha and, in turn, how much Yasha loved El'azar. Though he isn't one of the Twelve, he shares a deep connection with the leader of the Twelve. Somberness falls over the house, but Yasha seems unaffected.

Ben-Chalfai recalls Yasha's words from four days ago. "Wait a minute. Didn't you tell the messenger kid, 'This affliction is not unto death'?" *So, which is it?* he wonders.

The others pause and remember this declaration. Confusion swells. Hearts question. Doubt rises above faith. How could he? How could Yasha promise one thing and then deliver another? Can't he be trusted?

Yasha confirms with a curt nod, thinking of the day El'azar suffered the fallout from a rocket attack. "And I am glad for your sakes that I wasn't there. You're about to be given new grounds for believing," Yasha says with a grin. They're about to witness the unprecedented. "Now let's go."

Natan whispers to Faivel, "Come along. We might as well die with him." He's convinced that arriving in the vicinity of Ashkelon will ensure their deaths. After all, southern Israel is still under fire from Gaza.

Yasha retorts, "Why all these worried whispers? Runt believers! Haven't you caught on yet?"

Natan and Faivel grimace. The two cell members feel chastised and embarrassed. Natan, highly intelligent and self-motivated, reprimands himself. He values possessing vast knowledge and understanding of facts. Reality over fantasy. Normally, he catches on quickly to things yet not today. Natan vows not to make that mistake again. He watches the others collect their things in silence. As much as he wrestles with his thoughts, Natan determines that he's better off with Yasha than without—even if that means risking everything.

It takes the better part of a day traveling secondary roads to Ashkelon. The Twelve notice along the way that Yasha grows more and more brooding. The legitimacy of his friend's death looms ahead. When they enter the Barzilai University Medical Center, Yasha commands everyone but Arye, Kefa, Yochanan, and Yaakov to stay together near the entrance. They take seats in the waiting area, nervously looking around, wondering what's about to happen. Shimon and Mattiyahu go outside to smoke.

As Yasha walks through the sterile hallways, he takes in the sights and sounds of the sick, the dying. His heart beats loudly, in sync with heaven. Compassion swells alongside the tears. Soon they leak from his eyes. One drop, then two. Victims young and old subject to disease, to decay, to death…all because of one decision based upon one lie made ages ago. Yasha thinks of all these things, seemingly bearing every burden of every room he passes. Even his friend El'azar has suffered greatly too soon in life.

He rounds a corner and spots a door marked MORGUE at the end of the hall. Entering, Yasha sees friends and distant family huddled near Marta, quietly mourning. Miryam is down the hall handling the paperwork. Normally, Marta would have taken charge, but the trauma of losing their older brother has resurrected the trauma from their parents' deaths. She's locked in a place of mental paralysis as she struggles to accept the realization that the parental role now falls on her shoulders. Marta cannot concentrate on such basic things as medical paperwork. It's hard to see beyond the fact that the sisters are orphaned once again.

Yasha stands still, feeling the full weight of their sorrow. He closes his eyes, escorting more tears out. With a rush of emotion, he bends forward, hands on knees, feeling as though he's been punched in the gut. Quiet sobs cough out.

Marta notices the men for the first time and pushes past the others abruptly. She places a hand on Yasha's shoulder. He stands upright. They merely look at one another, eyes red, noses running. Marta takes a step and practically falls on him.

"Yasha," she squeaks through sobs, "if you'd been here, my brother wouldn't have died." She cannot bear the thought that El'azar is gone forever, that Yasha could have prevented this. But the fact is, he's dead. Just like her parents. And facts are brutal. The finality of it all washes over Marta again.

He doesn't answer but takes a deep breath, pulling her tighter against his chest. Compassion billows through him.

LOVE HOPES ALL THINGS, he hears.

"But I know…even now…" she says between breaths, "whatever you ask God, He will give you." Grace, forgiveness, redemption for mistakes.

Yasha smiles tightly. Truth spoken into the atmosphere. Though Marta doesn't know it, her statement has opened the door to the impossible. Yasha, eyes still wet, nods and kisses the top of her head. He answers matter-of-factly. "Your brother will be raised up."

Marta smiles wanly, thinking of the Torah's words. With some composure she says, "I know that he will be raised up in the resurrection at the end of time..."

Yasha pulls away from his friend, his hands gripping her shoulders. A gold necklace rests below her collarbone, the Star of David centered delicately. Yasha is reminded that he has come for all of Israel, for all the world, not just the ones in his close circle. He, like the One who sent him, desires for humanity to arise, to experience the power and personal love of God. What Yasha is about to do will reach far past one man, impacting both Jew and Gentile.

Looking deeply into Marta's sorrowful eyes, Yasha offers a promise. "You don't have to wait for the end," he says. "I am, right now, resurrection and life. The one who believes in me, even though he or she dies, will live. And everyone who believes in me does not ultimately die at all." He pauses, waiting to probe her heart. "Do you believe this?"

"Yes," replies Marta, wiping away tears.

The presence of Yasha puts Marta at ease. She has poured out her heart, and he, as always, has validated her. Yasha appreciates Marta's tenacity and strength as well as her fierce sense of justice, however imperfect. His gaze offers great consolation. No one can guess the totality of what Yasha brings with him when he walks into the room. No one can estimate his plan. He's a mysterious entity that they cannot live without now that they've encountered him. For better or worse, they need him.

"Where's Miryam?" Yasha asks.

Marta takes a deep breath and nods toward the room down the hall. She then instructs the mourners to go get her. When Miryam hears that Yasha asked for her, she jumps up and hurries down the corridor, paperwork in hand. She doesn't care that the hospital personnel call for her to return and finish the forms. Instead, she's focused on finding Yasha, knowing that he alone carries the comfort she seeks. Walking unsteadily, Miryam falls at his feet and begins weeping.

"Yasha," she whispers, "if only you had been here, my brother would not have died."

Yasha touches her head gently. Her crying pierces his heart. Miryam is fragile and compassionate; she seeks after the pure and the meaningful in life. His fondness for her is equal to his fondness for El'azar. Yasha looks up from where Miryam rocks on the ground to the faces of the Jewish friends and neighbors mourning alongside her. Grieving in large groups assures not only solace but honor for the family. Yasha groans, his soul extremely troubled. At this point, Yasha can no longer hold back his deep sorrow. Long streams of tears run down his face, blurring his vision. Those carefully watching him take note and whisper among themselves. His affection for El'azar is not lost on them.

A few paces away, an older woman whispers, "Well, if he loved him so much, why didn't he do something to keep him from dying? After all, he opened the eyes of a blind man." Although Yasha hears the question, he remains silent and laments internally at the thought.

What he wants to explain to Miryam and Marta and his cell members is that there are always two ways of seeing things: the natural and the supernatural. Facts versus truth. If they partner with the facts—that El'azar is dead—they will always be left wanting. But if they partner with the truth—how God views circumstances—it will set them free. He longs for them to understand this. Yasha attempts to give voice to his thoughts, but the sense of grieving he feels makes words difficult.

He'll just have to demonstrate.

"Where did you put him?" he asks after a few minutes.

A friend of Miryam's answers, "Come and see." She explains briefly that El'azar's body waits in the morgue's holding room, as Marta and

Miryam wanted Yasha to be present at the burial, their grief overwhelming. They've been waiting days for him to show up. Four, to be exact.

Once they pass through a secondary set of doors, Marta tells the director that she'd like to show the body of her deceased brother to Yasha. He leads them to the back room where bodies are held in-waiting. Miryam follows, as do Kefa, Arye, Yochanan, and Yaakov. Footsteps echo on the astringent floors. The director stops at a door marked ARRIVALS. He warns them that the room is cold and retains a distinct odor of decay despite the ventilation system.

A blast of frigid air sweeps over Yasha and Marta, who stand closest to the metal door. Yaakov thinks of industrial-sized freezers from his former life as a chef. Only this one contains bodies. The room is tall and narrow, a bank of large metal drawers lining one wall. Four across, three rows high. Twelve stainless steel coffins in all. Numbers mark each drawer.

The director walks over and pulls open drawer No. 7. A body covered with a white sheet slides out. The only part exposed is a pair of feet, one of which holds a toe tag indicating name, date, and ID number. The sisters slowly move into the room, while the men wait in the doorway to the hall.

From the doorway, Yasha says, "Remove it."

The mortician gives a concerned look.

"Yasha," Marta says, her brow furrowed, "by this time, there's a stench. He's been dead four days!"

Yasha looks at her and replies, "Didn't I tell you that if you believed, you would see the glory of God?"

Slowly, the director pulls back the white sheet to reveal El'azar's body, statuesque and ashy. Lifeless yet peaceful. His hair, short and sandy brown, remains soft as clouds even under the harsh fluorescent light. He wears the standard hospital gown and wristband. Marta covers her mouth and emits a sob.

For a minute, Yasha stares at the lifeless body. He walks over to El'azar, then lifts his eyes and palms toward heaven. "God, I'm grateful that You have listened to me. I know You always do listen, but on account of this crowd standing here, I've spoken so that they might believe You sent me."

Yasha closes his eyes, his head still tilted back. The director uses the moment to re-cover El'azar's body with the sheet. A deep groan causes the director to look toward Yasha. Suddenly, Yasha makes eye contact with him. The director catches a strange intensity in his gaze, and it throws him off balance. Electricity pings wall to wall. Around the room, neck hairs stand up. Out of nowhere, a loud voice booms through the silence.

"El'azar! Come up!" Yasha demands.

The white sheet springs up, and a loud gasp of air can be heard all the way down the hall. Marta screams. Miryam starts to faint, but Kefa dives in and catches her. Marta now latches onto her sister, keeping her upright. The director scampers backwards into a corner, his eyes wide with fear. The sheet falls from El'azar's head, revealing a perfectly healthy, albeit pale, body sitting up on the metal table. He blinks and looks around the room at the faces unfamiliar and familiar, getting his bearings. Confusion, then peace.

"Yasha!" El'azar exclaims.

Marta chokes amidst tears. She trembles out of excitement and wonder. *How is this happening? He can raise the DEAD?*

"What's with the smell in here?" El'azar asks, scrunching his nose, looking around. He mentally runs through a handful of questions. *Where am I? Why is everyone looking so startled? Why is it so cold?* Then he notices the toe tag. Revelation falls like lightning. The last thing he remembers is lying bandaged in the hospital bed, his sisters at his side. He had asked them to get Yasha. But Yasha never showed up. Until now.

El'azar yanks the toe tag from his right foot. "Won't be needing this."

Yasha laughs. The others stand fixed, trying to process the inconceivable miracle that's just happened. They are shocked and amazed. Are they hallucinating? How is this even possible?

The sisters hold onto each other, dependably. Never in a million years would they have imagined this scenario for El'azar. For their family.

"Tell me I'm not crazy," Kefa says in a low voice. "Tell me that I just saw a dead man brought back to life." He'd witnessed some aberrant things in the military but nothing close to this.

"*Dead* dead," Yaakov confirms. Yochanan nods, eyes bulging. Neither can move, as if glued into place.

El'azar swings his legs over the edge of the metal plank, the white sheet bunched at his waist. He shakes his arms, rolls his shoulders, gets the blood pumping again. Suddenly, he rubs his wrist. "Where's my watch?"

The mortician, aghast, fumbles for his bearings and finds the bag with El'azar's few belongings— a wallet, a ring, and a watch. In the wake of their grief, the sisters had forgotten to ask for these things.

El'azar takes all three and straps his watch back on. He looks at it intently, a mark of confusion on his face. He looks up, eyes wide. "Four days?!"

At first no one speaks. Then the director confirms the question. "Um, yes," he stammers warily, "you have been here four days."

Everyone looks toward Yasha.

"You left me dead for *four days*?"

Yasha shrugs, making a face of inconsequence. "Thought you'd enjoy the time," he teases.

El'azar hops off the metal plank and embraces his friend tightly.

With a full smile, Yasha whispers in his ear, "Checkmate."

He chuckles loudly. El'azar makes eye contact with his sisters and offers his outstretched arms. Miryam cries and laughs simultaneously while Marta shakes visibly. She can't seem to grasp what's just happened. Despite the shock, his sisters assault him with hugs and kisses and tears of joy.

Yaakov, Kefa, Arye, and Yochanan huddle out in the hallway, absorbing the unexpected surprise. Amazement and disbelief and elation pinball between them.

"This is incredible!" Arye bubbles with excitement for witnessing the miracle and for the miracle itself. He grabs onto the marvel with both hands, clutching the joy of the moment. His heart swells, his ruddy face glows, much unlike his brother's. Kefa keeps a straight face, keeps his lips pressed tight.

"Didn't see that one coming," Yaakov says to his brother. Yochanan shakes his head. They share astonished looks.

"No doubt this will upset some folks," he replies.

Who's going to explain it? Kefa wonders. He compartmentalizes the phenomenon. He glances back toward El'azar and Yasha. Nothing seems impossible for their leader. They yearn to rejoice yet hesitate considering the enormity of the miracle. Only God can raise the dead.

Unquestionably, they all see Yasha in a different way now. They've come face to face with the supernatural. Kefa whispers to himself, "Who is this man?"

As if hearing their thoughts, Yasha moves toward them, smiling. They look at him with trepidation, with awe. "Don't let facts define the story. Believing facts is easy but believing truth takes courage. Are you willing to look beyond what you see? Are you willing to see things the rest of the world doesn't see?" He moves in closer and pauses. "With God," Yasha declares passionately, "*nothing* is impossible!" He winks, that glint in his eye.

In the room, the mortician stands with his back against the wall again, mumbling under his breath. Perhaps he's talking to himself, perhaps praying. He determines that psychological counseling will be in his future. He's seen dead bodies make strange noises and even move temporarily but never stand up and walk again as if nothing had happened. Especially after four days. The director guffaws that he'll have to write "ALIVE: BACK FROM DEAD" in the file. Bureaucratic pushback won't be pleasant. *Maybe an early retirement is in order*, he thinks.

Yasha turns to the director and says, ""Get El'azar some scrubs. He certainly can't walk out of here in that flimsy hospital gown." He chuckles at the thought of it. "Then discharge him and let him go."

Yaakov looks at the pallid mortician. "Best of luck," he quips. The mortician is not amused.

Once El'azar has changed, he meets the others in the hallway. Marta clings to her brother. Miryam rips up the hospital paperwork. Yochanan and Yaakov whisper about the ramifications this will have on Jerusalem and the country at large. The world, even. Arye runs to find the rest of the Twelve, shouting the good news!

Confused and alarmed, they want to see for themselves. Yasha leads the group from the morgue back into the waiting room, where they join the other eight cell members. Questions are voiced, shouts of celebration thrown into the air. The volume of commotion rises and falls followed by hugs and slaps on the back, again and again. The followers of Yasha marvel at the unbelievable miracle they've just witnessed.

Ben-Chalfai cannot wrap his head around this phenomenon. Scientifically impossible. The tenth cell member questions everything he's been taught and everything he doesn't understand. Over and over, he mumbles, "I cannot believe this." If the rest of the group could only harness this power, this unstoppable force, think of the possibilities.

"He's a juggernaut," Natan says.

Ben-Chalfai grins, as if Natan just read his thoughts. He nods his head in agreement.

"A what?" Taddai replies.

"Does he always talk like that?" Toma asks Faivel.

"Always," Faivel confirms.

Yasha turns aside to his cell members and gathers them close. He throws an arm around ben-Chalfai and Shimon, one on each side. The others circle around. His eyes are alive with flames of fire. He whispers passionately, "Fortunate the eyes that see what you're seeing! There are plenty of prophets and kings who would have given their right arms to see what you are seeing but never got so much as a glimpse, to hear what you are hearing but never got so much as a whisper."

Once word gets out, attention on the Twelve will skyrocket. The recent healings and miraculous incidents are one kind of phenomenon; raising the dead is another altogether. Excitement and amazement overwhelm them. To be part of a divine assignment, a mission far greater than they could've imagined, inspires yet terrifies them. A couple members of the group allow fear to hijack their thoughts. Toma fears the power of his leader, Yehudas the power of his government's potential response. Both unnerved, both fighting the urge to rethink their commitment. Yasha senses this. He loves his twelve men, wants them to be fully engaged.

"See what I've given you?" he says with a delighted face. "Safe passage as you walk on snakes and scorpions and protection from every assault of the enemy. No one can put a hand on you." He looks from one to another, pulling them in with his eyes, with his words. "All the same, the great triumph is not in your authority over evil but in God's authority over you and presence with you."

While the Twelve absorb Yasha's insight and admonitions, some of the mourners who've witnessed the past few days have become unnerved by the resurrection. El'azar and his sisters stand huddled nearby, excitedly going over the events again and again. The mourners take it all in, discuss everything in hushed tones. Something isn't right, they say. They worry it's a gimmick. Perhaps the medical administration should be notified. Perhaps the authorities. Nobody notices as the troubled onlookers slink out the hospital door.

22

TWO DAYS EARLIER

The Israeli Diplomatic Grand Hall teems with round tables covered in crisp white linens. The room has the air of a state dinner, yet the occasion is an opulent birthday party for Prime Minister Ohred. Lights, crystal, and fine china adorn the decorated room. Hundreds of friends and dignitaries mingle. Spirits are high. Bodyguards and security details intersperse around the room. A band plays on a stage in the background.

Uri Ohred wears his finest Armani tuxedo, recently flown in from Paris. His second wife, Saidoreh, glides through the room in a red Versace gown. Harry Winston jewels embellish her dark olive skin. She radiates beauty, sophistication, and influence. She speaks four languages fluently. No wonder the prime minister wanted her for himself. His first wife fell far short of Saidoreh's qualities and charisma. It was icing on the cake that he stole her from his despised half-brother. The marriage caused more than a few political issues, but he harbors no regrets. None of the pundit commentary mattered to him, not even the more recent embarrassing criticism from the religious man known as the Immerser. His wife, on the other hand, is holding a deep grudge.

Dinner arrives and the guests find their assigned seats on this cold winter evening. A gourmet meal prepared by the most renowned chef in Jerusalem satisfies the crowd, even those who don't delight in haute couture cuisine. Lamb stuffed quince, pomegranate salad, and *sahleb*—a thick, sweet, and milky dessert—serve as three of the refined courses. At the end of the last course, Saidoreh takes the microphone on stage and thanks everyone for coming to celebrate her husband. She then announces a surprise.

Salome, Saidoreh's daughter from her previous marriage, emerges onto the stage. Dark hair, alabaster skin, stunning green eyes. Her dazzling aqua sequined Carolina Herrera gown gives the illusion of gliding through clear Mediterranean waters. Without forewarning, she begins singing a song written just for the prime minister in honor of his birthday. His surprise quickly turns to joy as her beautiful voice fills the banquet hall. He has never heard Salome sing in person.

The room becomes intensely quiet as everyone stares in awe while the striking sound emanates from the equally striking woman. Her voice rings out in a melancholy tone—the Fado style, tinged with destiny and fate. It is somewhat seductive yet praiseworthy. Every eye is fixed on Salome; she is hypnotizing everyone in the room. She could win millions—of people and cash—on American Idol. But she has everything she needs, as her mother is married to the prime minister of Israel.

Salome finishes and the guests offer a standing ovation. She blushes and bows gracefully. Ohred holds out his hands, beckoning her to come. She descends from the stage and embraces her mother's husband. The clapping ceases and the guests sit down. All eyes are on Salome and the prime minister.

"Ask me anything," he says loudly, alcohol and food swirling his senses, "I'll give you anything you want, I swear." He laughs and surveys the guests. They cheer approval.

Salome glances at her mother, who nods her head slightly. The signal has been given. Ohred has no idea that the next ten seconds will change his life.

She takes a deep breath. "I want you to give me right now…" she says to the crowd. Then Salome leans in and whispers into Ohred's ear, "*the head of Yochanan the Immerser.*"

Immediately, the prime minister's face goes white. He isn't sure if he heard Salome correctly, but she holds his gaze and smiles tightly. He tries not to show any shock in front of his guests, so a slow smile appears even though he feels extreme distress. He cannot reject her, not when he's made a show of granting any request. Given the fact that it's late December, Ohred ruefully considers that *Yom Kippur*, the Day of Atonement, has already passed. The annual time to repent and redeem. He bemoans this decision, knowing that it will weigh heavily on his conscience for the better part of a year.

The guests sit riveted with curiosity. "What?" they shout. "What has Salome asked for?"

With a forced chuckle, Ohred glances at his friends and relatives. He tries to find the right words. No doubt his wife, Saidoreh, has put Salome up to this—it wears her perfume of vengeance. He will be awake all night after making this decision. Ohred is furious with Saidoreh for making this request, for forcing his hand. She is using him, and it could backfire immensely. That cannot happen.

But Ohred, too, is a master at deception. As he thinks of his wife's twisted motives, the answer arrives.

"Peace," he says to the crowd with a forced smile. "She asks for peace in our land."

The audience claps and cheers and raises their glasses to a toast.

The prime minister kisses Salome gently on the cheek then turns and beckons his guard detail. He whispers into the man's ear. The order has been given. Saidoreh rises and lifts her wine glass. Her satisfaction overflows. She makes a quick tribute to her husband. The guests lift their glasses and toast in unison.

"To the prime minister!"

23

TWO DAYS EARLIER

Frazzled, a teenage boy approaches the door of the safe house. He is fatigued after traveling in makeshift ways from Ashkelon to a small town in western Galilee. But his message is imperative. Yasha needs to hear it from reliable lips. Technology is too easily traced by the authorities. It takes the boy some time to find the right house where Yasha and the Twelve remain out of public sight. Very few people know where he is—only his closest friends. The atmosphere in the Galilee region isn't nearly as volatile as Jerusalem, yet words and attitudes travel fast, especially in a place as small as Israel.

After questioning the boy, Kefa lets him in the door. He looks around at the men, noticing signs of fatigue on their faces. In a side room, Yasha sips hot tea. The boy enters and delivers the message.

"It's El'azar."

He describes the Palestinian rocket fired into the safe house in Ashkelon—a calculated attack launched on the doorstep of Israel's vulnerable citizens. The good news is that El'azar was alone; bad news is that he's wounded and in critical condition at Barzilai Medical Center. Might even need to be transported to Mt. Scopus in Jerusalem. The boy tells of the horror brought on by the rockets—the destruction, the carnage. Many structures were hit as the rockets, fired at random, connected with Israeli homes and businesses. It wasn't personal against the Twelve, though Shimon and Taddai harbor doubts.

Taddai knows from days in the IDF that Israel will retaliate, hitting Gaza hard, targeting the leaders of Hamas. After defending itself—or retaliating, depending on the perspective—Israel will eventually pursue a ceasefire. Will the tension ever end? Suddenly, flashbacks of his time in war begin to surface, unnerving him. Taddai feels the room spinning. Agitated and shaking, he stumbles from the room, but Yasha quickly steps in and places both hands on his shoulders.

"If the son sets you free, you are free through and through." Taddai looks at Yasha with his hazel, petrified eyes. Looking for that familiar lifeline. Silently, Yasha infuses Taddai with placidity, with serenity. He nods, feeling a strong peace settle over him. He's safe. Yasha's mercy had rescued his soul, making new the old. He'd run out of that darkness, that emotional tomb. No purpose in turning back now. Taddai lets Yasha's words wash over him again. *You are free. You are free.*

"Who sent you?" Yochanan asks the boy.

He tells them it was Marta and Miryam, who insist that Yasha travel to them immediately, fearing their brother is about to die. They cannot bear the thought of losing another member of their family. El'azar's life hangs on a cliff to eternity. The boy is also scared—he and his family have known El'azar for years. "You have to go back with me!" the boy pleads.

Yasha looks out the window for a few moments, waiting, listening.

The boy goes on to tell of rumors circulating around Jerusalem that El'azar was targeted intentionally because of his tight connection with Yasha. He did, after all, coordinate the safe houses around the country. Authorities are trying to undermine the cell in whatever means possible. Some of the Twelve agree wholeheartedly, but others doubt the reality of such manipulation. Why use the Palestinians to take him out when IDF easily could? Or maybe it was a case of being in the wrong place at the wrong time. Either way, El'azar is standing at death's door.

After some minutes, Yasha replies, "This affliction is not fatal. It will become an occasion to show God's glory."

Ben-Chalfai whispers, "What does that mean?"

"Stay tuned," murmurs Yaakov. His brother shoots him a look.

The boy doesn't know how to respond. Yasha gives no indication of urgency; he continues to sip his tea. The boy fidgets, hoping that Yasha will jump up and head back to Ashkelon with him. He tries to convey the desperation of El'azar's sisters. They are distraught that he might die. Their only hope is in the presence of Yasha. The boy has been instructed not to return without him. He's getting more agitated at the apparent lack of concern. Again, he pours out pleas on behalf of Marta and Miryam, pleas on behalf of himself.

But Yasha doesn't move. Some of the Twelve hover at the room's entrance. Arye and Faivel lean against separate walls in silence. Others are talking in whispers in adjacent areas. Toma, Natan, and Yehudas— more apprehensive than the rest—discuss the fact that going back toward Jerusalem and Tel Aviv would draw negative attention. Perhaps it will even incite violence. Shimon, of course, voices support for Israeli retaliation, wanting to make the Palestinians pay for El'azar. His temper flares, his passion for vengeance clouds his thinking. If only he could entice the others to revolt against everyone who fights Israel and the country's ordained destiny as a Jewish nation!

"Hope the IDF rains hellfire and brimstone on them," Shimon declares. "Wish I could pull the trigger."

"First things first," Yasha tells Shimon. "Your business is life not death. Follow me. Pursue life."

The Twelve weigh the words of their leader against the truth facing them. Death is a reality in this volatile land. Life must be fought for. Maybe there's more to what Yasha is saying than they understand. He's completely different from anyone else they've met in Israel. In the face of death and destruction, peace reigns in his heart, his demeanor, and his agenda. Despite circumstances or politics.

For long minutes, Yasha is quiet and pensive. Everyone waits to see what the decision will be. He then turns to the boy and instructs him to return alone. Yasha is staying in Galilee. The boy looks around the room for help. He can't believe Yasha refuses to visit El'azar. It goes against everything the cell stands for: caring for the poor, helping the sick, rescuing the oppressed. Doesn't he love El'azar like a brother? Doesn't he care? Didn't he just tell Shimon to pursue life? If Yasha waits, El'azar will die.

Yasha looks at him knowingly and reassures him that everything will turn out fine. "Don't let this throw you," Yasha says. "You trust God, don't you? Trust *me*."

El'azar and his sisters are going to have to ride out the storm. Ben-Chalfai stares at Yasha, trying to make heads or tails of his decision. He analyzes the situation, looking to compartmentalize and make sense of it. Why does Yasha heal some people at the drop of a hat, but others have to wait? Why the inconsistency? Yasha has healed scores of people in the last few months. Miracles of great proportion over and over. Ben-Chalfai wouldn't have ever believed them, but his own nephew is living proof— Levi, a stranger to Yasha, gets a miracle, but El'azar, a good friend, doesn't? The mystery confuses and borderline offends him. Something isn't right.

Faivel feels the same. It's yet another enigma for him to sort out. Yasha is full of them. Faivel wants to decode Yasha's decision, but his wheels spin. A few days from now, though, it will all make sense.

Again, Yasha says, "Just trust."

But the boy shakes his head, not knowing what he will tell Marta and Miryam. Slowly, in disbelief, he backs out of the room and retreats from the safe house.

Yasha looks out the window, watching the messenger disappear. Moments later, he slips out the back door, climbs a small hill above the perched house, and nestles into the landscape. Below lays the *Kinneret*, the Sea of Galilee—deep blue waters surrounded by mountains speckled green and brown. The largest fresh-bodied lake in Israel. Fished for centuries, traversed by many. Probably his favorite place on earth.

He thinks of his hometown of Natzeret, a city not far from where he sits. He thinks of his family. *What if it were my brother and not El'azar?*

he wonders. *My own flesh and blood?* A deep sadness penetrates his heart. He can sense the fear and distress that engulf Miryam and Marta. The next handful of days will, no doubt, be extremely difficult for everyone. Death has that effect. If it were up to him, Yasha would be on the road, reaching his friend in a few hours. But it's not up to him. He too must trust. And wait.

24

TWO MONTHS BEFORE

Photos clandestinely taken of all twelve cell members hang on the wall at the Shin Bet headquarters. A larger photo of their leader is tacked in the middle, dates and notations scribbled on it in black Sharpie.

Uri Ohred stands sandwiched between Moshe Reuven and Zvi Goren. They stare at the collage in silence, examining faces, looking for hidden clues. How did this cell pop up so quickly over the past few months? Where does the funding come from? What is their ultimate goal? If only they weren't so admired. So far, nothing illegal has transpired, but that doesn't mean plans aren't in the works. Two of the twelve are convicted felons; one good at managing money; another a legal defender. It's only a matter of time.

The prime minister, head of Shin Bet, and director of Mossad go over the rest. All of the cell members are Israeli citizens and Jews; two emigrated and most are non-religious. The student, the scientist, and the artist are clean—nothing on file. The Zionist, the former IDF soldier, and the tech geek have files but nothing incriminating. The erstwhile Orthodox Jew and the attorney have questionable yet non-threatening pasts. The sets of brothers, though, are a red flag. They have sizeable files but no former connections to the rest of the group. In fact, most of the men have never crossed paths before, so how they all ended up together remains a mystery. For the time being, that is. The Shin Bet is working around the clock to compile the pieces.

Why *these* twelve men? Was their assemblage orchestrated or merely organic? More often than not, groups like this are puppeteered by a superior force. Who, then, is the source?

TWELVE

"Twelve men, one leader," says Ohred.

"Yes, sir, twelve confirmed members," replies Reuven.

"I want a list of all their families," Ohred instructs. "I want to know every job, every neighborhood they've lived in, every person they've dated since puberty. I want names of connections to any organizations inside and outside of Israel. What are their passions? What are their vices? What are their secrets? I want to know everything about these twelve, down to their underwear size." Documentation, photos, eyewitness accounts—anything and everything they can find.

"Yes, sir, we're on that," replies Goren, director of Mossad.

"Nothing slips under the radar, is that clear?" demands the prime minister. He doesn't want any surprises down the road. Nothing that will catch him off guard.

The men nod in unison. Both departments, Shin Bet and Mossad, will work to uncover the mystery, competitively, of course. Both assume that each is superior to the other.

"Assuming the number twelve isn't accidental," Ohred continues, "what's the significance?"

"The leader frequently speaks of God. Potentially a reference to the twelve patriarchs," Goren offers, referring to the twelve tribes mentioned in the book of *Bereshit*, or Genesis.

"Perhaps," muses Ohred.

Moshe Reuven offers a different thought. "Numerologically speaking, the number twelve symbolizes power and authority as well as a perfect government."

The prime minister spins to face the Shin Bet leader. "Forming a coup, then?" he ponders aloud. "Not on my watch."

Behind them, the door opens and closes quickly. Ohred's deputy, Nakdimon, surveys the scene in silence. Something's afoot. Hairs on the back of his neck rise.

The prime minister says, "What have you got?"

Nakdimon shrugs, palms up.

"Why didn't you bring him with you?" He had instructed Nakdimon to lure Yasha into answering questions, to sort out the unanswered items. Not an arrest, just a conversation. He did not expect his deputy to return alone.

Nakdimon explains this morning's public rally. Yasha had addressed the crowd, challenging some and exhorting others—nothing condemning and nothing threatening against the government. Nakdimon fails to mention Yasha's sudden disappearance and his final warning, however; a reference to vultures circling overhead. That part is best left unmentioned. Ohred would take it personally, driving him to make an example of the Twelve's leader. For being the ruler of a democratic nation surrounded by enemies, Ohred has uncharacteristically thin skin.

Nakdimon tiptoes through his report, attempting to assuage any fears.

"Have you heard the way he talks?" he says, genuinely. "We've never heard anyone speak like this man." Charismatic, honest, engaging.

If looks could kill. "Are you carried away like the rest of the rabble?" asks Ohred. "You don't see any of us prominent leaders believing him, do you?"

The question goes unanswered.

"It's only this crowd," he continues, referring to the rally and the citizens of Israel, "that is taken in by him—and damned."

Nakdimon exhales audibly. His emotions are dangling from his sleeve. "Does our law decide about a man's guilt without first listening to him and finding out what he is doing? Maybe we should dig deeper before making rash decisions, to cover all the bases. His supporters will be up in arms if he's falsely accused. We could have a flash mob if we're not careful."

"Flash mobs don't scare me." The prime minister lowers his eyes at his deputy. He feels challenged by his subordinate, which irritates him. He scrutinizes Nakdimon silently. Has he, too, fallen under the spell of

Yasha and the Twelve? With a clipped tone, Ohred asks, "Are you *also* campaigning for him?"

Nakdimon pauses, unsure of how to respond. Does the prime minister know that he showed up unexpectedly at one of the Twelve's safe houses recently? That he had a long conversation alone with Yasha? Maybe he was followed and watched. Nakdimon silently wills his breathing to calm and his perspiration to stop. Ohred would have no hesitation in terminating him on the spot if he felt it necessary. Clearly, Nakdimon's boss is questioning his loyalty to him as well as to the Israeli government.

"People are saying that Yasha rivals Elijah the prophet. He demonstrates the impossible again and again," Nakdimon replies. "The reality is, Israel hasn't seen anything like this in centuries."

"Examine the evidence," Ohred demands. "See if any 'prophet' *ever* comes from Galilee." Natzeret, a town in lower Galilee that sits in a valley surrounded by mountains, is the largest Arab city in Israel. Not logical, or likely, for a Jewish prophet to emerge from such surroundings. Ohred will later learn that those prequalifications don't apply. For now, his dismissive statement halts the angle of conversation. He switches back to analyzing the Twelve and Yasha in particular. What is he missing?

From a classified file, Moshe Reuven pulls a list of documented "occurrences" or "disturbances," with Yasha at the center of them all. Hundreds of witnesses claiming miracles of all kinds: mental, physical, and emotional. Seemingly impossible feats done in the blink of an eye. Social media has captured dozens of instances, yet media manipulation isn't uncommon these days. Israel, a tiny country, seems to bulge with an influx of tourists. Public areas swell with crowds trying to capture a glimpse or an encounter with the leader of the Twelve. Reuven hands over the file.

"What about these so-called miracles?" Ohred asks the group after reading the list. He refuses to believe in such hocus-pocus. Somehow Yasha is manipulating the public for a specific reason. Ohred just needs to determine that reason.

"It's out of control. The world's in a stampede after him," replies Goren. He assumes it's a mass-delusion issue. He hates a herd mentality.

"Dramatic, don't you think?" says the prime minister. "Not everyone loves him."

"Sir," Goren replies, "our intelligence is tracking a high number of people flooding into Israel seeking to find him. The sick, the paralyzed, the mentally ill. It's like sojourners seeking the Fountain of Youth."

Ohred replies with disdain, "Fools."

"Some end up finding him—the ones desperate enough to believe in his proffered deliverance," offers the Mossad director. "But the vast majority are crazies looking to take a selfie with a celebrity."

"Do we need to close the borders?" Ohred asks.

"Not unless we stop this momentum before it gets challenging. We can put certain limitations in place, though. Strict limitations. Vetted business travelers and politicians will be permitted, most tourists will not." The fall season of Jewish celebrations has passed. The upcoming Hanukkah holidays will segue into a typical, quiet winter. Maybe, hopefully, it will even snow this year.

"There are reports of swarms of people currently making their way here," Nakdimon confesses. "You can't shut the borders now. Social media is blowing up." He offers to show them.

The prime minister and Mossad director exchange looks. Their generation inherently takes social media with a grain of salt, not Torah level of truth, as the millennials purport. But still, the notion needs to be double-checked.

"While I don't share in your distress," Reuven says, "I am alarmed at the seditious undertow spreading out from this cell."

The prime minister nods.

"Here he is, out in the open, saying whatever he pleases, and no one is stopping him." While freedom of speech is protected, speech that is perhaps designed to sabotage the government must be addressed.

"He's crazy, a maniac—out of his head completely. Why bother listening to him?" asks Ohred.

Why are the people so enamored? He also thinks about the Immerser, the outspoken critic of himself and his wife. Why do people follow lunatics like them? Little does he know that the Immerser and Yasha are closely related. Months from now, he will learn of the connection, fueling an even greater fury. But today, he vows that neither of them will be able to force him from office. *Fortunately, the Immerser's platform has been silenced as he now resides in a maximum-security Israeli prison*, he thinks. Saidoreh, his wife, had eventually worn him down and persuaded him to lock the Immerser up. While at first Ohred was hesitant to make that decision, he's now glad. The censorship has worked. Maybe that will placate Saidoreh's fury.

"I'm not so sure," Nakdimon replies sheepishly. He conveys snippets of testimony from various people: some healed, some restored, some fed and cared for. "These aren't the words or ways of a crazy man…"

The prime minister again second-guesses the loyalty of his deputy. While he appreciates constructive criticism and a difference of opinion, he feels that Nakdimon teeters on insubordination.

"Well, he's certainly more than a humanitarian giving away free health care," Goren comments derisively.

Nakdimon offers more. "This was recorded from a conversation Yasha had with Faivel, one of his cell members: *The words that I speak to you aren't mere words. I don't just make them up on my own. The One who resides in me crafts each word into a divine act.*"

"Divine, huh?" Ohred snorts. "I suppose he thinks he's the next Dalai Lama."

"Or Messiah," Goren concurs, rolling his eyes. *Fortunately*, he thinks, *Yasha didn't attempt to provide any rabbinical services on Yom Kippur a few weeks ago.*

"Crazy or not, we need to take action," says Reuven.

"Lay out a plan then," the prime minister says to his intelligence heads. Too much is at stake. Too much could go wrong if Yasha and the Twelve are left alone to do God-knows-what. Even if he must use unethical methods, Ohred believes he's doing the right thing for his country. He swore an oath, after all. Israel will not crumble from within. He will lie, cheat, and steal to secure the illusion of peace. The ends justify the means, he believes.

Surveillance, financial monitoring, setting traps, and spinning communication all get tossed on the table. All get approved. The tide will turn against Yasha and the Twelve. A Red Sea division will exist among the people of Israel because of this man. Government officials and skeptics on one side, ordinary citizens and believers on the other. Yet Nakdimon straddles the middle; he's not sure how things will play out. For now, he has one foot in each camp, but soon enough he'll have to decide. A separation of sheep and goats, like Yasha has warned. Is he willing to abandon everything he's worked for politically? Does he believe Yasha's mission will succeed and change Israel forever? Though he cannot answer, Nakdimon asks himself on what side of history he wants to land. Abruptly, his boss cuts into his thoughts and makes an unambiguous statement.

"This will be the end, not the beginning," snarls Ohred, "*of the Twelve.*"

25

Undercover agents alongside Nakdimon watch with intense purpose. They have been tasked with compiling information about Yasha and the Twelve. Incriminating information, to be exact. He has an agenda, they've been told. There's always an agenda. Once Yasha uses language that can be held against him—convincing evidence—the government agents are to detain him. Nakdimon has been instructed to bring Yasha in for questioning. Nothing serious, just routine information gathering.

The agents have taken in their surroundings at Dizengoff Square, a well-known Tel Aviv area with a large kinetic art fountain dubbed "Fire and Water" perched in the middle. An unspoken prophetic statement, no doubt. Yasha has intentionally chosen this location on a gorgeous fall day, an abundance of cafés and retail shops in the vicinity. Many ears available to tickle. Or anger, depending on the perspective.

Yasha and his cell of followers are unapproved activists. What they preach and practice conspires against the administration and endangers national security. Officials in high places feel that they incite supporters to contest the government because of alleged corruption. Yet it's just politics—impossible to expect nary a spot or a blemish upon Israel's political organization.

Yochanan the Immerser's arrest and imprisonment proves that the government tracks and traces vocal opposition. And that it often takes action thereafter. It's anyone's guess how long the Immerser will be jailed. Yasha knows that this, too, is part of the plan, though his followers do not. While both men were supposed to speak today, Yasha will take up the mantle for his cousin and forge ahead. He will not succumb to the bait of rage offered by government hands; he can feel the tentacles of malevolence in the atmosphere. Yom Kippur, the holiest day of the year, has recently come and gone. Prayer, fasting, and repentance. But it doesn't take long for people to lapse, once again, into sinful ways.

Yasha hears the familiar voice.

LOVE IS NOT EASILY ANGERED.

He and the Twelve escaped the confines of Jerusalem as Yasha had sensed a snare set for him there. He knows they want to apprehend him, perhaps even silence him—a reproduction of what happened to the Immerser. Tel Aviv, while more populated in the metro area than Jerusalem, holds fast as the financial center. Government resides in Jerusalem. The powers seeking to suppress Yasha are presumed to be seventy kilometers removed.

Yasha stands on the edge of the fountain and speaks to the engaged crowd. His voice rings loud and strong. "No one lights a lamp and then covers it with a washtub or shoves it under the bed. No, you set it up on a lampstand so those who enter the room can see their way. We're not keeping secrets; we're telling them. We're not hiding things; we're bringing *everything* out into the open."

The undercover agents bristle. Attendants cheer.

"When a strong man armed to the teeth," Yasha continues, "stands guard in his front yard, his property is safe and sound. But what if a stronger man comes along with superior weapons? Then he's beaten at his own game, the arsenal that gave him such confidence hauled off, and his precious possessions plundered."

Shimon and Taddai react as soldiers. They feel that Yasha is giving them a warning. A harbinger of sorts. The two members share a fervency for defending their homeland, even with Taddai's traumatic experience in the military.

"This is war, and there is no neutral ground. If you're not on my side, you're the enemy. If you're not helping, you're making things worse," proclaims Yasha.

Government agents spread out throughout the large crowd, recording these proclamations. This ringleader obviously seeks to divide people and to pit them against one another. His entire movement is supposed to be one of peace and tranquility. Or is it? On the surface, Yasha makes comments that sound enticing, yet the deeper message is grasped only by a few.

"Don't think I've come to make life cozy. I've come to start a fire on this earth—how I wish it were blazing right now!" Yasha declares. "I've come to change everything, turn everything right-side up—how I long for it to be finished! Do you think I came to smooth things over and make everything nice? Not so. I've come to disrupt and confront!"

Those sent to detain Yasha now have their proof. He's clearly forming a coup, to expose and depose the prime minister. They whisper to one another, believing they hold the upper hand. But Yasha knows differently.

From the north end, friends of Mattiyahu arrive at the demonstration—drug dealers, prostitutes, and thieves he has helped to exonerate in the past. A group of unseemly characters. Misfits, vagrants, and people just down on their luck. Mattiyahu welcomes them. Certain members of the Twelve, though, turn immediately uncomfortable. They are still acclimating to one another, not fully meshed as a group. Ben-Chalfai and Natan care about their reputations and what association with outcasts will mean. As they know, eyes are everywhere.

People nearby voice their displeasure, their opinions as unattractive as the offensive tattoos covering the disreputable. The holier-than-thou group begins to harass Yasha's close followers. "What kind of example is this from your teacher, acting cozy with crooks and riffraff?"

Mattiyahu—cocky, autonomous, often pushing extremes—rebukes them, using less than kind words in return. His colorful language retrieves smiles from his acquaintances but scowls from some of the Twelve. Even Shimon, who curses more often than the rest, is surprised. *Maybe this lawyer is the best of the worst*, he muses.

Yasha has come for them all, insiders and outsiders alike. They all need grace, they all need refining.

"You have minds like a snake pit!" Yasha declares. "How do you suppose what you say is worth anything when you are so foul-minded? It's your heart, not the dictionary, that gives meaning to your words. Every one of these careless words is going to come back to haunt you. There will be a time of reckoning. Words are powerful; take them seriously. Words can be your salvation. Words can also be your damnation."

Murmurs percolate through the crowd. His rebukes hit their targets. For some, it's convicting; for others, incendiary. Shimon looks up to find Yasha's eyes on him. It's a directive for them all, Shimon in particular.

"Guard your tongue from profanity," Yasha instructs.

Shimon winces. *Going to need an act of God to break that habit*, he thinks.

"And no more lying through your teeth," adds Yasha.

Mattiyahu feels his chest burning. Lying comes as naturally as breathing. He bends the truth more often than Natan recites the Torah. Can he really change at this point? Can Yasha expect that of him?

"Listen now!" Yasha shouts. "It's not what you swallow that pollutes your life; it's what you vomit—that's the real pollution."

Yehudas wonders if he's talking to the Twelve or Mattiyahu's friends. Who is the true target here? His eyes seem to hit everyone collectively.

"What are you trying to say?" someone yells.

"Are you being willfully stupid?" Yasha says, looking at those around him. "It's what comes out of a person that pollutes: obscenities, lusts, thefts, murders, adultery, greed, depravity, deceptive dealings, carousing, mean looks, slander, arrogance, foolishness—all these are vomit from the heart. *There* is the source of your pollution."

Mattiyahu, the tenth member to join, cringes at the list of violations. He's guilty of them all, save murder, though he defends murderers as an attorney. Natan and ben-Chalfai whisper about Mattiyahu being a half-step above his trashy friends. And Shimon murmurs to Yaakov about lawyers being bottom feeders—expensive to purchase but full of refuse. Did Mattiyahu invite his unseemly acquaintances today? Does he actually enjoy spending time with these people?

Yasha overhears them. "Why this gossipy whispering?"

One voice, then two and three grow louder, shouting criticism against the people deemed dregs of society. They don't have anything to offer, they say. They're a drain on the government. What possible interest could they have in political activism? Why not invest in people who can make a difference in this world?

Yasha shoots back. "Who needs a doctor: the healthy or the sick?"

Toma's ears perk up. *Is he talking about me?* he wonders. A few months ago, he was awaiting medical attention, speculating what his future would look like. The other cell members don't even look in his direction, even though seven of them were present when Yasha healed him. They have deciphered that Yasha's speech is multi-layered. Often it refers to something else altogether. But Toma, the eighth member to join this sundry group, has a lot to learn.

Though hesitant at first, Toma was intrigued at the invitation to join Yasha's inner circle. He had assumed, however erroneously, that he wouldn't be welcomed or accepted due to his flamboyant lifestyle. Though Israel's general population maintains a strong acceptance of homosexuals, none of the other cell members fall into that category. But they do all have a past, some more questionable than the rest. Yet Yasha extends love impartially, regardless. This love, unlike any other kind that Toma's experienced, happens just because he's breathing. No strings attached. He's learning, though, that there is a cost to following Yasha. That the past must be set aside. He must step into something altogether new, despite old habits and thought patterns begging for attention. He must trust Yasha to lead the way, moving forward not back. Even though it's foreign territory, even though it's frightening. But it's the same cost for everyone. Only what they surrender differs.

"All of Mattiyahu's friends, apparently," someone says, answering Yasha's question about who needs a doctor. Laughs from the crowd volley about. This, of course, sets Mattiyahu's friends on edge. They hurl curses in return, defending themselves. Tension escalates, voices intensify. Within a matter of minutes, this gathering has the potential to explode into violence. The high-and-mighty against the brash. Kefa, Shimon, Yochanan, and Yaakov move in closer, ready to act if necessary.

But Yasha invades. He points at the hecklers. "It's easy to see a smudge on your neighbor's face and be oblivious to the ugly sneer on your own. Do you have the nerve to say, 'Let me wash your face for you' when your own face is distorted by contempt? Wipe that ugly sneer off your own face and you might be fit to offer a washcloth to your neighbor."

Murmurs rise through the crowd. Yasha hears the pushback on his radical ideologies. He's not surprised it ruffles some feathers; in fact, that's his intention. To call out hypocrisy, injustice, and manipulation of people, no matter the race, gender, or religion.

"If you walk around with your nose in the air, you're going to end up flat on your face; but if you're content to be simply yourself, you will become more than yourself," Yasha explains. He looks at the faces before him. So many to reach. So many to love. "Go figure out what this means: 'I'm after mercy, not religion.' I'm here to invite outsiders, not coddle insiders—an invitation to a changed life, changed inside and out."

Extortionists, harlots, supremacists, and despots alike—he looks beyond reputation, beyond transgressions. Peace talks and moral accountability played out right before their eyes. Yasha demonstrates his heart. His love is always chasing someone down.

"You don't have to be a genius to understand these things," Yasha continues. "Just use your common sense, the kind you'd use if, while being taken to court, you decided to settle up with your accuser on the way, knowing that if the case went to the judge, you'd probably go to jail and pay every last penny of the fine. *That's* the kind of decision I'm asking you to make."

Mattiyahu narrows his eyes on Yasha. Not only does he preach a form of justice nearly opposite his own, he also practices what he preaches. Mattiyahu second-guesses being a part of this group. Why would Yasha invite him to be a cell member when he knows Mattiyahu's history? His utter moral failures? Other than legal advice, what does he bring to the table? Mattiyahu cannot answer his own questions. He should walk away, go back to chasing ambulances. Shimon would certainly be happy. But something will not let him.

Yasha looks up into the blue sky, talks to the One who commissioned him. "You've concealed Your ways from sophisticates and know-it-alls but spelled them out clearly to ordinary people. Yes," he says with a chuckle, "that's the way You like to work."

Kefa tries to decipher what Yasha is doing. The unexpected angles and counter-intuitive methodologies make it challenging to discern his agenda. Yasha continues to be an enigma. If only he would outline the greater strategy for the Twelve instead of giving impromptu instructions and obscure speeches. *What exactly is the plan?* Kefa wonders. Earlier words of Yasha come back to him: *Anyone who intends to come with me has to let me lead. You're not in the driver's seat—I am.* Kefa forces himself again to capitulate.

Looking through the crowd, Yasha spots the undercover officers. He sees their notetaking, understands their intentions and instructions. Yasha also notices Nakdimon. He thinks back to their private conversation just two months ago. He offers a silent prayer for the deputy prime minister. That his eyes would be enlightened, that his heart would surrender to the invisible pull that it feels. He knows that Nakdimon is surrounded by government officials dripping lies into his ear. Power and manipulation go hand in hand.

"Watch for the circling of the vultures," Yasha warns. People look up and around, not sure if he's being literal or figurative. "The world has nothing against you, but it's up in arms against me," he explains. "It's against me because I expose the evil behind its pretensions."

More evidence that he's planning on exposing top government leaders. Nakdimon formulates his assessment for the prime minister and the Shin Bet based on what he's seen and heard. He will not, however, confess that he's drawn into the unusual language that Yasha offers. He's never heard anyone talk with such ferocity yet kindness. Not a partisan political message, rather a direct approach that keeps all sides guessing. Nakdimon is fiercely loyal to the prime minister and will carry out his duty as prescribed. Yet, on a personal level, he is deeply intrigued. He's inexplicably drawn to Yasha. Fearing for his job, that secret will remain undisclosed.

Yasha wraps up his exhortations and hands out final thoughts like gifts to his supporters and detractors alike. Some become more enthralled, others more repelled. He won't compromise for the sake of making people comfortable. He will, however, invite everyone willing to enter into a conversation and experience that cannot be found elsewhere. Steer them toward a higher power with equal reigns of love and truth. Yasha steps down from the elevated platform into the crowd. A stark symbol of heaven coming to earth. If only people had eyes to see.

Nakdimon motions to his men. He had previously instructed the undercover agents throughout the crowd to close in on Yasha at the opportune time. But now, as they make their move, Yasha disappears. Literally. Mysteriously and miraculously disappears in a move reminiscent of Harry Houdini. They look around in confusion. He's nowhere in sight. No sign of him.

Yasha's cell members remain perplexed, moving outside the crowd. They too noticed the sudden disappearance. Where did he go? They look over the area, twelve heads swiveling to pinpoint Yasha's location. Nothing.

Nakdimon approaches the Twelve. Perplexed thoughts crowd his mind. What just happened isn't possible. They had Yasha surrounded.

"Where is he?" Nakdimon demands.

Kefa raises his eyebrows. Yochanan folds his arms, hands sliding into his armpits. Mattiyahu purses his lips.

Arye shrugs. "No clue."

"What do you care?" Yaakov barks.

Nakdimon answers, "I just want to talk with him."

Shimon notices Nakdimon's men hovering nearby. *Their undercover camouflage is pathetic*, he thinks.

"What's going on?" Yehudas asks as he begins to sweat. He doesn't buy Nakdimon's reason for a second. Something else is happening, something ominous.

"He seems to have just disappeared," Nakdimon points out. "Into thin air."

"Well, he's wily like that," Yaakov retorts curtly. He doesn't like Nakdimon nor his probing questions.

"He'll show up eventually," says Mattiyahu. "But I'm sure with your government resources that you don't need us." He tells the other eleven to move out. No need getting into potential legal waters with the deputy prime minister.

Nakdimon watches the Twelve vacate the area. After a minute, his men gather around.

"What do we do?"

"I'll take it from here," he assures them.

As deputy prime minister, Nakdimon has instructions, responsibilities. He stays fixed after the others leave, unspoken questions flying at him faster than answers. Why does he get the feeling that Yasha operates on a different level altogether? Normal restrictions and limitations do not apply. Disappearing into thin air? What is really happening here? Nakdimon remembers the conversation with Yasha a couple of months ago. Something about the wind and not knowing where it's coming from or where it's going. *That's the way it is with God*, Yasha had said. Nakdimon scans the area. No sign that Yasha had ever been there. Like the wind. Does this mean that Yasha is claiming to actually *be* God?

The square drains its crowd, returning to customary levels of activity. He rubs his face, reviewing the unexplainable event. They were so close, so assured of success. They essentially had Yasha within arm's reach. Then nothing. To the naked mind, it makes no sense. He can feel his emotions being tugged in opposite directions. Curiosity and a spiritual impulse war against reason and government orders. He has no answers. All Nakdimon holds now is a directive in one hand and a foiled attempt in the other. Ohred will be furious.

26

ONE MONTH EARLIER

Salome knocks softly on the door to the salon at the prime minister's residence. Her mother, Saidoreh, doesn't hear her enter; she's staring out the window, entranced by something unseen. The gray late-September day hangs heavily over the city. Rain feels imminent, though the wet season typically begins months from now.

"Mother," she says.

Saidoreh turns and smiles. Impeccable in her tailored, white pant suit, she radiates power and prestige. But Salome thinks her mother looks older. *Is it the stress of being the prime minister's wife? Or is something else causing her appearance to be changed?*

"Salome," Saidoreh says, embracing her. "How are you?" She knows that her daughter has just returned from a trip abroad training with world renowned opera singers. With a voice like hers, it was only a matter of time before being invited to join the elites.

"Tired but glad to be back." Salome's fair complexion radiates in the morning light. With her long dark hair, luminous green eyes, and high cheekbones, her beauty rivals that of her mother's.

"Come, sit here," Saidoreh instructs. She rings for her staff assistant to bring tea and food. They settle on the settee and exchange a few more pleasantries. Salome instinctively knows that her mother wishes to broach a serious subject. She waits while Saidoreh talks about trivial things. At last, the tea arrives. They serve themselves and enjoy a few sips.

"You look troubled, Mother. What's wrong?"

Saidoreh doesn't hide her confusion. Maybe her daughter hasn't heard. "I assume you've seen the recent news…"

Salome shakes her head. "Between training and traveling, I haven't had time to keep up."

"It's Uri," Saidoreh replies, referring to her husband. "He's been caught in an affair."

Salome bites her lip and eyes her mother with concern. She and Uri have never established a close relationship, despite her mother's urging. Salome admires and respects him as the prime minister of Israel, yet she still harbors resentment that he seduced her mother years ago during her first marriage. Once the woman committing the adultery, her mother now sits on the receiving end. *A bitter irony*, Salome thinks. *Probably wouldn't help to ask if she likes the taste of her own medicine.*

"What will you do?" Salome says. "Will you leave him?"

Saidoreh inhales slowly, steeling her resolve. "No. Just make him pay."

After a moment, Salome replies, "Is that wise, mother? He is the most powerful man in the Middle East, after all."

A fiendish smile crosses Saidoreh's face. Salome knows that look. Uri might have enormous influence, but she has her own methods of power and manipulation.

She will not be played a fool. Before, she was able to handle the public's criticism and distrust with the support of the prime minister; now, she feels left to fend for herself. She knows Uri will deny everything, seeking to bury yet another scandal. Saidoreh will play the part, defending him despite knowing the truth. She will use the situation to her advantage, of course, holding his indiscretion over his head indefinitely. Her anger will be placated one way or another. Money, state secrets, her own infidelity—the options are plenty to wield considerable control in this untenable situation. Saidoreh still loves her husband and her title, something she's not willing to relinquish just yet. But she will enjoy the opportunity to make him squirm.

A pregnant pause fills the sitting room. Salome senses another surprise coming and braces herself.

"Is there more?" Salome asks.

Saidoreh nods. "Yochanan," she replies, "the one they call the Immerser."

"I don't know him," Salome says, eyebrows furrowed.

Saidoreh provides a brief background on the Immerser—where he's from, where he lives, and most importantly, what he proselytizes. He is a rogue with many followers and supporters. He speaks out against government and injustice, causing many to do the same. His message of repentance and submission to a higher authority draws yet repels hundreds of people alike. Saidoreh and her husband are repelled. Yochanan has criticized them specifically.

"What did he say?" Salome asks.

"He told Uri this: 'Stealing, lying, coveting, and adultery are only some of the sins God holds against you. But pride will be your downfall. You were wrong to marry Saidoreh—that was the first adultery. And now the second. Sin upon sin. Your marriage is anathema to the inhabitants of this land. Your immorality a curse.'"

She proceeds to tell her daughter more details of the Immerser's public rantings: that Prime Minister Ohred has committed great evils against the people of Israel, that he is blind to his own sin that he contributes—leads, even—to the demise of his country.

Calls for his resignation circulate with petitions. Fortunately, it had not made front headlines, though *The Jerusalem Post* and *Haaretz* both gave it attention. Ohred had seethed at the condemnation and threats, taking immediate action to keep the finger pointing from spreading. He used inside sources in the media to spin the story in his favor, essentially ordering people to dismiss the words of an obvious madman.

Salome's eyes grow large. The pointed insults cross the lines of propriety. Even if the Immerser disagrees with Ohred's methods of running

Israel, he has no authority to harass the prime minister publicly, much less drum up support for his removal from office based on moral, not legal, issues.

Now Salome understands the deep lines on her mother's face. Rage, bitterness, retribution. Salome braces for what she knows is coming. The real reason Saidoreh called her to visit this morning.

"Something must be done," Saidoreh says with determination.

Salome nods, tentatively. "What are you thinking?"

"Uri finally ordered the Immerser's arrest. They found him on a kibbutz, cuffed him, and put him in prison."

"Good. He's still there?" Salome asks.

"Yes," says Saidoreh, pointedly. She stands and moves toward the window, putting space between them. "He's rotting away in solitary confinement, so I'm told. But, in my opinion, that's not enough. He, too, needs to pay." She waits a beat. "With his life."

Salome's eyes widen, her eyebrows rise in alarm. She hates when her mother confesses too much.

"In fact, I demanded that Uri have Yochanan the Immerser killed. Needless to say, our argument was heated," Saidoreh adds.

"What did he say?"

"He refused, of course, claiming it would incite unrest among various groups. Protests, potential riots, you know the drill," Saidoreh says dismissively. "He said that killing the Immerser isn't a wise political decision and that I should be grateful that at least he's imprisoned because his ramblings would reach no ears."

But Saidoreh isn't satisfied. She isn't afraid of the people or of the Immerser.

After a moment, she continues. "My husband fears that those who follow the Immerser will fight for their prophet," she explains. "But truthfully, I think that he fears the Immerser also."

"What do you mean?" Salome says.

Saidoreh draws a measured breath. "I believe that Uri finds him a 'just' man, perhaps even a holy man of some sort. A mystic worth noting." She rolls her eyes, demonstrating deep disdain. It amazes her that he retains strange esoteric notions. Maybe he's just trying to cover his spiritual bases.

Anger rises anew in Saidoreh's face. Salome watches the emotions stampede her countenance. She roils over the possibility that her husband might find the Immerser a righteous individual. Who is he to point a finger and shame Uri and Saidoreh this way? How dare he slander them? He would reprove the most powerful man in Israel and think there'd be no backlash?

"My husband has chosen the Immerser over me."

Her rage toward her husband is matched only by her rage for the wild kibbutz man. But Saidoreh will not be undone. Shame and disgrace have motivated her to formulate a plan. She will have her way in the end. Retribution against both men is due.

"What do you want me to do?"

Saidoreh smiles once again and sits back down on the settee. Salome's intuition cues right on time. "I will force my husband's hand," she reveals, "and have the Immerser beheaded."

Impulsively, Salome's hand covers her mouth, and she looks away. She doesn't believe the man should be beheaded for his ramblings, but her loyalty resides with her mother. It always has. She senses being trapped between her mother and the prime minister. Clearly, Saidoreh is plotting to manipulate her husband into getting her way. She almost feels sorry for him. Her mother possesses an aptitude for fierce determination as well as an unshakeable pride. Salome meets her mother's gaze. She knows Saidoreh has already assigned her a part in the fatal play.

"It's set for the night of Uri's birthday gala," she explains. "Hundreds of leaders and key political people will be there. According to the guest list, commanders and dignitaries and chief members of the Knesset. After dinner, you will sing a song created just for Uri, something sensational that will leave everyone breathless. Your voice is a rare and beautiful gift, you know," her mother confirms. *And I will use it as a weapon*, she decides. "Once the room has been awed, Uri will feel obligated to thank you by granting you something in return. It is then that you're to ask for the Immerser's head."

Salome hates being used this way. She hates the plan yet knows it will probably work. The blood of a man will be on her hands. Slowly, Salome pushes those feelings to the bottom of her gut, and she smiles tightly. Despite her better judgment, she acquiesces to the plan. *It's a battle between my mother and stepfather*, she thinks. *I'm just the messenger*. And in this case, the messenger will live.

Saidoreh pecks her daughter on the cheek and rises, offering up a silent thanks that she has one person who will never fail her. With only a few months' time, she has much to arrange before the state dinner.

27

FIVE WEEKS EARLIER

"Well," Kefa says, "we're obviously going to need a different hideout." Nakdimon's unexpected visit to the Bethany safe house twenty minutes ago has rattled him. Government officials up-close make Kefa and the others quite nervous. Especially when they show up at night, undercover.

Back inside, Yasha gathers his men. It's one thing for ordinary citizens of Israel to seek out the Twelve and its leader, but when top government officials move in close, the writing is on the wall. Time is of the essence. For the past five months—from April to late-August—Yasha has been making his mark on the land of Israel with the help of his twelve men. Word is growing, as is the momentum.

"We could spread out and communicate remotely," offers Faivel.

"No," Yasha answers. "We stick together. And we stay below the radar."

"Of course," quips Yaakov, "no problem for all thirteen of us. Our invisible capes should help."

Yochanan elbows his brother. "Think outside the prison."

Eyebrows go up around the room. They question whether Yochanan's comment is metaphorical or from literal experience. The Zavdai brothers, Yaakov and Yochanan, confirm their suspicions with a snide comment about Israel's harsh correctional facilities. Both Mattiyahu and Yehudas wonder what they've gotten themselves into; they have no desire to end up in such unpleasant locations.

"Let me tell you why you are here," Yasha says to the group. "To carry out the plans set in motion long ago."

They look at him, waiting silently. The plans for what? And who is orchestrating these plans?

"You're here to be salt, seasoning that brings out the God-flavors of this earth."

Yaakov glances at his brother. *You don't say*, he thinks. As chefs, they understand the reference and importance of salt. He's speaking their language.

Yasha continues, "You're here to be light, bringing out the God-colors in the world. If I make you light-bearers, you don't think I'm going to hide you under a bucket, do you?"

Bewilderment circles the room. They struggle to keep up with Yasha, to fully understand what he says. Faivel senses it's a code language like one of his many computer programs, yet he battles to crack it. His wheels spin.

Yasha adds, "My government is not a secret to be kept. We're going public with this."

His government? They all want clarification. Is Yasha planning to overthrow the current administration? What will he replace it with? Toma and Natan are nervous, thinking they've fallen in with a coup. Shimon swells with excitement. Ben-Chalfai worries he will be banished from the scientific community.

"This is hazardous work I'm assigning you. Stay alert. You're going to be like sheep running through a wolf pack, so don't call attention to yourselves. Be as cunning as a snake, inoffensive as a dove."

"What do we need?" Shimon asks, thinking of weapons and financing.

"Don't think you need a lot of extra equipment for this. *You are* the equipment."

The men glance around the room of the safe house, unsure of themselves and the others. It's a variegated group of Israelis that have no previous connections. Will they be able to work together for a common goal?

Can they overlook their individual motivations and personalities for a greater purpose? Yasha must believe so or else they wouldn't be here.

Yasha looks at Yehudas. "Don't think you have to put on a fund-raising campaign before you start. And no special appeal for funds. Keep it simple."

Yehudas nods, asking no questions. He has ways of channeling funds that don't flag attention. He has yet to understand, though, that Yasha can make money appear out of thin air. Yehudas feels out of his comfort zone yet strongly compelled to stay. He assumes correctly that the others judge him for being a former Haredi, the faction of strictly Orthodox Jews. Not exactly the most beloved sector of Israel.

Ben-Chalfai says, "We're tackling the public enemy?"

Yasha shakes his head. "Don't try to be dramatic by tackling some public enemy. You've observed how godless rulers throw their weight around and when people get a little power how quickly it goes to their heads. It's not going to be that way with you. Whoever wants to be great must become a servant. Whoever wants to be first among you must be your slave."

Exactly what Yasha has done. He was sent to serve not to be served.

Kefa doesn't like the sound of being anyone's slave. Even after being ejected from the military, he hasn't softened. Headstrong, defiant, impulsive. His pride follows him as closely as he follows Yasha. It will, eight months from now, bring him to rock bottom.

"Listen carefully to what I am saying and be wary of the shrewd advice that tells you how to get ahead in the world on your own. Giving, not getting, is the way. Generosity begets generosity. Stinginess impoverishes."

Yehudas wrestles with this instruction. He has made a living skimming a little off the top of people's wealth. A few shekels here, a few there. It's a secret no one knows, including Mattiyahu. Only Yasha is privy to the knowledge that Yehudas will exert the same dishonest, immoral behavior with the group's money. And then will betray him for even more money.

Yasha senses Yehudas's struggle. His eyes bore into the eleventh member. "Turn both your pockets and your hearts inside out and give generously to the poor." For some of the Twelve, they are willing to offer one or the other. For Yehudas, it's neither. Yasha presses in, despite all their shortcomings. Over the coming months, he will give them opportunities to practice.

"Some people will impugn your motives—"

"Just like my twin," Toma murmurs to himself.

"You have a twin?" asks Shimon in a low voice.

"A brother," Toma whispers back. "Fraternal, straight, and borderline malicious."

"Others will smear your reputation," Yasha continues, "just because you are with me."

"Sounds fun," banters Yaakov. "But some reputations already come smeared." He hooks a thumb at Mattiyahu. Ambulance chasers are pathetic. Shimon laughs.

Yasha shoots them a look. "Don't pick on people, jump on their failures, criticize their faults—unless, of course, you want the same treatment. That condemning attitude has a way of ricocheting."

Natan takes satisfaction in being kind to others. He genuinely desires to be a good person. But he still holds Faivel, his best friend, responsible for dragging him into this. Natan was the sixth to be chosen. There's clearly a hierarchy here, he thinks, ranking himself at the top for a life of goodwill and good deeds.

Yasha knows his thoughts. He looks at Natan with gentle eyes. "Be especially careful when you are trying to be good so that you don't make a performance out of it. It might be good theater, but the God who made you won't be applauding."

Natan feels mildly alarmed that Yasha has read his mail. *Can he hear everyone's thoughts?* he wonders. *How does he know?* Unnerving yet oddly compelling.

Like the others, Yochanan's mind swirls with questions he can't answer. He prefers circumstances and plans to be outlined in black and white, no room for margins or errors. He debates trying to pinpoint Yasha yet knows this won't work in his favor. So, he sits, arms folded across his chest, hands in armpits with thumbs pointing to heaven. The symbolism remains lost on him.

"At this moment, the world is in crisis," Yasha reveals.

Most of the cell members struggle to agree. Aside from the usual skirmishes between the Israelis and Palestinians, their world is relatively stable. And outside the holy land, there are no worldwide famines, no pandemics, no global wars. But the men fail to grasp Yasha's meaning. The supernatural comes first, then the natural.

"You expect us to save the entire world?" Faivel asks incredulously.

"Don't be naïve." *Maybe not the brightest of twelve men*, Yasha thinks. *Only one savior needed*. "The world will always reject God," he explains, "as a higher authority is anathema to self-centeredness. I'm trying to proclaim liberty from individual shortcomings and to proclaim truth. All have sinned against God and deserve punishment. *All*."

"Then who has any chance at all?" Toma asks, his skepticism in full force.

Yasha smiles. "No chance at all if you think you can pull it off yourself. Every chance in the world if you trust God to do it."

Collectively, it dawns on the twelve men that this group has potentially been commissioned by God Himself. None feels qualified for that level of work. Yasha thinks differently. He looks intently at his cell members, knowing full well they hold deep reservoirs of power within them. They've all seen and experienced the unexplainable. Miracles and supernatural phenomena speak volumes. They've been captivated by the impossible. Hooked from the start.

An unexpected peace floods the room, quelling anxiety, banishing doubts. Yasha places his hands on each member, imparting courage and confidence. Neither the masses nor government agencies can take from them what God has graciously given—faith over fear.

Yasha declares, "Anyone who intends to come with me has to let me lead. You're not in the driver's seat; *I* am."

The room is silent with dozens of unspoken questions. All the recruits wait for further explanation. Yasha looks them in the eyes. His gaze is intense yet enticing.

"Listen to me carefully," he says. "Haven't I handpicked you, the Twelve?"

They nod in agreement, from Taddai, the last member, to Kefa and Arye, the first two. All twelve, though, are unsure exactly what they were handpicked for. They all possess the same information—how each was chosen, how Yasha intervened after the terrorist attack, how rallies and provocative speech have landed the group on government watchlists. Months of behind-the-scenes action has surfaced. The Twelve sit not knowing their fate yet convinced to follow Yasha as he has greatly impacted their lives in such a short time. Questions loom and their worries emanate silently. Yasha knows their thoughts, their hearts. He knows they all want proof that they've made the right decision to follow him despite the unknowns. Proof that they will be the victors and not the victims.

"The mood of this age is all wrong. Everybody's looking for proof, but you're looking for the wrong kind. All you're looking for is something to stimulate your curiosity."

Mattiyahu bristles. He's been a master at manipulating proof, in legal terms, for decades. Shimon also chafes at Yasha's comments. Has Yasha guessed that his motives for joining the group also include a deep curiosity and love of adrenaline? He's not only zealous for Israel but also for spicy food and a fast lifestyle. *Not sure this will merge well*, he thinks.

"But you miss the forest for the trees. Don't be naïve. Again, some people will impugn your motives, others will smear your reputation—just because you believe in me." Believe in what he's doing for the hopeless, the tormented, the rebellious. "Don't run from suffering," Yasha continues, "embrace it. Follow me, and I'll show you how. Self-help is no help at all. Self-sacrifice is the way, *my* way, to saving yourself, your true self."

Eyebrows shoot up around the room. Is he talking martyrdom? The recruits are beginning to get cold feet. This is not what they had in mind.

"What good would it do to get everything you want and lose you, the real you? What could you ever trade your soul for?"

Silence. The twelve men let Yasha's question penetrate their hearts, their minds. For the moment, there are no objections.

"I'm not interested in crowd approval. And do you know why?" Yasha asks. "Because I know you and your crowds. And I know that love is not on your working agenda."

Each of the twelve emerged from different crowds—criminals, tradesmen, students, professionals, the strictly Orthodox. Each understands that Yasha speaks truth. Love does not drive their crowds; Shimon can attest. He recently stumbled upon Yasha at a peace rally two months ago. The message, so opposite the norm, rang full of challenges and intrigue. A call to action of a different kind.

"Love is the message then?" Shimon asks Yasha. "Not power? Not justice?"

Yasha smiles. "Yes," he admits, "love comes first. The rest follows."

Shimon questions further, as Yasha's approach is completely countercultural. "Great leaders do not begin with love," he challenges. "Passion? Yes. Determination? Always. But love? *Why?* That's sure to fail."

"Because a loveless world," says Yasha, "is a sightless world."

Yehudas and Mattiyahu absorb the message. It's antithetical to their backgrounds, their upbringings. Mattiyahu is drawn in, smelling an opportunity to make a statement, to stand out and revel in public attention. Yehudas, likewise, feels obliged to stay, but not understanding why. He senses unseen forces are in play, that fate has its hand in this decision. Though he tries, he no longer ignores unexplainable impressions.

"Love God with all your passion and intelligence and energy. This is the most important command, the first on any list." Natan nods vigorously, as he knows this Torah passage by heart. Lives by it. "But there is a second to set alongside it," Yasha explains. "Love others as well as you love yourself. These two commands are pegs—everything hangs from them."

Interesting, thinks Natan. *A twist on the Torah.*

Faivel silently runs through the instructions Yasha has given them. The commands. He feels like he's on the receiving end of one of his computer programs. He's not used to this as he would rather be the one in control. But in the Twelve, Faivel must surrender to Yasha, the Commander.

Yasha continues to clarify. "I came to bring everything into the clear light of day, making all the distinctions clear, so that those who have never seen will see, and those who have made a great pretense of seeing will be exposed as blind."

"Commander," Faivel blurts out, "does that mean you're calling us blind?"

Yasha grins at the new moniker.

The others think what Yasha has just said is cryptic. For most of the men, a handful of politicians come to mind as being blind instead of themselves. Government officials are notorious for demonstrating an inflated sense of self-worth and importance. But Yasha includes more than just those in government. It's a universal problem that continues to climb in numbers. The blind leading the blind.

"If you were really blind, you would be blameless, but since you claim to see everything so well," Yasha quips, "you're accountable for every fault and failure. But there's hope!" They need to trust in something greater to lead them instead of their carnal instincts, their pride, and their intellect. "I'm going to put it all together... put it all together in a vast panorama."

"All we have is your word on this," Mattiyahu says with uncertainty. His wheels spin with legal parameters. "We need more than this to go on."

"You're right that you only have my word," Yasha answers. "But you can depend on it being true. Sky and earth will wear out; my words won't wear out."

So many questions remain. Though the men have been brought in from all ends and sectors of Israel, they understand that their unity will be pivotal to this undertaking. Can that truly be accomplished? And though they have been given the option to walk away, none has chosen to do so. To be called is to be validated. Still, they wonder about their new leader. How trustworthy is he? How confident in the mission?

"A genuine leader will never exploit your emotions or your pocket-book," he promises them. "This is a large work I've called you into, but don't be overwhelmed by it. It's best to start small." Observe. Believe. Replicate.

They each have a role to play. They each have something to offer, yet success doesn't hinge on them alone.

"Remember a basic rule," he instructs them, "It's not what you do for God but what God does for you—that's the agenda for rejoicing."

Yasha reiterates that his methods are different. That they are counter-culture but non-violent. Humility and selfless service will be their mantra, aimed at the least, the last, and the lost. This way, they will create a mass movement greater than what terror or manipulation or persuasion can achieve. And with God directing, there is no limit.

Yasha looks at his men, studies them to gauge their commitment. Most believe what he has said and are willing. Some will believe along the way. And one will defy the rest. Even within this small group, Yasha will practice what he preaches—to love one and all, regardless of return.

Switching gears, Yasha establishes the ground rules for coming and going. Somebody is always watching, he explains with a glint in his eyes. His companions wonder if he's referring to God or to the government. Yasha instructs Faivel to work with El'azar on establishing new safe houses around the country. And to block unknown communication trying to come in. All phones must be protected, all computers safeguarded. Israeli technology is some of the world's best, but that's a two-way street, he explains. Yasha urges his companions to use extreme caution, to be off grid as much as possible.

"Don't miss what's happening right in front of you in order to capture or communicate something. You will have orders," he explains, "And you will execute them." All the members nod, as they all completed mandatory service in the IDF, Israeli Defense Forces. All but Yehudas, that is. Haredi Jews escape service. This fact is lost on nobody.

"All right," Yasha says, "Get up. Let's go. It's time to leave here."

In a moment, the cell known as the Twelve takes flight.

28

TWENTY MINUTES EARLIER

The deputy prime minister, Nakdimon, knocks on the wood frame of the Bethany safe house. It's close to 9:00 p.m. No one knows he visits the man causing excitement and unrest in his country. His moves must be inconspicuous. Nakdimon needs answers. His heart is caught between two worlds: government administration and the revolutionaries.

With a dark hat pulled low, he tries to make his appearance obscure. His face is well-known as a top government official, making it more difficult to hide. If he's caught, he will have to answer to the highest authorities. There's a lot at stake, though, and Nakdimon is apprehensive about risking his job and reputation in the pursuit of some explanations. If he gets what he came for, then he can report up the chain of command.

El'azar answers the door. He vets the man calling for Yasha, ensuring his identity. He instructs the man to go around to the back where he'll be hidden better. Yasha will meet him there.

Nakdimon second-guesses himself and debates leaving quickly. His plan is without form. He moves on instinct. This could be a terrible idea. Suddenly, he feels the warm, late-summer wind pushing at his back. A sign, perhaps. He moves around the safe house.

Within seconds, Yasha emerges from the dimly lit interior. He knows the man standing before him, as he's been a face in Israeli politics for many years. Yasha waits for him to speak. Nakdimon jumps right in.

He tells Yasha that the Twelve have popped up on government radar. Between the organized rallies, the recent terrorist attack at the hands of bar-Abbas, and the testimonies of various miracles, Yasha can't escape attention. The prime minister and heads of the intelligence community have been alerted, and the Twelve are being watched. Fiery language and supernatural occurrences will do that, he explains. Though a government agent himself, Nakdimon confesses that he's intrigued, enticed even. He may not speak for his boss, but he believes he can speak for a large segment of Israelis.

"We all know that you're straight from God. No one could do all the God-pointing, God-revealing acts you do if God weren't in on it," he says. Nakdimon fidgets, exposing his anxiety.

For months now, Yasha has been doing the impossible time and again. Curing physical ailments, providing resources out of nothing, restoring mental health. People near and far have rushed to find him, presenting inconceivable obstacles to amend. He never turns someone away. He never fails to meet their need. His fame goes viral. People love him. Social media calls him a hero. He and his inner circle have been dubbed the Twelve. Over a short period of time, Yasha had collected his men at the direction of a higher authority. Though newly formed, the group has captured the attention of Israel, the smallest country in the Middle East.

The government, in turn, stands at high alert, tracking this unexpected anomaly. Borders are being monitored to prevent an international scene. Both Mossad and Shin Bet are documenting everything in open files on Yasha and his companions. Nakdimon knows this yet keeps the information to himself. He too retains misgivings.

Yasha grins and nods. "Unless you people are dazzled by a miracle, you refuse to believe."

Nakdimon waits for further explanation. A warm breeze envelopes them. "What's the goal here? What's your end game?"

"The One who sent me gave me orders," Yasha says, "told me what to say and how to say it. Open your eyes and look beyond what you can see."

"I don't understand," he confesses. What is he missing? What can he not see? Something is there just beyond his grasp.

"The earthborn is earthbound and speaks earth language," says Yasha. "The heaven-born is in a league of his own."

Nakdimon fumbles for a cigarette in his coat pocket. He chides himself for not being able to quit. His vice helps calm the nervousness, the stress. He never imagined that being deputy prime minister would age him as fast as it has. Only a few years in, yet he looks ten years older.

"When you look at a baby," Yasha explains, "it's just that—a body you can look at and touch. But the person who takes shape within is formed by something you can't see and touch—the Spirit—and becomes a living spirit."

Nakdimon squints, as if he concentrates hard enough the answers will manifest. He needs concrete answers. For himself, for his boss.

"You know well enough how the wind blows this way and that. You hear it rustling through the trees, but you have no idea where it comes from or where it's headed next. That's the way it is with God."

Nakdimon answers, "What do you mean by this? How does this happen?"

The familiar voice speaks to Yasha.

LOVE IS NOT ARROGANT. IT IS NOT RUDE.

Yasha looks at him for a few moments. "You're a respected leader of Israel," he says, "and you don't know these basics? Listen carefully, I'm speaking sober truth to you. I speak only of what I know by experience; I give witness only to what I have seen with my own eyes. There is nothing secondhand here, no hearsay. Yet instead of facing the evidence and accepting it, you procrastinate with questions. If I tell you things that are as plain as the hand before your face and you don't believe me, what use is there in telling you of things you can't see, the things of God?"

Nakdimon tries to process what Yasha is saying. Does Yasha feel that God has sent him to overhaul the Israeli government? To eradicate corruption, evil, and defilement? If only Nakdimon could get Yasha to confess his agenda in clear terms.

In fact, he knows that Yasha is on the short list of people being watched and potentially subdued, forcefully if necessary. Should he warn him? Would that be a conflict of interest? Nakdimon cannot figure out why this man with his humanitarian approach is causing such concern at the highest levels. Unless something deeper is happening…unless ultimate power is at stake.

"You know what happens when a person crosses the prime minister," Nakdimon says, referring to the Immerser. He was arrested and thrown in prison a few weeks ago.

Yasha nods. He knows that his cousin is being detained for speaking out, for making political waves. But Nakdimon and the prime minister are unaware of Yasha's relation to the Immerser. That would only complicate things. They'll discover it soon enough. Yasha discerns that the hourglass of sand has been turned over. For himself and his cousin.

"That doesn't seem to intimidate you," Nakdimon comments.

Shaking his head, Yasha replies, "No." His perspective looms above the natural, unshakeable by human standards. His plan is set, his purpose clear. To be a ransom for many. "There is nothing to fear."

If Nakdimon expects to understand the power and influence that Yasha wields on the public, he will have to choose the right side. He thinks about the reality of following orders at the highest levels and yet wanting to do the right thing. This movement started by the Twelve could be the most significant in Israel's history. Nakdimon wants to end up on the right side, with the right party. But he's caught in the middle. Risk his career and everything he's worked for or join ranks with something that could change history? He starts to confess the inner turmoil, but when he opens his mouth, the words die.

Yasha understands. He watches the emotions play on Nakdimon's face. He looks up into the dark night and sighs. His whisper is soft but powerful.

TWELVE

"And this is the crisis we're in," Yasha says. He takes a deep breath and looks over his shoulder into the house. "That *light* has come into the world, but men love darkness rather than light because they practice evil. Everyone who makes a practice of doing evil, addicted to denial and illusion, hates the light, fearing a painful exposure."

The deputy prime minister fidgets, feeling as though he is being called out. Certainly, the government administration has carried out several shady operations of which he has been a part.

"Yom Kippur," Nakdimon states quietly.

Yasha nods. Next month, *Rosh Hashanah*—the Jewish New Year celebration with *mitzvahs*, special foods, and traditions—will be observed across the land. After that, Yom Kippur. The annual holiday remains the most important of the year. The day comprises introspection, prayer, and seeking forgiveness. A day to afflict the soul, seeking atonement for the past year's transgressions. For twenty-four hours, there's no eating or drinking, no bathing, no sex. Yasha knows that Nakdimon has much to confess, and when he does, his eyes will be opened to a deeper level of truth. The beauty of God's grace provided for those who humble themselves. The goal is Nakdimon's heart.

"But anyone working and living in truth and reality welcomes the light. Be governed by the heart, not by the people."

Nakdimon rubs the back of his neck and then fishes another cigarette from his pocket. A flame bursts quickly into the dark, and then instantly it's gone—a visual of Yasha's words. Nakdimon nods at Yasha and blows smoke into the night.

The leader of the Twelve puts a hand on his shoulder, bids him goodnight, and retreats inside. Nakdimon didn't get the answers he was after. What he got was more. Can he take the leap of faith that's obviously required? Can he believe without having all the explanations? Alone, Nakdimon remains captive to his thoughts and a glowing cigarette.

29

THREE WEEKS EARLIER

In the far south of Israel near Eilat, in a hot, darkened room, the Immerser sleeps as the atmosphere tingles with the presence of things unseen. The peace—heavy and concentrated—is severed by a sudden noise. He stirs and lifts his head. He'd been dreaming of angels and fully expected to witness the appearance of one. He rooms alone in a small hut-like structure. Commotion drifts in from outside, a sleepy kibbutz coming awake abruptly at 2:00 a.m. None of the residents had any warning of the clandestine raid.

Soldiers search for one particular face. House to house, room to room, furniture is turned over, wardrobes are emptied while dirty boots leave a wake of mud in hopes the person is found. He isn't. But a path of disarray trails behind. Residents yell at the soldiers, reprimanding them for the act of invasion. They are not Palestinians! They are not in occupied territory! But the military orders have been given to find the Immerser and bring him to Jerusalem. The soldiers do not care that he is also a Jew; they treat all offenders the same.

Suddenly, dark figures shrouded in black attire emerge from the shadows. Heavy boots, weapons, night vision devices. In less than three seconds, the Immerser is flipped onto his stomach, a powerful knee pinned against his back. A gun is pointed at his head. Zip ties bind his hands behind him. All the proper work of IDF soldiers.

A second pair of hands grabs him. Yanked up, wearing only shorts, the Immerser's skin rubs against the coarse uniforms of his captors. His long dreadlocks, held together loosely down his back, thrash about like Medusa's snakes. Tattoos cling to his arms, back, and torso. A large marking on his thick chest proclaims the word MALAK. *Messenger.* He asks for more clothes. Request denied. He'll get more where he's going.

"Where are you taking me?" he asks. Part of him doesn't want to know. The part that occasionally wavers under the enormity of his God-given mandate.

"To the palace, of course," mocks the commanding soldier. Others grunt in agreement.

Only the lone female soldier remains quiet. Nothing escapes her attention—not the Immerser's muscular frame, not his weathered face and unshaven chin, not the open Torah and maps of Israel stacked on a low table by the bed. She knows that he doesn't have any family and probably doesn't want one, as his mission in life remains his only focus. But she's inexplicably drawn by his magnetism, his aura. And those piercing blue eyes that even the shadowy room can't hide. Same kind of eyes that Yasha displayed—the kind that exude otherworldliness—the day she brought him the crimson guitar as a thank you for saving her last month. She wonders if the two men are connected somehow. There's been no report of that, but she feels the same electric atmosphere around them both.

The Immerser catches the female soldier's stare. Her ebony skin and black, almond-shaped eyes make him pause. An unexpected peace radiates from her. And he knows. He can feel her awareness of a greater presence in the room. His eyes grow watery, and he smiles, but to her, it's a sad one. One that understands human forces at play against those that are spiritual. She turns abruptly, picking up the maps and papers from the bedside table. Studying them, she looks for clues. *Who is this man, really?*

The Immerser knows inherently that his captors are operating at behest of top government officials. No information is shared. No leniencies granted. The Immerser expects a full interrogation at a holding cell, despite the fact that he never breaks the law—man's or God's. He does not anticipate, however, the fact that he'll never see his room or Kibbutz Samar again.

He starts to say something, but, without warning, a cloth hood drops over his head. His breathing speeds ahead of his body, and he tries to calm himself despite the panic rising in his chest. Internally, he prays. He then launches more questions at his assailants but gets no response. Deep down he isn't surprised. Israeli authorities don't have to answer to anyone, least of all a rogue man in the desert who espouses moral accountability. The Immerser wonders where they are taking him. *Maybe to Jerusalem? Maybe to an undisclosed airstrip for immediate deportation?* Hopefully, someone at the kibbutz will track down his whereabouts. It will take more than kidnapping to silence the spiritual man crying out in the wilderness.

"Go," the lead soldier instructs. The men proceed toward the door.

"Magda!" another barks. She's engrossed in the materials she found. *They are definitely connected*, she thinks. Yasha and the Immerser. Doesn't know how exactly, but she can feel it in her gut. She vows to secretly discover the truth.

"Move out!"

IDF soldiers march the Immerser out of the house.

Two hours later, he's escorted through what, he guesses, can only be a prison. He anticipates being among other guests who spout pointed opposition at their government. Political prisoners, government agitators. The Immerser will continue to proclaim his message of peace and right living, even behind bars, to prisoners and guards alike. But a last-minute decision by the warden lands him in a solitary cell in a separate wing. Ghosts of previous men call out in the silence. With the hood still covering his face, he can hear and feel their unwelcome presence. The Immerser mumbles under his breath, invoking the presence of God, attempting to find light in a place consumed with darkness.

One soldier waits outside the cell while the other ushers the Immerser into his new environment. Moments before the soldier leaves, he pulls the black hood off the Immerser and unties his hands. An orange jump-suit is thrown in his direction. No instructions, no explanations, just an emotionless face performing a government job. He turns to exit the cell. "Enjoy your stay."

The small cell throbs with late-July heat. No windows, no ventilation system, just heavy, stagnant air. Of all places, prison was the last on his list for visiting before the approaching high holy days. The fall celebration of Rosh Hashanah should be enjoyed with friends and meals and cited bless-ings. Not in solitary confinement. The Immerser closes his eyes, blocking out the reality before him. Instead, he thinks of the beauty and majesty of the high holy days, connecting their origins back to the creation of the universe and of the human race that began with Adam and Chavah. A new world, new life, and new year all rolled into one. Ten days after Rosh Hashanah, Yom Kippur will arrive. Observers will repent of their iniquity and seek absolution from God—a direct result of the first human beings opening the door to sin. He can only hope to be released before the feasts. But it's anyone's guess, truthfully.

Quietly, the Immerser prays. For his soul and the souls of those who placed him here. His mission remains the same: to call out wickedness and to immerse people in God's love and truth, the only thing that will cleanse them. Normally, he performs a ceremony called *Tashlich*, where sins are symbolically thrown into a moving body of water. Immersed in the Mediterranean, the Sea of Galilee, the Jordan—any body of water suffices. He quotes from the book of Micah: *"God will take us back in love; God will cover up our iniquities. You will hurl all our sins into the depths of the sea."* The Immerser can smell the water, can feel the forgiveness. Both he and his cousin Yasha proclaim the message of propitiation through God alone. A living picture of Rosh Hashanah and Yom Kippur.

Suddenly, his eyes pop open. His mind spins with the ramifications of his internment, of what the government is attempting to do. He must get word to Yasha. There's no time to spare. He formulates a plan, devising a way to send his cousin covert communication. Little does the Immerser know, the communication that ends up in Yasha's hands five months from now will be his last words on earth.

30

ONE MONTH EARLIER

Jaffa Gate, a stone portal in the Old City, sits open in the Jewish Quarter. Heavily trafficked, the gate links ancient structures inside with a modern plaza outside. Tourists and locals flow in and out all day. For this reason, a twenty-two-year-old Israeli sits outside the gate, a black guitar box open by his side. Homeless, hopeless. He plays on a beat-up six-string, panhandling for money.

The guy rests his back against the warm wall, eyes glazed over. The end of June is getting hotter by the minute. He sees people come near then far, some dropping coins into the box, some passing by without a second glance. But he doesn't really notice anyone. He doesn't look directly at anyone, rather stares around them. He plays music to quiet the noise in his head.

Four years ago, he found himself on the front lines fighting against Hezbollah near the Lebanon border. His first year in the Israeli army. The raw fear of combat held him immobile. He was supposed to take out the enemy holding a rocket, but instead the enemy took out his best friend. Shock, grief, and unbearable shame filled the space of fear. *It should have been me*, he thinks over and over, year after year.

Noises, smells, nightmares bring back unwanted memories. Posttraumatic stress renders him mentally locked. The enemy who once had a face is now only voices that taunt him mercilessly. All the killing around him ended up killing him inside. But he's too much of a coward to take his own life. Just like he was a coward that day. He cannot hold a job, cannot go back to the military, cannot afford medication for his post-traumatic stress. His family has rejected him. He lives and breathes alone. Despondency, pain, and despair dictate his days. Life holds no meaning, no value. He breathes but isn't alive. The weight of his shame has become his tomb. Utterly broken, utterly needing rescue.

Absentmindedly he sits, strumming the guitar in no particular fashion. Only the sound of music helps.

Shadows suddenly fall across his lap, many pairs of feet stopping near his spot. They are too close—close enough for him to feel uncomfortable. One pair of feet closer than the other eleven, a stranger who will soon become his leader. His eyes lift halfway up the stranger's legs, falling back again into place. He hunches more over his guitar. Something in the atmosphere around him has changed, but he cannot name it. He expects to encounter unspoken messages of disgust, pity, or contempt—the normal things thrown at him. Today it's none of those. It's something new, and although his body tenses as if reacting to fear, the fear never materializes.

In the guitar case sits a handful of shekels, not even enough for one meal. Yasha considers this and reaches into his pocket. He feels only fabric. No silver. No gold. He rarely carries money. Mostly ideas and passion and motivation against the status quo, as well as the power to change things. And people.

Swiftly, Yasha swings something from around his back. The former soldier detects a large object out of the corner of his eye but refuses to look directly. It isn't until he hears the strumming of a second guitar that his attention takes focus. A beautiful guitar, deep crimson red, comes into view. The soldier is intrigued and catches himself staring at the instrument. Images of blood pulse through his mind. His heart races at the memories that haunt him, yet he can't tear his eyes from the instrument. His own plucking slows to a whisper as he listens to the notes streaming from Yasha's guitar. For countless seconds, he sits mesmerized at the beauty it's producing, clean and light. As if climbing a ladder, the soldier's eyes ascend slowly to Yasha's face. There he discovers something shocking. A face of approval, of knowing. *But how?* he wonders.

Without words, Yasha nods his head at the soldier, encouraging him to play. He hesitates, unsure. Never has this happened. Soon, a makeshift duet unfolds in the afternoon air. The soldier has silently partnered with this stranger, and everything changes. The gross weight in his chest dislodges from his ribs. As the two men play together, energy grows around them and around those watching. Soon, hands clap to the rhythm and feet begin to bounce. Yasha remains attentive to the soldier, offering years' worth of acceptance and validation.

A warmth spreads to the four corners of the soldier's heart. With every beat, the noise in his head lessens. *Wasn't there an old story from the Tanakh about David playing music for a tormented Melek Shaul?* he thinks. Something his mother had told him as a boy. He looks up at Yasha, who nods and smiles confidently, as if reading his mind. *Don't try and analyze what's happening*, the soldier tells himself. *Just enjoy the brief freedom.* He feels as light as before joining the military. Before the death of his friend, before the PTSD enveloped him.

An ancient Hebrew song emerges from the chords, a song of deliverance. Like a national anthem, it speaks of the Jews emerging through difficulty into victory. Local residents stop and join in the ensemble, while tourists stop and absorb the scene. Videos are taken to be broadcasted in minutes. Yaakov, the third member to join the Twelve, anticipates potential backlash if the videos go viral. It will undoubtedly be viewed as inflammatory: Yasha singing and playing music of Jewish deliverance from their enemies. And near the Temple Mount a few months after Passover, no less.

"Maybe not the best idea," Mattiyahu says under his breath to Yehudas. Both men raise their eyebrows, sharing a look of agreement.

Shimon overhears, disgust fomenting inside. *Charlatan*, he grouses internally. Not only does he despise smug lawyers like Mattiyahu, but he also condemns those who fight against Israel's total sovereignty. *How does Yasha expect us to work together with such contradicting ideologies?* he wonders. Shimon, full of zeal, views what Yasha is doing differently than the rest of the group. Yasha clearly loves this nation, checkered history and all. Shimon rejoices in this and hopes it sets in motion a turning of the tide to reclaim the property their enemy controls.

Yasha, fully engaged in the music, continues to watch the soldier, eyes marking the invisible passage of deliverance occurring inside him. It appears as if the two musicians are playing for the gathered audience, yet Yasha knows it's about the one lost soul. Ten full minutes pass, then fifteen.

All at once, the soldier looks his duet partner directly in the eyes. Like snapping out of a trance, he lets out a curt laugh. The hypnosis is gone. He stands up, strumming more intensely on his old guitar. Strings verge on rupturing. He doesn't care. The music broke through when nothing else could. He feels normal again. The two guitars sing high and loud. A veritable melee ensues, pulling everyone into melodious joy. Another ten minutes pass like a handful of seconds.

Yasha wraps up the song with a tremolo, brushing back and forth quickly on the last chord. The crowd claps and cheers. Handfuls of money drop in the guitar case. People slap each other on their backs and smiles drift into the web of Jerusalem. Yasha rotates his guitar to his back, giving the soldier a final nod. They clasp hands as soldiers would.

"What's your name?" Yasha asks.

"Taddai," the soldier replies.

Before he hears the internal voice, Yasha knows. An otherworldly sense, as experienced with the other eleven.

Taddai. Number 12. *Gentle soul, big-hearted, loyal; loves to throw out clever comments without cracking a smile.*

Yasha takes him in. Dark eyes lined by dark circles. Once military-short hair now hangs greasy and long in his face. Nails bitten down to the quick. Heart broken by tragedy and despair. Soul on the precipice, longing for hope yet trapped by lies.

For the first time in years, Taddai smiles. Yasha radiates love in return. He doesn't understand how, but Taddai knows he's different. *What just happened?* he wonders. *Who is this person?*

Yasha jerks his head toward the Old City, telling his followers the next direction. The eleven members begin to depart. It seems, though, that Taddai misses the invitation. The crowd shifts like a school of fish. Streams of people usher Yasha and his followers through the Jaffa Gate and into the Old City. Taddai watches them disappear like water.

Some minutes later, the area quiets to its normal pace. The soldier sits back down against the wall, anticipating the return of noises and voices in his head. After all, PTSD doesn't just disappear in thirty minutes. But as he searches for the familiar ties that bind, he cannot find one. He searches deeply for signs. No depression. No heightened anxiety. No despair. No feelings of trauma. Regardless of conjured images and memories, the emotional response doesn't manifest. *How is this possible? What in the world?*

Shocked and motivated by an unseen force, Taddai bolts up and grabs the money from his guitar case. He sprints to follow the man who resuscitated him.

"Wait!"

31

THREE DAYS EARLIER

El'azar moves around his house in Bethany, glancing through windows and closing curtains. His sisters, Marta and Miryam, offer food and drinks to their guests. For weeks, El'azar had been watching every movement of Yasha's cell, ever since the terror attack on Moshe Baram Street. And he rightly assumes that others are watching the small group as well. El'azar loves chess and senses a game has begun. But before Yasha could extend an invitation for him to join the group, El'azar explained that he and his two younger sisters are orphans; he cannot leave them on their own. What he can do, however, is offer his house as a safe place, a hideout whenever necessary. Off and on, Yasha and his nine companions have gathered here following the tragedy. Finding seclusion, establishing camaraderie.

Shimon, the newest member, watches and speaks little. He studies everyone, absorbing everything. Though the men here have known each other for only a short while, there's a collective excitement in knowing that they've been chosen. Shimon sits off to one side, and El'azar moves in to ensure that he feels welcome in the safe house. A noticeable energy hangs in the air. Something unknown is building. Yasha moves about engaging with his companions, listening for divine instructions.

From the corner of the adjoining room, Arye glimpses a breaking news report from Jerusalem. He urgently motions the others over. Faivel grabs the remote and cranks up the volume. Suddenly a face fills the screen. Those eyes. That scar. Kefa furrows his brow and makes eye contact with their leader. They know.

For the last week, the report continues, security forces—including counterterrorism and undercover patrol—have been deployed throughout the State of Israel. A joint investigation launched by the police and Shin Bet has led to the arrest of a Palestinian man named Isan bar-Abbas, a resident of the Aida refugee camp near Bethlehem. He killed more than a dozen people in a recent terrorist attack in Jerusalem. Bar-Abbas denies allegations but has confessed to swearing an oath of jihad to Allah. His conviction awaits.

A loud knock on the door startles them, interrupting their focus. Faivel mutes the TV. The others move into adjacent rooms, out of sight from the entry. Outside, a portly man, short and sweaty, fidgets at the door with his tattered briefcase. He adjusts his flat cap that sits atop his scruffy gray hair, shifting it to cover his growing bald spot. His hazel eyes double-check the motorcycle parked on the street.

Mattiyahu. Number 11. *Insecure, opportunistic, twice divorced; has more than a few enemies.*

Alongside him stands Yehudas, Mattiyahu's financial advisor. They're in the throes of discussing current legal cases that Mattiyahu is litigating for his various clients—thieves, extortionists, abusers of the law. Both men push boundaries where morals and money are concerned. Wealth, power, and a measure of prestige fuel them. Secretly, of course.

El'azar answers the door and sees the two men. They seem to be an odd pair. Could pass for door-to-door salesmen or proselytizers of a strange cult. El'azar doesn't like the look of them.

Mattiyahu blurts, "I was able to track down Yasha…"

Immediately, El'azar grows tense, frustrated that the safe house has become compromised already.

"How exactly?" El'azar challenges.

"My sources are confidential," Mattiyahu replies, curtly.

El'azar begins to close the door, but Mattiyahu throws out his arm, keeping it open. Yehudas stands motionless, a smug display of confidence on his face. He knows that Mattiyahu usually gets his way.

"I want to speak with the group," Mattiyahu says, "even briefly."

El'azar vets Mattiyahu and Yehudas for a full five minutes—name, occupation, political party, purpose—then checks with Yasha. He nods, despite El'azar's misgivings. *Maybe Yasha can't detect the smell of an opportunist*, he thinks. El'azar opens the door wide, and the men cross over the threshold into something completely unexpected.

Mattiyahu notices the ticker on the news channel mentioning bar-Abbas. "He's why I'm here." Mattiyahu points at the TV. "The terrorist."

Yasha asks him to expound, knowing full well the lawyer's objectives. It doesn't take a genius. Even Faivel can answer this one. On supernatural direction, Yasha has already decided to offer Mattiyahu a place in the cell.

The other nine slowly emerge, listening and watching the two men. Yochanan silently hopes that Yasha will not invite them into the group. He doesn't trust them. As the fourth to join, he has closely observed the process with Faivel, Natan, ben-Chalfai, Toma, and Shimon. Yasha seems to choose his men at random, yet Yochanan understands there's an intentional method to the seeming madness.

Mattiyahu admits that he had tracked them all down, as they'd allegedly witnessed and aided people in the aftermath of the terror attack. He introduces himself, touting his credentials and ability to provide legal counsel for those impacted by such horrific events. He will sue the State of Israel, the Palestinian Authority, the Transportation Department, whoever is necessary to have recompense for injuries both physical and mental. For his clients, of course. Justice is imperative, he proclaims, though it seems obvious to the others that his motivation is financial. That and recognition. Never mind that he consistently bends the law to fit his agenda.

"You weren't there," Yochanan says, "you don't know." His heart for injustice can identify an imposter immediately. He silently criticizes this man dressed in a leather jacket and wrinkled jeans. Yochanan doesn't trust anyone going through an obvious mid-life crisis. He assumes that Mattiyahu isn't particularly religious, despite the head covering. A coverup for something else, perhaps.

"Doesn't matter," Mattiyahu replies.

"It wasn't just a peccadillo," Natan says curtly, "he blew up *a bus!*"

Shimon throws Natan a side glance. He uses the strangest words.

Mattiyahu nods. "I've seen enough terrorism in my life to know how this operates." His tone bears the edges of personal experience. Yet the arrogance and seemingly blasé perspective is off-putting.

"Fairly certain this is complicated enough," Yaakov states.

"Spoken like an amateur," Mattiyahu retorts.

Both men glare at one another. Shimon steps forward, trying to break the building tension. His dislike and distrust of lawyers is reaching new heights. He would like nothing more than to slam the door in Mattiyahu's face, forgetting him indefinitely.

From across the room, Yasha interjects. "Don't say anything you don't mean. You only make things worse when you lay down a smoke screen of pious talk. When you manipulate words to get your own way, you go wrong." He knows Mattiyahu's propensity to be divisive with his comments. Years of being around morally compromised people has created a hard edge to his façade.

Mattiyahu feels chastened by Yasha, this stranger that he's pursuing, but certainly doesn't show it. He redirects, hoping to shift the focus back to the terrorist. He holds out a business card. "In case you want to pursue legal action…"

"You can't use legal cover to mask a moral failure," Yasha answers, looking intently at him.

For a moment, the room is quiet as the men contemplate this proclamation. The lawyer fumes, wondering if Yasha's referring to him. He does not enjoy having a room full of eyes pointed in his direction.

He lets out a snort. "Tell that to the prime minister." Ohred has certainly been attempting to cover his immoral tracks, especially since the Immerser called him out publicly a few weeks ago.

"Who's this?" Shimon asks, pointing to Mattiyahu's companion.

Mattiyahu eyes his friend, the accountant. "Yehudas."

Clad in black pants and white button-down shirt, Yehudas waits prudently, hands in his pockets. Frame tall and lean, hair short and dark, eyes luminous and brown. Remarkably attractive.

"What's he want?" Kefa inquires.

"He works for me," Mattiyahu explains. "He's good with money."

Yasha looks at Yehudas for long moments. He hears the familiar voice.

Yehudas. Number 10. *Raised strictly Orthodox; casual charlatan; good at manipulating numbers; addicted to pain medication.*

Normally, strictly Orthodox Jews don't fraternize with people like Mattiyahu. But Yehudas, after his near-death experience, walked away from the sect and from his family. Following the freak work accident that almost killed him, Yehudas got connected with Mattiyahu, an attorney for such matters. That was two years ago. They ended up exchanging services—legal help for financial assistance. Everything under the table, naturally. No one in Yehudas's family knows of this connection. Nor do they know of the meds.

Like the others, he too will be an integral player in the cell that Yasha's forming. He knows that Yehudas carries the potential to ignite the group into fury, like a match to gun powder. But he also knows that Yehudas has already been chosen. He can feel it with clarity.

"I don't anticipate using your legal expertise," Yasha explains to Mattiyahu. "Rather, I have a proposition for you. For both of you."

Yehudas and Mattiyahu exchange looks. Normally, this isn't how their business acquisitions play out. To their surprise, Yasha invites them to become part of their faction. Shimon groans audibly. Yochanan closes and rubs his eyes. Is he surprised though? Every level of society is being represented. The dynamics are becoming more and more interesting. No doubt this is intentional. The group is shaping up to be as varied as Israeli wine varietals.

Unexpectedly, the doorbell rings. El'azar mumbles that they definitely need a new safe house. He moves to the door, finding a beautiful, African, twenty-five-year-old woman in an IDF military uniform. On her chest, an Israeli flag is sewn onto the olive-green fatigues. El'azar stares at her for a moment, taken in by her beauty and by her unexpected presence. She offers a tight smile, and the breath catches in El'azar's chest. He's never met an African Jew before, though many live in Israel. His respect for her military service makes her even more intriguing. And appealing. After questioning her intentions, El'azar shows her into the living room. His eyes follow her and betray him. Enamored, he vows to find her again and pursue her.

She, however, only has eyes for Yasha. Her brusque mannerisms catch everyone's attention, as does the aura around her. She carries a heaviness, a darkness that's hard to miss. The demons that oppress her begin to agonize in the proximity of Yasha. They know that he has more power than they do, so they turn up the heat. She fights for control—something that she practices daily and has learned to mask. If she can cope enough to get by, then she feels secure. Even though she's far from it. Making eye contact with Yasha, she carefully weaves her way through the curious men to the room where he sits. A guitar the color of a deep red sunrise hangs by her side.

"You left," she says, "before I could thank you."

He looks at her arm. "And the bones?"

"Whole," she replies. "No breaks."

Yasha smiles at her, and for a moment she forgets why she came. His eyes, his demeanor are magnetic. The weight of the instrument at her side eventually redirects her thoughts. She holds it out.

"For you."

He looks at it with admiration, for its lacquer shines a beautiful, crimson color even in muted light. A glimpse of the future flashes before his eyes; he momentarily closes them and sighs. The beauty and value of the guitar is evident. He raises an eyebrow, silently asking if she's positive of the sacrificial gift. The woman nods.

"Thank you…?" Yasha says, waiting for a name.

"Magda," she replies. "That's what my fellow soldiers call me, anyway. My family emigrated to Magdala from Ethiopia. It stuck."

Suddenly, a curious look crosses her face as thoughts of a previous life flash through her mind. Yasha sees this, understands she's carrying a huge burden. He knows, instinctively, that evil has triumphed in her life. That men have taken advantage of her for years. That she was lured into being trafficked in order to help her family after the death of her father in Ethiopia. The subsequent abortions only added to the shame, fear, and depression. Her demons—seven in all—followed her to Israel and into the military, where she'd hoped to escape the mental and spiritual torment. That proved to be a mere distraction. The daily harassment persists. Even now, they are greatly agitated and screech for her to run! *Run!*

Yasha's heart melts. Compassion soars. Deep scars hidden beneath such beauty. He stares at Magda, eyes brimming with unconditional love. She begins to well up, unsure of the apparent connection her heart feels with this stranger. Captivated. By just one look.

"A treasure," he says.

Does he mean the guitar? she wonders. *Or me?*

Yasha throws the strap around his neck and playfully plucks at the strings. Magda looks at her watch and bids goodbye. She doesn't glance at the TV or else she would've seen the face of the terrorist who had shattered her arm more than a week ago. Fortunately, Yasha had immediately healed her that day. Her demons had raged against the encounter with Yasha, just as they seethe now in his presence once again. Most everyone can sense the darkness that Magda carries with her, though they don't understand the reasons for it. Perhaps she dabbles in the occult. African nations are known to practice witchcraft.

As she makes her way back to the entrance, Yasha plays a tune that's familiar to her. Only when she steps through the threshold does she realize it's the song her deceased father sang to her as a little girl—the one he made up solely for her. It had always brought her peace. This time, however, enormous power hits her from across the house, knocking her off-balance. One by one, the demons that torment her flee against their will. Even the ones she cannot name. Years' worth of pain vanishes in an instant. The heaviness, the shame—gone. Her knees buckle and she trembles under the substance of something unseen. A force more powerful than the demons. She grabs the doorjamb, steadying herself. Shock sets in, then unmistakable peace. Unmistakable freedom.

Magda whips around in surprise, finding his face. Those penetrating eyes, that kind smile. Yasha has given her things not even asked for. Liberty. Tranquility. *But how? Why? Who is he?* Her thoughts run wild in confusion, in excitement.

Yasha winks, then segues into another, unknown tune. Magda slowly returns his smile. A turning point in her life. She closes the front door behind her, though a chasm within her has flown wide open. Tears run down her face. *This won't be our last interaction*, she thinks. *Some unseen force will keep our paths crossing.* She vows to discover more about Yasha and to protect him however possible.

Inside, it's clear to the others that something significant, perhaps even miraculous, has just taken place. The atmosphere has shifted dramatically. Whatever darkness or heaviness that Magda carried in with her disappeared in an instant. An air of electricity now fills the house.

The eleven men turn and look at Yasha. Some are more familiar with his approach, others more surprised. Some have been in the group longer, others newly acquired. But even if they think they understand, they do not. So much has yet to happen, so much has yet to unfold. The spectrum of personalities gathered varies like the twelve tribes of Israel. They all have been chosen; they all have a role to play. But none of them will ever be the same.

Yasha looks over his new recruits. He knows there is one more out there, yet he silently gives thanks for these eleven. The last cell member will be made known in due time. He understands the forces controlling the timeline. His job, quite frankly, is to listen and follow orders. Everything else will fall into place.

32

ONE WEEK EARLIER

Hundreds of people—Israelis, Palestinians, and foreigners alike—stand ready to lobby at a pro-peace demonstration at High Tech Park in Be'er Sheva. Once a mere camel town, Be'er Sheva, the largest city in the Negev desert, now takes its place as a technology and cybersecurity hub. Rally participants yearn for peace in their region, calling on government officials to change regulations that affect Jews and Arabs in the land. Recent terror attacks in Jerusalem have motivated the current administration to exact stricter legal and military measures throughout the country. Tensions mount as different factions voice their opinion. Today, on a parched mid-June day, calls for peace rise up from this bustling city anchored in the southern portion of Israel.

Eagerly awaiting the next speaker, people converse and share stories and ideologies, projects and theories. There's no lack of innovation or motivation in this town. People strive to make a difference.

Auditory difficulties keep the technicians busy behind the stage. Yasha and his eight companions stand at the edge of the crowd, waiting. Silently, their leader slips from their side and makes his way onto the platform. Was he planning to speak or was it a spontaneous decision? No one knows what he will say, what he will do. He's an enigma to them.

Suddenly, speakers start to crackle, and a shriek from the microphone alerts the crowd. Yasha paces the platform. Praying, seeking, watching. With the fervor of a rabbi on a high holy day, he launches into a tacit manifesto. Yet it sounds different than the usual ones proffered in such rallies.

Yasha speaks a different message: a culture of honor. He's not political or military minded. His message goes deeper than changing the government and the party in power. He yearns for a just society that has mutual respect for one another in actions as well as words. He speaks of communal acceptance that is then franchised out. His mission, though not bluntly decreed, seeks to reach the masses with a commitment for honest living flanked by policies of mercy and love. Prosperity of soul to the people of this tense region. Though there are enemies all around lying in wait, the aim is not to sew discord but to use creative energies to promote peace as a matter of principle. Terrorism belongs to those seeking to dissolve any reconciliation achieved. Hate to replace peace.

"It's urgent that you listen carefully to this!" Yasha begins. "Don't look for shortcuts to God. The market is flooded with surefire, easygoing formulas for a successful life that can be practiced in your spare time. Don't fall for that stuff, even though crowds of people do. The way to life—to God!—is vigorous and requires total attention. Anyone here who believes what I am saying right now and aligns himself with God is no longer condemned to be an outsider. They've taken a giant step from the world of the dead to the world of the living." Yasha paces the stage, impassioned and resolute. "It's urgent that you get this! The time has arrived—I mean right now!—when dead men and women will hear the voice of God and come alive."

Close behind Yasha, a large modern footbridge dubbed the DNA bridge spirals out and over the adjacent railyard. Shaped as a double helix, the bridge stands as an homage to the technology sector, though Yasha views it otherwise. Symbolically, it represents his own life—God's DNA in human form. The two strands, of heaven and of earth, inextricably intertwined. His message must also be intertwined. Yasha's words tickle their ears, offering them a new platform for an improved life. But not everyone is receptive.

"What does God have to do with this?" a voice demands. "We prefer enlightened ideas."

"Modern ideas!" another voice shouts. Get rid of the religious tone, they demand. Technology and cyber-security rule in this growing town. Tangible, factual philosophies, not arcane ones.

Faivel, the group's lone technology geek, tends to agree with his fellow vocational experts. He prefers formulas and patterns over concepts and vague perspectives. What's provable not theoretical. Yet Faivel feels that Yasha encompasses both systems of thinking—that he coils together, like the double helix bridge, seemingly opposite ways of promoting progress. And promoting peace.

"Hate me, hate God—it's all the same," Yasha declares. "It's interchangeable; you either love both or reject both. But my purpose is not to get your vote and not to appeal to mere human testimony. If I turned the spotlight on myself, it wouldn't amount to anything. I'm not out to get my own way but only to carry out orders."

"From whom?" a man yells. "Who gave the orders?"

The One who sent Yasha outshines him. If only they could see that. "You haven't recognized Him in this. But I have."

The crowd cannot pinpoint this rogue man. Who he is, what his true agenda is. Some feel that Yasha speaks in riddles, never giving straight answers. A tactic, perhaps. But more often than not, his words carry double meanings.

"You all saw and heard the Immerser," Yasha says. "He gave expert and reliable testimony about me, didn't he?"

Someone yells at him. "Just who are you anyway?"

"I am here," Yasha says loudly, "to announce pardon to prisoners and recovery of sight to the blind. To set the burdened and battered free."

Some cheer, yet some hiss their disapproval. Whistles of praise next to shouts of resentment. Not everyone at a pro-peace rally seeks peace, especially given the attack in Jerusalem three days ago. Tension hovers at an elevated height. Terrorism must be condemned, especially when committed at the hands of Muslim neighbors. Bloodshed has left a fresh residue in the mouths of Israelis. Some believe peace can only be obtained through a strong response. An eye for an eye. Others believe strong diplomacy must be employed to avoid further escalations. Peace through compromise and concessions.

"Is he talking about releasing terrorists?" Natan says to the group.

"All bets are off," Yaakov replies in a conspiratorial whisper.

Yochanan smirks, then shrugs a shoulder. "Just go with it."

At the moment, from center stage, unconventional ideas are being launched. Yasha wars not against governmental wings but against mindsets and cultural practices. His wings of leadership offer healing. He confronts the way people think in order to bring freedom. He invites the demonstrators to engage in a countercultural underground movement that doesn't seek the approval or permission of governmental leaders. Even those in power who claim to champion the poor and downcast use those same souls for political and monetary gain. Their motives are far from pure. True power lies in the hands and feet of our communities, he proclaims. Honor, purity, *love*. Those things cannot be taken away or manipulated for specific agendas. Calling people to live extreme lives as history makers.

"I am not trying to get anything for myself. God intends something gloriously grand here and is making the decisions that will bring it about," Yasha declares.

Yochanan raises his eyebrows, throwing his brother, Yaakov, a look. *That could be a thorny problem*, he thinks. *A secret grand plan? Blueprints for shaking up the nation? Such talk can kill the prospect of peace… or get the speaker killed.*

"I say this with absolute confidence," Yasha continues. With animated passion, he gives a final shout. "This is God's year to act!"

Down front, off to the side stands a man with probing, pale-gray eyes. Rust-colored hair cut short, freckled face donning a goatee, soft around the middle. He sports a kippah and a hooped earring. He is seeking to make waves in the land he believes belongs solely to the Jews. Yasha takes note of him and hears the voice.

Shimon. Number 9. *Zionist and political activist; adrenaline junkie; craves change; hates lawyers and lobbyists.*

Yasha will soon discover Shimon's idiosyncrasies—hot tempered, swears often, loves hookah pipes and nightclub music, all paired with a contagious smile. Born in Israel, raised in Morocco. For someone who has traveled the world, Shimon remains convinced that Israel is the only place to live. His volatile personality makes Yasha grin. So much potential.

At twenty-six, Shimon believes less in diplomacy and more in taking action. He admires Yasha's ideas but thinks they're too subdued. If it weren't for the language or implied methodology, Shimon would write him off as just another voice. But the obscure speech, odd sounding to most, offers the invitation he's seeking.

Yasha is a man who pursues justice and virtue. He accepts people for who they are yet calls them to step out of the things that create bondage. He changes circumstances to demonstrate his compassionate heart. Different from everyone, Yasha somehow identifies with even his enemies. He seems detached in ways but fully invested in his country. Without a doubt, he keeps people on their toes. Some are unnerved, others adore him. Bottom line, his grassroots revolution is aimed at bettering the Middle East and, ultimately, the globe. He's the only speaker at this rally to motivate Shimon to participate in something much bigger and more profound.

Shimon deciphers all these things, deciding that Yasha is a secret Zionist—one worth joining in the fight for a better Israel. He smiles at the thought. This label, however, comes with a price. Zionism is tinder for fire in Eretz Yisrael. Some see it as aggressive and discriminatory, others as ideology and destiny. Shimon tells himself he will draw out the Zionist dogma from the speaker. He will bend him toward a more radical approach, drawing crowds bigger than this. The time has come, he decides, to promote someone passionate for such change. He believes he's found his agent. The new face of the Zionist movement. Yet everything that Shimon maintains will soon be turned upside down.

Thirty minutes later, as Yasha exits the area, Shimon follows. He feels the same adrenaline rush as when he cliff jumps in Akko, an old town on the edge of Haifa. The remains of the ancient city date back thousands of years, its archeological stone walls a symbol of strength and endurance throughout centuries of discord. One section of the wall offers a favorite spot for those seeking the thrill of hurtling themselves off the ramparts, falling some thirteen meters, and landing in the turquoise waters of the Mediterranean. Shimon loves it. Jumping feet first or flipping backwards, he revels in the thrill as well as in the tempting of fate. Though there's potential for things to go seriously wrong, Shimon doesn't allow fear to dictate his decisions or to distract him from pursuing adventure. A true adrenaline junkie.

And following Yasha is no different. He knows, without a doubt, the tell-tale signs. His pulse races, his mind darts, he wants to plunge into the unknown. Shimon isn't aware that he will be the ninth member to join the cell, a fact that will surprise and challenge him. What he does know, presently, is that this opportunity comes around once in a lifetime. He assumes the experience will be like no other.

He won't be wrong.

33

THREE DAYS EARLIER

Bus No. 22 pulls up to the stop, releasing its passengers. Children and their parents, teenagers, and elderly citizens emerge from the confines of the large vehicle. Yasha and his eight companions arrived moments before on No. 71 and now make their way up the sidewalk.

"We got here in record time," Faivel comments, looking at his watch.

"Yeah, that bus driver has a metal foot," Arye says.

Yasha laughs. Kefa rolls his eyes. "Lead foot, Arye. It's *lead* foot."

"Same thing," he replies, brushing off his brother's correction.

Within thirty seconds, a second crew of passengers steps onto the bus, filling most every seat. No. 22 runs Moshe Baram Street, a major thoroughfare in the southern part of Jerusalem.

Right before the doors close, a young man in medical scrubs with dark circles under his eyes makes an impromptu decision and hops off the bus. He moves quickly up the sidewalk, glancing back after a few seconds. He doesn't notice how near he is to passersby and bumps into Yasha unexpectedly. Yasha stops and looks at the young man—deeply into his ghostly eyes, his sinister soul. This unnerves the man even more, but he can't seem to tear away from the gaze. It's as if he's seeing a vision of his past and future simultaneously. His eyes register shock, then fear, then defiance.

From the bus, an older woman shouts to the young man. He's forgotten something; left his medical bag underneath the seat. But before she can finish, the bus explodes in rockets of glass, fire, and metal. For a few brief moments, the street is silent except for the background noise of flames and falling glass. No birds, no voices. Perhaps the volume of explosion deafened every ear nearby. Then, in the blink of an eye, the sounds return full force.

An inferno engulfs bus No. 22. Soon it will be reduced to charred metal. Half of Yasha's companions have dropped to the pavement, the others cover their heads, ears, and eyes. Yasha, though, watches the young man who bumped into him—the one with a pronounced scar under his right eye—now rapidly rounding the corner, disappearing amid the chaos.

The screams and noise of flames bring Yasha's attention back to the bus. Immediately, he grabs the arms of Yochanan and Arye—one looking at the carnage, the other looking away—and sprints toward injured people strewn on the sidewalk. Ben-Chalfai, a member of the medical and scientific community, barks commands, identifying the wounded in order of life-and-death status. Kefa runs around looking for the suspected terrorist to catch him but soon gives up. He's gone. The rest of the men follow and pair up with the victims. They offer help, comfort, anything they can.

Natan pulls off his shirt and makes a tourniquet for a Palestinian woman. Toma wipes blood from an Israeli child's eyes, while her mother wails in shock and anger. Kefa and Yaakov lift an unresponsive body out of the street and onto the sidewalk. Faivel grabs water from his bag, offering some to the victims, his boots crunching broken glass up and down the walkway. In minutes, the sounds of sirens approach, reaching out an invisible arm of comfort to everyone on the scene.

Despite this, Yasha moves among the wounded, even the dead, performing miracles undercover. He touches the arm of a crying African-Jewish woman, the bones reversing its break; he puts his hands on the belly of an Arabic man, stopping the unseen flow of blood; he stoops down and puts his fingers to the neck of a little boy who isn't breathing, and blows on his face. Love is on the move.

TWELVE

Once the paramedics and police descend, Yasha retreats into the shadows. He listens to the explanations and confusion of the survivors. He watches them load the boy onto a stretcher, a medic declaring his death. But as the white sheet is draped over his face, the boy lets out a moan. The other medic hollers that he's breathing, and the sheet falls to the sidewalk. Yasha smiles to himself.

No one has witnessed these things, save one Israeli man, watching with acute curiosity. His gentle blue eyes burn with interest. The compassion and the miracles have not escaped his attention. He cannot understand why the miracle worker shies away from the authorities, both law enforcement and medical. While assisting the wounded in getting attention, the Israeli man watches as eight other men join in the shadows, conversing in low tones. Most have a mixture of blood and dirt on their faces, their clothes.

"Are we leaving?" Arye asks.

"Lickety-split," Yaakov suggests. Flashbacks of prison taunt him. He doesn't want to get accused of doing the wrong thing. It's an upside-down world.

"I think the authorities have it under control," Yasha offers. He knows that demonstrating too much too early will cause him to be out of step with the orchestrated timeline.

Within moments, they are headed away from the scene of the explosion crafted by a terrorist. None know where they're going exactly.

Making a split-second decision, the young man with gentle blue eyes runs over to the group. He introduces himself as El'azar and confesses what he saw. He knows that Yasha can identify the murderer, that he stood face to face with the Arab "doctor" moments before the explosion, and that it's clear Yasha doesn't want to talk to the authorities. It won't be long before those same powers come looking for Yasha and the eight men who aided the wounded and dying. Glances dart around the small group. Hearts pound with trauma and uncertainty. El'azar offers a safe house in his neighborhood only a few miles away. Yasha nods. In silence, they retreat to an undisclosed location to decompress and reassess, the face of the terrorist and human carnage filling their minds.

34

ONE WEEK EARLIER

A parade of men and women streams through the streets of Tel Aviv in the heat of the day. Moving down the beachfront promenade, Herbert Samuel Boardwalk, rainbow flags fly and signs of pride fill the landscape. Voices cry out, some chanting, some cheering. Music steps in time with marching feet. Hours of celebration in the streets from residents and tourists result in the largest parade of its kind in the Middle East region. Both political and social, the parade swims along, ending by the seashore in Charles Clore Park. A boisterous, flamboyant party stretches through the day and into the cool Mediterranean night, sending runners of noise to the edges of town.

Five kilometers east inside the Central Bus Station sits a small walk-in health clinic. Free HIV tests available during June for immigrants and the uninsured, the sign reads. Fifteen men who've emerged from the festivities wait patiently in the main room for time with the medical staff. Privacy is mandatory.

Toma leans back against the plastic chair, checking his phone. The others around him are engrossed in conversation about the week's activities as well as the participating revelers. Toma, an uninsured modern artist, is shorter, slighter, and dressed more chaotically than his fellow patients. His appearance borders on homelessness, though he's far from it. He doesn't care what he looks like as long as his art is selling. He pushes up his thick, black-framed glasses, noticing through the window a group of men moving toward the clinic. He assumes they're heading downtown to experience the annual gathering—an essential part of that community. *Probably just got off the bus from Haifa*, he thinks. Once closer, though, Toma decides they are devoid of the telltale markers. He can't pull his eyes away from the men as curiosity and strange magnetism lure him.

Yasha takes note of the clinic sign and smaller testing sign and slows down. He glances at the cluster of patients in the waiting room. Some display clear indications of disease, others don't. Toma does, though he tries to disguise it. Yasha feels the familiar unseen pull in his heart, fierce and unmistakable. He steps into the waiting room, but his seven companions hesitate.

For a dozen reasons, they'd rather let Yasha enter alone. Natan, in particular, holds a solid disdain toward the homosexual community in light of what the Torah says. Faivel and Yaakov step toward a nearby exit to smoke. Kefa, Arye, and Yochanan launch into a discussion about politics. Ben-Chalfai, brainy and focused with a perpetual professional demeanor, looks up the latest medical research for victims of HIV, expanding his thirst for knowledge.

Within moments, Yasha strikes up conversation about the medical clinic with a couple of patients who think he's inquiring for himself. Bolts of compassion pound through his chest for the pain these men have suffered, both physically and emotionally. Their stories, their realities cross every kind of boundary—familial, cultural, educational, religious. While all different, the men share a history of struggle, rejection, and uncertainty for the future. Disease is an all-too-common presence, early death its partner.

Out of the blue, one patient begins confessing to Yasha his fears. That the disease has gotten much worse. That he won't have much time to live. That none of his family will attend his funeral. Yasha nods, listening. The patient unfolds many apprehensions common with a positive diagnosis.

A message sounds in Yasha's ears.

LOVE DOES NOT DISHONOR OTHERS.

TWELVE

Suddenly, he steps in and hugs the man. Eyes around the room stare in disbelief. Most people do not want to touch HIV victims, much less embrace them fully. Knowing this, Yasha goes around the room, proffering himself sacrificially, human touch breaking down barriers. He affirms some of the patients, says nothing to others, but smiles deeply at each. Lastly, he reaches Toma.

Number 8. *Artistic, moody; thinks in abstracts; questions everything.*

Toma stiffens as Yasha approaches. He wants to run from the room, yet he can't move his limbs. This man scares him. Guarded, he doubts Yasha's motives and questions his uncomfortable-looking companions who lurk outside the clinic doors.

But Yasha reaches out, touching his shoulder. Immediately he stands, his muscles ignoring instruction. The embrace is awkward on Toma's part, as his arms never leave his sides. Yasha, though, folds him into his strong arms. A heat unlike anything he's ever experienced envelopes his body. Something is happening but he's blind to it. Toma wonders if this is what a father's embrace feels like. Something he has craved all his life. He feels years of shame, manufactured pride, doubt, and rebellion melt away. The warmth spreads beyond his limbs, reaching into his soul. His emotional wounds match his physical ones. Without permission, Toma's eyes begin to water.

Shunning fanfare, Yasha emerges back into the station corridor. He catches a last look through the clinic window; the patients carry on with their lives. Toma, however, holds his gaze.

Forty-five minutes later, he sits in the small, cluttered office of a clinic staff member. Toma finds himself thinking of his Jewish family, of his religious childhood. A family of four, they were God-fearing, financially stable, and well educated. Love was present though never demonstrated. At around eight years old, however, Toma was exposed to graphic, salacious materials, the intensity of which grew with each passing year. By the time he was a teenager, illicit same-sex materials had entered his world, propelling him toward a different mindset. A different attraction. Soon thereafter, thoughts became actions, and experiments were conducted. He had crossed a threshold, uncertain of the future but unsure of a different way.

After fifteen years, he wonders about the choices he's made, about the relationships he's allowed, about the beliefs and mindsets that have dictated his path. He is, after all, secretly waiting for the results of his latest blood test in a clinic at a bus station. Time is ticking.

The staff member closes the door and sits at her desk across from Toma. She puts the folder down and exhales loudly. Her eyes lock onto his for what seems like an eternity.

"I'm not sure how to tell you this," she begins. Toma sinks a few inches down in the chair. His stomach cinches, his breath catches. He fights tears by biting his tongue until it trickles blood in his mouth. None of his family knows that he's there. That he's waiting for an official time-line on death.

"We ran your blood test not once, not twice, but three times because there was some confusion."

Toma blinks but cannot respond.

"We even called the clinic from your previous test to verify. They assured us you were given a positive HIV diagnosis three years ago. Is this correct?"

Slowly, he nods. Still no words form. He feels terrified that he has mere months or weeks to live, that his situation is worse than expected.

The clinic nurse shakes her head. "Again, I don't know how to say this, but your situation is... *unusual.*"

Toma inhales audibly. "What does that mean?" he says quietly.

"Your blood tests that we just ran confirm that you...*do not*...have HIV."

A long pause. "I'm sorry?"

"Have you noticed any recent changes in your health?" she asks.

TWELVE

"What?" he says more to himself than the staff worker.

"Have you noticed any recent changes in your health?" she repeats, agitated.

He shakes his head, still trying to absorb this new information. *What on earth is going on? Does she have someone else's file?* he thinks.

"Are you taking any prescribed medications for HIV?"

"No, I prefer..." he confesses, "more natural remedies." He feels ridiculous at offering this statement.

"So, you are not on any sort of medical program to combat this disease then?"

Toma indicates no. He second-guesses himself—again—doubting his previous choices. Internally, he begins to berate himself. Natural remedies have never cured HIV. But then again, his test is negative, quite unexpectedly.

"Has anything out of the ordinary happened that might explain this?" she probes further.

"What?" he says. He begins to shake his head "no" but stops. His eyes move toward the door, his brows furrow. The clinic worker follows his gaze.

"Toma?"

His mind jumps back to the waiting room. The man who sat and listened. The man who innocently hugged everyone. The heat flooding his body, the strange sentiments. *What happened out there? Some kind of illusion? Magic?* He chides himself for even thinking such things. He doesn't believe in anything other than the physical world—what he can see and hear and touch and prove.

But blood tests don't lie.

Impossible.

"Toma?"

He snaps back to awareness. "What? No, nothing," he replies, his mind spinning.

"As you know, this is impossible…medically speaking."

"Yes."

"You can always get another test done somewhere else," she offers, "but as I said earlier, we ran it three times."

"May I have a copy of my test results?"

"Of course," she says handing it to him. "Who knows? Maybe it's a miracle." Her laugh is sharp, mocking the idea.

"I don't believe in miracles." He's too much of a skeptic. But medicine certainly didn't cure him, nor did natural remedies. So, what did?

She shrugs. "Me neither. It's possibly remission, though that doesn't happen without specific drugs." She shrugs again, feeling compelled to investigate further but knows she won't because of the sheer number of cases the clinic maintains due to free testing. "So, unless you have a better explanation…"

Toma thanks her and folds his paperwork. Holding the confirmation, he passes through the waiting room, searching the faces of others who also received hugs. He doesn't notice any outward difference, yet the atmosphere carries a vastly different feel. Toma walks quickly out the clinic door, fear and exhilaration hand in hand. Foot traffic is sparse, the hour in between arrivals and departures. He moves toward the exit, picturing Yasha.

"Okay," he whispers, "you have my attention."

35

TEN DAYS EARLIER

Jerusalem's Mahane Yehuda market spreads out before them like an elongated circus tent. The pitched roof dotted with metal fans, the bright signs, the merchandise piled high. Yasha and his six cell members dodge and weave among locals and tourists from dozens of countries. The covered marketplace that smells of coriander and turmeric stretches long with hundreds of vendors lining both sides. Colorful and noisy, the market offers fresh fruits and vegetables, baked goods, meat, and fish. Cheeses and nuts, spices, wines, and textiles. Clusters of round pita bread stacked like *yarmulkes*, Jewish skullcaps. Sellers call out to potential customers as they meander the market, or *The Shuk* as it's known.

Along the way, Yochanan and Yaakov pick up falafel and kibbeh from familiar vendors.

"Haven't seen you around lately," the vendor remarks. "You close down?"

"No," Yaakov replies. "Taking a break. Seeing some sights."

"What do you mean? You're out of money?"

Yochanan shakes his head. "Not exactly." He wipes his mouth of tzatziki.

"If you're still in business, where are you getting your supplies?" the vendor asks. "Don't tell me it's Yuri; he's dishonest and will rob you blind!"

"Not him," Yaakov laughs.

"Who then?"

Yochanan glances at Yasha. "Kind of a different source right now."

The vendor knows that's all the information he's going to get. The Zavdai brothers are known, in certain circles, for keeping a tight lip. A practice they honed from years of internment.

A small coffee shop catches Yasha's eye. At the entrance sits twenty gallon-sized bins brimming with coffee beans in a dozen shades and sizes. Handwritten signs, in Hebrew and English, depicting their origins—Kenya, Costa Rica, Brazil, Tanzania, Peru—sit perched atop the mounding beans. Yasha leans into them, breathing the fresh aroma that reminds him of incense rising. Inside, he and his followers order Turkish coffee. It's his favorite. Dark, nutty, strong enough to raise the dead.

Little do the first half-dozen members of the cell know but they are being followed. For days now, a man has been watching from the shadows, making detailed notations yet keeping the information to himself. Today, this man is being led around by a young boy, also intent on finding Yasha. Hand in hand, they don't bear any resemblance to each other, yet it's obvious they're related. Merchants call out to them offering deals too good to ignore. But the boy and his companion tune out the cacophony. They are on a mission.

When coffee cups sit empty, Yochanan and Yaakov make a motion to leave.

"Not yet," Yasha instructs.

It seems to Faivel that Yasha is possibly hiding, trying to get lost in a crowd. Or maybe that Yasha is people-watching, looking for another participant to join his eclectic group. Why else would they be waiting here?

Arye pulls out his deck of playing cards and ropes Faivel and Natan into a game of spades. Kefa rolls his eyes and gives the others a warning.

"Arye takes cards seriously," he says. "Borderline addiction."

Ignoring his brother, Arye deals. The game heats up, voices grow louder. Yasha eyes them silently.

Natan, the latest member of the cell to join, becomes self-conscious. He doesn't want to jeopardize anything.

TWELVE

"Maybe we should bring it down a skosh," he says nervously.

Arye shoots him an interesting look. Faivel chuckles. He loves that Natan weaves unexpected words into everyday conversation. Half the time nobody knows what he means. Eventually, the others will get used to it.

"Done!" Arye shouts, winning the round and slamming his hand on the table for good measure.

"Told you," Kefa replies, talking to the newcomers.

Suddenly, the boy spots Yasha, and his eyes light up. He pulls the hand of his companion and moves quickly toward their table.

"Levi," Yasha greets him cheerfully. "Good to see you!"

The boy smiles broadly, his countenance lighting up the coffee shop.

"Everything alright?" asks Yasha.

"Yes!" Levi answers. The joy emanating from him is contagious. "He wanted to meet you," he says, looking up at his companion. "My uncle."

Yasha meets the man's gaze. Medium height, salt and pepper hair neatly parted, glasses rimless, clothes spotless. Eyes light brown, eyebrows bushy. Cheekbones set high against a square jaw. Gives off an air of having money and privilege. Roughly fifty-five years old. Before he speaks, Yasha knows this man's profile.

Yaakov ben-Chalfai. Number 7. *Quiet; nerdy to a fault; potential Nobel laureate; passionate about finding scientific cures.*

Yasha introduces himself and the others, cordial conversation ensues. Yaakov works for a company that makes medical devices for kids living with impaired conditions. With dual degrees in science and economics, Yaakov found himself drawn to medical technology and healthcare innovation. Israel is among the world's leaders in medical and scientific breakthroughs. His muse has always been Levi, his young nephew, who has been physically challenged since birth. Yaakov holds a soft spot in his heart for him. Continually picked on and teased, Levi has endured more than his seven-year-old psyche should.

And yet all of that has radically changed. Medically speaking, a complete transformation isn't possible, or likely. Finding help for children like Levi has been Yaakov's driving force for almost a decade. It's what he thinks about, dreams about, pursues with an intense passion. To make life a bit easier for the underdogs.

But now?

"Follow me," Yasha says, getting up. He drains the remaining coffee dregs and walks back into the market melee. Yaakov ben-Chalfai, silent but intrigued, follows, as do the other six men and Levi.

Arye compliments him on his new smile. The young boy beams with pride.

Yasha turns to his unsuspecting new cell member. "All right if I call you ben-Chalfai?"

Yaakov ben-Chalfai furrows his brow, the question obvious on his face. He isn't aware that Yasha is offering more than a desired medical explanation. For the moment, he can only focus on getting answers. But Yasha has already called him.

"Less confusing than having two Yaakovs," Yasha answers, nodding to the other Yaakov. The cook nods and smiles at the scientist.

"Sure," he acquiesces. A minute later, ben-Chalfai finally inquires, "How'd you do it?"

"What?" Yasha asks. He stops at a vegetable vendor, eyeing some produce.

"Change Levi."

A soft voice resounds in his head.

LOVE DOES NOT BOAST.

"I didn't," Yasha replies. "God did."

Ben-Chalfai sighs. Not the answer he's looking for. "But it *was* you," he insists. "Levi said you were the only one… the only one there to… reach out to him."

Yasha nods.

"So?" ben-Chalfai demands.

Yasha shrugs. He buys some fresh figs, popping a couple into his mouth.

"What you did was impossible." Ben-Chalfai is getting frustrated with the lack of answers. He can feel his blood pressure rising. "Was it witchcraft? Sorcery? What? Did you bargain with Levi for something in return?"

"Levi owes me nothing," Yasha replies kindly.

"Then how?" demands ben-Chalfai. "And why?"

Yasha smiles at his new inductee, eyes twinkling. "Love."

Ben-Chalfai narrows his eyes, brows furrowing.

"It was love."

A shift has happened. Ben-Chalfai lines up the crosshairs in his mind with the face of Yasha in the scope. His intensity has found a new target. He will disprove him and ultimately embarrass him. Science and medicine are the authority here, not imaginary forces. He feels like he's being tricked somehow. *Perhaps bribery? Blackmail?* He scours his brain for plausible objectives. His family members, though idiosyncratic, are upstanding and law-abiding Israeli citizens. Most of his relatives have been duped into thinking it's a free gift. But ben-Chalfai knows no such thing exists. *There's always a tangible explanation. There's always an angle.*

Ben-Chalfai, of course, keeps these last thoughts to himself. No point in divulging his goal of proving that there's something subversive about Yasha. He doesn't anticipate that the mission will take long. His deep sense of duty to family and to medicine will expose the fraud.

In turn, Yasha just winks, bidding the scientist to follow.

36

FOUR DAYS EARLIER

Humidity hangs in the afternoon air, clinging to Yasha and his cohort as they walk through Jerusalem with a purpose. They're on a mission, though the six members remain uninformed. As they make their way among the neighborhoods, Yasha catches wind of something. He slows down and turns his ear to the north. He thinks for a moment and abruptly changes direction. His heart strings have been tugged. The men ask where they're headed, but Yasha gives no reply. They have learned to follow regardless.

Soon, sounds of laughter and shouting become obvious. The voices of children are unmistakable. They round a corner and see, in a nearby courtyard, a group of boys kicking a well-worn black and white ball. The cell members wonder why Yasha takes interest. After ten minutes of watching the boys holler and nudge each other as they run toward two makeshift goals, the group starts getting restless.

Kefa says, "Let's go."

But Yasha doesn't move. He continues to stare at the raucous boys and mutters quietly to himself. A small boy in ragged clothes scores a goal suddenly, and his teammates rejoice. Yasha claps then turns to exit the courtyard when one of the older boys catches his eye and runs over. The other boys follow suit. The boys feel enthralled that adults have been watching them play.

Immediately, Kefa, Yaakov, and Faivel run interference, rebuking the kids. "Go away! Go back to your game."

Yasha glares at them. "Don't push these children away. Don't ever get between them and me," he says, irate. "They're at the very center of life in my realm." His companions look at him in confusion. Children at the center? Makes no sense.

One of the youngest boys looks Yasha in the eyes and says, "Come! Do you want to play?"

Yasha glances at his men, who frown and scowl and shake their heads. Don't they have better things to do with their time?

The older boys begin yelling with excitement, "Yes! Yes! Play!" Hands big and little grab Yasha's arms and pull him toward the makeshift field. To his followers' chagrin, he doesn't resist. In fact, Yasha races them back to the courtyard and captures the ball first. Everyone falls into play. The children run and shout, thrilled to have an adult kicking the football with them. Cheers and groans, laughter and competition bounce in every direction. Some of the cell members stare in wonder, others glance around to see if people are noticing. None know what to do exactly.

Fifteen minutes later, Yasha strides over to his followers and wipes a sleeve across his drenched forehead. Out of breath, he leans over, hands resting on knees. The May warmth only adds to his unexpected physical exertion.

"Mark my words," he says panting, "unless you accept God's realm in the simplicity of a child, you'll never be a part of it."

An eruption of celebration rises from the courtyard as another goal is scored. The game ends, and once more the children run to Yasha. He picks up a couple of the youngest ones, barely five years old, and holds them close. Heads of dark curls and big eyes look at him with admiration and awe. Yasha tickles the ones in his arms, and they squirm back down. Before anyone can object, he lays his hands on their heads and affirms each boy, proclaiming his worth and ability to make a difference in the world.

Suddenly, Yasha notices a set of eyes hiding by a wall on the east side. He motions for the boy to come over, but instead the boy withdraws.

The others inform Yasha that the child's name is Levi and that his face is deformed. A severe cleft lip. When he was born, the boys explain, Levi's parents were ashamed and embarrassed by his deformity, so they immediately had procedures done to fix it. The treatment was done too early, as it turns out, and as he grew older, his features became more distorted. A gaping hole separates his top lip, stretching up from there through his gums and into his nose that is bent sideways. Clusters of flesh-like small balloons congregate where smooth skin should be. The deep scars only add to the visual conglomeration. Everything is affected—his speech, his breathing, his eating. All that on top of his heart defect.

And so, he hides. None of the boys invite Levi to play as the deformity vexes them. Scares some, even. He doesn't attend school, doesn't have friends. Has felt universal rejection all his life.

Compassion surges through Yasha's chest, and he stays the arrival of tears. Within seconds, Yasha nears a timid Levi, who's peeking around the corner yet trying to blend in with the cement wall. He cannot be more than six or seven years old. Levi digs his chin into his chest to hide his face. Slowly, Yasha bends down so the two are eye level.

LOVE BELIEVES ALL THINGS, Yasha hears within.

Especially in the impossible.

The cell members watch him talk to the boy, expecting him to encourage Levi as he did the others. A running commentary from the older boys fills the air, some expressing fear, some disdain. Why would Yasha pay attention to Levi? No one else does. Yet after some minutes, the boys and the cell members see Yasha walking toward them with Levi riding piggyback, his face buried into Yasha's shoulder blade.

All the chatter stops once Yasha arrives. His face betrays nothing.

"He wants to play," Yasha says. The top of Levi's head peers over Yasha's shoulder, eyes reading everyone.

The boys look at one another, their feelings transparent. They hesitate and shuffle their feet. Some groan. They suddenly are bereft of chatter.

"Oh, for Peteness' sake!" Arye says, conflating phrases, his compassion for Levi evident.

"For Pete's sake," his brother whispers in his ear. "Or goodness' sake. Take your pick."

"Oh, for goodness' sake," Arye repeats, "let him play!"

The eldest boy reluctantly nods consent. In the end, respect for Yasha trumps all uncertainty. "He can play."

Yasha smiles and swings Levi around, plopping him in front of the boys. Immediately, they start screaming and pointing. A few cell members flinch; Faivel and Natan instinctively look away. Levi tries to cover his face, burying it in Yasha's arms, when he realizes what the boys are shouting.

"It's not…it's not…" stammers one child.

"Something strange happened to you!" says another.

"He looks *normal!*"

Levi looks up at Yasha with huge eyes. *What happened? What did you do?* he wonders. But Yasha just chuckles. The look on Levi's perfectly formed face sends ripples of love through Yasha's body. Levi begins to touch his face. Normal lips! A normal nose! Smooth skin! Arye pulls out a phone and takes his picture, showing it to Levi. He sees himself with unmarred features for the first time in his life. Touching his face with shaky hands, Levi confirms that he's not dreaming, that his mind isn't tricking him. He traces his lips, his nose, his teeth and gums, searching for any malformations. None. Even the scars are gone. Tears form in his eyes, each one declaring bottomless thanks. He cannot speak.

Yasha nods to the field and says, "Go!"

Levi touches his chest. "My heart?"

"Also normal," Yasha promises.

The two stare in silence at one another, smiles tethering their hearts. Levi lurches forward, wrapping his arms around Yasha's waist. The six cell members marvel at this miracle, wondering if Yasha knew that Levi would be here today. Was it mere coincidence or a divine appointment? And how exactly did he heal him?

Levi debates running home to show his family—they will be dumbfounded yet overjoyed—but he's never been included in football games. Yasha, sensing his dilemma, removes Levi's arms from around his waist and bends down.

"Go," he says gently. "Go play."

Levi nods and decides his family can wait. Squeals of laughter erupt from the boys. They gather around Levi and cheer, jumping with excitement. Levi beams, his cheeks flushed and pinched from a surplus of smiles. En masse, they run to the makeshift field and divide into teams. Both sides argue over who gets to have the new player. He has become a celebrity.

Yochanan's eyes bulge with disbelief. *What is the probability of that happening?* he thinks. His brother notices and reads his thoughts.

"I'm sure it's just a fluke," he quips sarcastically.

Faivel smiles at Natan, as if to prove Yasha is who Faivel claimed he was a couple of days ago. "You're welcome," he whispers. Natan hates that his best friend has an annoying propensity to always be right. It's infuriating yet somehow comforting. The two exchange looks, both comprehending the adventure they've fallen into.

Kefa stares hard at Yasha. He sees beyond the circumstances, beyond the miracle. Normal limitations are missing. These types of occurrences won't stay uncelebrated for long, though. Word will spread and ignite everything. For better or worse. Kefa has no clue that the next year will change his life. As well as the world.

37

TWO DAYS EARLIER

Arye and Kefa, Yochanan and Yaakov follow Yasha as he moves around the capital city on a beautiful early-May morning. The first four members of the cell, soon to be known as the Twelve, keep their eyes open and mouths shut. They know that Yasha is on a mission—that he's searching for more men. Soon the next member comes into Yasha's view.

Number 5. *Analytical; automation savvy; generally disheveled; bad at solving riddles, which infuriates him.*

Yasha approaches the café in measured steps. A small outdoor table at the end of a largely empty patio sits covered with a laptop, phone, and other electronic devices—a buffet of technology. Fingers on everything at once is Faivel, tech geek. Absorbed in his work, the young man eventually notices that he suddenly has company. He lowers the expensive headphones covering his ears. Yasha moves in close and drops a riddle in his lap. One he's never heard before. One pertaining to himself. And to the Messiah.

Faivel stares up at Yasha. Smooth black skin, brown hooded eyes, goatee. A short salt and pepper afro that could stand some grooming. Not concerned with fashion, as his old cargo pants and shrunken graphic tee shirt declare. He could probably make a living hacking into corporations and foreign governments, but his Ethiopian mother would kill him faster than the Israelis would. His brain scrambles to unlock the riddle.

He regards Yasha's companions, scanning them quickly like one of his computer programs. Nothing is making sense. *Why has this man solicited me with a riddle? Who are the others? What's their agenda?* After a minute of awkward silence, he surrenders.

"Tell me," Faivel says.

Yasha grins and points at Faivel. "Come, follow me. You will find out the answer and much more," he promises.

"Who are you?" asks Faivel.

Yasha turns back, looking straight into his dark eyes. "Yasha ha Natzeret," he says.

"Natzeret?" says Faivel. "The Palestinian town in Galilee?" Another piece of info that doesn't make sense. *Somehow it must all fit together*, he thinks, *the riddle and his place of origin.* What is he missing? And why does this stranger with palpable magnetism want Faivel to follow him?

Yasha waves his hand, beckoning the new recruit. He and the four others begin moving in a different direction, away from the café. Faivel waits a beat, calculating the odds of missing something important. He often operates on intuition, regardless of circumstances. A quick glance around confirms that he's not being watched. Though he knows nothing about these men, he knows when to recognize an intriguing opportunity. Faivel jumps up and packs his gear. He catches up with the small crew, sizing them up.

A low hum begins to form among the men. What is happening? Where are they going? What exactly will they be doing? Yasha explains to the five of them his invitation to impact the world, bringing deliverance, bringing hope. None has a clue as to what he's talking about. Not to worry, Yasha conveys, others have been required to trust blindly through-out the history of their people. Usually ends better than expected.

Ten blocks away, a throng of young Israelis push forward toward the makeshift stage. Atop stands a thirty-three-year-old man known as the Immerser speaking loudly. Long dreadlocks thrash down his back, thick muscles push at his clothes. His eyes are fiery and intense. He investigates the faces below him, searching for those eager enough to make a change.

Their eyes declare a hunger, their body language a thirst. He must give them the message, the one he received while out in the desert.

Most are willing to recognize the need for revolution in the land of Israel, but some remain resistant. The Immerser senses these individuals the way he senses the proximity of water with a supernatural olfactory awareness. The naysayers—soldiers and members of government—murmur loudly enough for plenty of ears to hear. Criticism thrown like missiles. They represent the current administration's lack of morality. The Immerser once again voices his opinion that evil and corruption continue to reign at the highest levels. He once again calls out Ohred and Saidoreh—reminds the crowd that the prime minister, his wife, and the entire Israeli governance are moral failures. No one is outside the law, especially God's law. He knows intuitively that these men, the naysayers, have been sent by the government to discern agendas. Potential uprisings make them nervous. And vocalized judgment raises their hackles.

"Brood of snakes!" the Immerser yells suddenly. He glares at the government men with a fierce passion. "What do you think you're doing slithering down here? Do you think a little water on your snakeskins is going to make any difference?"

They glance sideways at one another, unsure of the right response. They claim to want peace yet the weapons at their sides and in their mouths demonstrate otherwise.

The Immerser continues his confrontation. "It's your *life* that must change, not your skin! That is why I came here—to immerse you in truth so you can get a fresh start with God."

Contrition cannot be found in soldiers' backpacks or politicians' pockets. People of all spheres drift in to catch a glimpse and an earful of this renegade preacher. Treated as a show more than a service, a selfie opportunity.

"We are descendants of Avraham—true Israelis," a voice cries out in defiance.

The Immerser predicts this outburst. He smiles and chuckles at the cavalier proclamation.

"That's neither here nor there. Descendants of Avraham are a dime a dozen," the Immerser replies. "God can make children from stones if he wants. What counts is your life. Is it green and blossoming? Because if it's deadwood, it goes on the fire."

Murmurs amid the protesters arise further. "Then what are we supposed to do?"

The Immerser answers, "If you have two coats, give one away. And do the same with your food."

Others from the political arena speak out, challenging the Immerser. Taunting him, essentially. "What should *we* do?"

"No more extortion—collect only what is required by law."

Some are satisfied while others push for more. A soldier in the back demands, "And what shall *we* do?"

The Immerser looks past his eyes into his wounded soul. "No shakedowns, no blackmail—and be content with your rations." He knows that the naysayers have been sent from Jerusalem by men in high authority. Peaceful protests against the status quo come to attention as the volume and attendance increases.

"It's who you are and the way you live that count before God."

"Who are you?" a government man in front questions. "That we may tell those who sent us."

A second voice chimes in. "What do you have to say for yourself?"

"I'm Yochanan the Immerser," he confesses, denying nothing. "I'm thunder in the desert!" His loud cackle reverberates throughout the crowd.

Looking around, he catches the eye of a certain man. The face is familiar and immediately he feels a rush of excitement and hope. Hair stands up on the back of his neck. Electricity suddenly pulses through the air, and the Immerser wonders who else can feel it. This is it! Yasha has arrived! He and the Immerser lock eyes.

"Listen!" he booms. "A person you don't recognize has taken his stand in your midst. He comes after me, but he is not in second place to me. I'm not even worthy to hold his coat for him."

The crowd looks around trying to pinpoint the man. Commotion escalates, bodies sway. Is it a superstar? A dignitary? Even the five cell members who stand near Yasha wonder who the Immerser's talking about.

The Immerser shouts again what he's been saying for months. "The *real action* comes next! The main character in this drama—compared to him I'm a mere stagehand—will change your life. He'll place everything true in its proper place and everything false he'll put out with the trash to be burned."

Kefa and Arye exchange looks. Didn't they just talk about this yesterday? The Immerser, how he mentions "the real action," how Yasha had suddenly materialized in the middle of their conversation? What are the odds? Arye gets goosebumps.

The Immerser jumps off the platform and weaves through the crowd. Voices banter, heads crane to get a glimpse. He finds and embraces his cousin Yasha with a hug that lifts him from the ground. He kisses the side of his neck. They both laugh, extending the embrace, slapping each other's backs. How long since they have seen one another? Where have you been? How's your mother? That beard!

"So, you know each other?" Kefa asks.

Yasha and the Immerser laugh. "For a while now," Yasha answers. In true form, he leaves them wondering. Eventually they will discover more. For now, it's enough.

"Did you like what I told them?" the Immerser says.

Yasha smiles yet thinks of the crowd's obstinacy. "How can I account for the people of this generation? They're like spoiled children complaining to their parents." *Oy vey*, he thinks, rolling his eyes. His cousin laughs. "Their eyes are open but don't see a thing. Their ears are open but don't hear a thing."

The Immerser smiles broadly. "And that's why we're here!"

Swiftly, Yasha's cousin pulls him onto the stage. The crowd cheers, eager to hear more. Yasha takes the microphone and declares over the holy land a campaign of peace. A revolution is coming to the land, he proclaims, one of authority and proper allegiances. A countercultural movement aimed at change for those who crave it.

The first five members of the Twelve absorb Yasha's declarations. None of them, though, understand that the calling goes beyond a brief adventure. Instead, a lifetime decision that will echo throughout generations to come hangs in the balance. Will they accept? Will they turn away from Yasha for the promise of something less provocative and potentially dangerous?

Faivel's wheels still spin the riddle Yasha posed to him. It drives him mad to be stuck on the answer. Typically, he prides himself on these types of mental puzzles. Taking things apart and reassembling them comes naturally to Faivel. His brain thrives on such cognitive challenges. This one, however, has him stumped. Only when he shifts gears to decipher hidden meanings does the answer come to him. His face immediately brightens as the unseen light bulb illuminates in his head.

An opportunity to partner with the impossible.

Faivel quickly disappears, looking for a small shop on the main thoroughfare. An old Arab man with a large colorful hookah sits in the doorway adjacent. Inside, he bounds over to his best friend from Galilee. They had essentially grown up together despite their vastly different backgrounds—a ying-yang relationship.

"Natan," Faivel says with a mischievous smile, "I think we found him."

"Who?"

"The one Moshe wrote of, the one told by the prophets…" Faivel pauses for dramatic purposes. He knows that his best friend studies everything from ancient literature to the Holy Scriptures to modern bestsellers.

Natan is a perpetual university student, moving from degree to degree. For years, he studied the Torah and subsequent Hebrew writings looking for the key to unlock the mystery of the Jewish Messiah. He knows every theory, every prophecy, every angle ever written. And yet it remains a mystery. But Faivel claims to have found him?

"His name's Yasha…"

"Who?"

"From Natzeret!"

Natan guffaws loudly. "Natzeret? You've got to be kidding. I don't have time for your silly riddles," he says. "Nothing worth anything comes out of Natzeret." They banter for some minutes, Faivel promising it's no riddle and Natan spouting rapid-fire reasons that the Messiah cannot possibly emerge from Natzeret. They talk over and around each other like only best friends can—animated and passionate. When they both reach the end of their respective arguments, Natan attempts to resume his work. But Faivel stops him.

With an odd smile, he says. "Come, see for yourself."

Minutes later, Faivel is at the foot of the stage with Natan a few steps behind. He is wary of his best friend's exposition. And he is completely unprepared for a radical encounter.

As he comes around the edges of the crowd, Natan hears a pointed shout. "Now *there's* a real Israelite, not a false bone in his body." Yasha smiles at him broadly. He stops cold.

Natan. Number 6. *University student; trustworthy; good judge of character; currently memorizing Dostoyevsky and the Torah.*

Yasha hops down from the stage and makes his way to his new cell member. Tall and skinny, clean shaven, receding hairline, round glasses. Driven by knowledge, prestige, and intellectual pride. Doesn't get easily persuaded, especially by unestablished doctrines of any nature.

Natan says, "Where did you get that idea? You don't know me." He's leery beyond belief. Something isn't right.

"Before Faivel called you," Yasha replies, "I saw you under that fig tree."

Natan narrows his eyes, furrows his brows. He peers at Yasha from behind his glasses. No one had seen him wander through the orchard a few days ago. He made sure of it, or so he thought. He needed time to process parts of the Tanakh, the Old Testament, that he had long misunderstood. Had his cries of clarity to God worked? Was this man bringing him the answers? He whispers to himself with a mixture of confusion and fear, "A prophet of God...?"

Yasha chuckles. "You've become a believer simply because I say I saw you one day sitting under the fig tree?" His laugh resonates deeply but does not offend. It is mysterious yet innocent.

The other men exchange looks. Everyone is trying to make sense of the strange conversation. Is Yasha some sort of mystic sage? An oracle?

Yasha knows their thoughts. And their doubts. He cannot wait to open their eyes to a different realm. He replies, "You haven't seen *anything* yet!"

And, with a quick turn, he heads out of the crowd moving toward the Armenian neighborhood. The men, though somewhat guarded, quickly fall in step. In one day, their lives swing from predictable to unimaginable. They haven't the faintest idea of what awaits them. That twelve seemingly unrelated men would be thrust together in a group and collectively change the world.

Behind them, the Immerser has taken command of the stage again, grasping the attention of the crowd by telling stories of his past and making proclamations of the future. Citizens and officials alike are forcefully challenged to change ways, to unite under the heading of peace and justice. This won't be the last rally for the Immerser. Word of him is spreading rapidly despite his grassroots operation. The Immerser has taken his rhetoric far outside the kibbutz, and others will follow. Social media and cyber technology, while key to disseminating information rapidly, are a double-edged sword. The future of Israel depends on the ability of the government to squash all uprisings that undermine the delicate balance of the land. Months from now, the Immerser will learn this the hard way. His divine assignment, however, cannot be thwarted.

He watches Yasha move to the outskirts of the crowd, giddy with anticipation. Yasha turns and makes eye contact with his cousin, giving the secret signal that they had created years ago. Nothing can hold them back. Not now.

38

48 HOURS EARLIER

Hovered over a low fire, Yochanan ben Zecharyah—a man known as the Immerser—sautés onions and some dried fruit in a cast iron skillet. The aroma wafts throughout Kibbutz Samar and draws a small crowd. Behind them, a blazing sunset covers the dry desert sky. The mountains and plateaus burn with color. Cool air begins to settle upon them, the temperature dropping handfuls of degrees at a time. He adds date honey to his mixture and then some walnuts. Pairs upon pairs of eyes watch his skillet while ushering in the peaceful evening. Soon, he spoons the mixture over prepared rice, and bowls are filled.

The Immerser loves to cook but hardly eats. Mostly vegan, really. His body betrays stereotypes. Short, muscular, and tanned from long years in the desert, he looks more like a well-honed wrestler than anything. His thick hair, dreadlocked and long, has never been cut. His clothes are oddly patterned, his molded shoes unconventional. His eyes glow with fire, a spiritual burning deep within.

He thinks back to earlier that morning at the Dead Sea. Images of him floating in the densely salted, emerald waters bring back a swath of emotions. Every so often, he escapes there to clear his head, to receive direction. On a makeshift island in the middle of the saltiest body of water on earth stands a small lone tree surrounded by white salt flats. The Immerser feels a strange connection to this unusual feat of nature. Odd, meaningful, unique. A lone tree and a lone voice. Life surrounded by death yet emerging fixed. As he floated in the shallow waters beneath the tree, he felt an overwhelming sense that the time had come.

For months, the Immerser has been disseminating ideas of righteous living in the kibbutz, in smaller cities, in desert enclaves. Picked up by social media, spread by wagging tongues. Again and again, he's announced imminent change coming to Israel. His message is a wakeup call followed by a call to action. He's been a lone voice, unwavering in passion, undeterred in mission. Many people have ignored, ridiculed, or questioned his message. Few have heeded the call. Fewer still will end up joining the real action.

Now, the Immerser stares out into the dark heavens and listens for that still, small voice. He knows when to question and when to obey.

A woman with a mouthful of food asks if anyone has heard about the latest scandal regarding the prime minister. Eyes roll, breaths huff in disgust. But he looks intently at the woman, feeling an impending significance. Allegations of illicitly receiving money, bribery charges, and financial wrongdoing, she explains. This is after Prime Minister Ohred has recently emerged from a different scandal involving previous governmental affairs. Though Ohred fights for his people, accusations of misdeeds have plagued him for years. Somehow, he's been able to evade the fallout from his scandals as prosecutors search in vain to locate concrete evidence.

This time, the woman explains, it's not just the prime minister. His wife, Saidoreh, is in on it too. Apparently, she's been using state funds for her personal use in several ways. And not just a small amount. Tens of thousands of shekels.

The others chime in, calling their prime minister and his wife names, spewing hatred at their country's corruption.

"It gets worse," she explains.

"What do you mean?" the Immerser asks.

"It turns out that Saidoreh is stealing money to punish her husband and placate her own anger…because the prime minister was caught in an affair with another woman."

The Immerser bolts up as if hit by a spark from the fire. He paces back and forth, murmuring under his breath. The woman glances at him, sensing that the atmosphere has shifted. In mid-stride, he stops, turning to the small crowd, his face full of indignation.

"It is *wrong!*" he tells them. "The only reason she married him was to gain access to political funds. The coffers of the people have been gleaned in an unjust, illegal manner. It's manipulation—pure manipulation! And now her sin has escalated his sin!"

The Immerser continues his virtuous diatribe, calling for her arrest and punishment. Calling for the prime minister to step down, to be indicted. Accountability must be rendered. His passion for righteousness is as densely wound as his waist-long dreads that whip around in serpentine motion as he paces back and forth. His voice rises and falls as he shouts out for people—all people, including the nation's leaders—to turn from inherent wickedness and embrace a more just and pure way of living, outlined by the God of the universe. There's no time for foul play anymore, he argues. The world has seen enough injustice and cruelty and immorality, and it's groaning for change. Broad is the path to destruction. Narrow is the one that leads to a better, more secure life.

Those around him, the Immerser's supporters, agree and join in the chorus of a righteous denunciation. He bathes his listeners with ethical and virtuous ideologies, baptizing them into a new mindset. A young teenager sitting with the group logs into a social media account, posting quotes and videos as fast as he can type. A verbal firing squad against the highest Israeli office ensues. Feeling a holy righteousness upon him, the Immerser proclaims an end to the madness that surrounds the prime minister and his administration. Too much has gone on for too long. This must *end.*

In an instant, the people of Jerusalem and all of Israel will hear that voice—a sole voice crying out in the southern desert wilderness. The video and the message will eventually spark events to bring about his downfall. But all of that is still months away.

"It's time the people had a God-fearing, Torah-abiding leader. Someone who will follow the honorable ways of our ancestors, like Moshe and Avraham," he declares. "Cheating, stealing, lying, corruption…and now adultery! Where does it stop?" He stops and shakes his head. "Only murder is left."

Suddenly, the Immerser feels a twinge in his belly. No vision, no voices, just an overwhelming sense of certainty. He can't explain the meaning, but he knows somehow that Prime Minister Ohred will eventually have blood on his hands. The forces behind this are already in motion. He can't identify it, and he can't stop it. The Immerser sinks to his knees, humility and submissiveness taking over. His heart switches direction toward a posture of genuine, reverent concern. He begins to pray silently, rocking forward, minute after minute. Tears spring up. Human life is precious, yet spilled blood is coming. The question is, whose?

With this thought lingering, the Immerser rises and begins to move quickly toward his sleeping quarters.

"Where are you going?" the teenager yells.

Turning his head, he yells in return, "To the city! The time for action has come!"

39

EIGHT DAYS EARLIER

Mid-afternoon, dozens of people weave in and around the open-air shops of Jaffa's flea market. Art studios, clothing boutiques, restaurants, and bars call to patrons, foreign and domestic. A few blocks over, the ancient port of Jaffa shores up against the Mediterranean Sea in stark contrast to the modern buildings of Tel Aviv/Yafo, a stone's throw north. A pastel rainbow of arched doors lines the main thoroughfare that parallels the coast. Centuries-old limestone buildings sit stacked up a hill overlooking the blue-green waters. A red and white lighthouse perches faithfully by the marina. Slews of colorful boats bob, tied to the dock.

Yasha moves purposefully up and down cobblestone streets, looking, listening. He tries to make eye contact with strangers, desiring to pass on an unspoken message of grace and peace. But few people look his way. They are absorbed in their own tasks, interacting with those who are familiar, shunning those who are different.

Suddenly, the aroma of warm spices wafts toward him. Yasha looks around to identify its source. Tucked on the far end of the marina sits a modest food truck. The sign is obscured from this angle, but as he draws near, a smile forms.

"5 LOAVES 2 FISH NOMADIC KITCHEN"

Normal crowds are absent as it's 3:00 p.m. Sounds, though, of a motor humming and knives chopping run steadily. The menu board displays a few culinary options: *shakshuka* with tomato, egg, peppers, and onions; grilled fish with Israeli couscous; braised lamb pita with tomato-cucumber relish; and *shish taouk*, a spicy kebab dish.

Yasha watches the two men working inside the food truck, unaware and sweating from the heat and the tight quarters. Early forties, he guesses. They move around the truck with a rhythmic cadence as if they've been in this environment for years. The younger-looking one hums and focuses on assessing spices. The older one starts for the back door when a set of penetrating green eyes stop him cold. The face is benign but somehow enticing.

"Return after four," the cook says, pointing at the hours posted.

Yasha places a large amount of money on the ledge, enough to feed the two others with him, Kefa and Ayre. That's when the cook notices them also. *Can't people read the operating hours?* he thinks. He looks back at Yasha. *Maybe this guy doesn't speak Hebrew. Maybe he's hearing-impaired. Looks like a questionable character, what with the odd tee-shirt and all.* Yaakov wonders what his logo "THE ACTION" means. The cook again points to the sign and turns away.

"Whatever you've got," Yasha says firmly, placing the order.

Those eyes, that smile. The cook inhales deeply, then acquiesces. A few minutes later, sandwiches, pitas, and some couscous salad appear on the ledge. The three men take their pick and spread out on the nearby curb for a mid-afternoon snack. Yasha is mouth-deep into a fisherman's sandwich when the cook appears next to him, stained apron around his thick middle. His dark eyes, thick eyebrows, and bushy, black beard offset his bald head. Muscular frame covered by a black t-shirt, scores of tattoos revealing themselves. Intimidating features. He hands Yasha his change, but Yasha waves it off. Nobody refuses to take that much money back. The cook eyes his patron warily.

After profusely complimenting the cook, Yasha wipes his sticky fingers on a paper napkin. He feels for sauce on his face and finds a section. Laughing, he again praises the cook for the delightful surprise. Food truck options normally aren't that flavorful.

"Tell me," Yasha says, wiping his mouth again, "what's your story?"

The cook gazes at his truck and sighs with satisfaction. He might as well sit. Forearms resting on his knees, he's twice as big as an average man. "For many years, I worked in a prison kitchen."

He unwinds the threads of his past, moving in reverse order. He and his brother, the other chef, had pooled a little money because they wanted to buy a food truck. A mobile kitchen. Years of cooking in prison facilities forced them to be creative with limited supplies and sparse spices. It caused them to dream of cooking better food on the outside, of trying their hand at something different. The prison kitchen, challenging and severely restricted, was better than the interrogations, though. Torture methods by Israeli intelligence meant long periods without sleep, being tied up in contorted positions, being cuffed and beaten. Information was squeezed out of them using intimidation, humiliation, and psychological torture. Political activism had its price, landing him in jail. That's where he joined his brother, incarcerated a month prior. Both accused of firebombing different places. Both convicted.

Yasha takes it all in. He looks up into the sky, silently acknowledging how he'll experience much of the same physical torture. All of a sudden, he hears the voice inwardly.

Number 4. *Ambitious, intense; sarcastic and brutally honest; somewhat bloodthirsty; outstanding chef.*

"And you are?" Yasha asks.

"Yaakov," he replies. "Yaakov ben Zavdai."

"And your brother?"

"Yochanan."

Yasha glances into the truck. Medium build, short hair under Moroccan style cap, extra-long black beard. Same dark eyes and eyebrows like his brother. Prefers plain white V-neck shirts to Yaakov's perpetual black t-shirts. Looks, and is, younger than his sibling.

Again, the voice.

Number 3. *Black-and-white outlook; fights for justice and integrity; secretly desires to be famous.*

"And who are they?" Yaakov nods toward the other two men sitting further down.

"Arye and Kefa," answers Yasha.

Yaakov eyes them curiously. Both spotted with grease and grime—on their clothes, on their skin. He reads a different name on the work jumpsuit worn by Kefa. Odd and disconcerting.

Knowing his thoughts, Yasha says, "Used to be called Shimon. But I call him Kefa. Brothers like you and Yochanan. Sons of Yonah."

Yaakov ponders the proffered information in silence. Prison taught him to always be two steps ahead. He recognizes that something's afoot, though he can't determine if it's auspicious.

Arye and Kefa acknowledge the introduction, Arye offering compliments of the food. Words are brief, more left unspoken than spoken. Yaakov reads people well, another gift of incarceration. He opens his mouth to probe further but thinks better of it. He slaps his knees and rises. But Yasha grabs his thick, tattooed arm, pulling him back down.

Reams of potential stretch within Yaakov, as Yasha sees it. He can channel the passion, the lightning into something greater than political activism. He can use this man to start a counterculture movement based on peace and compassion rather than violence that will ripple for generations to come. Yaakov's weakness is actually his strength.

Yasha lays out a proposition for the Zavdai brothers. One that offers great power and promise. A chance to make an indelible impact on the world. Yaakov shakes his head, tight grin on his lips.

"Yochanan won't go for it," he replies.

"Afraid of repercussions?" Yasha asks.

"For some reason," Yaakov deadpans.

Though they have sworn off activism for good—not worth the potential prison torture—a small part of him still yearns for it. Makes him feel alive. Like he's leaving his mark. But Yaakov worries about the rami-fications, about his business. As will Yochanan. *What'll they do with all the supplies: the spices, the meat, and fresh fish?* His thoughts float out toward the boats tied up some yards away.

"Don't worry," Yasha says with a grin, as if reading Yaakov's mind. He hands him the empty paper bowl, remnants of fish sauce dotting the bottom. "From now on, you'll be fishing for people."

40

THE DAY BEFORE

Yasha sits atop the tower overlooking Mar Saba monastery, backpack at his side. It is a windy April day. Streams of cool and warm air alternate, brushing his stoic face, rustling his dark hair. The seasons are changing; spring is here. Passover has been celebrated. *Shavuot*, the Feast of Firstfruits, waits patiently in the wings.

Below, the stone fortress—an imposing castle of sorts—nestles tightly into the cliff, cascading down hundreds of feet toward the green Kidron valley that sits halfway between Jerusalem and the Dead Sea. Yasha knows his life, his purpose also sit halfway between two places: heaven and earth. Mar Saba, an ancient bastion of solitude and peace, emanates decades of spiritual connectivity. Foundations laid long ago send up the incense of prayers, sweet and fragrant. Yasha breathes deeply, a slight aroma of frankincense and myrrh filling his senses. Faint echoes of monks reciting holy incantations drift on the wind.

He reaches into the backpack looking for an apple. Instead, he finds a white envelope with his name on the front. He examines it for other information. None. Surprised, he looks around but sees no one. Inside is a letter. Two paragraphs really. The first indicates a green light to proceed. The second gives instructions for the assignment. Finances are in place. Accounts are secure. One voice fills his heart.

You are My son, chosen and marked by My love, pride of My life.

He no longer questions its origin, as he instinctively knows. He's tuned into the frequency of heaven. Aligned perfectly like a dial on the

AM radio, picking up direct messages.

Again, the voice. *Love through change. And change it all through love.*

Yasha understands the system, he sees the challenge. It will be anything but easy, though it will be worth it. He turns, paper in hand, and kneels down, folding forward until his forehead rests on the ground. His hands are outstretched in resignation. Words of the *Shema*, the declaration of faith, fill the space.

Hear O Israel, the Lord our God, the Lord is One.

Immediately, a fast-moving reel of images plays in his head. Graphic scenes are prophetic pictures of the next year. Each of the Twelve, all the enemy groups, and everyone in between. From government officials to friends to enemies. Ohred, Reuven, Goren, and Nakdimon; El'azar, Marta, and Miriam; Saidoreh, bar-Abbas, and even Yehudas. Images of Magda and the Immerser also weave in and out. Joy, intense pain, severe loss, victory. To be the rise and fall of many in Israel. To be a sign from God. To reveal the thoughts of many hearts. He can feel it acutely. So much will happen in a condensed amount of time. The next twelve months will bring extraordinary highs and extreme lows—life, torture, death, and everything in between. From this April to next, the world will become a different place.

He sits up and inhales sharply, eyes wide. He is terrified yet senses a familiar peace. Closing his eyes once more, he offers a deep sigh of acceptance and nods his head ever so slightly.

His assignment is clear: to love. The outcast, the marginalized, the sinner and the righteous. Love for humanity will lead him to call out those who commit injustices. It will lead him to find people, to meet people where they are, and to beckon them to a life of more. Inviting them to know the One who sent him. He will influence people who will influence nations. All through love. Love is the motivation, the currency of heaven.

The last words on the folded paper pulse through his mind.

LOVE NEVER FAILS.

TWELVE

• • •

Hours later, Jerusalem comes into view, spread out in shades of warm lime-stone. It's potentially the most volatile city on the planet. Domes, spires, and minarets freckle the landscape. *The epicenter,* he thinks. Though not born within its walls, he knows everything starts and ends here.

Yasha walks alone around the city as if looking for something lost. Or perhaps *someone* lost. He stops every now and then, looking at certain people, evaluating them silently. After late morning turns to afternoon, he suddenly stops.

An old mechanics' garage sits open, yawning grease and carbon fumes. In the back, a man who appears to be eighty sits on a low stool listening to modern Arabic techno streaming from the radio. Two men donned in well-worn jumpsuits work on a forty-year-old car resting on blocks. Yasha observes that the car is just a metal shell, though he imagines the finished product gleaming with glossy paint against the BMW hood symbol.

One of the mechanics lies on his back on a creeper underneath the car, twisting a wrench in endless circles. He eventually slides out and rests against the door, and one side of Yasha's mouth rises in a grin. The young man is stocky and medium height with kind eyes. His dark hair, held back by sunglasses, falls in curls at his shoulders. His ruddy face is flushed from the stagnant air and Israeli sun. He wipes black smudges on his face with his sleeve. He yells to his partner over the music, asking how much longer they're going to work. Jokes are thrown over the car like rockets, meant to get a reaction.

After a few minutes, the one on the creeper begins talking about a guy making waves in Israel. He describes him and his approach to impacting the masses. Comes from deep in the southern desert. On some kibbutz.

"Have you heard?" he asks.

"About the Immerser?"

Listening, Yasha switches his gaze to the taller mechanic on the other side of the car. He's big and muscular with concentrated, dark eyes and darker eyebrows. His bald head and skin are noticeably tanned. No hair on his oval face, just smudges of grease and sweat. The man doesn't smile as much as his coworker, and Yasha reads in him a well-defined intensity. He's focused on putting back together the original engine, the task of reassembly challenging and time-consuming.

"Yes," says the one on the creeper.

Seems like another humanitarian with an agenda, the older mechanic confesses. They come and go, like volunteers at a dig site. What they leave behind has little impact, in his opinion. Besides, he doesn't trust anyone sporting dreadlocks and, no doubt, a strong patchouli odor.

"His ideas are interesting," the shorter one says, "but he keeps referring to someone else…someone significant, supposedly. More powerful and influential."

"Does he give a name?"

"No," he says.

"Then why give it attention?" the taller one asks.

"Because of what he declared recently."

"And that was what?"

"He said, '*The real action comes next.*' Whoever he is, the Immerser sure thinks he's going to make a huge impact."

The tall mechanic absorbs this statement and considers how it might influence the land of Israel. He desires to see real, positive change in his beloved country. Too much hatred, too much unrest. If only he could fix it like he fixes cars. Deep down he craves being part of the action. He always wanted to make his mark on Israel in a lasting way. Not fame, necessarily, just influence. He thought that was supposed to happen during his military service with the paratroopers, a coveted role of service, but his stubborn pride landed him discharged and humiliated. Ever since, his attitude has progressively soured. Negative and disillusioned, he hides in the family auto shop. Waiting, hoping somehow for another chance.

"Sounds like bad intel to me," he snorts.

Yasha watches from a short distance. The mechanics are obviously related, most likely brothers or cousins. Their nonchalant banter amuses Yasha, and he thinks about his own cousin Yochanan, called the Immerser. Fondness wells up in his chest. They had spent holidays together as children, laughing and wrestling like all other boys. As they grew older, their sense of calling and God-driven identity kept them close despite physical distance. Word of Yochanan's operation has reached Yasha, the implications set in motion: Yochanan is the prototype for Yasha. Their counterculture methods advance the same message. Yochanan has been laying the groundwork; now Yasha's time has come. Apparently, word has spread.

A voice begins to fill Yasha's ear with information, as if from an unseen earpiece. Supernatural communication.

Arye. *Jovial, approachable, optimist; loves playing cards.*

Shimon bar-Yonah. *Older brother to Arye; good with cars; passionate, headstrong, general pessimist.*

Number 2, Number 1.

"You are Shimon bar Yonah," Yasha says loudly, getting the taller man's attention. Shimon stops in mid-turn, squinting in the sunlight to focus on the stranger's face. The hairs on his neck spring up. He looks around, scanning the area. Nothing seems out of place. The strange man is alone.

Who is this guy? How does he know my name?

The mechanic gets the sense that this stranger has been watching, listening. But he just appeared out of nowhere. Wasn't there a minute ago. The brothers watch as he moves in—the older one skeptical, the younger one with piqued interest.

"Now," Yasha proclaims with a glint in his eye, "you shall be called Kefa, the Rock."

Shimon, now Kefa, stares hard at the man, flickers of recognition running through his mind. He has seen that face before. But where? A dream, perhaps? He cannot recall any details but has a strong sense of déjà vu. A strange feeling rises up in his chest, yet it's not fear. The captivating eyes penetrate his soul. Long moments pass without words, the intensity mounting.

Equally as noticeable is the shirt the man's wearing: navy with a white logo that reads "THE ACTION." Arrows shoot off the letters in every direction like a compass. Though it pays tribute to a British mod band from the 1960s, the owner couldn't resist the symbolism. A touch of self-appointed humor.

Kefa is stunned by the uncanny timing of it all. Could it be the mysterious man that he and Arye were just talking about? The one who the Immerser had referenced? The one who is supposedly the *real action*?

The brothers look at each other, perplexed. Intrigued. Coincidence? Arye grins at Kefa, his look saying it all.

"How about that?" he says.

Kefa furrows his brow, admitting nothing. *Impossible odds*, he thinks.

"Come on," Arye encourages, "let the dawn fall on you, then put the dots together."

Kefa suppresses a smirk. He loves Arye's unusual idioms and propensity for positivism. *What exactly is going on here?* he wonders. Kefa can't put his finger on it, but something feels significant. Long ago he learned to pay attention to possible coincidences, to the things that seemingly have no connection. If the Israeli military taught him anything, it taught him that. And to take calculated risks.

Arye jumps up off the creeper, wipes his hands on a towel, and makes his way toward Yasha. Kefa stands confused, hesitant. Yasha sees both of their hearts, both of their inclinations. Arye is willing and trusting, while his brother remains the inverse. *Some just need more of a jolt*, Yasha thinks.

TWELVE

Yasha glances up to heaven. Looking back at Kefa, he fixes his eyes on him. Suddenly, Kefa can hear nothing save the pounding of his heart in his ears. The music on the radio has gone. The sounds of the garage have ceased. The voice of his companion faded. Silence in the waiting. It's coming, yet Kefa doesn't know what *it* is. Anticipation mounts. Yasha, eyes locked on his first cell member, calls to him.

"Kefa!"

The sound of Yasha's strong, commanding voice hits him in the chest with full force. An adrenaline rush like he experienced with the paratroopers surges through him. Every cell in his body is electrified, every thought pinging. It's what he's been seeking. He doesn't know how, but he just knows. An invitation. An opportunity not to be missed. He has no idea that the next twelve months will radically alter his life, and that from here on out nothing will ever be the same. For him, for everyone.

Yasha jerks his head toward the city.

"Follow me!"

ACKNOWLEDGMENTS

I never thought I'd write a novel, much less two. But God keeps dropping creative and inspiring and challenging ideas into my head, into my heart; and I just cannot say *no*. I'm learning to have faith in myself for these projects because, well, He apparently does. All thanks and praise go to Father, Son, and Holy Spirit.

Thank you to my wonderful and devoted husband, Tyler; and my beautiful, sweet, and spunky daughters, Madalene, and Hannah. Your love, continual encouragement, and belief in me to write books keeps me going, especially when I encounter those unwelcome periods of writer's fatigue. Here's to doing all things—hard things, unexpected things—through Christ, who gives us strength.

To my parents for their unwavering love and excitement, and for promoting my work with great passion year after year. Particular love and affection to my Dad, who unexpectedly went to be with Jesus mere weeks before publication—I know you're the first person to hold a printed copy of TWELVE in heaven's magnificent library.

To my sisters who inspire me to achieve and make an impact.

To my Bible study, church, and prayer group friends who cheer me on faithfully.

To friends and family alike who read copies early, late, and whenever I asked.

And special thanks to Sherrie Clark, Kaye Falls, Emily Hitchcock, and the Storehouse Media Group. It was a joy and privilege to work with such amazing women.

ABOUT THE AUTHOR

TRISTAN KENWORTHY HODGES holds fine arts degrees from Pepperdine University and Brooks Institute of Photography. Her first novel, *Seven*, depicts the redemptive biblical account of Mary Magdalene, combining historical fiction with compelling spiritual truths. She currently lives in NE Florida with her husband, daughters, and two adorable dogs.

For more information visit www.tristankhodges.com and follow her blog for TWELVE at www.twelve.press. You can also find her on social media: